THE PATH TO SOMERSET

Book Two of the Seymour Saga

By Janet Wertman

Printed in the United States of America
First printing 2018

ISBN 978-0-9971338-3-7 (Kindle edition)
ISBN 978-0-9971338-4-4 (Paperback edition)
ISBN 978-0-9971338-5-1 (EPUB Edition)

Library of Congress Control Number 2018911241

Cover designed by Jennifer Quinlan of Historical Editorial
Front cover image (Edward Seymour, by Antonio Moro) is from the collection of the wonderful Sudeley Castle and used with permission.

Table of Contents

This one's for my mom...

PART ONE: ANNE OF CLEVES

God Send Me Well to Keep...

Chapter One

March 3, 1539—Tower Hill

London was a city of contrasts. It was England's expansive soul, the center where some twenty small rivers came to nourish the majestic River Thames, that main thoroughfare whose banks were dotted with the glorious manors and expansive gardens of its noblest citizens. It was also England's warped mind, a maze of twisted streets and lanes where rickety houses stopped the light from shining on the faces of the poor.

Today, more than three thousand people crowded Tower Hill, the intersection of the two Londons, the grisly site where the King's justice was meted out to the high born. The Tower itself, its white stones glinting ghostly bright against the dismal gray sky, had just disgorged another prisoner to his fate, and now a murmur of anticipation was rippling through the assembly.

Edward Seymour, Earl of Hertford and brother-in-law to King Henry VIII, swallowed to relieve his dry throat as his onetime mentor, Sir Nicholas Carew, mounted the three steps to the scaffold. Edward held his breath when Carew turned around to look at the section where Edward sat with the rest of the King's Privy Council. Thankfully the death stare never reached him. Instead Carew's lip curled when his gaze fell upon Thomas Cromwell, the man responsible for this moment, and then Carew's eyes turned back to the distance above the crowd.

Edward looked down at his hands. His long thin fingers were carefully interlaced in his lap, their pallor stark against the peplum of the black silk doublet that covered his hosed thighs. He didn't want to be here, but the presence of the Council confirmed the legitimacy of the sentence; they had little choice but to attend.

Carew began his speech, his eyes blank. "Good Christian people, I am come hither to die, condemned by the law against which I will speak nothing."

Carew's thin voice faltered with the uncertainty of a man shocked by his fate. He had failed to bring treason to light, had claimed to be unaware of the treachery when he corresponded with the traitors, but his excuses were riddles that could be taken several ways. That was all it had taken to plunge from power to death, despite his closeness to the King.

"Instead I will urge you to study the Gospel, all of you, to keep your minds on what is good and true, for I fell because of my false views."

Interesting turnaround for the conservative Carew, given that his quest to restore Roman Catholicism and roll back religious reforms had given credibility to the charges against him. Men said surprising things on the scaffold.

"And thus I take my leave of the world and of you all, and I heartily desire you all to pray for me."

Carew handed the executioner a small bag of coins – a bribe to do his job well – then knelt before the block and spread his arms. Edward felt a shattering rush of life as the axe rose, glinting in the light, then a sudden void when the weapon struck with a dull thud. He hid his flinch by scratching at an itch in his beard, trimmed to match the King's. Edward kept his thinning hair almost shaved, as well, since the King himself was bald.

"So perish all the King's enemies," said Thomas Cromwell.

The other Councilors kept their eyes downcast as they rose to pass through the crowd, parted for them by the guards.

Edward walked down to the Thames for the ride back to Whitehall Palace. The water had been blue and calm this morning, but it was gray and angry now. A sign from God? Perhaps, but whether it was wrath for a traitor's crime or outrage over false witness was not clear.

Edward wondered again whether Cromwell had taken advantage of the King's anger. Carew had refused His Majesty's request to trade some lands and had insulted him after a game of bowls. Had Cromwell manipulated the evidence, as some claimed? It would not have been the first time.

As Edward scanned the dock for a boat for hire, a quiet voice behind him asked, "Would you like to share mine?"

Edward looked over his shoulder. Cromwell's black eyes were uncertain, almost nervous. He had lost many allies over his prosecution of Carew. Edward made his choice and nodded at his friend. They walked over to the small shallop whose hull displayed the arms of Cromwell's three-year-old barony. The crewman handed them cushions; they, too, trumpeted Cromwell's title.

They sat, and Edward fixed his eyes on the rough waters. Blessedly, Cromwell held his tongue so Edward could indulge in the moment's natural melancholy. Only the slap of the oars punctuated the silence.

Once the boat docked at Whitehall Palace, the two men went directly to Mass in Henry's private oratory, a sanctuary whose wood-paneled walls exhaled incense even when none was being burned. Reverence was required, though business was welcome. This was the King's favorite time to get things done – though he frowned on others attending to any needs other than divine or royal ones. Attention could be diverted from God to the King but no further.

Edward joined the King for Mass every day. Favor and fortune came from proximity to the throne, and Edward was determined to remind the King in a thousand small ways that they were still brothers, that he deserved to be advanced. Edward's younger sister, Jane, had succumbed to childbed fever after giving birth to Henry's heir three years ago. Had she lived, Edward would surely be a duke by now. After all, it had been the quest for a male heir that led the

King to destroy two wives and tear asunder his realm's religion. Edward had been appointed to the Privy Council when the King took an interest in Jane, was named Viscount at their marriage, and was elevated to his earldom at Prince Edward's birth. A second son would have completed the trajectory, but Jane's death made her brother's influence uncertain. He needed to work hard now.

Edward and Cromwell waited at the door until the priest turned a page in the Psalter, then took their seats. The King's eyes flickered at their entrance, and they bowed their heads in ostensible prayer. They had arrived during the readings. Edward usually arrived early so he could speak with the King before the service; Cromwell usually came late and spoke with the King afterwards. Cromwell's lateness was calculated, though Edward could not tell whether it was meant to signal industry or disdain for traditional Catholic practices.

Such an interesting man, Cromwell. Unlike Edward and most other highborn courtiers, Cromwell's black hair was long and his face was beardless. Cromwell downplayed any physical similarities to the King – a backhanded way for a commoner to demonstrate loyalty. Another example of the insight that had earned him a barony and three of the most important posts in the land: Lord Privy Seal, Principal Secretary, and Chancellor of the Exchequer. He was a good ally and a true friend, albeit one whose outspoken dedication to religious reform, among other things, had earned him numerous enemies.

The Eucharistic prayers were beginning; Edward knelt. He was enough of a reformist to no longer believe in the host as actual body and blood, but he did hold it sacred. Not that he discussed this with the King: denying the Real Presence was dangerous. Only Cromwell and the Archbishop of Canterbury, Thomas Cranmer, dared broach this issue, and even they tempered their arguments to avoid angering the monarch whose only real quarrel with Roman Catholicism was the Pope himself.

Mass over, the King stood and called to the page in the

corner, "Have some food sent to the library."

In the months after Jane's death, Henry had shut himself in his rooms, emerging only to worry about his son and impose rules to protect him from pestilence and assassins and whatever new evils came into the King's increasingly suspicious mind. Food became his only solace, and he had steadily expanded until his arms were larger than an average man's thighs, and his pages had taken to opening both sides of the double doors when he passed through. He had resumed hunting and other active pastimes; these seemed to keep further expansion in check but made him more ravenous than ever.

The page bowed with a flourish and ran out.

"Now then," said the King, leaving the chapel for the library.

The room had been rearranged to accommodate the King's latest conceit, a new illuminated manuscript he'd had commissioned, and which stood open on a tall lectern. Four of his other favorite texts graced stands of complementary heights. The King was obsessed with the beauty of this art, and only commissions truly indulged his obsession. The thousands of other manuscripts he had acquired from the dissolution of the monasteries tended to be of modest quality - like the men who had peopled the houses - and would not do.

The King chose a chair and settled in. Edward poured him a cup of wine.

"You were late today," the King said to Edward.

"Sir Nicholas Carew departed the earth this morning."

The King took a breath and his eyes flashed to Cromwell. "It is a sad thing when men turn traitor."

Cromwell nodded. "He redeemed himself at the last and recognized his false views."

The King sniffed. "Why is it that men's eyes only seem to open when death is imminent?"

"The certainty of their eternal sentence turns many men to the truth," Cromwell replied.

"Amen," said Edward, even though Carew might simply

have been trying to protect his wife from further retaliation. The King would brook no criticism of his Church, which he created when the Pope refused to annul Henry's twenty-year marriage to his brother's barren widow so he could marry Anne Boleyn. The Church of England was guided by the King's own conscience; only fools believed he would abandon it just because he had turned on Anne.

The King looked out the window.

The silence was broken by a familiar voice from the hall. "Prepare for a feast," it called, and suddenly Edward's brother Tom was bowing melodramatically and waving in a parade of pages. Each carried a large tray heavily laden with food: meats on one, custards and savory pies on a second, desserts on a third.

"Ah, thank you, Tom," the King said. "Of all my men, you know my appetites best."

Tom smiled and tucked his reddish hair behind his ears. He was well suited as a gentleman of the Privy Chamber. Tom had inherited the Seymour ambition but not the Seymour talent; he was all show, no substance. Edward prided himself that those traits were reversed in him even as he secretly envied Tom's *bonhomie*.

The King lumbered over to the table and took generous portions, then gestured to the men to join him. Edward and Cromwell piled their plates to match the King's, but Tom took only some baked pears with scraped cheese and a small marzipan subtlety. The men were quiet for a time, as the King smacked his lips and licked his fingers.

A knock came at the door, then a page's face appeared. "Doctor Butts asks leave to attend you."

"I saw him in the hallway," said Tom to the King. "I told him to give you some time."

The King clapped Tom on the shoulder. "This is as good a time as any. Better to be distracted, eh?"

The three men bleated their agreement, and Butts entered, his black and scarlet robe billowing behind him. Two assistants followed with his supplies. The King pushed his chair sideways and stuck out his leg. "Well, how does it look today?"

Butts crooked his finger, and one of the assistants set a footstool on which the other placed the King's leg. Butts started to remove the bandages that began just below the knee and went all the way up the King's thigh. The inner layers were stained yellow and brown; a putrid odor crept into the air as the ulcerated sores came into view. Edward quietly pushed his plate away.

The King had injured his leg three years ago from a bad fall during a joust, and the wounds had plagued him since. On good days he hid his pain well enough, but on bad ones he could not hunt or even walk comfortably. Such a sad state for the man who had once been the golden prince of Christendom. And probably one of the reasons he hadn't remarried. Not that Edward wanted to push a new wife. He was quite happy being the brother of the King's one true love. Indeed, Edward dreaded the day when some other brother would come along to take his special place...

March 3, 1539—Whitehall Palace

The trip back from Tower Hill had been long enough for Stephen Gardiner, the Bishop of Winchester, to tell a meditative rosary. At the end of the journey, the fifty-six-year-old looked up at Whitehall Palace, formerly York Place, and shuddered. It had been built by Gardiner's former patron, Cardinal Thomas Wolsey, to demonstrate the magnificence of the Catholic Church and his own wealth and power, but the King had come to resent its superiority to his own palaces and had seized it for himself. It was now the principal royal residence and a warning against the sin of overstepping one's place.

The King, fully satisfied his seven rooms were far grander than Wolsey's five, had made no changes to the semi-royal suite Wolsey had created for himself. Instead, the King passed those accommodations over to Thomas Howard, third Duke of Norfolk, premier duke in the peerage of England. Norfolk had more royal blood in his veins than even the King himself, though this was never discussed.

Outside Norfolk's grand apartments, Gardiner paused to adjust his white cassock and the fur collar that peeked out of it: the great Duke noticed such sartorial details and adjusted his opinion of people accordingly.

Gardiner made the sign of the cross to calm himself and entered Norfolk's Privy Chamber, the private reception area that guarded his inner sanctum. Striding through, the Bishop barely noticed the magnificent tapestries brightly lit by expensive wax tapers. He found Norfolk in the library, sitting at the rosewood marquetry table he'd commissioned for his jade chessmen. Busy contemplating his next move, he didn't look up when Gardiner entered.

The Bishop bowed. "My Lord."

He caught his reflection in the mirror and straightened the biretta on his head. Norfolk still did not acknowledge Gardiner's presence. The Bishop took another look in the mirror and smoothed the straight gray hair that ended in a careful inward curl just above his collar.

Norfolk put an index finger on a rook and slid it to a new square. He sat back in his carved, tall-back oak armchair and spread his arms over the sides. He narrowed his black eyes on Gardiner and motioned for him to sit. "You play the next move."

Gardiner was used to such requests: the Duke used random intrusions to spice up the games he played against himself. Gardiner slid into the empty chair.

"You were at Tower Hill?" Norfolk asked.

Gardiner nodded and looked down at the board. "Carew is dead."

Norfolk crossed himself. "A good man gone."

A Catholic man gone. This was the latest in a line of executions. It was a dangerous time to be conservative.

"*Sumus omnes in manus dei*," said Gardiner. We are all in the hands of God.

"Damn Cromwell to hell," Norfolk said.

Though he knew he shouldn't be, Gardiner was surprised by the ferocity in the Duke's voice. Norfolk hated Cromwell and was understandably agitated by attacks that were coming perilously close.

"I'm just glad Carew did nothing to compromise either of us," Gardiner said. "You dined with him several times; I did also. We could have been accused."

"Don't be a fool," Norfolk said. "Carew never conspired against the King. That blacksmith trumped up the charges against him."

That blacksmith. Gardiner was not sure whether Norfolk hated Cromwell more for his reformist views or his humble family origins. The Bishop had often heard Norfolk say only people of gentle birth were fit to converse with the King or any other nobleman. Thankfully, Gardiner thought, the Duke made an exception for churchmen. Sometimes.

Gardiner shook his head. "Carew wrote to the traitors, knowing of their plot. I don't believe he was part of it, but he should not have risked involvement."

"Cromwell was going after him regardless," said Norfolk. "All for complaining about the secrecy with which the investigations were conducted. It was revenge." Norfolk paused. "Carew died for actions against Cromwell and not for any against the King. Just like my niece."

Norfolk's niece, Anne Boleyn, had inspired the King to create chaos in his court and outrage throughout the land. The King had pursued her for seven years, married her against the directive of the Pope, then had her executed on false charges. False charges created by Cromwell.

Norfolk stood up abruptly, knocking the chess pieces to the floor. "I want him dead," he snarled before stomping over to the side table. "Him and anyone who wishes him well."

Norfolk poured a goblet of wine and downed it in a single gulp. He poured another and motioned for Gardiner to serve himself, then moved to the tall windows that overlooked the gardens.

The harsh midday sun streaming through the leadlights

highlighted the deep creases on Norfolk's leathery face. Gardiner was thankful the two men were on the same side. Norfolk was sixty-six years old in an age when most men were dead before fifty, and his compact frame still looked indestructible. He was a soldier at heart, with a reputation for ruthlessness earned through countless battles.

"I mean it," Norfolk continued. "I will not endure any more of this. That bastard was aiming for me. And you. We must have him gone."

Gardiner sniffed. Easier said than done. Thomas Cromwell had a way of anticipating and procuring the King's every desire - women, wealth, even food - by means of religious reforms, moving the King further and further away from the true faith. The King had even recently authorized the Holy Bible to be translated into English - *English!* - and ordered that a copy be placed in every parish church so any peasant or merchant might come to look upon and dispute the word of God. Where did this leave priests, even bishops, except in the dust? Gardiner felt acid in the back of his throat and willed himself to calm down. "He seems to be in a position of strength right now," he said.

"Better to remove him when he is lulled by confidence."

"You have a plan?"

"Cromwell has gone too far with reform. It was one thing when he separated England from Rome, or when he persuaded the King to dissolve the monasteries. Now he wants to eliminate rituals - sacraments even - and remove holy decorations from places of worship. The cur calls them 'superstition.'"

What about how he wants to curtail the power of the clergy, Gardiner screamed silently. That was the more important issue, this idea that men should develop their own relationship with their savior and forego the intervention of learned priests. How in the world had the Archbishop of Canterbury, that idiot Thomas Cranmer, come to agree with that?

"So, you have a plan?" Gardiner repeated.

"The King is Catholic at heart," Norfolk said. "He will

swing the pendulum back, given the right impetus. If we can arouse his suspicions against Cromwell's motives, we will triumph."

Gardiner crossed himself. "*Ita amen.*" So be it.

"And when order is restored, I will run the country for the King, and you will replace that heretic Cranmer as the highest prelate in the land."

For a moment Gardiner felt his soul sing. He bowed to the Duke in a show of submission. May his will - and His - be done, the Bishop prayed.

May 18, 1539—Hertford Hall

"Halloo," Edward called out as he and his companions tossed their reins to the page. They dismounted in the courtyard of his home - Hertford Hall, as his wife liked to call it. It wasn't yet grand enough for such a name, but she liked to remind them both of how far Edward had climbed and how much farther he could yet reach. Yet another way the formidable Anne Stanhope Seymour presented the ultimate foil to Edward's first wife, who had made him feel inadequate in every possible way.

Anne appeared in the doorway, squinting slightly, and all was well again. Anne truly was the perfect wife. Some called her cold, but the same people called Edward cold, and they were wrong. To Edward, Anne was the ultimate loving helpmate, possessed of a discretion that matched Edward's own. She was slim and capable, pious and smart. She could ingratiate herself to anyone, though she did not tolerate fools.

She also was right about Hertford Hall. The site was ideal - on the south side of the Strand, the most coveted location in London. It was walking distance from Whitehall and Westminster, where the court spent most of its time. It was also just off the River Thames, which made it convenient to the King's other London residences. Denizens like the Dukes of Norfolk and Suffolk and the Marquesses of Dorset and Exeter had turned the neighborhood into an expanse of large mansions and walled gardens, a proud paradise. The Hertfords' house was the least impressive around, but there was ample space to expand it: the property boasted several other buildings, even chapels. Eventually Edward would build a grander residence, but for now he was happy to collect the income that would help finance those dreams.

Anne smiled at Edward, then to the two men he had brought to dinner: his brother Tom and Ralph Sadler, Cromwell's closest friend and former ward. With a warm "Welcome, Ralph" she walked over to kiss Sadler. "We are honored."

"What about me?" joked Tom. "Are you not honored to receive me?"

"You are too well aware of your great welcome," Anne replied airily as she walked over to kiss Edward. "Come, gentlemen. Archbishop Cranmer only just arrived."

The men followed her to the Great Hall, where the dining table was ready. This time it was only the five of them, the core group Edward knew he could trust. The court had become a dangerous place as the King's views shifted more frequently and his temper frayed more easily. It had become difficult to give even good advice since any mistake could cost a man his career or his life.

Thomas Cranmer, Archbishop of Canterbury, was sitting by the fire, staring into the flames with the same soft look he wore in prayer. When they entered, his brown eyes brightened. He stood and made the sign of the cross over them. "Ah, my lords, may God protect you. And our ailing friend."

This was a reference to Cromwell, who had spent the last three weeks at home, hoarse and hacking, feverish too. The King was terrified of illness, and Cromwell had been quickly banished from court until every symptom was gone, which would likely be a month or two. His absence was proving to be a disaster for the reformers' religion, as no one was left to counteract the whispers Norfolk was dropping into the King's ear, urging a return to orthodoxy.

Edward closed his eyes briefly at the blessing. Thomas Cranmer's very presence was soothing, even holy. So different from the orthodox Catholic priests like Stephen Gardiner, the Bishop of Winchester, whose vanity and greed lent peckishness to their tones.

"What is the latest news?" Cranmer asked. He had been away from court this past week, attending to duties in Canterbury.

"Were you there for Norfolk's tantrum?" Sadler asked.

"Norfolk had a tantrum?" Anne broke in, surprised.

Norfolk had taken advantage of Cromwell's absence to create a committee in the House of Lords to settle religious issues in the land. Two days ago he had upbraided his committee in front of the King for not agreeing on anything. Of course, the lack of consensus stemmed from fear of contradicting the King, but the stunt had driven the monarch back to conservative principles.

"It was all planned," Edward said. "It had to have been. He proposed they boil everything down to six doctrinal issues."

"Six?" Anne raised an eyebrow.

"I expect they reaffirmed Christ's real presence in the Host," said Cranmer. "The conservatives cling to the idolatry of that superstition. As if the Lord could be commanded by the hands of man."

"They went far beyond the Real Presence," Edward said. "That was their opening gambit."

"I'm going to guess they also continued the system of indulgences," said Anne. "Norfolk is a sinner who is looking to an eternity of private Masses to secure the Lord's forgiveness."

"He was probably goaded to that by that weasel Gardiner, who wants to be well paid to say them," Tom said.

"An eternity of masses in which only people of noble blood will share the cup during Communion," Cranmer said, shaking his head. "I take it that was on the list as well."

"Of course," Edward said. "Norfolk is the ultimate

snob."

"What else?" Cranmer asked.

"Confession is once again a sacrament, and they stressed the binding character of vows of chastity." Edward paused and bit his lip. "They reaffirmed clerical celibacy."

Anne gave a sidelong glance at Cranmer. "This is far more conservative than the King has been in some time."

"How did he react to this proposal?" asked Cranmer. "Did he realize this would return us to the early days of the break with Rome, when our two Churches were identical in all but their leaders?"

"Whether he did or not, he gave his approval, and the points were quickly gelled into a disastrous bill that Parliament is sure to pass: the Act of the Six Articles."

"The whip with the six strings," snorted Tom.

"Call it what you will," Edward said dryly. "It rolls back all the progress we've made."

"It might yet be amended," Anne said. "Surely when the King sees the bill in writing he will change his mind."

They all looked at Edward. "Without Cromwell, we have lost all our influence."

Anne turned to Cranmer. "But surely, Your Grace, you can discuss some of the most extreme—"

"No," Tom broke in. "Cranmer must stand down on this. It is too dangerous for him."

"And Margarete," added Ralph.

Thomas Cranmer had made a foolish mistake several years ago: he had taken a wife. The Lutheran reforms permitted clergy to marry, and at the time Henry seemed to accept the wisdom of the practice. But he had veered again, and thus the Archbishop's secret had been buried for years.

Cranmer cradled his head in his hands. "Praise God, I have managed to smuggle her out of the country."

Edward nodded, relieved. Still, there were spies everywhere. God forbid someone should inform the King of his Archbishop's sin. Cranmer would be burned.

Cranmer continued. "I pray my misstep does not destroy our cause."

Sadler patted Cranmer's arm. "Norfolk seems to have planned with exceeding care. He has been meeting with the lords, privately and publicly, to garner support."

"The only support he needs is from the King," said Tom.

"It would appear that he has it," said Edward. "And so we have lost."

"But might Cromwell return in time to change things?" Tom asked. "Ralph, how is he?"

Sadler shook a heavy head. "No better. It is up to us."

Anne quickly cut him off. "You would be fools to even try."

Edward cringed. She was right, but it hurt to hear it, let alone comply. Could Edward really abdicate all authority? The King's shifting allegiances made it dangerous to take a stand, but could Edward really do nothing?

If he wanted to earn the power he craved, he needed to do something to save the reforms that meant so much to so many. Gently, to be sure, but he had to act.

Edward took a deep breath. "She is right. We'll not stop the Act." He watched his guests glance at each other. "But we can perhaps soften its outcomes. That's where our focus should be."

"That would do it." Sadler drew out his words. "We can contain the enforcement until we muster the strength to change the rules—"

Tom clapped his friend on the shoulder. "Then we can let Norfolk have this empty victory and take away his toy when the time comes."

Edward felt Anne's approving smile. He could do this. For so long others had discounted his merit, but now they looked to him for guidance. This was the bright spot of Cromwell's absence, the light to focus on.

Chapter Two

The morning's Privy Council meeting was almost upon them, and Edward was reviewing notes in his lodgings at court. Although he preferred going home to Anne, he slept at court at least three nights a week. Only members of the Privy Council and nobles who were barons or higher were lodged; his comfortable apartments not far from the King's were a badge of honor. Edward had learned from Thomas Cromwell to be around often enough that the King could rely on you - but not so often as to make Henry bored or cranky. It was a fine line. Every day and three nights seemed right.

Edward heard low voices outside his door, and then a page announced "The Lord Privy Seal" as Cromwell strode in, sure of his welcome.

His round face was thinner and more lined, but his color was good. He wore a broad smile and moved with all his usual vigor.

Edward jumped to his feet to hug him. "Welcome back. Sadler said you would be returning today. I didn't know whether you would make it to the Council meeting."

"You know me better than that. I have been here since Matins."

"Matins?" The man who avoided church services had chosen to attend the pre-dawn Mass usually attended only by monks and fanatics?

"I thought it an auspicious start to the day." The look on Cromwell's face was completely bland.

Edward kept his face equally bland to give Cromwell his due. "How better to return to court in the middle of a holy war?"

"No war. The Act is a certainty, and only fools would dispute it."

"Though we can try to minimize the penalties that will be imposed for violations."

Cromwell picked at a cuticle. "Sadler told me you'd suggested that."

Edward held his breath, almost annoyed at how desperate he was for his mentor's approval.

"You are quite right," Cromwell finally said. "I have given your idea a great deal of thought. I had a lot of time."

Edward laughed. "You did indeed. You gave us a bit of a worry, old friend."

Cromwell nodded. "I know I did, though I passed all danger soon and have been well for more than a month. As I regained my strength I accomplished a number of happy projects. New orchards for my house in Stepney, even some building plans."

"I knew you would be well occupied."

"I also had time to review some of the King's correspondence, to make sure I was not returning to any problems."

"I suspect you did more from home than most do at their desks," Edward said and smiled.

Cromwell shrugged. "I found an interesting item to share with the King. A married priest in Kent who begs the King's pardon." Cromwell rifled through the papers he had brought with him. "He says he wishes the King could have found it lawful for priests to marry, for he and his wife would have been to the Crown doubly faithful, first in love, and secondly for fear of the Bishop of Rome."

"Have you gone mad, Cromwell? If Norfolk hears of this—"

"He won't. But listen to the rest. He says, 'But as the King has established a contrary order, I have sent the woman to her friends three score miles from me and come straightaway to ask pardon.'"

"You can't speak to the King of this. What if someone makes the connection with Cranmer?"

"I received the letter. As His Majesty's Principal Secretary and the holder of his privy seal, I am obligated to discuss it. And I thank God for the opportunity."

Edward covered his face with his hands. "But the danger."

"This honest priest is a blessing. He gives us a chance to set a gentle precedent – for he will surely be forgiven, him and all those similarly situated. And this will move the King further towards mercy for greater sins. But most important, it blunts any weapon Norfolk might think he has."

Edward lowered his hands. That was Cromwell's genius. Edward's fear that the King would discover Cranmer's marriage had blinded Edward to the real issue: how to manage the discovery if it happened. Power was a game of chess, and winning depended on how many moves a person could see in advance. And protect against.

"I should never have doubted you," Edward said.

"And now, it is time to greet the rest of the court." Cromwell swept his hands toward the door. "Shall we?"

They walked to the King's apartments. When the King was in residence at Whitehall, the Council met at least twice a week in the King's study rather than at Westminster.

The massive Council table, which took up the western third of the room, was backed by a console against the wall and piled high with papers and maps. Across from this setup, the King's workstation for his potions and medicines took up another third of the room. And in between, moderating the influences, perched the King's throne. Crowded in front of it were three stools on which he could rest his legs or invite people to sit. Although the hour of the meeting had not yet arrived, Henry was already seated on his throne, resting and looking out the giant window before it. On the tapestry behind him, the apocryphal Judith held up the severed head of Holofernes.

"Cromwell," the King called. "You are fully recovered?"

Cromwell bowed. "Your doctors confirm I am in better health than I have ever been, Your Majesty. I am rested and ready to take on the world for you."

The King relaxed and smiled. "Excellent."

The rest of the Council members ambled in, greeting the returned minister. Some did so with less grace than others. Norfolk, for one, whose fake smile accompanied a tepid welcome and disingenuous concern that perhaps the return was premature. The old duke walked quickly to claim his place at the head of the table. The others followed automatically.

Edward's seat was near the middle of the table, facing the throne. As the Earl settled in, he noticed Cromwell had not stirred. He was still beside the King, waiting quietly.

When everyone was seated, Cromwell turned to the King and continued their conversation as if it were still just the two of them. "Sire, it is an honor to return."

Henry smiled benignly. "Ah, Crum, it is good to have you. I am not so well served when you are absent."

Cromwell brightened at the compliment; Norfolk darkened.

"Thank you." Cromwell bowed. "While I was away, I was consumed with horror over not being able to serve Your Majesty. I spent part of each day pondering what I could be doing, even from my sickbed, to ease your days."

The King nodded smugly. "An admirable thought."

"And I succeeded."

"Ah?"

"I heard the Bishop of Rome was pushing France and the Empire to war with us, and set my mind to enhance our defenses."

"Which we have been doing," interrupted Norfolk, "by strengthening the castles on our coast." He was the military expert who always urged battle to a ruler who glorified war. So different from Cromwell, who saw war as an unnecessary expense - especially for a monarch who lavished enormous sums on luxury. Cromwell had saved the treasury by seizing the vast riches of the Roman Catholic Church. That opportunity would not recur.

Cromwell made a show of turning back to the King. "I thought for days how best to establish our strength and then communicate it to Francis and Charles. As I was considering the possibilities, the answer presented itself to me."

"Eh?"

"I wanted to trumpet our German alliance, and then I remembered the Duke of Cleves has a sister whose beauty is universally praised, a woman who is said to be learned and graceful. Your Majesty is in need of a wife—"

"You want us to get into bed with the Lutherans?" Norfolk interrupted. "Next you'll be advising the King help the poor by giving away his riches."

Cromwell narrowed his eyes. "I fail to see the connection."

"Luther pretends all men are equal before God - his philosophy leads to a state where men share all things in common."

"That is an abomination," said the King.

Edward held his breath. This argument had become the conservatives' main weapon. The King harbored a natural antipathy toward social welfare policies that implicitly demeaned his status - and condemned his extravagance.

"My good Duke," answered Cromwell, "while we may reject many of the Lutheran views, we both understand that the Bishop of Rome is not the Vicar of Christ on earth. On that basis alone, we are tightly connected. And this way perhaps His Majesty can enjoy the bedding."

Henry snickered.

"She cannot be so beautiful as the widowed Duchess of Milan," Norfolk snarled. "We would have heard if that were true."

"Ah my good Duke," Cromwell bowed, a smug smile on his face, "you are absolutely right to think so. And yet" - he turned back to the King - "Christina of Milan's outer beauty is ruined by her bad temper."

The King grimaced. None of them could forget the girl's curt reply to the King's suit: "If I had two heads, one would be at the disposal of the King of England."

Cromwell spread his arms. "I say it is time for us to look for a better choice, and Cleves may give it to us. We have the promise there of a true beauty who could bring peace and prosperity."

Henry nodded slowly. "You speak true."

"Let us commission Hans Holbein to paint Anne of Cleves – to capture her as she is, for good or bad. And she has a younger sister, Amalia. Holbein could paint both – or whichever is fairer. And then you can decide for yourself and see whether your heart wants to proceed in the matter."

"We would have heard if she was exceptional," Norfolk repeated.

"I trust Holbein," said the King. "Let it be done. Have him leave within the week."

Edward wrung his hands under the table, hurt that Cromwell had not thought to share his strategy beforehand. *But it would be good for England,* Edward reminded himself, and smiled with the other reformists, while Norfolk and Gardiner tried to hide the gnashing of their teeth.

June 29, 1539—Lambeth Palace

The waves of the River Thames lapped gently against the side of the royal barge as it approached the torch-lit dock. It was just light enough that the deep red of Lambeth Palace's façade was still visible, its white stone dressings glowing with a holy light.

The palace, the official residence of the See of Canterbury, was just across the river from Whitehall and Westminster. Archbishop Thomas Cranmer had organized a formal dinner for the King and the court. Edward was glad to have been invited to make the crossing on the King's barge, along with twenty or so of the most influential people in the realm.

Wives had also been invited, though the King, the churchmen, and Cromwell had none. Norfolk, estranged from his spouse, brought his mistress. It was a strange contradiction that a man who so despised commoners was so committed to Bess Holland, his former laundress. But he insisted she be accepted at court, and right now she was deep in conversation and unapologetically holding her own with Anne and two other ladies, while the Duchess of Suffolk occupied the men.

Catherine Willoughby Suffolk was a striking woman, desired by almost every man at court. At twenty years old and after six years of marriage, her face had finally lost enough of the plumpness of youth to make the Suffolks look more plausibly a couple rather than a father and daughter.

"Sit here by me," Henry said, patting the cushion next to him. "As much as I enjoy gazing at you, I want to enjoy your perfume."

She smiled and did as she was told. Edward was amused to see the women roll their eyes as the men clamored to also catch a whiff. Even Bishop Gardiner lifted his nose. Only Cromwell looked bored. To Edward's knowledge, Cromwell had not been entangled with any woman since his wife died a decade ago.

Edward took a deep calming breath to clear away thoughts of death. Far better to summon the gratitude commanded by the Lord and bless his sister Jane for catapulting him to this position.

Edward ran his fingers over the rail's silky polished wood as he admired the rich details of the King's barge. She was a light shallop that could attain almost magical speeds: fully manned with eight rowers, she could travel the thirty-five miles from Hampton Court to Greenwich in only four hours – this jaunt from Whitehall to Lambeth offered barely enough time for them to get comfortable, sheltered by rich tapestries hung between carved and gilded columns. Even open, the arrases maintained privacy but allowed a clear view of the sprawling river.

Edward's reveries were interrupted by Norfolk's angry voice. "No, Lady, you are wrong."

Edward turned.

"I don't see why the cup should be kept from the people at Mass," the Duchess replied icily. "I find it of great comfort; everyone should share that holy moment."

In contrast to her older husband, Catherine Willoughby Suffolk often took positions of reform; the allegiance to reformation was often generational.

"It certainly would elevate the common man," Edward said. "God's grace is a blessing to all."

Cromwell snorted. "And yet we reserve such reverence for priests."

"Would you go against the King's own beliefs then?" Norfolk's voice was a purr, and Edward could see Cromwell's lip curl in response. Edward hoped no one else noticed the clear disgust; it was a rare weakness on Cromwell's part.

"Play that again," the King called to the musicians. "Louder, for us to enjoy."

Further discussion was thus stifled by recorders and lutes until the barge pulled up to the Lambeth dock. Thomas Cranmer was waiting there with a full complement of servants. The first few carried trays with wine and sweetmeats.

The King stepped off first, and after a quick exchange of greetings they all crossed the small lawn to the palace, whose doors stood wide open to welcome the group.

Cranmer bowed. "Please don't leave until you have visited the library. I have a new volume to share with Your Majesty. From Flanders."

"Let us repair there now," the King said, his head giving a gleeful jiggle from side to side. He was an avid reader of theological tomes, and Cranmer was an avid collector of books, tracts, theses, and biographies - anything written with a philosophical or academic bent. As a churchman who could read not only English but also Welsh, Latin, Greek, French, Spanish, and German, Cranmer had assembled seminal texts in all these languages to create the largest library in England - a conceit that was forgiven because he was the Lord's man, and his great learning reflected well upon the King.

The main collection was housed in a vast room with shelves all the way around, topped by a second story of shelves then a third story of windows. More collections crowded other rooms. Shelves were arranged by topic. They were not all filled to the same capacity, since they varied in size to accommodate both the taller ancient manuscripts as well as the more compact leather-bound volumes of recent provenance. Every book contained Cranmer's annotations; they not only marked important points, but also proved he'd read the tome.

"Have you any books for me?" asked the Duchess of Suffolk.

"I have books for anyone who wants them," said Cranmer, waving his arms.

The perfect repartee burst into Edward's mind. "It would be a fine pastime to compete to choose the right book for the Duchess. Your Majesty could judge."

"That would be splendid," said Cromwell. "And if we disagree with a person's choice and offer our own alternative, we should also declare the person we think should read that book."

"Or if it should be burned," said Gardner.

"I would love such a chance," said Anne.

"Challenge accepted," said Norfolk.

There were still more murmurs. Edward felt the warmth of Anne's proud smile.

"Does that mean I get to suggest books for others?" asked Catherine.

"Don't look at me," said Suffolk, even though she hadn't. "Your Majesty?"

Smart man, Edward thought, *giving permission to the King to be the gallant one.*

"Anyone may suggest if they open themselves and their recommendations to judgment," said the King with an expansive wave. "The question is whether you have the confidence to play."

The Duchess smiled and turned to Suffolk. "Husband,

have I the confidence?"

"You can always wait to see how the game goes before you decide to commit," said her husband. "Let's begin. I would suggest a text that teaches you about wifely duties. Ovid's poetry comes to mind."

Henry snickered as the women blushed from the mention of the erotic verse.

"If it's passion you seek, you seek Petrarch," said Norfolk's son with a pompous shake of his carefully coiffed head.

Henry Howard, Earl of Surrey, was as insufferable as his father, but had turned his conceit to the arts instead of war. Surrey constantly challenged Sir Thomas Wyatt for the title of greatest poet at court; Wyatt deserved it but Surrey inhabited the role. He was tall and wiry, with a perpetual smirk and a rooster's strut. He constantly quoted his own verse in a stage voice that lilted and trilled, and he favored Italian fashions to suggest he possessed the Roman genius. Actually, Surrey cared more for his appearance than anyone at court, even Tom, and his allowance from his father's fortune allowed him to indulge that interest. His embroidered velvet sleeves were finer than anyone's but the King's: puffed, slashed, and turned back to reveal contrasting linings that matched the *passementerie* on his doublet.

The Duchess shook her head. "I've read him. We've all read him, thanks to you and Wyatt."

Surrey was inordinately proud of how he and Wyatt had discovered and translated Petrarch's poetry. That's what had spurred Surrey to write his own verse, to extract the personal praise he considered his due. According to Surrey, God meant him to be superior to his fellows because he was born to a superior family. He did not believe commoners possessed intelligence or deserved to enjoy any rights. *God help us,* Edward thought.

"Ah, but how much?" Surrey pressed. "Petrarch goes deep. There are always more lessons from the love he bore for Laura."

"If it is models you seek, I would suggest Dante's

Commedia Divina," said Gardiner. "So you can be as Beatrice to your husband and lead him to *Paradiso.*"

Edward stifled a snort. Of course Gardiner would choose a Catholic text. But at least his suggestion had shifted the conversation away from Surrey's pretentiousness.

"Bishop Gardiner was kind to you," said Anne. "I would have chosen to outrage you with the twelfth-century master Capellanus. He claims in his *De Amore* that we women are slaves to our bellies, and love a fine meal."

"That tome is not for a woman to read," said Suffolk. "But I suggest it is perfect for the King as he contemplates his next bride."

"That will depend on the bride," said Edward. "If you want something practical, I would suggest *Secretum Secretorum,* or *Secret of Secrets,* the letter from Aristotle to Alexander the Great. It speaks of the philosophy of governance, and strategies of war and peace. Important ideas in today's dark times."

"I know that one," said Henry. "I read it many years ago. It might be good to read again now."

"That choice might give concern to my Lord Norfolk," said Cromwell. "The volume gives advice on whom princes can trust. He'll not fare well in that analysis."

Edward winced. Ever since Norfolk had taken advantage of Cromwell's absence, the two men had become so much more combative.

"I'm not afraid of any analysis," Norfolk said. "But I don't see the need for any text beyond the *Aeneid* and its reminder that divine intervention might delay, but will never avoid, our ultimate destinies. Like Wolsey, rising so high but ending even lower than the day he was born."

"Now, now," said the King. "I intend to read the volume that Cranmer has for me. But I award the first point to the Bishop for his suggestion of Dante for the Duchess. I have always admired the fair Beatrice myself."

"Not the lovely Laura?" Surrey asked.

Edward's annoyance over how Gardiner had managed to outshine him was soothed by the King's easy dismissal of

Surrey: "I think the journey is a good reminder of our earthly duties," Henry said. "And I heartily approve of that – almost as much as I would approve of dinner. Cranmer, might we repair?"

"Your Majesty's desire is my own," Cranmer said, nodding to a page in the corner before taking his place at the King's side. As the host, it was Cranmer's privilege to lead the procession to the Great Chamber, though still a half inch behind His Majesty for protocol.

Strolling down the hallway to the sound of trumpets, they passed the portraits of two hundred years of Cranmer's predecessors, then empty walls that left room for several hundred years of successors. Finally they reached the imposing room whose magnificent arch-braced roof had been built around the same time as the one across the river at Westminster.

They took their seats quickly, spurred by the royal appetite. Edward soon lost track of the dishes; since the King's presence had removed the sumptuary limitations, Cranmer had organized a ceaseless parade of platters heaped full of delicacies. He'd beautifully handled every detail with the exception of a very important one: he'd committed the ultimate folly of placing Thomas Cromwell and the Duke of Norfolk at the same table. The King's table.

Cranmer was too naive to realize two rivals could never be friends. Each resented the other for his hold on the King, one earned through efficiency and ability, the other born from blood.

So now Cromwell and Norfolk sat across from each other, midway down the long table. The narrow white expanse between them was a raging battlefield, the flickering candelabras beacon fires. Nothing could hold back the animosity that rose between the two adversaries as they took opposing positions on every topic from appropriate vestments for the clergy to the seasoning of the chicken dish. Edward cursed his placement near the two fighters, since the King was paying attention only to the four people seated around him. All the witty remarks Edward had prepared were wasted.

"I'll take some of that," Norfolk growled when a server almost made the mistake of serving his hated rival before himself.

Cromwell conceded with a twisted smile. "Age before beauty, my good Duke."

"Pearls before swine," came Norfolk's reply.

The disagreements reached their apogee after dinner, when the conversation returned to Wolsey. As always, Norfolk heaped calumny on the lowborn Cardinal who'd once eclipsed him. "Some churchman," Norfolk sneered. "They say he killed himself on the road to the Tower. Apparently he was less afraid of hell than facing the King he'd betrayed."

"He was just a sick old man who died fortuitously," said Cromwell before turning to Gardiner, who was seated closer to the King. "What say you, Bishop?"

Gardiner had been a protégé of Wolsey's, along with Cromwell and Edward, but had turned his back on his mentor to help create the Church of England that placed Anne Boleyn on the throne. It was a sneaky trick for Cromwell to bring Gardiner into the conversation now: Gardiner still clung to Catholic beliefs. It was also risky to bring the dispute closer to the King's attention. Edward cast around for another conversation to join, but like a raging fire the fight had consumed all the air around it.

"The King is the representative of God on earth. I see how Wolsey could prefer Purgatory to judgment," said Gardiner.

Cromwell snorted.

"He lined his pockets with gold, as if that could hide his common blood," Norfolk snarled.

"Many of his offices were Church commissions," said Cromwell quickly. "And their revenues—"

"And their revenues built palaces to rival the King's." Norfolk was firm.

"That the King now owns. One of them freely given to

the King upon its completion." Cromwell was equally firm.

Edward felt his stomach tighten. It was dangerous to defend a traitor, however faintly, even though Wolsey had been right about the Boleyn. The King never spoke the name of his former wife, and wouldn't let anyone else use it around him.

"Freely given?" repeated Norfolk, dripping with sarcasm. "Freely given after he realized his extraordinary hubris was deeply insulting to the man to whom he owed everything."

"And you are an expert on hubris, as we all know," Cromwell said.

"Aye, it's a talent that comes from generations of service to England. It lets me see it in others. Like you."

"But not yourself?" Cromwell sneered. "You fought against the King's father at the Battle of Bosworth. Tell me, my good Duke, did you enjoy your time in the Tower for that betrayal?"

"I fought for the anointed King of England despite my misgivings," Norfolk sniffed. "You could never do that, since you serve only your own interests."

"Liar."

"Pretender."

Edward thought he felt the King's eyes on him, but when he looked the King was deep in conversation with the Duchess of Suffolk.

Edward was unnerved. Had the King sent a signal?

Edward silently cursed Cromwell. Where was the sage mentor who counseled patience and dissimulation?

Edward cut into the conversation. "My Lord," he said to Cromwell, "I hate to interrupt, but I was hoping to have a moment with you before the dancing started." He stood and spoke to the rest of the table. "Please excuse us a moment."

The second they were away, Cromwell leaned over, hands on his thighs, breathing hard. "Thank you," he said to Edward. "Though I wish you had found a better ruse."

Edward stiffened. "You should be glad I stopped you when I did."

"Bah. I've put up with that arrogant ass long enough. Who is he to treat me like that?"

He's the most powerful man in the realm after the King, that's who. "You shouldn't challenge him like that."

Wildness swirled in Cromwell's eyes. He raked a hand through his hair. "I must discredit him. He will destroy me."

"If you pursue him after an exchange like that one, your advice will be discounted. You must let him hang himself."

"Oh, I'll make him hang himself," said Cromwell, making light of Edward's advice. "I'll not let anger cloud my judgment."

Cromwell's attitude vexed Edward, but he shrugged it off. This was not the time to let anger cloud his own judgment, after all. "Well, just now you quarreled openly with the Duke of Norfolk."

"He looked to belittle me in front of the King. I am the Lord Privy Seal, the King's Viceregent. His insults bear on the realm as well."

"You must learn to ignore the insults and let your actions speak for themselves."

Cromwell shook his head. "Ignore? Perhaps. Forgive? Never."

"I wish you well with that," said Edward, allowing some of his exasperation to show. It was time for Cromwell to stop acting like a petulant child.

"He thinks himself too high; the King will pull him down. The lion in the jungle tolerates no competitors." Cromwell looked off, and suddenly seemed to make up his mind about something. He turned to Edward and bowed abruptly. "I will leave now, find a boat for hire. The air will do me good. Please make my excuses to Cranmer, and to the King too if he notices my absence. I wish you good night."

Edward's discomfort grew as Cromwell walked away. It was selfish of Cromwell to indulge his temper like that – it could endanger everything they'd worked for. An open rift with Norfolk could damage Cromwell's credibility, and even push the King back to orthodoxy. The people would lose their Bibles and their voices. That would be a sad thing for England.

With a sigh, Edward turned and walked back to the dinner.

October 2, 1539—Windsor Castle

Stephen Gardiner stifled a yawn. The Privy Council was meeting in the King's Presence Chamber, but the King had not yet joined them. Although this lateness had become habitual, the councilors were expected to be on time – a policy the King enforced by coming early on random days to surprise them. Woe to the lord who was not yet in his seat! As a compromise, on the late days Cromwell began on time with business that did not require the King. Most often this involved letters he had already discussed with His Majesty, or letters that need not rise to royal attention.

Which made this part that much more painful. Bishop Gardiner tried to look as if he were listening, though Norfolk didn't bother. His favorite pastime was cleaning his fingernails with the gold-tipped dagger that always hung from his belt, and which he did mostly to annoy Cromwell.

Since that June night when Cromwell and Norfolk revealed the extent of their enmity, the King's two chief advisors had been forced into an ostensible truce. The King told them bluntly he valued them both, called them jealous dogs fighting over a crumpet, and ordered them to get along. They did when both were before him. Behind the scenes, they argued as much as ever, understanding that the King secretly enjoyed baiting his ministers against each other.

Gardiner could feel his lip curl; he forced his face slack. It still grated on him how Thomas Cromwell refused to accept the way of the world. How dare a recent baron challenge an ancient duke, whatever civil offices Cromwell might hold? How dare he even challenge Gardiner for precedence? Gardiner, a bishop in the Church. Cromwell pretended he and Gardiner came from the same commoner background, but Gardiner's father had been a wool merchant. A substantial one. There was a hierarchy even among common folk, and Cromwell was at the bottom of that one too.

A whiff of decay alerted Gardiner that the King was at the door, and the energy in the room changed as the monarch lumbered in. Short greetings were exchanged, and things settled down enough for the King to clap his hands. "Where are we?"

Cromwell responded. "Discussing the latest correspondence and what it says about the military goals of France and Spain. The way both sides intend to reject our offers, however generous they may be. Also our concern about what they will discuss in private when Charles passes through France on his way to the Low Countries."

Gardiner caught a slight smile on Cromwell's face. Of course he was smiling. The threat of war with Catholic countries benefitted Cromwell's push to escalate England's alliance with the German states, the ultimate harbor for lowborn Protestants.

Admittedly, the alliance was a smart political move – it had already tempered the threats from Francis and Charles – but with the vast sums of money spent to enhance England's fortifications, it soon wouldn't need the Lutherans. Thank God the Cleves woman was not known to be a great beauty, whatever Cromwell claimed.

"Well," said the King, "whatever those two scoundrels discuss, we should be safe for a time behind our new coastal defenses. What news there?"

"We spent a little more than eight hundred pounds in September for twenty-four masons and twelve laborers. And of course the materials for the four bulwarks they built during the month – a hundred and fifty thousand bricks, and wagons of lime, chalk, and timber."

"Good, good. Was that all here?"

"Yes, Sire. We also spent about five hundred pounds in Calais. Mainly on masons and bricklayers."

"Good. What else?"

Before Cromwell could say anything further, Norfolk broke in. "Your Majesty, you should send me to France to speak with Francis. Perhaps I could cool his anger and remind him of your great friendship."

Gardiner groaned inwardly. Leaving the country would open the field to Cromwell. One needed to be around the King to have any influence.

"You are welcome to try," the King said. "You should plan to leave within the month."

"Excellent idea, Your Majesty," said Cromwell. "But in the meantime, there may well be another tool to add to your arsenal. May I move on to the final item on our list?"

Cromwell put his papers down on the table and rubbed his hands together. The Earl of Hertford, Edward Seymour, picked his head up and smiled. *He knows something,* Gardiner thought. He felt Norfolk's quick glance at him but didn't return it.

Cromwell walked to the far corner of the room, where shadows all but obscured an easel covered by a purple cloth. *What trick is this?*

Before making any move to dispel the mystery, Cromwell paused and looked around, then quickly moved to open the window's curtains. The sudden light from two stories of leaded glass lent a theatrical note to the display, which Cromwell heightened with a bow. "The portrait has arrived from Cleves," he said. "It might be fitting to unveil it at this time."

The King sat back in his chair and raised a hand to stroke his beard. The lords leaned forward.

With a flourish, Cromwell tore off the cloth to reveal the painting beneath, a study in rich oranges. The King gasped. They all gasped.

Hans Holbein had outdone himself. He had captured a gentle, intelligent face. Clear white skin, and full lips smiling as if at a private joke. Strong shoulders that tapered to a tiny waist. A regal beauty, not a showy one.

Even Gardiner found himself stirred, then just as quickly horrified both at his own reaction and at what that portended. The King recovered from an open-mouthed reverie to rise and walk over to the portrait. From only inches away he gazed into the girl's eyes. His face was reverent, and it was clear to everyone in the room they were looking at the next Queen of England.

"But what about the dowry?" Norfolk broke in. "Can Cleves provide an appropriate settlement?"

The King's eyes did not leave the painting. It was Cromwell who turned and responded. Was it deliberate or inevitable that he looked down his nose? "They have promised unparalleled military assurances," said Cromwell. "Safety for the entire realm is a better aim than some gold coins quickly spent."

"We have their assurances without the marriage," said Norfolk. "I fear such a close commitment to the Protestant faith."

"Her brother is the Lutheran," Cromwell said. "The Lady Anne was brought up a strict Catholic, though she is said to be open to England's reforms."

"You go quite far in pushing the King to marry," Norfolk said.

"The King needs sons," Cromwell said.

"I don't like that your thoughts go to a time when sons might be needed," Norfolk said, his voice menacing. "It is treason to speak of the death of the King."

Cromwell arched an eyebrow. "Tis you who discusses death, my Lord. All rulers need sons, and I want to give ours the pleasure of getting them."

Norfolk shrugged off the turnaround and bowed to Henry. "I too wish you pleasure, but this situation feels forced. Can you really trust Holbein's—"

"Enough!" The King shouted, turning around violently. The King liked Holbein, and the artist had perfectly captured many people before this. "This portrait shows more than beauty," he said, and his tone was ice. "The girl's face calls to me. Let us sign the treaty and get her here as soon as possible."

The King left them, Cromwell on his heels. Hertford

ran out too. The rest of the Privy Council sat back, stunned into silence.

Norfolk walked over to the painting. He looked at it up close as the King had done. "Bah," he said and walked out as well.

Stephen Gardiner felt a chill in his spine and crossed himself. Cromwell had, impossibly, turned things around and bested them all.

Chapter Three

January 1, 1540—Rochester Castle

Edward took a deep breath of the English coast's salty air. Perched high on the site of an old Roman settlement, Rochester Castle's white Kentish ragstone battlements loomed over the charcoal waters of the River Medway, just inland from the English Channel. Henry had chosen this castle to receive Anne of Cleves because its massive exterior showed the strength of England's fortifications while its interior offered as much majesty in its hangings and furnishings as Hampton Court Palace. It was also a clue, likely inadvertent, into her husband-to-be's character, though with the symbols reversed: a majestic exterior hid a harsh temper.

The future Queen had pronounced herself charmed by the accommodations and happy to meet the family members sent to greet her: Edward and Tom; Ladies Mary Howard and Margaret Douglas; and the Duke and Duchess of Suffolk. No mention was made that these connections were through dead people: Edward and Tom through their late sister, Jane, of course. Lady Mary Howard was the widow of Henry FitzRoy, Duke of Richmond and Somerset, the King's bastard son who had died at sixteen. Lady Margaret Douglas, Countess of Lennox, was the daughter of the King's older sister, Margaret. And Charles Brandon, the Duke of Suffolk, had been married to Henry's younger sister, Mary, until her death in 1533, and was now married to the much younger Catherine. Edward hoped the macabre coincidence was not an omen.

He pushed the thought away and focused on the bull-baiting they would soon enjoy, once the animal had been tied to its stake in the courtyard. The sport would show off the skills of the English dogs and improve the flesh of the meat they would eat the next day, after which the company would begin their leisurely trip to London, stopping in every village to accept the greetings of the English people. Cromwell had planned every detail, including the gradual increase of the size of the crowds so Anne would meet the King before the largest gathering of all.

The quiet was shattered by a clatter of hooves. The rider was a gentleman, judging by the cut of his furred cloak. Edward recognized Sir Anthony Browne, Master of the Horse.

"Prepare for His Majesty's arrival," Browne called as he reined in his lathered mount in the courtyard.

"His Majesty?"

Browne dismounted and handed off his reins to a page. He pulled off his gloves, finger by finger, as he spoke. "The King grew impatient. In the middle of the New Year celebrations, His Majesty announced he could wait no longer to meet the woman he's been dreaming of for months."

"The King is coming?"

Panic gripped Edward. He didn't like sudden changes, didn't like being put on the spot without time to consider or plan. To calm himself he sprang into action, pointing at the page. "Tell the Duke of Suffolk he will be giving up his rooms – he and his wife can have mine." He turned back to Browne. "How many are you?"

"Three besides me. Two men of his Privy Chamber and Cromwell."

"Then one additional room and some pallet beds should suffice," Edward said to the page. "And make sure the kitchens are prepared."

The lad nodded and ran off.

Further conversation was stifled by the toll of a bell from Rochester Cathedral. Not the hour bell, but the death knell. Not the main one, one of the smaller ones.

Browne crossed himself. "At least it's not anyone important. Just a merchant or a farmer."

Edward stifled a caustic reply on the value of a human soul. This was not the time for a fight.

Browne continued, oblivious. "How goes it so far?"

"Quite well, The Princess is most gracious. She has praised all the preparations."

Suffolk's approaching voice sounded behind them. "I hear my wife and I are being dispossessed."

"As am I, on your behalf," Edward said.

"And the King's. I think it an excellent sign that he wanted to come greet his bride."

Edward was still uneasy. The formal meeting had been carefully choreographed. This one would be much messier, with more room for errors.

The King's party arrived, their large smiles leading the way.

"Sire," Suffolk boomed as he grabbed the King's reins and motioned for a page to help with the dismount. "We hear your patience could not stand another week."

"Ah, Charles," the King answered, "how could I pass up the opportunity to greet my new bride?"

Suffolk guffawed. "You've a few days left before the wedding, but I'm sure Your Majesty will want to prime her for that."

"We don't want her too prim, after all," Henry snickered. He allowed the men to help him from the horse. With his feet on solid ground, he took on a more serious tone. "What do you think of her?"

Suffolk smiled and nodded. "She is a sweet, kind lady. She will be a credit to your throne."

Henry nodded back, clearly relieved. "I have brought gifts with me, rich furs to adorn her new estate. I was going to offer them myself, but on the ride I had a wonderful idea."

"Sire?" Edward asked, and his pulse pounded from another change of plans.

A smile spread across the King's face. "I will not reveal myself right away; I will pretend to be a simple messenger."

"You always did love that game," Suffolk said with a chuckle.

Edward was thrown for a moment, then memories flooded back. Sir Nicholas Carew had told countless tales of how the young Henry had played the romantic knight, riding disguised to villages to seduce young maidens before revealing his true identity with a gold sovereign for the girl to remember him by. And here he intended to resurrect that old pleasure with European royalty.

It was a terrible idea, but the King was devoted to the ideas of chivalry, honor, gallantry. There was no way to dismiss a belief that was the essence of how he saw himself, even when it was no longer how he actually was – *especially* when it was no longer how he actually was.

Henry and Suffolk giggled. "Edward," the King called, "give me your cloak and you take mine."

The weight of the King's jacket was unexpected: Edward hadn't realized how heavy gold thread could be, had forgotten that jewels were rocks.

The King lost his majestic aura when he donned Edward's coarse woolen cloak, which up until now had been a point of pride for the young Earl. Age had weighted the monarch's face; his eyes, already shrunken by his bulk, had turned beady and suspicious; and his thin lips had gone from authoritative to cruel. Women cleaved to their husbands in service to God – but this young woman would not know this was her future husband. Would she react well to this angry old man who stank of disease?

"Shall we accompany you?" asked Suffolk.

"Nothing would please me more," added Cromwell, though his crooked smile betrayed nervousness.

"Fine," said the King as he entered Rochester's cavernous Great Hall, where excited servants bobbed and bowed and scurried all the faster to complete the preparations for the royal visit.

When they reached the Princess's rooms, Henry stopped and pushed Edward forward to precede him. "I am not your King. Don't let protocol betray my identity. Suffolk knows how to do this."

Suffolk guffawed and led the way to the Cleves' bedchamber, where the group had already been announced. The Princess awaited them, regal as any queen, dressed in a gown that could have been the one from the portrait that had captivated the King.

"Your Grace," Suffolk said as he entered, holding his bow until the King was in the room as well. "The King has sent a trusted messenger to welcome you."

"Thank you," she replied with a curtsy.

The King pushed forward and bowed, rising with a pained smile. "Welcome, my Lady. His Majesty did not want you to fear he had neglected your New Year's gift."

"His Majesty has been most gracious," she said in her heavily accented English. "I have no gifts - no need for gifts."

"Ah, but he would give you anything you desired. He fell in love with your portrait, but I must say it is nowhere near as fine as the original."

She blushed and looked away. A roar came from the courtyard and they all looked out the window to see the first dog leap for its attack. Unfortunately, the King quickly lost interest in the event so Edward and the rest of the attendants were forced to pull their attention back from the sport.

The King glanced at Suffolk and smirked. Henry slowly bent to one knee, grunting all the way - he hadn't knelt to anyone in a long time. When he was settled, he grabbed her hand and kissed it while gazing up into her eyes like a young, lovesick swain.

Anne of Cleves looked back at him with an impatient smile. "Kind thanks, good sir."

The kisses continued until she gently pulled her hand away and turned back to the window. Unruffled, the King stood, with a discreet hand from Suffolk. "We shall take some wine," Henry called, and a page came running in with a tray and several cups.

After the drinks had been poured and distributed, the boy glanced around furtively and sweat broke out on his forehead. He sidestepped to the door, bowing spastically as he went, and Edward realized he was desperately trying to leave the room without turning his back to the King. He needn't have bothered: the Princess had eyes only for the bull-baiting.

"I trust your journey has been pleasant," the King said loudly to draw her attention.

"Yes, quite." She glanced at him and turned pointedly back to the window.

"And your accommodations lavish."

Another glance. She clearly had little interest in speaking with this rough representative.

The King changed tacks. "You have a lovely shape, my Lady," he said. "Your bridegroom is a lucky man."

Anne of Cleves slowly looked over at him, then at the rest of them, clearly upset that they were not discouraging this kind of talk. This time she did not turn back to the window, but pursed her lips and lowered her eyes.

"A toast to the wedding night," the King said.

They all smiled uncomfortably and raised their glasses, all except for the Princess.

"When it will be the warmest bed in Christendom," he continued.

The Princess blushed and flinched like a stricken horse.

Unfortunately, the King did not stop. Instead, her stern reserve caused him to lose control.

"Sweetheart, you bewitch me," he cried, stretching out his arms and lunging at her.

Edward froze, mouth agape, with the rest of the room. Only the Princess responded, gasping and shuddering, arms crossed against his advances.

That did not stop the King. "Praise God, I shall be your true husband," he bellowed as his hands grabbed hers.

The Princess screamed and threw herself to her knees.

"*Mein Gott! Mein Gott!*" she spat, eyes bulging and wild. Edward recoiled; even the King halted.

Suffolk stepped up and bowed deeply. "My apologies, Princess. This messenger is no messenger; he is the King. I suggested this ruse so you could meet without the pressure of protocol. I apologize for my mistake."

Her eyes still darted, but she took a deep breath. Suffolk held out a hand for her to stand and she took it.

The King grimaced. "I am sorry for my enthusiasm," he said and bowed stiffly. When he rose his face was a careful blank.

She took another deep breath and curtsied, yammering in a patois that Edward could not understand. All he could do was pick out the repeated word "virtue" and the phrase "the German court is different."

The King edged closer to the door. "I shall wait on you again tomorrow before I leave."

The words calmed her. "I look forward to the day," she said, eyes still averted.

The King left the room, and the group followed him out. He then returned to the door and bowed a last time before shutting it behind him. His face was grim when he looked at them.

"I am ashamed that men have so praised the Princess."

"Your Majesty?" The strain of maintaining a casual look raised Cromwell's voice by more than an octave, and it cracked like a teenaged boy's.

"I like her not," the King said.

"Sire?" Cromwell croaked.

"Must I really put my head in this yoke? Is there no way out?"

Cromwell could only stammer. "You don't...is she...Your Maj—"

"I don't want to be here anymore," said Henry, his shoulder sagging.

"It's late, Sire. Stay here tonight," said Suffolk. "Things may look better on the morrow."

The King shook his head. "I have no energy to travel

further; I will retire now. But I will need wine. Much wine."

"My page and your men will accompany you to your rooms," said Suffolk. "I will follow momentarily with provisions."

Henry nodded curtly and slung his cape over his shoulder. Slowly he trudged down the hallway, dragging his feet as he went. Edward's heart felt heavier with each step.

"I am so sorry," Edward said to Cromwell.

Cromwell shook his head. "It's fine. All will be well."

"How can you say that after such a meeting?" Suffolk asked.

Cromwell waved his hand as if brushing away a gnat. "He liked her," he said. "Enough to forget himself."

For a moment Edward found the logic vaguely persuasive, but then his annoyance returned over Cromwell's obstinate optimism. "She refused him."

"No, she refused the messenger to save herself for the King," Cromwell said. "It is understandable that a young princess of refined morals would refuse to entertain the advances of an unknown gentleman."

"I know the King," said Suffolk. "He expected her to discern his majesty through the disguise."

"A woman assaulted in front of her betrothed's representatives is in no position to discern majesty." Cromwell wagged his finger. "Or to appear at her best."

Suffolk's eyes narrowed. "She was indeed a woman in panic," he said slowly.

"The Princess acted in accordance with the great estate to which she has been called. Surely the King will come to understand this. I will tell him myself, and I trust you will mention it as well?"

Suffolk looked at Cromwell appraisingly. "Aye," he said. "I will."

A page appeared with a large flagon of wine. Suffolk grabbed it. "Wish me luck."

"Skill, not luck, my good Duke," said Cromwell with a knowing smile.

Before Suffolk had gotten three paces away, Browne

spoke up. "I shall check on the horses. We may be riding out quite early tomorrow." He ran off, leaving Cromwell and Edward alone.

Edward turned to Cromwell. "You can't really think this will blow over? She looked disgusted by him. He will never forgive her for that."

"Innocence should not be easily ceded."

It sounded plausible when he said it, but still Edward doubted. I think it is a mistake."

Cromwell shrugged. "She will rise to this. It is her duty. And the King's."

Edward shook his head, but Cromwell only leaned forward and clapped him jovially on the shoulder. "This is what kings do. And the Princess is a lovely lady. The people will love her and so will the King."

"It is not the opinion of the people I fear," said Edward.

"She gives his country peace. She assures his people's safety. This is the closest thing to his heart. His legacy."

Edward remained unconvinced, but he had no energy or stomach for a fight right now. Surely it would all be fine. Cromwell was rarely wrong. Not on things this momentous.

January 7, 1540—Greenwich Palace

Early in the morning after the royal wedding, the page set a tray on the trestle table in Edward's small Presence Chamber and bowed out of the room. Cheeses, dried fruits, and biscuits still warm from the kitchens; Edward would not have to leave for some time. He bowed his head to say a quick grace before breaking his fast. His ear was cocked for any hint of movement in the hall from the King's room.

Given how reluctant the King had been to enter into the marriage, Edward intended to hide away for as long as he could. He didn't want to be associated with disappointment, if that's what it turned out to be. Cromwell maintained that the situation would smooth over if the new Queen had wit, and she clearly did. But still Edward doubted.

A quiet knock startled him. "Hertford?" It was Cromwell's voice.

Edward considered silence but decided against it. "Come," he said.

Cromwell entered, his jaw set.

"Well?" Edward asked.

Cromwell closed his eyes and shook his head, then sat heavily at the table. Edward jumped up to grab a glass of ale for him, and the choicest morsels from the tray.

Cromwell reached for the cup and stared at it, fingering the Tudor roses in the heavily worked silver. "Is this from the set the King gave you as a New Year's gift, the year your sister was Queen?" he asked.

Of course Cromwell recognized it – he suggested all the New Year's gifts.

"The very same," Edward answered. "A reminder of better times, and a hope for future ones."

"To better times," Cromwell toasted and drank deeply.

Edward was suddenly filled with melancholy for days when the future really did look bright. "You have spoken to the King?"

Cromwell stared into the fire, anguished. "I waited upon His Majesty in his Privy Chamber." He paused. "I found him not as pleasant as I expected."

"Perhaps he was just tired?"

"I was so bold as to ask him outright how he liked the Queen."

Edward inhaled sharply.

"He answered me soberly. He said, 'Surely, my Lord, as ye know I liked her before not well. But I like her now much worse. For I have felt her belly and her breasts and thereby as I can judge she should be no maid.'"

"No maid?"

"It gets worse."

Edward strained to imagine how such a thing could be possible. "Worse?"

"He said he was so struck to the heart when he felt them that he had neither will nor courage to proceed any further in other matters."

Edward felt the blood drain from his face. "He didn't consummate the marriage?"

"Not yet," said Cromwell. "He is punishing me in this. Withholding pleasure from himself to express the extent of his anger."

"So where is the cure?"

"He is a king, for sweet Jesu's sake," said Cromwell. "He must act like one. What is wrong with the man? Does he really think he can act like this before all of Christendom?"

Dangerous words. Edward kept silent.

"I will grovel as I always do," Cromwell continued. "I will praise his great fortitude and the love for his country that prompted him to do this. Remind him this is the only move that assures England's security." He took a drink and squared his shoulders. "He'll get over his pique soon enough."

"God willing."

Cromwell nodded as if trying to convince himself. "A few masques, that's all it will take to reveal the Queen's charms. That and wine."

"And if you are wrong?"

"All he needs to do is close his eyes and think of other things. He can get sons by her, and seek his real pleasure elsewhere. It's a simple enough matter."

"You are not worried at what mischief Norfolk and Gardiner will cause when they hear of this?"

"What mischief can they cause? Besides, Norfolk is in France, and His Majesty does not speak of these things to Gardiner."

"Still," Edward said.

"I know I am right."

Edward looked into Cromwell's flat, black eyes and shuddered.

"You will see," Cromwell said. He slapped his hands on the table and stood. "And now I must get to work before I give the King cause for any new criticism."

After he left, Edward eyed the food left on the table.

Regardless of what Cromwell said, Edward still intended to keep to his plan of hiding for some time.

February 28, 1540—Whitehall Palace

"That's impossible," said Stephen Gardiner in shock, his mouth agape. Norfolk had returned to court after three months in France, and Gardiner had come to Norfolk's apartments to welcome his friend and ally. But instead of finding a man happy to be home, he found a Duke snarling from the letters that had awaited his return.

Apparently, Thomas Cromwell had taken advantage of Norfolk's absence to wreak mischief: he had closed Thetford Priory, the resting place of centuries of Howard family remains. For four years, Norfolk's considerable influence had exempted the house from the monastic dissolutions, but the King had changed his mind.

"It's fact," said Norfolk. "His Majesty has rejected entirely the single-minded pursuit of holiness, has deemed worthy of shelter only those who serve a flock."

"But surely the order can be countermanded, surely you can persuade the King. It's not just your relatives, it's also his own dead son—"

"No." Norfolk's voice was flat and final. "The closure has been completed."

Gardiner looked at his hands, at the frantic letter the Abbot had sent to the Duke only ten days prior. "How?"

Norfolk handed him a second letter, even more impossibly recent, informing him it had taken the commissioners only three days to present the dissolution order, turn the monks out of the house, cart off the plate and household goods, and remove the lead and slate from the roofs.

Gardiner sat back, stunned by the alacrity of the implementation. And concerned for Norfolk, who would have to scramble to find holy ground into which to re-inter dozens of proud ancestors. An ignominious position unworthy of the Duke.

"Cromwell's doing. I will destroy that scum, mark my words. He has gone too far, by God." Norfolk's eyes were hooded and his face was dark.

This thrust should not have been unexpected to the old warrior. When Cromwell was absent, Norfolk had moved the country toward Catholicism – a move that made the Baron's retaliatory gesture seem petty.

Truly, Cromwell's advantage was not as extreme as it could have been. The King was not so carried away by love of his new German bride as to continue to sweeten that alliance. Indeed, he was tiring of both.

"Cromwell thinks he rides high in the King's favor right now," Gardiner said matter-of-factly. "He has been rude to me as well. But the pendulum will swing back. I feel it already shifting."

Norfolk nodded, and Gardiner mentally crossed himself to atone for the unholy conceit that filled his breast at such vindication.

"He will regret his arrogance," said Norfolk. He nodded and raised a single eyebrow as he leaned in to share a quiet piece of news. "The King wants my niece Catherine."

Norfolk's words took a minute to sink in, then understanding exploded. Catherine Howard was a slip of a girl barely seventeen years old, with a swaying walk and a flirtatious smile. Of course. She looked faintly like Suffolk's wife, the former Catherine Willoughby – another woman the King had always desired.

"Does she know?" Gardiner asked.

"Of course she knows." Norfolk's voice was harsh. "She came to me."

Gardiner closed his eyes and bowed his head. A king's mistress was in the perfect position to influence policy: Catherine Howard could be the divine instrument that brought England back to the blessed Catholic fold. Gardiner would surely get a cardinal's hat for that. He made a trembling sign of the cross. "All her necklaces should be crucifixes. She must attend every Mass, spend her life telling the rosary. Invite the King to share her faith in between their pleasures."

"I have told her to keep her knees tightly shut."

"What?"

"I think she might unseat the Flanders Mare."

Marriage. Of course. Not just a temporary toy but a permanent force – for of course her whole family would rise with her. And their friends. Gardiner nodded. "She could well do that."

"I have instructed her to share her yearning for an honorable marriage. To summon innocent outrage if he should try anything." Norfolk's smile did not reach his eyes. "To play her cousin's game."

Anne Boleyn had indeed set the path for a maid of honor to supplant a queen. Another niece of Norfolk's who had contributed to the advancement of the Howard family until she was replaced by the same method. Could this trick really work a third time?

Gardiner changed his tone. "It is a dangerous project."

"Not if we simply let things happen and guide them when we can. That is a small risk for a large reward."

"It still seems unlikely," Gardiner said. "What of the alliance with the German states?"

Norfolk curled his lip. "Each new day reminds France and Spain how much they have always hated each other. Meanwhile, Francis has followed up the fine New Year's gift he sent to the King with kind words and wishes I have been instructed to pass on. I believe we are well beyond the danger that required the marriage. And so it can be dissolved and a better one settled."

"Would that it were that easy, but what cause can we use?" asked Gardiner. "Her precontract to Lorraine? We tried to raise that to avoid the marriage and failed."

A small smile played at the side of Norfolk's mouth. "That was before the marriage. A term I use loosely."

Gardiner was confused. How could Norfolk question the marriage? It had been consecrated by the Archbishop of

Canterbury in front of the court and the world, then—

A blinding thought gripped him. "Has he still not bedded the woman?"

"Still not," smiled Norfolk. "Or so my niece tells me."

Gardiner's knees weakened. As if he understood, Norfolk sat so Gardiner could collapse without breaching protocol.

The marriage was not yet fully a marriage. The King understood the significance of consummation - it had been at the heart of his fight to dissolve his marriage to Catherine of Aragon. This must be deliberate restraint.

"Who else knows about this?" Gardiner croaked. "How is this not more widely spoken of?"

"The Queen has little English. And this is not a topic easily discussed."

"Praise the Lord," Gardiner said, and made the sign of the cross again.

They sat in silence for a moment. Norfolk was uncharacteristically calm, a small self-satisfied smile playing around his mouth.

Gardiner's mind was racing. "Praise the Lord you came back when you did," he repeated. "So you could instruct your niece."

"She is a Howard," Norfolk boasted. "She was quick to see the possibilities herself."

"The King loves gardens," Gardiner blurted.

Norfolk raised his eyebrows. Gardiner shook his head apologetically. "She should be asking him about plants, talking to him of cures. Queen Jane made much of that trick."

"Excellent point," said Norfolk. "I will pass on the advice. As for you, my dear Bishop, I would hope you would find some way of hinting at the blessing of marital bliss. I want us all to be singing the same tune."

"Of course." Gardiner looked down at his hands as if they held some sort of answer. "Though I think we also should glorify pure love and chivalry - we don't want to inflame him so much he destroys our advantage."

Norfolk nodded. "Do it," he commanded, and turned away.

Gardiner bowed out, wondering to himself at the mysterious ways of the Lord, at how His Church could be saved by a mistress and a dissolved sacrament. God's fight sanctified any weapon.

Chapter Four

March 29, 1540—Hertford Hall

Mist enveloped the hired barge, making the forty-minute trip from Hampton Court to Hertford Hall seem endless. They had been late getting started and almost missed the tide. Part of Edward wished they had, given the oppression that mounted as they approached the city. The feeling was mirrored by scenery that gradually changed from empty fields on both sides to congested masses of humanity hidden behind squat walls, their doors shut tightly against the gloom.

They were on their way to visit Edward's wife, Anne, for dinner. She had not returned to court as Edward had hoped: she was too often with child to serve as a lady-in-waiting to the Queen. So Edward returned home four nights every week, and Anne insisted on holding a larger *soirée* on at least one of these; it let her feel a part of things. This was the first time Edward resented the obligation, even though tonight involved little more than family. He longed to crawl into bed and pull the curtains tight around him.

His siblings, Tom and Elizabeth, had made the trip earlier in the day. That left the four of them on the boat now: Edward, Sadler, Cromwell, and Cromwell's son, Gregory, who married Elizabeth just a short time before Jane died. They rode in silence. Only the grunts of the rowers, tired from the slight drag of the unhelpful water, broke the quiet, raising the tension that made it hard for Edward to inhale fully.

Earlier that day, the King had required their presence for no clear reason, hemming and hawing over cards and dice for more than an hour before finally blurting he wanted a discreet way to annul his marriage to Cleves. Then he'd quickly gone off to some amusement with the Duke of Norfolk.

Edward hated feeling like he was sharing the blame for this matter, and leaving with the others for this gathering only exacerbated things.

Anne ran out to the courtyard to greet them, arriving before the stable boy. "The King intends to put aside the Queen," she hissed.

Edward stiffened. *How does she know?* "Why do you say that?"

"Listen to what your brother tells you and see if you disagree."

She turned on her heels and strode away. Edward looked at Cromwell, whose face had turned ashen.

"He told me he wanted this secret," Cromwell muttered. "That he'd told no one."

They walked in silence to the Great Hall, where Tom and Elizabeth were seated at the long trestle table, chatting over walnuts.

Tom laughed. "I knew your wife would not wait to tell you."

Edward stopped in his tracks. "Where did you hear this news?"

"No news yet, but he is courting Catherine Howard," said Tom.

Edward's relief that this matter was still technically a secret was quickly drowned out by horror. "What?"

"Last night during the dancing I saw him giggle like a young girl. You would have thought he was the innocent and she the doddering monarch."

Edward searched his mind for what he knew about Catherine Howard. Seventeen years old and newly come to court from the country. A middling beauty, but with the coquettishness of her cousin Anne Boleyn. His shoulders slumped and he took his place at the bench. His companions joined him, and they each grabbed a walnut and a bronze nutcracker.

"There was no way to miss it," Tom continued. "I could feel a tingle in the air from across the room."

"Mention how he defended her," said Anne, hovering over Tom.

"I was getting to that," Tom said peevishly.

No matter how many times Edward told her, Anne always forgot Tom thought himself the showman and whined when anyone rushed him through a story. A common failing, actually, though it was more annoying coming from his brother.

"Thomas Culpeper, ever the rake, made bawdy comments when we were preparing the King for bed. Talked about how warm that bed would be if he married such a woman. The King cuffed his ears and said she was too good for such a rogue."

"Who in the world allowed a Howard girl to join the Queen's household?" Cromwell asked.

Elizabeth shook her head at Tom. "The King squeezed the Queen's hand last night, and smiled kindly at her. You are making too much of his attention to Catherine."

Gregory sat forward. "He is right that she may be above Culpeper's attentions. Didn't he rape a gamekeeper's wife?"

"That was his brother," said Tom, bristling at his sister's disagreement. "What's more important is that she could sway the King toward the Catholics."

Elizabeth laughed carelessly. "He can't leave the German alliance."

Edward winced, and felt Cromwell, Sadler, and Gregory do the same. Even Anne, who didn't yet know the facts, rolled her eyes.

"Unfortunately, he can and will," said Cromwell. "Our coastal fortifications are complete, peace with France is assured – he does not need Cleves anymore. And what the King does not need, he discards."

"But how could he put aside a foreign princess?" Elizabeth continued, ignoring Geoffrey's hand signals to hush.

Cromwell leaned forward and looked ominously into his daughter-in-law's eyes. "His Majesty today tasked me with finding the answer to that question." His face was twisted as if the words tasted foul in his mouth.

Three sharp intakes of breath. Then silence.

Anne groped over to a chair and lowered herself.

Elizabeth was the first to speak. "I still don't believe he will marry Kitty Howard. And I don't know if she expects it either. She has not changed at all in her manner with the Queen, and she's no more or less kind to the rest of us. I would think she would hold such an advantage over people."

"She's smarter not to, actually. And now that Norfolk's back, he'll coach her," said Cromwell. "Too many mistresses have risen to become wives."

"Still, it means little," said Elizabeth.

Anne tapped her fingers on the table. "If only he would bed the Queen."

The whole court had discovered the Queen was still innocent when she told the Countess of Rutland how her husband came to bed each night: he would kiss her, take her by the hand and wish her a good night – then in the morning he would kiss her again and bid her farewell. "We'll have to see more than that, ere we get a Prince of York," the cheeky Countess had replied, but the Queen shook her head and said she was more than happy with the state of affairs. Every lady had shared the story.

"That's the scariest piece," said Edward. "It means—"

"Stop," Cromwell shouted. His eyes were wild. "His Majesty did not mention this fact to me this afternoon. A key piece of information that would make my assigned task easier, and he didn't tell me." Cromwell paused, and a smile spread across his face. His eyes narrowed and he looked around the table with a smirk. "Why do you suppose he did that?"

"He assumed you knew," said Edward.

Cromwell shook his head excitedly. "His Majesty is always dissembling. Everything he does is deliberate and sneaky – he weaves a tangled web. He didn't tell me because he didn't want me to use the Queen's innocence. He doesn't really want to leave her, he just wants the girl to think he will."

It was an interesting view of Henry. Edward knew the King was calculating enough to do something like this, but this didn't seem likely.

"My Lord, I am not following you," Anne said.

"The little Howard tart is likely to spread her legs now that Norfolk knows I've been instructed. Don't you see? He just wants the girl to cede – he wants me to fail."

Edward opened his mouth to speak but closed it when he saw Anne's warning look. She was right: this was not the time or place to question Cromwell's judgment, especially if the minister was just putting a brave face on things.

Two pages entered with the silver finger bowls that presaged the start of the day's final meal. Edward tried not to grumble. It was a Friday during Lent, so dinner would not delight. There would be no flesh, no eggs, no dairy. Just fish and parsnips. Oh, Anne would probably offer a roasted pike to tempt their appetites, and might even add an eggless rice pudding to soothe their angry stomachs, but still. For a man who loved his buttered bread, this was as good a reason as any to embrace religious reform.

Conversation was strained during the meal. By silent agreement they turned to gossip. As early as possible, Edward sent their guests off to their rooms for the night so he could finally enjoy the peace he'd been craving.

Apparently Anne had different ideas. The second they were alone in their rooms, she turned to him with a hiss. "Make friends with Norfolk."

Edward sighed and slumped in a chair to untie his tall leather boots. "Act the hypocrite? Would you also have me pretend corrupt priests hold the key to our eternal life, turn my back on the common—"

"I would just have you friends with the next Queen's uncle. Your conscience need not trouble you over that."

"Easy for me," Edward sighed. "Impossible for Cromwell. Not after he has openly baited the man as he has." It was ridiculous how Cromwell and Norfolk battled. And frightening that the King seemed to enjoy pitting the two men against each other, as if their enmity assured him of greater loyalty from both.

Anne pressed her lips together. "It's too late for Cromwell. You've seen for months his judgment can no longer be trusted. You must save yourself."

"What?" Edward asked, although he understood quite well.

Anne removed her hood and shook her hair loose before flouncing over to her dressing table. She grabbed her prized ivory-handled brush and began to stroke her locks. "Cromwell has known for some time the King is unhappy, and he has done nothing. He has also known for some time the King has not bedded his wife. That is dangerous enough, but now if your brother is right and the King desires Catherine Howard, well..."

Edward's stomach turned over. "If the King does indeed desire Catherine Howard, perhaps Cromwell is right to do nothing – except pray this fancy will pass."

"As Wolsey did?"

Edward cringed. She was right. Wolsey had dragged his feet on securing a divorce for the King from Catherine of Aragon, in the hope the King would tire of Anne Boleyn before the deed was done. He'd died a broken man. "Poor Cromwell."

"Poor Cromwell, you say now, but we all knew all along the King liked comely young things. Look how he acts with the Duchess of Suffolk."

Edward shook his head, pained at how stupid his wife was making him feel. "But he also loved my sister. And Catherine of Aragon in her own time. He values propriety."

Anne shook her own head. "Who are we to say what will attract him? Such a mercurial man. It was doomed from the start."

Edward took a deep breath. "I will think on this, but I don't want to do anything rash."

Anne had solved the puzzle that bothered him. Again,

Edward blessed his good fortune at having a wife who could advise him so well – despite her sharp tongue. The truth was sometimes cruel, after all.

"There is another danger you must consider," said Anne. "The flaw in Cromwell's logic."

"Which one?"

"He disregarded the bigger secret the King kept. The fact he desires Norfolk's niece. He knows this information would make Cromwell drag his feet."

Edward's mind spun. She was right. The act of the secret and the secret itself were equally significant. Another variant of Cromwell's lessons: if you look to see why the King does something, look at the people he tells about it or doesn't. Still, one detail rankled. "But if we take Elizabeth's view as correct, he also is keeping his intentions from Catherine Howard."

"Your sister is an idiot," Anne said. "And if she were right, that would just make things worse." Lips quivering, she put down her brush and clasped her hands to plead with him. "I beg of you, befriend Norfolk. Before this goes any further. When this is done, Cromwell will not be so welcome at court. You need new friends."

April 14, 1540—Hampton Court Palace

Of all the King's palaces, Hampton Court was the most magnificent. It would stand to reason, then, that the apartments allocated to the Duke of Norfolk there would be most impressive – but they weren't. Oh, they could still make Gardiner's jaw hang open, but they were not as fine as they could be. The walls had no marble or gilt to complement the carved wood paneling, and they were hung with dour portraits instead of inviting tapestries. They were the rooms of a weathered warrior, not those of a refined artist. More fitting for a man working to implement an important strategy.

Catherine Howard had come to report on an innocuous

walk with the King, and the conversation had quickly shifted to the latest news, which inevitably provoked disgust from the old Duke. Norfolk hawked loudly and spat into the fireplace that dominated his study. Gardiner cringed inwardly but was impressed with how Catherine merely paused, her smile unchanged, and allowed the offending gesture to pass as if it had never occurred. Praise God, he thought, that she was not sensitive to an old man's displays.

And there would surely be more spitting from Norfolk: in three days, Thomas Cromwell would be elevated to the Earldom of Essex. *Essex.* The title was created in the twelfth century – two hundred years before the dukedom of Norfolk arose. So while Norfolk would still be England's premier peer, Cromwell would boast a more ancient lineage.

"*I* should have been given the Essex title and revenues," Norfolk snarled. "I deserve them more than that cur."

Gardiner let him sputter. Ranting would calm him. Happily Catherine too remained silent, gazing with the same calm smile that could mark her as either angelic or simple. Gardiner still couldn't quite tell which.

Finally the Duke slumped into a chair and drummed his fingers on the wood claws that peeked out from the padded *manchette*, a signal he was ready to discuss tactics. Now Gardiner could reason with him.

"This may have been his reward for closing the abbeys, but that service has already faded from memory," said Gardiner. The last abbey had submitted to the King the week before, ceding the final pile of Church wealth that would accrue to the English treasury. "Now Cromwell has nothing to distract him from dissolving this sham marriage. Now he has to succeed."

Norfolk's face twisted. "He had to succeed anyway. We all must do the King's bidding. There was no need to change the station of a blacksmith's son."

Gardiner took a deep breath. The man's personal animosity was clouding his judgment. "This tightens the noose," Gardiner continued. "The King has given Cromwell a higher platform from which to fall."

Norfolk leaped out of the chair to pace. His mantel billowed behind him, the white lynx collar glowing in the room's darkness. "He can't fail. Catherine must become Queen."

Catherine gave a small start. Her smile widened, and she smoothed her damask skirt. It was a well-chosen garment: it had a formfitting shape, and its dusty rose color highlighted her reddish hair and enhanced her coloring.

Gardiner shook off the vision to continue the discussion. "Remember there are many ways to fail. You cannot allow yourself to be distracted by Cromwell's title. The King expects this done quickly and his patience will wear thin – we just need to spur the wearing."

Norfolk bared his crooked yellow teeth. "We must spur it hard. What if the King gets drunk one night and beds Cleves?"

Gardiner nodded and was about to respond when Norfolk stopped pacing. His mantel sagged for a moment then swirled again as he spun to face Catherine, eyes blazing. He raised a finger at her. "You must yield to him."

"Your Grace?" Gardiner was shocked. Just last week they had agreed this would be folly. With any man this would begin the countdown to indifference – and with this King, so quickly bored...

Catherine lowered her eyes and nodded, smile unchanged.

"Wait," Gardiner began. "I commend your loyalty," he said to Catherine, "and I know your uncle must appreciate your trust, but much of your appeal lies in your innocence. I worry its loss might harm your position."

"The King believes he is not married to the Queen," she replied, her voice firm. "Therefore if we pledge our troth to each other, and we consummate our vows, we will be married in the sight of God."

Her reasoning was sound, as if she had considered the issue. Interesting. Surely Gardiner's should not be the only voice urging caution. He turned to Norfolk. "I wish to understand your sudden change. If he beds Catherine and does not hear the angels sing in chorus, all is lost."

"He will not be disappointed," said Catherine quietly. Finally, the smile was gone from her face.

Norfolk nodded approvingly at her confidence and turned back to Gardiner. "He is less likely to be tempted by Cleves if he is bedding my niece."

"And I can be careful to avoid pregnancy," Catherine said quickly.

"No," Norfolk cried. "Just the opposite. We want you with child. That will force the issue. As it did with your cousin."

Norfolk was right. After seven interminable years of holding out, Anne Boleyn had changed her strategy. The King bought her maidenhead by elevating her to Marquess of Pembroke and presenting her as his intended to the French King. The resulting pregnancy had hastened the plans for the Church of England. An heir had to be legitimate, after all.

"Yield," he agreed.

Norfolk clapped his hands together, and walked to the table to pour himself some wine. "Here's to rubbing the blacksmith's face in his downfall," he said, smiling for the first time since he'd heard the news about the Essex title.

"But not yet," warned Gardiner. "Right now, our priority is to see Catherine safely on the throne. Once that happens, you have all the time in the world to destroy Cromwell – your niece can speak of how she mistrusts him, how she doubts his loyalty."

"My uncle has already instructed me to do so," Catherine said.

Norfolk laughed. "Ah, Gardiner, she was magnificent yesterday. She compared the court to market day in Lambeth." Norfolk turned to his niece. "Say it as you did to the King."

Catherine nodded and turned to Gardiner for the performance, tilting her head so her smile looked up at him. "Oily men, standing in the middle of the path to peddle their wares, forcing their terms on you until you forget which are your own and which are theirs." She tilted her head to the other side, eyes far off, then turned back to Gardiner and looked at him full in the face. "Much like your Thomas Cromwell."

Gardiner made the sign of the cross in homage to such wit. "That is wonderful, though for now do it only when you are alone. Cromwell should be lulled into a false sense of security by his damned title."

"Like a dog distracted by a meaty bone," Norfolk snickered. "Easier to destroy." He poured two more goblets of wine and handed them out. "To happy plans."

"Happy plans."

They drank deeply and sat back. Catherine broke the silence. "So you don't want this change known, Uncle? That will be difficult."

"Why?"

"He should be uncertain of me until the very last moment, but that leaves no chance for him to give orders we not be disturbed."

Gardiner's stomach tensed. "You need a private place for this love to bloom," he said. "I can hold private dinners for you at my Palace of Winchester. Then whatever happens..."

Norfolk's eyes narrowed, then he nodded. "This is good. You and I can repair to your library after dinner so you can say Mass for me for a vassal who died. They'll be alone for an hour." Norfolk turned to Catherine. "Take your time. There will be many such dinners."

Gardiner looked down at his hands and saw they were steady. He cared nothing for the fact that church grounds were being offered for fornication. If it served to restore God's true Church, it was a holy act. After all, He did move in mysterious ways.

June 10, 1540—Westminster

The Privy Council met at Westminster at least twice each week, and some of its members also met as the Star Chamber, a special judicial body mandated to enforce laws against powerful people that regular courts might be too intimidated to try impartially. It had broad power to impose punishment, even on actions that were technically lawful, and was therefore much feared, even though most of the time it merely heard petitions of redress from subjects around the country.

The lords of the Star Chamber slumped around a massive oak table in the center of the room, eyes cast down, listening to Cranmer read the facts from the case before them. Or pretending to. They were the fifteen most powerful men in the land - all but Edward appointed because their governmental posts assured membership - and they disdained administrative details. Not Edward. Edward was constantly reminded he was the only one who did not hold an office, who sat on these councils at the pleasure of the King.

Edward looked up to the ceiling, at the gold stars dotting the blue background, the same ones that had given the group its name centuries ago. As always, the consciousness of history and the tenuousness of his position made him straighten his back and focus his gaze, reminding himself that every English subject deserved justice, and it was an honor to confer it.

The captain of the scarlet-liveried guards caught Edward's eye. He was approaching from the back of the gallery and had continued on past the railing toward the Council table. He must be delivering a message to one of the lords, though Edward could not imagine why a page had not been sent on such a menial task. Clanking swords signaled the appearance of more yeomen, two by two, at both of the doors across the room. Edward looked over his shoulder and saw there were also guards at the doors behind him. The Council was surrounded.

What was this?

The captain went directly to Cromwell, started to bow, stopped, then resumed. Cromwell stood, eyes wide.

"My Lord, I have a warrant to arrest you for high treason."

There were gasps and a rustle throughout the room. For a moment none of it made sense to Edward. His mind replayed the words, trying to decipher what they could have been. Then the Duke of Norfolk stood and faced Cromwell, a grim smile on his face. "I always knew you for a vile serpent, unworthy to walk among us. Now the world knows it as well."

Cromwell looked back at the guard. "There must be some mistake."

Without a word, the guard unfolded the paper to show him the King's signature. Edward's first confused thought was that the document lacked a seal, so it could not be official, but then he remembered: Thomas Cromwell was the keeper of the seals.

Cromwell grabbed his bonnet and threw it on the ground. "This, then, is the reward for loyal service?" he cried.

Edward's insides froze and he looked around. Sadler and Cranmer looked shattered. Norfolk and Gardiner kept calm gazes on Cromwell. Wriothesley and Suffolk wore smug smiles. Browne and the others seemed carefully noncommittal, especially Sir William Kingston, who must have known. Of course, Kingston had served as Constable of the Tower for more than a decade and had intimate experience with such surprises.

"Gentlemen, I appeal to your consciences," Cromwell said. "You know I am no traitor."

"You are a Lutheran who seeks to subvert the King's policies," said Norfolk.

Cromwell drew himself to his full height. "I am the King's faithful minister who does only his bidding. If I thought I had offended, I would renounce all pardon for such a heinous act."

The Duke of Suffolk banged the table and leaned forward. "And yet you are a traitor according to the laws you yourself made." A Catholic duke siding with a Catholic duke, forgetting his own humble origins. "Many men have been brought to death over words spoken with good intention. Perhaps now you understand the standard you have set."

Edward felt bile rise in his throat. The irony was clear. Cromwell had spun treason from whole cloth to bring down a dozen men - even a queen. And now he himself was trapped. For beliefs Edward shared. He suppressed a retch.

"Take your prisoner," the Duke of Norfolk ordered the captain. "But first" - he lurched forward and grabbed the Order of Saint George that Cromwell wore around his neck - "you are not fit to wear this."

Cromwell looked down, defeated, at the empty place on his chest. Norfolk dropped his voice to a cruel whisper. "You never were."

Cromwell raised his fists and lurched forward, but the guard darted in front of Norfolk to protect him. Edward's heart ached as Cromwell's shoulders slumped and Sir William Fitzwilliam, the Lord High Admiral, leaned over to untie the garter that adorned Cromwell's leg. Another honor removed, this time by a man who had been a friend during times of prosperity. Edward imagined he heard the room sigh, but that could just have been his own breath.

The guard clenched Cromwell's shoulder and led him to the side door that opened onto the river. Cromwell fixed his moist eyes straight ahead and moved stiffly, like a child's toy. The other guards followed close behind, ten armed men for one prisoner. They left the door open behind them, and Edward could see them hurry Cromwell onto a boat waiting to take him through Traitors' Gate to the Tower. Cromwell did not look back.

Edward felt numb, surrounded by a hard shell of fear.

Norfolk turned to the group. "And now, gentlemen, let us discuss the Bill of Attainder that we must present to Parliament forthwith." A Bill of Attainder. A legislative declaration of guilt without the opportunity for defense. The method Cromwell had himself popularized for removing enemies.

"What are the charges?" asked Cranmer.

"Corruption, heresy, and plotting to marry the Lady Mary," answered Norfolk.

The words shocked Edward. Plotting to marry the King's daughter? What invention was this?

"Shall he have no trial?"

"The Star Chamber can condemn him, his guilt is clear enough," said Norfolk in a clipped voice. "Besides, why should he receive anything more than any of his victims?"

Cromwell had made much use of this judicial vehicle. *Those who live by the sword shall perish by the sword,* Edward thought. The irony was gripping, and he wondered whether Gardiner had a hand in that decision.

Norfolk cut short the discussion. "I will prepare a draft of the Bill, to keep things simple." He turned to Sir Thomas Cheney, Treasurer of the Household. "You'll need to get your men together for the inventory - no need to tarry on that."

The inventory. Again Edward's stomach turned over. A man convicted of high treason forfeited all his goods to the Crown. A quick inventory, before frightened heirs could think to hide valuables, kept everyone honest.

"For now I shall return to Greenwich to inform the King his orders have been carried out. Who is coming?" asked Norfolk as he stalked out.

Gardiner and most of the other councilors crowded behind him toward the door that had just swallowed Cromwell. Fitzwilliam looked over his shoulder at Cranmer and Edward, then at Sadler; he left to go with Norfolk's troop. Edward felt a tug, uncertain what to do. Part of him wanted to go with them, to find out more of what had just happened, to see the King's reaction. But he had planned to return to Hertford Hall, which was just a short trip from Westminster. If he went to Greenwich he would never make it home that night, and he needed to see Anne and seek her counsel even though he knew she would be angry he hadn't gone with Norfolk, hadn't thrown his lot in with the winners.

He just couldn't bring himself to do it.

"Archbishop, would it be presuming upon your hospitality to keep our plans for supper?" Edward asked.

Cranmer's face showed no sign of the subterfuge. "Would it be presuming on your friendship to ask you to do so?" he replied.

"Thank you," said Sadler, joining in.

The room emptied, Norfolk with his large and boisterous entourage going to one barge, Edward, Cranmer and Sadler slinking to another. Edward prayed there was no danger from Cromwell's shrunken circle of friends grouping together so conspicuously.

"Your Grace, I beg you," Sadler said to Cranmer as soon as the oarsmen had cast off and they would not be overheard, "may I borrow a messenger? I want to warn Cromwell's servants to remove anything dangerous. No reason to give Norfolk ammunition."

Edward's throat tightened. That was another of Cromwell's own tricks, to use an arrest as a way to secure the evidence to justify it. Half the charges against Anne Boleyn were the product of her own hysterical rantings after her arrest. Now it was another method that would be used against him.

"How will you avoid compromising the messenger?" Cranmer asked.

Sadler kept his eyes down. "The servants have instructions to remove a particular shelf of books and destroy his letters."

Edward took a ragged breath. This was calming and disconcerting at the same time. How many possibly heretical books could be found in his own home? If he were arrested, it would matter not at all that some had been given to him by the King himself. Edward needed to clear out his own collection immediately.

Cranmer dropped his face into his hands. "How in the world could this have happened?"

Sadler shook his head. Edward did likewise. How indeed? All Cromwell had ever done was the King's bidding. With one exception. But even then, the King had made a great show of naming Cromwell Earl of Essex not two months ago. How in the world had the King changed so drastically in a matter of weeks - and how had he concealed his plans? That was the most terrifying part.

"How have we come to this?" Sadler wailed. "Where a simple mistake can be cast as treason? We are none of us safe."

It was true. In his youth, the King had delivered clear warnings, but now his displeasure was all that presaged danger. Edward sighed. "We never have been, we just never recognized the risk."

"But Cromwell was a loyal friend. The King loved him well."

Edward held his tongue, but the list of the King's dead friends tolled in his mind. Thomas More. Bishop Fisher. Anne Boleyn. George Boleyn. Henry Norris. William Brereton. Francis Weston. Nicholas Carew. So many more. Now Cromwell.

"His Majesty has made a terrible mistake," Sadler said. "I pray he will realize Norfolk's accusations are all lies and twisted truths."

"Amen," they both answered.

The three men sat back in their seats, lost in thought as the waves lapped against the boat. Edward thought of Cromwell on his way to the Tower.

The shadow of the axe chilled his very bones.

Chapter Five

The gardens at Greenwich Palace were magnificent this time of year, a heady mix of spring and summer flowers at the height of their beauty. At every opportunity the entire court streamed outdoors to feel the still-gentle sun and light breeze on their faces. Their flighty mannerisms annoyed the careful politicians who took to the gardens, regardless of the weather, for conversations they didn't want overheard. Gardiner was walking now with Thomas Wriothesley, his former protégé and continuing friend. Almost two decades ago, Gardiner had taught law to the then-seventeen-year-old at Trinity Hall, Cambridge. The aspiring courtier was able, enterprising and tenacious, and now served as one of Henry's principal secretaries and Secretary to the Council.

"God was with us in this," Gardiner said. He allowed his smugness to show, as much over their defeat of Cromwell as his own ability to recognize talent.

"Amen to that," said Wriothesley. "Let us pray He is equally kind in the matter of the divorce."

"Aye," Gardiner nodded. "Have you given any thought to how you will proceed?" Gardiner and Norfolk had agreed Wriothesley should take the lead. He was closest to Cromwell in zeal and ability.

"Of course, Your Grace," Wriothesley replied. "You will tell me what points I must prove, and I will see that the evidence exists to prove them." He dropped his voice and leaned in. "By whatever means necessary."

Gardiner felt the blood drain from his face. Not from

the quiet promise – that was why Wriothesley had been chosen for the task – but rather from fear of the responsibility that now looked to be falling onto his own shoulders. "You expect me to advise you as to the law?"

Wriothesley hastened to explain. "I was hoping for your guidance on the religious side – that will rule the legal aspect."

The religious side largely centered around the lack of consummation. Gardiner was at a loss as to what this meant on a practical level. This would be a nightmare if the woman did not corroborate the facts.

Gardiner brought his hands together as if in prayer, his automatic stance when he needed to think. As they rounded the corner of the rose bed, the Duke of Norfolk strode up to them on his way back to the palace. "The King has sent for me. Apparently the cur has written to him from the Tower. Both of you come with me, and agree with everything I say."

Norfolk turned on his heels and the two men fell in quickly behind him. Gardiner had to take several small steps to match Norfolk's long, angry strides. The Bishop's mind spun over what Cromwell could have said in his letter. It would be a plea for mercy, surely, written even though Cromwell knew the King hated such missives. The King avoided any mention or thoughts of death, especially ones he had – or would soon – cause. But what other choice did a prisoner have?

They quickly reached the royal apartments. The King was standing at his worktable preparing a salve for his leg. As the three men entered, he put aside the pearls he had just ground and turned to the lead. The King loved medicinal pursuits, and it was as good an opportunity as Mass was to discuss important matters with him. This was a blessing for Gardiner, whose position as a bishop lost him the privilege of conversing during a holy rite.

They all bowed, Norfolk lowest of all. "I understand there has been a letter?"

The King motioned with his chin to the desk. "Over there. Read it to me."

Gardiner let out the breath he didn't know he'd been holding. The King had not read the letter yet. *Praise God.*

Norfolk picked up the document covered in Cromwell's cramped scrawl. The Duke looked at the King, keeping his face a careful blank. All their faces were carefully blank. Any satisfaction over Cromwell's plight would exude a tone too close to hubris, and fake sympathy might prompt mercy. An inscrutable countenance was safest until indignant outrage on the King's behalf could emerge. "Shall I?"

The King grunted.

Norfolk cleared his throat but shook his head instead of beginning. "Before I do, I should inform you the guards who searched Cromwell's home found letters to Lutherans he had written. Your Majesty, he proved himself a heretic; it made me sick to my stomach."

The King looked up from his work, eyes narrowed. "What did he say?"

Norfolk shook his head again and looked down. "He will never abandon the Protestant heresies, even if you do, Sire."

Gardiner's cheeks grew hot. He looked down to hide his eyes and to emulate Norfolk's pretended distress, while silently absolving Norfolk for the lie.

The King pressed his lips together and went back to his work. "Go on."

Norfolk cleared his throat and began to read. "'Prostrate at Your Majesty's feet, I have heard you wish me to write such things as I think concern my most miserable state.'"

Prostrate at Your Majesty's feet. Echoes of the letter Cromwell had years ago dictated for the Lady Mary to sign, which had earned the King's forgiveness for his daughter's obstinacy. Of course, it had been proffered before the punishment stage. Gardiner could think of only one instance where any monarch had backed down after an arrest: when Norfolk himself had been charged with treason by Henry VII - with much more validity - and had not only escaped his fate but regained his fortunes. But he was a Howard. Cromwell did not have the blood to pull off something like that.

Gardiner still felt amazed at how the trap had been so easily sprung. Thomas Cromwell would be convicted, with no more evidence than he assembled for his own victims, because his political choice of royal bride had been recast into an intent to put his own interests ahead of the King's. Add to that Cromwell's failure to accomplish the annulment of the marriage, again for personal advantage. Disloyalty was treason – and how much more disloyal could a man be?

Norfolk continued. "'And where I have been accused of treason, I never in all my life thought to displease Your Majesty.'"

The King began to stir the paste, leaning over the mixture and paying careful attention to his work. Gardiner could hear him humming quietly. He had clearly stopped listening.

"'If it were in my power to make Your Majesty to live ever young and prosperous, God knows I would; or if it had been or were in my power to make Your Majesty so *puissant* that all the world should be compelled to obey you, Christ knows I would.'"

For so long Cromwell had produced miracles for the King, releasing him from Catherine of Aragon and then Anne Boleyn, refilling the treasury he'd emptied in Wolsey's time from buildings and wars. But all by destroying the Church. So yes, Cromwell would employ sorcery to help his King, and perhaps had.

The King put a dollop of salve on his knife and held it up to examine it in the light. Not satisfied, he continued the stirring. And the humming.

When Cromwell's letter moved to excuses for his transgressions, Gardiner straightened his shoulders and set his mind to be as blank as his face. He marveled at how prisoners could be kept so thoroughly ignorant of the accusations against them. He knew this was one of Cromwell's tricks, but Gardiner had never realized just how powerful it was. Cromwell believed he was in prison for having retained more servants than he was allowed, in violation of the sumptuary laws. And that the King's anger for this crime had been provoked because Cromwell had shared a personal communication involving the Queen. Fascinating.

It was a shame the King was not listening; he would be annoyed over these offenses. A personal communication involving the Queen could only mean a problem like the one he'd had with Anne Boleyn, when the court learned he sometimes lacked skill and virility in bed. There, as here, because of consciousness of sin. It had never happened with Queen Catherine or Queen Jane. Maybe the King had agreed to the arrest because of such pique. God was clearly on the side of Norfolk and Gardiner in this.

"'Written with the quaking hand and most sorrowful heart of your most sorrowful subject, and most humble servant and prisoner, this Saturday at your Tower of London.'" The Duke of Norfolk let his voice trail off and waited for the King's reaction.

"Is that it?"

"Apparently so, Your Majesty. I take it you are as little impressed as I am. The man makes no move to try to right the terrible wrong he has done to you by saddling you with a woman unworthy of your great attention."

The King brushed his hands together to rid himself of invisible dirt. "He should get me divorced. Then he may consider apologizing."

Gardiner forcibly suppressed the sign of the cross he longed to make at the reprieve he had been granted. The King was right: they still needed Cromwell to help arrange for the divorce from Cleves. Gardiner hoped Norfolk would not be so foolhardy as to spurn such assistance – Cromwell might be a lowborn cur, but he was an efficient and effective administrator. It would be a narrow path to tread – to ensure the King's gratitude did not lead to a pardon – but they had no choice. They needed Cromwell's help.

"You made him an earl and still he did not do his duty to you," Gardiner said. "Let's see if the threat of judgment spurs him any the quicker."

Norfolk shot the Bishop a look he could not interpret then turned back to the King. "And how much more of a traitor is he if he succeeds only with such a threat? When it was for love of you, he failed. Now that it is to preserve himself, he succeeds? Nay, Your Majesty, even if he succeeds he must die."

Gardiner suppressed a smile. The King sucked his teeth and nodded. The Duke had clearly struck a nerve and laid out the perfect progression from the original argument that landed Cromwell in the Tower. Again, Stephen Gardiner thanked God that the Duke of Norfolk was on their side. He was too formidable a man to have as an enemy.

June 16, 1540—Hampton Court Palace

Steam rose from the bathtub and fogged the windows. The King sighed and lay his head back against the marble tub, his face a deep crimson. "Another reason I love Hampton Court Palace."

Edward nodded. The King's Privy Closet bathroom was a wondrous place. Deep, plush window seats of dark blue velvet ringed the room, crowned overhead by gold battens carefully stenciled onto a white background. But the tub was its most marvelous feature. Great expense had been lavished more than a decade ago to install actual taps, one for hot water and one for cold. The charcoal-fired stove that fed the cistern was right behind the wall, in another room, but you'd never know it – somehow the pages worked it silently.

Although the space could easily accommodate all the King's gentlemen, today only Edward was in attendance. For which Edward was supremely grateful. "I'm surprised you ever leave, other than to Windsor or Beaulieu," he said to the King. Those were the only two other places such a miraculous contraption existed. And the Tower, though the King no longer stayed there.

"I must work, not idle all my time away. Though I daresay, today has been quite productive."

Edward knew what he meant, but wanted to let the King tell the story. After all, the King's version would be the ultimate truth. "Ah?"

"Yes. Cromwell will be busy in his cell."

Edward's chest contracted. He needed to get past this automatic fear every time the man's name was mentioned. His future depended on it. "What sort of activity do you propose to permit a prisoner?" he asked, in as noncommittal a voice as he could muster.

"Wriothesley is crafting for my divorce a list of every fact relevant at law or to the Church and a corresponding list of the people who can supply evidence."

Wriothesley was crafting the list? Of course that is how he would have presented it to the King. Had Wriothesley mentioned he had first met with Cromwell and written down his instructions? Edward forced himself to calm down. "So he plans a trial?"

"No, it will all be done through depositions we all supply."

"We?" asked Edward even though he already knew he wasn't on the list. The names had been assembled in that morning's Council meeting.

"Me, Norfolk and Suffolk, Wriothesley, my doctors, and some of the Queen's ladies."

Also the Bishop of Durham, Lords Audley and Cobham, Sir Anthony Browne, Anthony Denny of the Privy Chamber, and Thomas Cromwell himself, Edward thought. Such a long list, and no mention of Edward. Edward cursed his decision to pretend ignorance – and resolved that in the future he would try to be more honest. "I would not shy to add my name as well."

The King's shoulders closed in on themselves. "I'm sorry, brother, I never shared my deepest misgivings with you... I...I thought it disloyal to Jane somehow."

Edward hadn't expected such a personal rationale, and it touched and reassured him. He happily allowed all the sorrow and sympathy he felt to show on his face, and added more. "I wish you had," he said. "I wish you had, and that I found some remedy for you."

"The only person who needed to find a remedy was the man who thrust me into such a horrible position. And finally he will start working to that end."

The King let out a loud sigh and slipped his head under the water for a moment. Edward watched until His Majesty reemerged, and then, keeping his voice as noncommittal as possible – since any passion might awaken Henry's suspicions – Edward said, "I would think Cromwell should be happy to have an opportunity to remind you of his efficiency and persuade you of his loyalty."

The King paused a moment. "Perhaps," he finally said, then sat up. "There is a letter from Cranmer on my desk. Bring it in here."

Edward found the letter in the King's office and skimmed it quickly, picking out the name *Cromwell* and the words *sorrow* and *innocence*.

Cranmer was defending Cromwell, and he was clearly going much further than anyone else dared. He had done the same for Anne Boleyn years ago; until now, it was the only instance of anyone defending an accused traitor. Of course, Cranmer was known to be a close confidant of each of the accused, and therefore at risk of being associated with their crimes. In such cases, it might be prudent for him to bring up the issue himself, rather than leave a question to fester in the King's mind. But it was still admirable bravery.

Edward kept his eyes away from the letter on his return to the bath chamber. A good thing, as the King locked eyes with him. "Read it."

"'Most gracious sovereign—'" Edward began.

"To yourself."

Edward nodded. For a time, the King watched, hawk-like, but then relaxed into the hot water, head back and eyes closed. Edward kept his face a mask of perplexed skepticism, just in case.

Despite his resolve, Edward felt himself softening with every line of the letter. Cranmer had written of how he loved Cromwell as a friend, and of the love Cromwell seemed to bear the King. Cranmer also noted Cromwell's vigilance against treason in others – "King John, Henry the Second, and Richard II would never have been overthrown had they had such a councilor" – before stepping back to concede the heaviness of his heart if the accusations were true. He couched seeds of doubt in concern for the King – "Whom shall Your Majesty trust hereafter if you may not trust him?" – and his heartfelt closing was a reminder of Cromwell's skill: "I pray God would send you a counselor who could serve as well as he had."

The letter made Edward wistful for a time when such arguments might have been compelling. Now they were not: once charges were brought, protestations of innocence suggested the King must have been unjust. Whatever Edward said now was dangerous, though because of their long friendship Edward might have some leeway. He hoped he did, since condemning Cromwell would make Edward feel like Peter denying Christ.

In the end, he decided his natural reaction was the right one – especially in light of his recent commitment to greater honesty. "His Grace has captured the dismay of all of us who love you, Sire," Edward finally replied. "And the consternation of all of us who thought of Cromwell as a friend."

Henry opened his eyes, looked at him sharply, and then nodded. "It makes me worry for your sister and her husband," he said.

Edward felt himself start. The King must have seen it too, because he continued. "I don't blame her in the least, or the boy. Please tell them that from me."

It had not occurred to Edward they might be at risk, and he stifled a shudder. "She will be happy to hear of your continued love," he said. "When she heard of this affair, she wept for not having any idea of the great harm you had suffered at her father-in-law's hands."

Henry sniffed in clear self-pity, but his face quickly twisted. "I tire of the bath. Call my men. I need Heneage."

Sir Thomas Heneage, the King's Groom of the Stool.

Edward bowed and backed out. As he watched the King's men stream into the bathing room, Edward reviewed the conversation in his mind. It had been a good one, for many reasons. He had nourished the seed of Cromwell's innocence that Cranmer had planted, and sown one of his own. He had secured the King's mercy for Elizabeth and Gregory. And he had gotten the King to agree to keep him closer in the future. But he still felt numb.

June 29, 1540—Hertford Hall

The clatter of hooves on the cobblestones jolted Edward out of his reverie. He was sitting in the Great Hall, pretending to relax after supper but was actually on edge, waiting for news of Cromwell's fate. Anne and Tom were with him, as well as Elizabeth and Gregory, who had been living at Hertford Hall since the arrest. Without Cromwell, Edward was the undisputed head of both families, and the couple had little choice since all Cromwell's goods had been seized, including his beloved old house at Stepney and his new mansion at Austin Friars. Cromwell had built it on the land of a dissolved monastery; the new property was one of the largest private homes in London, with more than fifty rooms arrayed around three courtyards – another coal that had fueled Norfolk's hatred.

Anne swept to the window and reached out a finger to pull back the curtain. "Green," she said between tight lips. The royal livery meant the messenger was coming from court.

Elizabeth crossed herself. Edward pushed himself slowly to his feet and went to stand beside Anne and wait. Through the space between the curtains he could see the stable boy leading the horse away and the fast-paced messenger already being admitted to the house.

Too quickly, Edward heard the clanking of heavy boots measuring long strides across the stone floor of the corridor. At the entrance to the Great Hall, the messenger paused to glance around the room, discounted Gregory and Tom and headed straight to Edward. After a quick bow of only his head, he silently held out a letter with Sadler's seal.

Edward's hand trembled as he took the message. He pretended not to notice Elizabeth's whimper, and felt rather than saw Anne's eyes looking over his shoulder. He opened the seal and scanned the short line of writing, then nodded to the messenger. "Thank you. There is no reply."

"Well?" Elizabeth and Tom asked in unison the second the servants had left the room.

Edward shook his head. "The Act of Attainder passed both houses. He's been condemned."

Tom fell back in his chair as if he'd been pushed. Gregory lowered his face into his hands, and Elizabeth reached out to stroke his back. "The King may yet remember what your father means to him," she said in a gentle voice.

Gregory shook his shoulder as if to shake her off. She continued. "He sent him money in the Tower. Why would he do that except to give him hope of life?"

"And he allowed him to pursue the divorce from Cleves," Anne added. "This might well be the chance for the King to show mercy."

Up until ten minutes ago, Edward would have agreed. Indeed, for a time he had good hope Cromwell's arrest might have been just a cruel warning. But no one had ever returned from this fate, not after having been attainted. It was time to make the necessary shifts. "You must write to the King," Edward ordered Elizabeth.

Anne sucked in her breath. "That is too dangerous," she said, her words clipped. "And will do nothing. You cannot defend a traitor; you are barely allowed to pray for one. Cranmer was foolish to try. Elizabeth cannot make such a mistake."

"I didn't mean she should write to the King on Cromwell's behalf," answered Edward. "That would be pointless." Elizabeth broke out into sobs, and he raised his voice to make her listen. "It is time for you to write for yourself. The King told us almost two weeks ago you and Gregory are not suspected in this mess. I assured him of your eternal gratitude, but now he needs to hear it from you."

"Why now?" asked Elizabeth.

"The attainder gives you no choice. Having been judged guilty, your father-in-law is guilty, and you must condemn his crimes."

"Judas would write such a letter," said Elizabeth.

"That is only part of moving forward. You must remind him how you have been caught up in this, so he can help you. And soon, before he gives away all of Cromwell's assets."

Elizabeth looked at her brother as she would look at a monster. Edward shrugged it off. "You must write to the King to tell him how his assurance of continued love relieves the extreme indigence brought upon you by Cromwell's heinous offenses. To thank him for the mercy he has shown to you – and to Gregory through you."

"My father-in-law might yet live through this," Elizabeth said.

"If he does, he will thank you for it," Edward answered. "This is the best and surest comfort you can give to him right now: to know his son is safe."

"And mercy towards Elizabeth might soften him towards Cromwell's plight," added Tom. Edward had almost forgotten his brother was even there.

Elizabeth threw a guilty glance at Gregory. "What excuse do I make for waiting so long to write?"

"You didn't want to make any suit for fear of being troublesome," Edward said firmly, centering the argument around the King. Cromwell had taught him that.

Edward took a deep breath. He needed to step up, to step into the void created by Cromwell's departure. It was time to stop trying to hold the place for his friend, or Norfolk would soon fill it. That was the last thing Cromwell would want. Reticence wasn't loyalty.

Gregory raised his head. There was great force behind

his quiet voice. "You should sue to be part of Catherine Howard's household."

Gasps, then silence.

"He's still married to Anne of Cleves," Elizabeth finally said. "Should I not wait?"

"I will mention it to the King when I give him your letter," said Edward. "And I will explain that you did not wish to be too forward." He paused. "I will also speak to Norfolk about it."

"I would not have wagered I would ever see the day we all decided to bow to Norfolk," drawled Tom.

Edward tried not to roll his eyes. "The man is uncle to the next Queen and has just engineered the death of a member of our family. Yes, we bow to him. You must learn strategy, Tom. If you cannot defeat an enemy, you should not engage him."

Indeed. It was time for Edward to revive his interest in military pursuits, time to do whatever it took to emerge victorious. Norfolk craved power and riches, and Edward was the only man who could temper the Duke's influence.

Edward had to dare. He had to make his voice heard and his opinions respected. Whatever it took, he had to do it. For his nephew. For England. For God.

July 15, 1540—Hampton Court Palace

Gardiner again tried to curb his impatience as he followed Norfolk and Hertford in slow steps behind the King and Catherine Howard, who were walking under the covered colonnade at Hampton Court Palace, out of the rain. To their left, the palace's tall windows alternated with brick and marble. To their right, large raindrops chattered and hissed on the gravel *parterre*.

The King's pace faltered; he winced but quickly recovered. Hertford and Norfolk were looking elsewhere and missed it, probably deliberately so. Gardiner cringed; loyalty called for an attendant to express concern, but the

King would likely resent his weakness being noted in front of his seventeen-year-old ladylove. Unfortunately he should not have been walking. He was having a hard time that day, and the odor of his decaying leg was particularly strong despite his desperate attempts to mask it. Still, he insisted on showing off his manly strength, so there they were.

"I need you to read Cromwell's letter again," the King said.

Gardiner stifled a groan. This would be at least the third time the King asked to have Cromwell's latest groveling letter read to him. It had arrived almost two weeks earlier, right after the attainder, and it still crowded the sovereign's mind. The weasel might yet escape.

"Let us sit for a moment so you can read," the King continued. He raised a hand to call for a chair that arrived so quickly the pages must certainly have been eavesdropping.

The King lowered himself into the seat and propped his feet out toward the gravel *parterre*. No one commented on the grunt he was unable to suppress.

Gardiner brightened. This might just be a ruse to justify a rest. *Please God.* He exchanged glances with Norfolk. Hertford noticed and didn't drop his gaze. Was that challenge or complicity?

"This is lovely!" exclaimed Catherine. "Another way to enjoy the fresh air."

The King smiled and grabbed her hand to kiss it. "Your constant delight is a rare jewel," he said, staring deep into her eyes.

"Ah, Your Majesty has found a much better focus than a barely coherent letter," said Norfolk.

Hertford raised his hand and ordered another page to bring the letter.

Gardiner stiffened when Norfolk nodded at Hertford. The Duke was nicer to Hertford than he had ever been to Gardiner. More respectful. It wasn't fair.

The page returned quickly. He held out the paper to Hertford, but Gardiner seized it to hand to Norfolk: Norfolk needed to be the one reading. Hopefully the Duke would understand the great service Gardiner had just done.

"Go on," said the King, looking into Catherine Howard's eyes. He cradled her hand in his and stroked his thumb across her dainty fingers, most of which boasted one or more rings; she batted her eyelashes and smiled at secret, silent jokes between them.

God bless the wench, playing the game for all it is worth, Gardiner thought. It was, after all, worth a great deal.

"I shall skip the parts pertaining to the divorce from Cleves," Norfolk said.

"Fine," said the King, still rapt.

"'Most gracious and merciful Sovereign Lord.'" Norfolk's monotone made the flowery words sound ridiculous, and almost guaranteed they would not be heard. "'Beseeching Almighty God who in all your causes hath always counseled, preserved, opened, maintained, relieved and defended Your Highness – I pray He will now vouchsafe to counsel you, preserve you, maintain you, remedy you, relieve and defend you, as may be most to your honor, wealth, prosperity, health, and the comfort of your heart's desire.'"

Catherine sighed loudly. "This makes me glad we are not married."

The King recoiled. Norfolk looked like he was about to fall forward in a feint, and Gardiner felt sick. Only Hertford remained unperturbed.

"What?" asked the King.

"If we were married, it would be my duty to defend such a scoundrel. To beg your mercy for him, as queens do. But he doesn't deserve it."

Gardiner was careful to keep the smile off his face. The girl was brilliant.

"But go on with your reading, Uncle."

"My Lady," said Norfolk, inclining his head gallantly. The deference in his voice disappeared as he returned to the letter's drone. "'I most humbly beseech Your Grace to pardon this my rude writing, and to consider I am a most woeful prisoner, ready to take the death when it shall please

God and Your Majesty; and yet the frail flesh incites me continually to call to Your Grace for mercy and pardon for my offenses.'"

Gardiner's heart pounded. The pathos of Cromwell's letter increased with each reading. Any minute now would come its final words in all their intensity. "'Most gracious prince, I cry for mercy, mercy, mercy.'"

Norfolk let his voice trail off. They were all silent for a moment, then the blessed girl saved them. "The rain has stopped," she cried. "I shall run and fetch some herbs. Lady Rochford gave me a recipe for a poultice I want to try for your leg. You are all just talking about terrible things here anyway." She gave a quick curtsy and ran off, her blue silk skirt swishing across the marble walkway.

They all watched her retreat down the colonnade, turning every few feet to turn back with a smile and curtsy for the King. Because he was facing sideways, she got to display such coquettishness while not technically turning her back on him. Her interpretation of protocol might have been overly daring in another, but her teasing held the King rapt. Still staring after her, Henry spoke. "She shall have Cromwell's manors."

Gardiner's chest swelled with pride, as if the girl was part of his own family. Norfolk bowed in thanks, and Hertford pretended indifference.

The King turned to Gardiner. "And you," he continued, "I will need someone to take over the post of chancellor to the University of Cambridge. Will you do that, Bishop?"

Gardiner was speechless. This would allow him to make a permanent mark on the educational system, make sure the next generation was properly instructed. Only Oxford was an older institution. He bowed low in reverential thanks. "Your Majesty."

The Bishop's triumph swelled from the twisted grimace on Hertford's face, the closest Edward Seymour could come to a smile at this news. Norfolk was jubilant.

"Ah, Sire, that is brilliant," said the Duke. "Under Cromwell's leadership, Cambridge has been encouraging reformists and heathens. The Bishop is the perfect man to lead the institution back to its core."

"Don't go too far, Gardiner," the King warned. "I don't want to embolden the Catholics. In fact, those three priests being held in the Tower? If they have not yet recanted, it is time they should die. Bring me the warrant and I will sign it."

Gardiner felt heat in his face and tightness in his chest. For a moment he thought he saw a slight smile play around Hertford's lips, but it was quickly gone. Hertford was impassive, as was Norfolk. As Gardiner would be too.

Nothing was ever safe.

July 28, 1540—Tower Hill

An early morning mist hovered above Tower Hill, lending it a ghostly quality particularly suited to the occasion. Edward stood in the third row of spectators ringing the scaffold. The other members of the Privy Council stood to his left, Sadler and Sir Thomas Wyatt to his right. Thousands more packed behind.

Edward's lips trembled, and he pressed them together. Every gesture would be noted; it was not politic to show too much sorrow.

The bells from the city's churches began to peal for the top of the hour, their discordant tones forming an unholy cacophony that sounded as anguished as Edward felt. The moment they ceased, a wave of jeers arose and spread. Cromwell must have emerged from the Tower. The high born were not the only ones who hated a commoner who rose to join their ranks; the low born also resented anyone who escaped their sad fate. Both groups were openly gloating over this impending death.

The jeering grew louder as Cromwell, in chains, approached the scaffold. His eyes were almost closed, his black hair matted. A man utterly defeated.

"The axe is too good for you," screeched a voice.

Edward shuddered. Without Cromwell's most recent title, that would have been true.

The low born were hanged but cut down quickly and eviscerated alive, their organs held up to still-seeing eyes, then their bodies cut into quarters. Brutal as beheading was, it was sweet mercy compared to the end Cromwell had just barely escaped.

"Take care, my Lord," Surrey called sarcastically as Cromwell passed by. He was wearing yellow, celebrating the event.

Edward tried his best to keep a sneer from lifting the side of his lip. Cromwell flinched but his gaze didn't waver.

He paused when he came to the steps, and his shoulders heaved before he mounted the platform. Once on it he looked around into the distance, as if he hoped to see a messenger with a reprieve. It seemed like that moment of action renewed his strength, or perhaps the view of the crowd reminded him to make a good end. He walked to the block at the front of the scaffold, keeping his eyes on the crowd, this time focusing on those close by. He teared up on seeing Sadler and Edward, then his gaze wandered further afar. Bewilderment and worse spread across his face as his eyes passed over Suffolk, Wriothesley, Gardiner, and so many others.

"Praise God he was spared the sight of Norfolk triumphant," whispered Sadler.

"Where *is* the good duke?" Wyatt asked. "He is the type to spit on the severed head of his enemy."

Sadler and Edward exchanged glances. Even more quietly, Sadler explained, "Norfolk forfeited his final victory to be at Oatlands Palace. With the annulment finalized, his niece weds the King today."

A low whistle escaped from Wyatt's lips. "Now there's a secret Surrey never shared."

"The King told only Edward and Tom," said Sadler.

"Norfolk gloated that the ceremony would take place right after the axe's swing," Edward said. "As if Catherine were Salome earning the head of John the Baptist."

"Did he say that?" Sadler asked.

"Of course not," Edward said. "Though I did ask why he had not insisted the head be brought to him first."

"How did he respond?" Wyatt's eyes widened with the fascinated fear of a man staring into a beehive.

"It took him a moment to close his mouth," Edward said, and Wyatt and Sadler nodded at Edward's audacity. He kept to himself how, after the initial shock had worn off, Norfolk had broken out into a cackle and clapped Edward on the shoulder.

Wyatt shook his head. "The King could be convinced of anything right now. Have you seen him when he's near the girl? He can't keep his hands off her; they travel over her."

It was indeed a sobering reminder of how easily the King could be controlled.

Suddenly Cromwell was looking quizzically at them, mouthing "Gregory?" They shook their heads. The lad knew his presence would not be a comfort. The rest had little choice: loyal subjects were expected to relish the King's justice.

Cromwell took a deep breath and focused his gaze above the crowd. "I am come hither to die," he began, as they all did, submitting to the law that condemned them. His voice quavered a bit but grew in strength as he went on. "I have lived a sinner and offended my Lord God, and I ask Him heartily forgiveness. I have been a great traveler in this world, and being but of a base degree was called to high estate. Since the time I came thereunto I have offended my prince, and I heartily ask him forgiveness. And I beseech you all to pray to God with me, that he will forgive me."

Cromwell closed his eyes to recite a semiprivate litany. When he opened them, they blazed with the fire of the hell he feared. "I pray you to bear me record: I die in the faith of the Holy Church of England, not doubting in any article of my faith, nor doubting in any sacrament of the Church."

Carew's same claim. Everyone's same claim. Anyone could be condemned by the apostolic Church that Henry had created and whose doctrines he continually changed.

While salvation, on earth and in heaven, depended on believing as the King believed, precisely what that was depended on the day. They were all dogs, hoping not to be whipped. *Just tell me what you want me to think.*

"I heartily desire you to pray for the King's grace, that he may long live with you, in health and in prosperity. And after him that his son, Prince Edward, that goodly imp, may long reign over you. And once again I desire you to pray for me..."

As his words trailed off, he looked down at the block for the first time. He knelt before it, touched its edge cautiously before resting his elbows on it. He clasped his hands in prayer and buried his face in them for a final quiet moment.

When he emerged, his eyes were wide and wild. "May God have mercy on my soul, into God's hands I commend my soul," he said as he lay his head on the block and flung his arms wide.

Knowing such resolve would weaken with every passing second, the executioner hastened to swing the axe.

The haste was a mistake.

The first blow missed the neck and bit deep into Cromwell's shoulder. He shrieked, immobilized.

Edward pitched forward in shock and horror, as did his friends to his left. The crowd roared.

The second blow, thank God, severed the head.

So perish all the King's enemies, leaped to Edward's mind. But Cromwell hadn't been an enemy of the King, only of Norfolk.

More catcalls and yells as the executioner held the head high and placed it on its spike. Edward turned away from the berserk wrath still displayed on the face, and placed a hand on his own throat. The guards went into formation to parade the head back to the Tower. It would be flaunted atop the main ramparts until it rotted off.

The crowd fell in behind, laughing and chattering as they dispersed. Edward, Sadler, and Wyatt held back, silent and hollow, watching as the workers carted off the body and splashed buckets of water to wash the worst of the blood off the block. Soon nothing was left of Thomas Cromwell.

Memento, homo, quia pulvis es. Remember man that you are dust. Edward made the sign of the cross over the scaffold and walked away.

PART TWO: CATHERINE HOWARD

The Rose Without a Thorn...

Chapter Six

August 8, 1540—Hampton Court Palace

Edward took a deep breath of the incense-laden air of Mass and let his spirit derive comfort from the magnificence of the Chapel Royal. Most people loved it for its royal blue, pendant-vaulted ceiling where dozens of gilded angels held escutcheons emblazoned with Tudor heraldry. Edward loved it because his sister Jane's coat of arms was featured on both sides of the West door. Try as Norfolk might, he would never erase that piece of history.

Edward leaned forward as he closed his eyes and thanked God all the harder for granting him such grace in his life, even as he prayed for the strength to make it through the banquet later – and an excuse that might help him avoid it.

The Eucharistic prayers of the Mass soon ceded to the Responsory ones. This was it. This was the moment.

"Pray, Lord," said the priest, "that King Henry and Queen Catherine shall so use their power that your people may lead a quiet and peaceable life in all goodliness and honesty."

And just like that, Catherine Howard was announced to the world as Queen of England. Now letters would be sent to every foreign ambassador, and messengers dispatched across the land to bring the news to the country's hundreds of churches, so every Englishman could pray properly.

Edward sighed. The first time the King used this technique, parishioners had left in protest over having to exalt Anne Boleyn after two decades of loyalty to Catherine of Aragon. Since then, people had learned not to get too attached to their queens.

Edward felt an imperceptible nudge from his wife and glanced at her. Her eyes remained fastened on the priest, but her chin tilted up and right to call attention to Norfolk. The good Duke had turned around to study the crowd. Edward caught his eye, smiled and nodded. Norfolk returned the gesture, prompting Anne to greet him in turn and extend the goodwill they were all working so hard to display.

It was all lies.

Another wave of emptiness came over Edward, leaving vague unease in its wake. He felt Anne's glance and forced a smile. Anne didn't appreciate the malaise he'd suffered since the sight of Cromwell's severed head on its spike. She saw Edward's newfound fatalism as weakness.

"Are you ailing?" she whispered.

He nodded, his jaw tight, but was comforted by her loving squeeze of his knee. She was right that his resistance weakened him. He needed to accept the new situation. He would eventually, it was just a question of when. Life would be so much easier by doing it sooner.

Edward's resolve faltered when the procession began down the aisle. The enormous energy it would take to socialize with the other guests weighed on his shoulders. But Anne squeezed his hand and her understanding strengthened him. Enough that he joined the line and exchanged gracious pleasantries all the way to the Great Hall, where the first of a full month of banquets and feasts and hunts would celebrate the King's new marriage.

To escape the crowd that had congregated in front of the doors, Edward pulled Anne to the side as soon as they entered. From this quieter vantage point, they surveyed the room. As always, hundreds of eavesdroppers stared down at them. Constant reminders that there were no secrets at court, these were tiny heads carved into every one of the ceiling's fine Irish beams, carefully painted with eyes wide and shrewd.

Anne pointed out the King and Queen near the center of the room. The King was dressed in thickly jeweled white damask for this feast day. The rich padding on his massive shoulders made him tower over the Queen, whose magnificent robe of moss green silk clung to her petite frame.

"Good symbolism," Edward conceded. "Green for freshness and fertility."

"And the necklace," said Anne. Indeed, Catherine Howard's neck was ringed by a strand of pearls as large as eggs, as if her head were sitting in a nest. The image was vaguely disturbing.

"Oh, and there's your sister."

Elizabeth was just behind the Queen, clad in the same light green worn by all the ladies-in-waiting. Edward was glad his sister had secured the post. The King had already referred to her as Lady Cromwell; he might be considering restoring Gregory's courtesy title.

A peal of bold laughter from one of the women surrounding the Queen caught Edward's attention. *A forward chit,* he thought derisively. Her French hood was perched far back on her head to show an overwide expanse of hair. "Who is that?" he asked.

"Joan Bulmer," Anne answered. "She served with the Queen in the household of the Dowager Duchess of Norfolk."

"Not high born, from the looks of her," said Edward.

"She's quite young," said Anne. "She needs maturity and discretion. Of course, so does the Queen."

Edward shook his head. "The Queen had maturity and discretion enough to treat Anne of Cleves with respect."

"But not enough to refuse inappropriate friends."

The laugh had drawn the King's full attention. He must have said something cutting, because the Bulmer girl blushed deeply and bowed low before running away. The King paid her little mind after that; his eyes were only for his wife. His left hand rose to the side of Catherine's bare neck; he lowered it slowly to her shoulder and down her back to her waist. She leaned into him and lifted her mouth for the kiss they all knew he wanted to give her. He quickly lowered his hand to cup her buttocks and draw her closer.

She pulled away with no hint of annoyance. Instead she looked up at him from under her lashes, a playful smile on her face. "What, in front of the Archbishop? And the Spanish Ambassador?" Her confident voice rang around the room.

"In front of the world," he shouted, punctuating the last word with a sweep of his arm.

"*Non aultre volonte que le tienne,*" she said with a curtsy. No other will but yours. In keeping with her motto.

The King looked around with pride, and Edward found himself transported back thirty years to the household of Henry's sister Mary, then eighteen, when she had wed the fifty-four-year-old Louis XII of France. The monarch died three months later, supposedly from his exertions in the bedchamber. *Was this Norfolk's secret plan?*

Edward put the blinding thought aside for later. He raised his glass to his brother-in-law and walked over, Anne barely a half step behind.

"Congratulations, Sire," Edward greeted the King. "I pray for many fine brothers for my nephew."

"I promise to do my duty often," the King replied. That set off chuckles among his gentlemen, standing right behind him. Tom was there, Thomas Culpeper too. Edward nodded to them but his greeting was lost as Norfolk's son, the Earl of Surrey, joined the merriment.

The Earl was wearing a burgundy jacket that verged dangerously close to the purple reserved for royalty. As always, the silk linings puffed aggressively through the slashes in his brocade sleeves. Edward tried to smile in greeting but Surrey turned to speak to the King.

It irked Edward the way Surrey considered himself above Edward. Edward was twenty years older and had earned his earldom, while Surrey held only a courtesy title through his father. But Surrey had the lineage that inspired the people; they revered him despite his scorn for them.

"Sire," Surrey bowed, "I know how love doth rage upon a yielding mind, how small a net may take, and mesh a heart of gentle kind," he recited. His own verse, of course.

The Queen clapped her hands at her cousin's cleverness, and the King beamed.

Tom, even more irked by Surrey than Edward was, seized the conversation back. "It is always our pleasure to accompany you to the Queen's chamber. We'd be happy to escort you there now," he said.

"That would be a far better choice than a banquet," said Thomas Culpeper. "We could make your excuses. Surely no one will notice the absence of the guests of honor."

That quickly brought out giggles among the Queen's women. "Master Culpeper, you are a scamp," called out Lady Rochford.

"Your Majesties," said a small voice behind them that quickly dampened the ribaldry.

Edward quickly turned. The Lady Mary was in a low curtsy before her father and new stepmother.

"Welcome, child!" the King exclaimed, raising her.

"Yes, welcome child," said Catherine.

Edward thought he saw a hint of disgust flit across Mary's face, but she curtsied again. It was hard not to laugh: Mary was nine years Catherine's senior.

"It is my honor and pleasure," Mary said to Catherine before turning her full attention to the King. The two of them spoke a bit while Catherine fidgeted and finally turned away with a loud sigh; she was said to dislike Mary as much as the girl disliked her. Surrey rolled his eyes and wormed his way into the King's conversation with Mary, for whom Surrey's eyes widened with gentle admiration.

Another line from the man's poetry jumped into Edward's mind: *Hampton Court taught me to wish her first for mine.* Surrey had written it about the fair Geraldine, his anonymous love. Gossip had been quick to point to Lady Elizabeth Fitzgerald, but was it Mary? Could Surrey be in love with Mary? He had a wife, so any pursuit of Mary could only end in dishonor, a sure way to death..

Edward turned to Anne, half expecting her to have read his mind, but she only looked at him, puzzled. Still, the exchange returned his senses: he was surely wrong and his time would be better spent on real issues.

"My husband will answer that. He knows all," the Queen declared with a hand on the King's arm, drawing him away from the conversation with Mary, who lowered her eyes. The girl had a great deal of practice at closing her eyes to distasteful situations.

Edward's mind flashed back to Cromwell. If only he had been similarly patient, enough to ignore Norfolk's baiting. A man bowed to the person who had the King's ear – or privates – and waited for better times.

Edward had always known that.

A sudden clap on his shoulder made him turn around. It was Norfolk. Edward forced a broad smile onto his face. "My good Duke, all of England rejoices with you today," he said with apparent enthusiasm.

August 20, 1540—Windsor Castle

Edward's leg started bouncing, but he caught it after a single twitch: he did not want to betray his annoyance. Gardiner was prating on about Cambridge, bragging about his latest reversal of a policy instituted by Cromwell. Taking advantage of the unexpected presence of the King, who had made a surprise appearance as he did sometimes to test them. He loved to find his ministers unprepared or disorganized – it gave him a chance to berate them. Today, the King had slipped in unannounced and caught the Master of the Horse, Sir Anthony Browne, examining his shoes.

"Your job is to pay attention to my horses' shoes, not your own," Henry roared. "If you cannot draw such a basic distinction, how can I trust you in your post? You have many rivals, they work behind your back to take it from you. Tell me why I should not dismiss you now?"

Browne had thrown himself on his knees and cried real

tears, spoken of his gout and a pain in his foot from a rock before conceding that none of these were excuses. Finally, with a grunt, the King had waved away the jumble of words. A terrible experience for the councilors, but it would put His Majesty in good spirits for hours afterwards.

A rap on the heavy wooden door interrupted the Bishop's self-congratulations. "Master Burke for the King's Secretary," announced the page

Henry waved the man in. "Burke? The cryptologist?"

When he saw the King, Burke's rheumy eyes opened wide; he slumped into a deep bow and hid his face in his black robes. "Sire, I did not expect this great honor. I am so sorry to have interrupted. I thought I was importuning only Master Wriothesley."

Wriothesley. Not the Council. Edward wondered once again whether information was being withheld, and he resolved to befriend Burke.

"Importuning Wriothesley?" boomed the King. "Nonsense. My Council exists to serve me and the realm. They cannot be importuned. What is your business?"

"O-Only to bring the letters I have deciphered."

"Ah. Good man."

Wriothesley raced over. "Marillac or Chapuys?"

The two ambassadors, of France and Spain, respectively, would be the only men – besides Henry himself – who would use a cipher in their correspondence. They also would be the only men unaware Cromwell had long had their letters delivered to the King's Principal Secretary with the keys to the codes. Edward glanced heavenward in acknowledgement of his late friend's cleverness.

"Marillac's."

"That eel." The King nodded. "Wriothesley, read it."

This startled the cryptologist, who grabbed the letters back and held them close to his chest. "Beg pardon, Sire, but I—"

"Thank you, Burke. Wriothesley?"

Burke opened his mouth again, then closed it. He thrust the papers into Wriothesley's hands and bowed out.

Wriothesley harrumphed, as though he had been the one to introduce the topic. "There are two letters here, Your Majesty. One to Francis and the other to his chief minister enclosing it." He put the cover letter aside and began the missive to the French King. "'Sire, I wrote before of the executions of Thomas Cromwell and Lord Hungerford – but they were followed two days after by that of six doctors. Three of these (Pol, Abel and Dancaster) were hanged as traitors for speaking in favor of the Pope, and three (Barnes, Gagard and Hierosme) burnt as heretics. It was wonderful to see adherents of the two opposing parties dying at the same time, and it gave offence to both.'"

Edward's first thought was that the sentence was typical of the French Ambassador: as insightful as it was smarmy, and pretending to grace. Edward's second thought was to fear the King's reaction to this unexpected truth – but Edward quickly put a bland smile on his face to hide it. To expect disaster was to court it.

The King looked at each of his ministers in turn before breaking into laughter. "He's quite blunt, but he clearly conveys to his master that I favor neither party."

Edward relaxed. The Council members exhaled as well. Wriothesley continued with the rest of the letter, which contained a similar combination of facts and interpretations. It grew in insolence, but Marillac was French, after all. There was no love lost there, but no intention to war either.

"The French Ambassador always leaves a foul taste in my mouth," the King said as he stood. "But a fine meal will cure that."

As the Council members jumped to their feet, Wriothesley bowed self-importantly. "I will review the other letter and report to you if it contains anything of note."

Henry waved. "No, no, I had forgotten." He sat back down, and the lords raced to follow.

Wriothesley launched into the letter Marillac had written to a peer, not his king, and Edward quickly realized this was not just more of the same whining. "'The English permit their king to interpret, add to, take away, and make, more divine law than even the apostles ever dared to attempt. They make of him not only a king to be obeyed, but an idol to be worshipped.'"

Edward felt a chill. *Please God, let this be the worst of it,* he thought, but the crack in Wriothesley's voice said there was more.

"'This prince seems tainted, among other vices, with three which in a king may be called plagues.'"

Wriothesley stopped and looked up, eyes bulging. The King spoke, his jaw tight and the telltale vein in his forehead bulging. "Go on."

"'The first is...the first is that he is so covetous that all the riches in the world would not satisfy him. Hence the ruin of the abbeys, the spoil of all churches that had anything to take, and the suppression of the Knights of Rhodes. Hence, too, the accusation of so many rich men, who, whether condemned or acquitted, are always plucked. He troubles even the dead, even those revered as saints, witness Saint Thomas of Canterbury, who, because his relics and bones were adorned with gold and jewels, has been declared traitor. Everything is good prize, and he does not reflect that to make himself rich he has impoverished his people, and does not gain in goods what he loses in renown.'"

There was utter silence. Wriothesley's voice was barely a whimper. "'Thence proceeds the second plague, distrust and fear. This King, knowing how many changes he has made, and what tragedies and scandals he has created, would fain keep in favor with everybody, but does not trust a single man, expecting to see them all offended, and he will not cease to dip his hand in blood.'"

Edward closed his eyes to put aside the fear and excitement that gripped him, and to commit Marillac's words to memory to share with Anne. The Ambassador had done a particularly good job of describing the King, capturing a number of nuances Edward had never quite put into words.

"'The third plague, lightness and inconstancy, proceeds partly from the other two and partly from the nature of the nation, and has perverted the rights of religion, marriage, faith and promise, as softened wax can be altered to any form. The subjects take example from their prince, and the ministers seek only to undo each other to gain credit, and under the color of their master's good each attends to his own. For all the fine words of which they are full, they will act only as necessity and self-interest compel them.'"

"Your Majesty, I think we have heard enough," said the Duke of Norfolk. "I suggest a sojourn in the Tower might teach this damn Frenchman some manners."

The King's face was stony.

"And a whipping," added Gardiner.

The lords took the King's silence as assent, and started to talk among themselves of punishment. Fear rose in Edward's throat. To harm an ambassador was to declare war. Something that despite their coastal fortifications they were not prepared right then to do.

"We cannot," Edward said. His words silenced the room. The King turned to him with a death stare that turned Edward's knees to jelly. But the die was cast. When all was said and done, Edward needed to advise the King and protect England. This was Edward's value and his opportunity. Let others play to the King's weakness; Edward must inspire trust. That was the only way to keep the throne safe for his nephew to inherit.

"To take any action would permanently ruin our access to these letters. Much as I want to see the nails torn from Marillac's fingers, we must be prudent."

Norfolk was the first to scoff. "You are a damned coward, Hertford. Or are you in league with the man?"

"I serve none but His Majesty. And I do it better than you."

Norfolk stood. "I would lead an army to avenge our King. You would—"

"Would you avenge the sky if a simpleton called it yellow?" Edward said, jumping to his feet to take advantage of the more than three inches he had over Norfolk. "More fitting revenge is to use France's own secrets against them."

Edward paused. Norfolk's lips trembled, but no sound came out. Edward waited until the good Duke took a breath, then Edward delivered the final blow. "You would put England at risk."

Norfolk turned his head toward the King without taking his eyes from Edward's. "What is your opinion, Sire?"

The King sucked his teeth and looked down at his fingernails. "My brother-in-law is right. Marillac is safe from his perfidy. For now."

Norfolk shut his mouth and looked deep into Edward's eyes. Edward felt the pull and worked to turn it around until he felt as though he were plunging the depths of his adversary. Like a beaten dog, Norfolk turned away.

Edward had won. But at what price?

August 28, 1540—Whitehall Palace

Edward relaxed into his high-back chair and looked up at the arched ceiling whose every inch was carved with roses or cherubs or scrolls. He was with Sadler and Cranmer, sitting in the King's office, at the conference table the King kept for Council meetings. The court had left on its annual summer progress – a small one to survey the coastline – and the King had rewarded Edward for his sage advice during the Marillac mess by putting Edward in charge along with Cranmer; they would implement the decisions of the Privy Council until the men joined the King's retinue in October.

Edward had placed his seat at the head of the table. Despite his ambition, or perhaps because of it, Edward had been careful not to use the King's chair of estate. Instead he took the next finest one and moved the throne to a perch slightly behind his left to symbolically supervise the goings on. It would insulate Edward from criticism. There was no reason to take foolish chances, after all.

"What has arrived?" he asked, resting his elbows on the *manchettes* and steepling his fingers as he looked back and forth expectantly at Sadler and Cranmer.

This was Edward's chance. He needed to prove himself now that the world had changed. His position had always depended entirely on the King's goodwill, though that was true of anyone, but Cromwell had helped make Edward relevant. Now, Norfolk was working to dismiss him, to replace the Seymour influence with Howard blood. If Norfolk succeeded, his son Surrey would be the one to guide England's next monarch, not Edward. And Surrey's way would do it with policies that would destroy everything. He would turn the country Catholic, purge the Council of men who were there because of their ability rather than their blood. Worse, he might well look to subvert the succession and place a Howard on the throne – not such a difficult leap once the Queen whelped a son.

Edward could not let such a travesty happen. His nephew had Seymour blood in his veins; this was the family's chance to become royal, immortal. Edward was the only one at court who was totally loyal to the boy, totally committed to his dynasty. Edward needed to make sure the Prince was powerful enough to take his rightful place.

Sadler bit the inside of his lip as he rifled through the short stack of papers carefully arranged before him. "Letters from Calais, Norfolk. And this one from the Privy Council. We are to create new standards for appropriate behavior."

"Eh?" Cranmer looked confused. He'd been away the last few days and had missed all the excitement.

"A priest at Windsor spoke unwisely of the Queen," Edward explained. "Questioning her integrity for meddling with the King while he was married to Cleves, that kind of thing. The fool was imprisoned."

"Actually, no." Sadler looked amused. "This morning's courier related another incident."

"Another one?"

"Just yesterday. The Queen's vice-chamberlain was drunk and disorderly in the King's presence."

"Edward Baynton?" Cranmer looked as shocked as Edward felt.

"The same," Sadler said.

"So, this is not about the Queen," said Edward.

"Well, the King wants orders issued that people behave more soberly in his presence. He wants nothing to contaminate the purity of the Queen."

Other than himself, Edward thought but carefully bit back the words. Derision was treason.

"Of course," said Cranmer. "We shall put together the formal instructions."

"I would have thought this would be the kind of thing Wriothesley would insist on doing himself," said Sadler. "There must be some pitfall we are not aware of."

Edward turned that idea over and discarded it. More likely it stemmed from the rivalry that had sprung up between Sadler and Wriothesley, a rivalry that was quite bitter on Sadler's side. The two gentlemen were both secretaries to the Council, but Wriothesley acted as though he were senior to Sadler – and the pretense appeared to be working. Repeat a lie often enough and it will be believed, Cromwell had always said, and he was right. It didn't help that Sadler was intimidated by Wriothesley's gentle birth and legal training. It was never a good idea to show weakness: the scent of blood only encouraged a hunter.

"If we need to, we could have him be the one to present the draft to the King," Cranmer suggested.

Spoken like the man of the cloth he was, not like the political animal Edward needed.

Let him be himself. The whisper blew through Edward's mind as if Anne were right beside him. Cranmer was an innocent whose naiveté was endearing, and the King trusted him. That perspective was too valuable to tamper with, though it did require occasional correction.

"Nay," Edward said firmly. "As long as our draft acts to protect the Queen's sensibilities, we need not fear. Your way would allow Wriothesley to steal our ideas and present them as his own – that is much more dangerous in the long term."

Sadler nodded, a glimmer in his eyes. "Hertford is right. Cromwell's death has left a large void of power. We must not cede anything we don't need to."

Cranmer shook his head, still not grasping the complexities. "There is no void left – Norfolk has seized it all. We are lost."

"Wrong." Edward slammed his fist down on the table, more for show than from anger. He needed them to pay attention. "Norfolk has the King's ear for a time, thanks to his niece, but influence is temporary. We have the chance to put our stamp on things here, to assemble power and forge alliances that will serve us far into the future." He paused. "And wait for the good Duke to make a mistake."

"You think we can bring him down?" Sadler was too eager; he needed to learn that inaction was equally a strategy.

"No," said Edward. "He is the Queen's uncle, after all, so he is safe." He watched as the two men looked down and fidgeted with the quills and papers and tiny crumbs on the table. "But we must stop him from overreaching."

They both fixed their gazes on Edward and waited.

"Norfolk has the vanity of Midas and the hubris of Icarus, and I worry for my nephew," Edward explained.

Cranmer's face softened. "How goes our royal imp? Have you seen him recently?"

"I visited last Sunday and he is quite well." Edward smiled at the memory of the pudgy three-year-old's delight at the spaniel puppy his uncle had brought him.

"Then what is wrong?" Cranmer asked.

"The more power Norfolk amasses, the more mischief he can – and will – cause. We need to provide a consistent counterweight."

Sadler narrowed his eyes. "How?"

Edward felt the hoarseness in his voice. "By banding together to do what is right for the realm. By speaking up when Gardiner tries to shove orthodoxy down our gullets. By supporting each other's policies and futures."

"This is nothing new," Sadler said. "We have always agreed about the important issues."

"It is more important than ever to show agreement," Edward said.

"The Lord will strengthen our just cause," Cranmer said.

Edward prayed the Archbishop was right.

October 25, 1540—Windsor Castle

Stephen Gardiner hurried to keep pace with the young page who guided him down Windsor's main corridor to greet the Duke of Norfolk. The court had just returned from its two-month progress, the King's annual chance to connect with his people and escape the pestilence that gripped London during the hottest days – a blessed situation where motivation and reward were interchangeable. As always, Norfolk eschewed the event.

Gardiner knew it was torture for Norfolk to watch the King enjoy himself with anyone lower than an earl, or perhaps a baron. On a progress the King would parade himself before the peasants, and that offended the old Duke's sense of propriety.

Of course that was just Gardiner's secret guess. The more obvious explanation was that Norfolk used the time to visit and oversee his many properties, a task he avoided while the court was hard at work. Besides, Norfolk had nothing to gain from a progress. Gardiner did. During the first half of the trip, Gardiner served as the King's right-hand man, with Wriothesley as the perfect assistant. Even better, those gentlemen who might unseat him – that opportunist Hertford, for one – hadn't joined the progress until after Gardiner had left, so he hadn't had to share the King's special favor with anyone.

And now Gardiner was on his way to Norfolk's apartments, summoned by the good Duke's messenger. With each step, the Bishop reviewed what he would say. He had been preparing all summer a witty list of things the Duke needed to know. Part of Gardiner's new, more powerful persona.

The two men turned the corner of the long corridor. A cassocked figure in the distance filled Gardiner's vision: Archbishop Cranmer, coming toward him.

Cranmer hadn't been invited on the progress: he had been left in London to play the workhorse. In his absence there had been no one to offer a heretical twist during the King's daily theological discussions. Every day Gardiner brought the monarch ever closer to the orthodoxy of the true faith. And every night, alone behind his bed curtains, Gardiner delighted to repeat and expand on those interpretations, reliving them and anticipating them at the same time.

The thought always warmed him. He was finally the King's favored religious advisor. And this was the Bishop's moment of triumph.

"Greetings, Your Grace," he said. Though bowing first as required, he did so nonchalantly so as to signal strength.

"Ah, Your Grace, you are arrived." Cranmer's bow was meticulous, equally low – the appropriate response to signal strength. "I did not think to see you until supper."

Was that a slap? An implication that Gardiner would carve his schedule around meals because he had nothing of import to do? It was so hard to tell with Cranmer. He was acting as if he was unaware of the power shift, as if it did not exist. Was this ignorance or a deliberate challenge?

The King would ascribe it to ignorance – the monarch believed Cranmer apolitical, even naive. Gardiner knew it was all put on; it always had been. How could the King not see through Cranmer's machinations?

Gardiner swallowed to clear the bile that had risen in his throat. "I was on my way to wait on the Duke of Norfolk, who has also arrived for the court's return."

"Of course. The Council is meeting at three. I am on my way to meet with William Paget, also newly arrived."

Paget had been Secretary to Anne of Cleves. Was he a Lutheran heretic? Or was Cranmer trimming his sails and courting the moderates? Or being politic and fawning before the conservatives? Damn him.

Gardiner steeled himself. He would not let Cranmer best him again.

Norfolk's messenger shifted his weight to the other foot,

and Gardiner was glad of the excuse. "Ah, yes," he said to the youth. Turning to Cranmer, he bowed. "I apologize for my haste, but I must be off."

Cranmer bowed back, and his serene expression infuriated Gardiner. But he reined himself in and continued with the page to Norfolk's apartments, calming himself to better deliver the news of the King's increasing orthodoxy.

For once, the opulent tapestries that lined Norfolk's walls felt inspiring rather than intimidating. Scenes of England and battles, they served as constant reminders of the Howard history of greatness. Unfortunately, Norfolk was not wearing the smile Gardiner expected. Instead the Duke's face was closer to a snarl. "Where the devil have you been?"

Gardiner allowed the anger to wash over him. Total acceptance was the only way to calm the Duke's temper. Same with the King. "My Lord, it is good to see you."

Norfolk harrumphed and poured himself wine.

Gardiner kept his aplomb and continued. "I hope your time away was as well spent as mine. I would be glad to hear your news. Or share mine if you prefer."

"Lady Margaret Douglas meddled with my nephew during the summer progress."

"Which nephew?"

"Charles Howard. The Queen's brother."

Gardiner's good mood dissipated. "Is Lady Margaret such a fool as to have not learned her lesson? And how could your nephew court such danger?"

Lady Margaret Douglas was the King's twenty-five-year-old niece, in line to the throne immediately after the King's daughters. Four years earlier, she had become secretly engaged to Norfolk's younger brother, Lord Thomas Howard, a foolish move for both of them: Prince Edward had not yet been born, the King's daughters had been disinherited, and the King's bastard son, Fitzroy, had just died. An unapproved marriage between the next heir and an ancient and powerful family reeked of treason. Lady Margaret had eventually been forgiven, but the idiot Howard had been left to rot in the Tower, where he died only a year later.

"Bah." Norfolk swung his arm. "The lad is married. This was more dishonor than treason. And has been treated as such."

"Dishonor can too easily rise to that level with this King."

Norfolk snorted. "She's been packed off to Syon Abbey to contemplate her sins."

Gardiner pursed his lips. "You must condemn your nephew."

"I have."

"In strong enough terms? This is dangerous."

Norfolk stormed over and grabbed Gardiner's arm, pulling him in to growl into his ear. "I've had great practice in denouncing people over the years."

Norfolk's obvious intent to intimidate had the opposite effect. Gardiner shook off Norfolk's grip and took a step back. "You have many relatives who have angered the King."

Norfolk lifted his chin. "All without any mud splattered on me."

"And the Queen?"

"The Queen had nothing to do with the intrigue," Norfolk said. "The King is holding nothing against her."

Gardiner looked down. "That is fortunate."

Of course the Queen must have known, yet she had not discouraged it. How could she have failed to realize that such an affair would have serious political consequences? Was that naiveté or recklessness?

"Is that all you have to say?" Norfolk's voice was close to a snarl.

"What would you have me say? Do you really need me to tell you the King's reaction is a warning to keep her ladies in check? Not to mention a warning to us to keep the Queen in check."

Norfolk looked intently at him, then shrugged and walked away to sit on one of the cushioned window seats. "I had expected you to come up with a plan but I see you are right. There is nothing to be done but to wait for this to blow over."

Gardiner's good mood returned. Norfolk had given him credit not only for his ideas but also his logic. "And pray nothing comes up in the interim that will test the Queen's influence in other matters."

"Unfortunately the French are up to their old tricks again."

Gardiner nodded. The French always proclaimed great love for the English, and their words rang all the louder when they were cheating them. "There is no threat though, only posturing."

Norfolk grimaced. "Nevertheless, I don't want the King to regret dissolving the Cleves alliance."

"Regret Cleves? No, the alliance is still strong. My Lady of Cleves has written her brother to assure him of her good treatment. And Spain is a better friend than ever." Suddenly fear took hold. "Is there some...other problem with the Queen?"

Norfolk looked down at his cup. "My niece continues to captivate the King. I just fear the King's mind will swing back."

It was true the King veered, like a pendulum, between extremes, but not over something like this. "I don't know that we need to worry about that, my Lord."

"I am concerned there has been no talk of the Queen's coronation."

Gardiner pressed his lips together to hold back the annoyance that first came to his mind. He moderated his words to sound kinder. "He's probably postponing the expense until she births a child. He did that with Queen Jane as well."

Norfolk shook his head. "Yes, yes, but that means we must press harder."

"Harder?"

"Too many of Cromwell's old friends are left at court. We must remove Cranmer too."

Gardiner's heart soared. Eliminating Cranmer would open the path to the Archbishopric of Canterbury. Still, he restrained himself. "That will be difficult."

"Not if we start with Sadler," Norfolk said. "He might give us evidence of the comfort Cranmer offers to heretics. Thomas Wyatt is another lever we can use."

"I thought Wyatt was a friend of your son's?"

"That needn't spoil our plans."

Henry Howard and Wyatt were poets, great poets. The King loved them as he loved Holbein, believing in a noble comradeship in art. Yet Norfolk saw only a man of barely gentle birth distracting his son from more important pursuits.

Gardiner pushed aside his misgivings and nodded. "I will start to draw both of them into religious debates, in front of the King or not, and see what happens."

"I'll make Sadler seem inept – that will discredit him to the King. We'll use Wriothesley too, to report on their conversations and collect copies of their correspondence."

"If only your niece would get herself with child."

"I've spoken to her. She understands it is her foremost duty. And she attends to his lusts often."

"I did see the King was in a good mood all day on the progress. He even ate less and mentioned to me that he intends to continue this new regimen. Said it made him feel younger, the way his new wife did."

"Good," said Norfolk. "We need him to sire a son. A Howard son, so my blood can live forever."

Gardiner was about to remind the good Duke that a Howard son would not be the heir, but it was unlikely Norfolk had forgotten such an important point. As much as a good, Catholic, Howard King would be preferable to a reformist Seymour monarch, that was not a plot in which Gardiner would participate.

November 26, 1540—Woking Palace

They were as high as man could get in the hills surrounding Woking Palace, and the cloud of Edward's breath glowed blue in the thin morning light. The King had brought a coterie of favorites with him to this relatively small manor to enjoy the pleasures of the countryside. Mainly young men, not old ones – reformists, not Catholics.

May it always be thus, Edward thought.

It was easier to strengthen his bond with the King when Norfolk was not there. It was also easier over an activity like hawking, at which Edward excelled. The King appreciated and rewarded skill.

There were twenty courtiers hunting for red grouse, but only six entrusted with hawks. The rest were either happy to be included or pretending they weren't miffed, depending on how close they felt themselves to the King.

At Henry's signal, Edward pulled back on the reins with his right hand, holding the left steady for the peregrine perched there. The bird hadn't been flown yet, and Edward didn't want her to become prematurely excited or spooked.

An open field stretched before them, and Edward caught sight of a white rabbit's tail fleeing. The King turned to the handler, who quickly handed him a goshawk. Not the most noble of birds, but the King was not about to let game escape. With rabbits, the goshawk was the bird of choice for every English cook, every man who needed to fill his pot that night: its stubbornness and speed were most likely to capture this prey. The King did not like to fail.

The King quickly released the predator, and the black and white barring of its mail glinted in the light. It took off horizontally and gained steadily on its quarry, keeping to a deadly straight line even through brush. With a final stretch its talons dug into the hare, and the two rolled over in a sudden cloud of dust.

The King pounded the pommel of his saddle with pleasure. His party pressed in to congratulate and follow him to the victorious bird, who was already atop its victim, ready to tear it apart.

The King didn't dismount for this next step; it had been more than a year since he had made the effort. Instead he nodded to the handler, who leaped off his horse to retrieve the goshawk with a choice treat. The man quickly placed a second morsel on the King's glove to coax the bird over to the royal perch where it belonged.

"That was wonderful to watch, husband," said the Queen.

Henry puckered his face to blow her a proud and grateful kiss and looked around at his company. He held his bird higher, a wide smile on his face.

Edward exchanged glances with Tom, who tried to make his way around Suffolk and his wife to nudge Wriothesley out of his choicer spot.

The King had been in rare form lately, rising between five and six, hearing Mass at seven, then riding out hawking until the mid-morning meal. It wasn't clear whether he could ride so much because his leg had improved, or whether his leg had improved because he rode so much. Either way, he was far more trim than he had been in years, and far less moody. Even Marillac's secret letters had noted the improvement, a fact Edward knew pleased the King, who feigned indifference.

The bells on the goshawk's jesses jingled, and the King stroked it gently with his meaty hand. "There is no greater moment than the triumph after a kill," he said.

Edward let the deeper truth of the statement wash over him, much better than to let it strike him in the chest. In the calm he found an opening. "We should train birds ourselves this season," he said warmly. "There is nothing better than molding a bird to its destiny."

"I heard Jane say that too," Henry laughed, but there was a catch in his throat.

"We Seymours were taught young," said Tom as he pressed his horse closer, through the crowd that parted for him. "The chief falconer at Wolf Hall was quite a philosopher."

"Jane once told us you had similar instruction in your own youth," said Edward. "She loved how the two of you equated birding to life."

The King nodded at Edward, a rueful smile on his face.

"And apparently you as well, brother." The King continued in a different tone. "If only the Dowager Duchess of Norfolk had provided such lessons to her own household," he said, and his sidelong glance at his wife caused titters in the crowd. "That is the one flaw in my Rose Without a Thorn."

That was what the King had started calling his new wife. He had even given orders for a commemorative coin to be struck in her honor featuring the words *Rosa Sine Spina* on the reverse - a homage that came much cheaper than a coronation.

Even without looking at her, Edward could sense the Queen's eyes flashing at being found wanting, in front of a crowd yet. Her discomfort amused Edward, but Tom, ever the gallant, came to the rescue she did not require. "It is woman's lot to be flawed because of Eve, and man's lot to endure it. This is barely a bristle on your rose's branch, still a miracle."

The Queen shook her head at Tom before she too turned to the King. "Would I could see myself through your eyes, for I see many more flaws. But I do know I see no thorns in you so I see how love might blind you to mine."

Henry grandly swept out an arm to her. "Was ever a King so blessed in his wife?" he asked the company. Spirited applause broke out among the courtiers, and the occasion quickly devolved into a contest of compliments for the King and Queen. It was a regular pastime, as Henry rarely tired of such efforts, and Catherine had grown accustomed to it as well. She thrived on admiration, like her cousin Anne Boleyn before her.

Such a flirt, Edward thought. No, that was unfair. She was simply at ease with people. The trait would be forward in a girl but worked well for a monarch. Especially one who had to make an old man believe he was as young as he ever was.

Edward caught himself and looked around, but everyone was still smiling and laughing in that shallow way designed to project the deeply loyal insouciance that was the universal affectation of a courtier.

The hawking party continued onward. Tom rose up next to Edward and whispered, "What is wrong? Your face is twisted as if you ate something bad."

It never failed to annoy Edward that Tom didn't waste his charm on family members. "Nothing. At least, nothing more than worry for our nephew."

"Worry? With the King so hardy, he is sure to get a younger brother soon." Tom threw a backwards glance to confirm the trailing riders' distance. "Or sister."

The words exploded in Edward's head. Of course. All this worry about the King siring another son – if he did manage to get his young wife pregnant, it was far more likely to result in another daughter. Henry had discarded several wives over their failure to provide him an heir, but surely by now it was clear the fault was with him.

The game was not lost.

I leave it to the Lord, Jane had always said. Edward could do that, too.

January 3, 1541—Hampton Court Palace

The Great Hall at Hampton Court Palace was the ideal spot for the New Year revels. Edward wondered idly how many times he had seen this exact scene, and whether the sight would ever cease to inspire him. Thick pine garlands, strung with crimson holly berries and white popped corn, ringed the room where the stained glass panels began some twenty feet above the floor. The fir chains on the sills of the scenic windows created the illusion of a forest floor and turned the decorative trusses of the soaring hammerbeam ceiling into virtual tree trunks. Earlier in the day, Edward had brought his royal nephew to experience the room without the pressure of the crowds, and the sight of it had caused the normally reserved four-year-old to lift his arms and twirl in glee.

Anne nudged Edward to look at the King, resplendent in white with silver and diamond accents, sitting in his magnificent chair of estate on the dais before the fireplace. Both his feet were on the floor, a sign his leg didn't pain him today.

"He looks both terribly happy and horribly sad," Anne whispered.

The King's eyebrows were melting down the outside of his eyes while his mouth attempted a wobbly smile. *Good.* His mawkish joy would be perfectly served by Edward's story about the Prince's awe at the decorated hall. The Queen would be entertained as well; she was happier to speak of her stepson than of Jane, even though she had completely eclipsed Jane.

Right now, the Queen sparkled. The King had lavished more presents on her than on any of her predecessors, and her slight frame was dwarfed by a heavy rope necklace of two hundred large pearls around two pendant laces that held ten clear table diamonds and one hundred and fifty-eight fair pearls.

"How many abbeys were dissolved to pay for that finery?" Anne asked.

Edward shot her an amused glance, and her green collar caught his eye. The present he had given her on the birth of their first son. It paled beside the Queen's finery, but it was worthy of pride forever: a stunning band of four emeralds the size of grapes, separated by smaller diamonds, with everything held into place by a double layer of gold links. From it hung a pendant, a larger emerald in the middle of her chest. Anne had gasped when she first opened the package, and joy had filled his heart. She loved fine things.

With a rustle of skirts, Lady Mary was before them. Her light curtsy gave them honor. "Such a pleasure to see real friends," she said. "My father was looking for you."

"We just arrived," said Edward. "I hope he wasn't—"

"Not at all," Mary rushed to interject. "He just wanted to share a moment with you."

"Lovely," Edward answered. "Will you bring us?"

Mary looked over at her mother-in-law on the dais and hesitated.

Just then, the Queen stood and raised a hand to issue a loud command. "A galliard, gentlemen."

Courtiers ran to the center of the room to take part in the dance, jostling for choice positions.

"Husband, will you join me?" the Queen called, stretching out her arm to him.

Henry raised his glass to her. "Nay, my sweet, I will watch you. Your grace will bring joy to me and all the court."

Edward was glad to see him decline the invitation. The King had exerted himself heavily this season with his young wife. There were limits to his endurance. Even if his leg did seem fine.

Catherine curtsied her happy acceptance. "I cannot dance alone," she answered coquettishly.

Henry looked at the gentlemen standing to his right. Thomas Culpeper was closest, and he got the slap on the arm. "Go partner the Queen. All of you, dance."

Culpeper smiled widely and added a flourish to his bow. "If we cannot serve you with dance, Your Majesty, we are happy to so serve the Queen."

"Better work than they usually get," said Tom as he walked up behind Edward.

Mary looked at him quizzically. "Sir?"

Tom laughed as if caught in mischief. Given his childish humor, he was probably referring to the amount of time the King spent on his close stool. "T'was but a jest" he said. "And a poor one at that."

The court turned to watch as ladies ran to face gentlemen in lines. The dancers bowed to each other to begin the ritual, then clasped hands to start a circle around the room. After eight paces, four sideways, the couples stopped to take turns kicking up their heels for each other before bowing and clasping hands again. The steps were controlled and stylized, each gesture exaggerated. The Queen and Culpeper were well matched, of similar age and build, and the same bold smirk cut across their fetching faces. It made sense, as Culpeper was distantly related to the powerful clan.

"Unless you would prefer to dance," Mary said with a smile, "I would love to bring you to the King right now."

Edward smiled. It was wonderful when things worked out so well. They approached the King, who was indeed glad to see them. The four were able to gather comfortably on the dais, watching the rest of the court and gossiping among themselves. Family.

The high activity eclipsed the arrival of the seven-year-old Lady Elizabeth. The page could not announce her properly over the music, but the Queen saw her standing in the doorway and stopped dancing. The rest of the dancers quickly followed suit; a few banged into someone else.

"Sweet cousin, come join me," Catherine called out, holding out her hand.

Edward leaned his head in close to Anne before whispering. "A Howard always advances another Howard."

Anne raised an eyebrow. She had noticed - everyone had - how the Queen had shown great favor to the younger princess during this Christmas season, seating the girl across from her and keeping her close during the day. Much better treatment than she had given Mary.

"If only your brother and sister were equally skilled at such promotion," she whispered in response.

Touché, Edward thought, though his siblings weren't as inept as Anne often made them out to be.

Elizabeth bowed to the Queen, then her father, before running over. Smart child.

"You shall be my partner," the Queen said to the girl and the room applauded.

"She could have no better," Culpeper said with an easy smile. He backed off in a gallant surrender of his place.

Before the dancing could resume, a page announced Anne of Cleves. She had arrived that day with wonderful gifts - two great horses with purple velvet trappings - for the King and Queen.

"Welcome, sweet sister," called the King. "We are happy to see your smiling face."

"It is a joy to see my good brother and his cherished

wife."

The King descended from the dais to greet her, and the Queen raced to his side, Elizabeth in tow.

With an apologetic glance at Anne, Edward offered his hand to Mary so they could follow. It was wrong to remain on the dais when the King was on the floor.

Henry held up his arm, and a page appeared bearing sables on a gilt platter, which he knelt to offer to the King. Henry took the furs in one hand and presented them to Cleves, who marveled over them, though the present seemed a bit light given the contrast to the Queen's finery.

"And since I am giving gifts," he said, turning to his wife, "I shall give you tonight's now."

He proffered a large ruby ring with one hand and waved the other again. This time two pages appeared, each carrying a tiny beagle puppy.

The Queen clapped her hands in delight. Lady Anne did the same, as did every woman in the Great Hall.

The Queen reached out and took one in her arms. "They are wonderful," she said. "They will make excellent hunting companions."

"May I?" asked Lady Anne, doing the same. The women laughed at the wriggling bundles craning to lick their faces.

"You must have one," said Catherine. "He will be brought to your rooms. And this ring, too." She motioned for the pages to take the dogs and placed the ruby on Lady Anne's finger.

Anne of Cleves took a step backwards. "I couldn't..."

"Nonsense," said Catherine. She turned to the King. "You don't mind, do you, that I love your sister as you do? You have given me so many wondrous gifts; it is my great joy to share my good fortune."

Nicely done, Edward thought. He leaned over to Anne and whispered. "You think her uncle put the idea in her mind?"

"Norfolk hates to part with riches. He would have told her to stop at the dogs."

Edward stifled his laugh and turned back to the scene before him. But still one thought nagged at him. He leaned back to Anne. "Why is she so easy with Cleves but so uncomfortable about Jane?"

Anne rolled her eyes. "Catherine has no cause to be jealous of the Flanders Mare. Your sister gave him a son."

Edward closed his eyes. That one fact was the fount of everything.

Chapter Seven

January 16, 1541—Hampton Court Palace

The tall hedges of the Pond Garden acted as screens against errant winds and prying eyes. Gardiner, Norfolk, and the King were walking, and less jealousy would arise if no one knew about their little outing.

Gardiner took a deep breath and turned his face to the sky to smile. It was one of those winter days a man dreams of, sunny and crisp. A stroll was a far better choice than the hawking so many people favored. Gardiner went, of course, but he was a mediocre horseman and never got a bird to fly. Not like Hertford, who had grown up with a model stable and a fabled aviary.

Gardiner forced himself to pull back from the jealousy that had surfaced. This garden stroll was ideal, he reminded himself, just him, Norfolk and the King. Norfolk was dominating the conversation, seizing opportunity – Wyatt had bested the King at cards earlier, and had acted smug, even aggressive, about the victory. From small acorns like this mighty rages could grow.

"They say Wyatt corresponded with Cardinal Pole," said Norfolk. "Why would he deal with that traitor except to support his evil aspirations?"

As always, the mention of Reginald Pole brought out the throbbing purple vein in the King's forehead. Traitors wanted to replace Henry with his Catholic cousin, one of the few other men with royal blood still alive.

The King nodded but then crossed his arms. The vein faded. "No one has seen any letters."

"I say it was Sadler who helped conceal them," Norfolk accused. "He makes my blood boil, him and Wyatt. Two who don't love you."

The King stared down at the pebbled path as he walked. His eyes scrutinized the rocks as if there were some answer there. "I fail to see it," he finally said. "Sadler has been my close companion for more than five years, Wyatt for twenty."

"And yet they wish you dead," said Norfolk. "The two discussed a time when you would no longer be with us; the whole court heard their treason. How are they not in prison right now?"

Gardiner lowered his eyes. The poet had said words that could be so construed, speaking with Sadler and in front of a crowd. Of course, he would likely deny the meaning Norfolk was placing on those words, but Wyatt wasn't there to defend himself.

The King stumbled and grunted. Gardiner and Norfolk thrust out their arms, but he waved them away. Instead he bent over, hands on his thighs just below his haunches, catching his breath.

Gardiner and Norfolk stood in silence until the King had straightened, taken a deep breath, and exhaled the incident like a dog shaking off water. When he started walking again, Norfolk jumped back in. "Wyatt has always disdained your generosity. He chased my niece even after your interest was known, probably sullied her too."

The King halted and narrowed his eyes. Gardiner's heart stopped. It was a dangerous game to remind the King of Anne Boleyn. Worse, of a time when he was under her spell. Of course, the current Queen's blood relationship to the unfortunate woman had rendered some such reminders inevitable. And less deadly.

"That was long ago," the King finally said.

Norfolk, to Gardiner's amazement, was still not dissuaded. "I say this, Your Majesty, because he cares nothing for sin, he cannot be counted on for loyalty. The man has defied divine law for fifteen years by refusing to do his duty by his wife. He cares nothing for yours."

Another dangerous argument. The King might fully empathize with Wyatt's refusal, having been unable to bring himself to bed Anne of Cleves. But again the danger of the reference lent an aura of honesty to the argument. *Fortune favors the audacious,* Gardiner reminded himself.

"You really think he is a traitor?" There was a catch in the King's voice. Was he wavering?

"I know he is. He should be arrested before the sun sets. Him and Sadler. I cannot forgive as Your Majesty does; God in His wisdom has not granted me such grace. I hate all who harm you, forever and completely."

Norfolk finished, and Gardiner realized he had been holding his breath. The speech had been powerful, compelling.

"Draw up the warrants so they may be questioned." The King's lower lip trembled. "Draw them up and I will sign them."

"I've had them ready for days. I told you I hated those two." Norfolk waved his arm to summon the page posted at the garden's entrance for just this request. "Bring a pen for His Majesty," he called.

The page must have run the whole way, for he returned with an inkwell and quill before the men had gone ten paces.

Norfolk grabbed the youth's arm and spun him around. "Bend over," Norfolk said, placing a wide right hand on the boy's back to speed the process while his left took the papers out of his breast pocket and shook out their folds.

"Sire," he said, placing the papers on the page's back and holding out the quill he had already dipped in the ink.

The King picked up the top sheet. He started to read it but quickly put it back down.

Gardiner held his breath as the King signed first one page, then the next. It was done. The earth would soon be cleansed of two more vestiges of Thomas Cromwell.

Gardiner still could not believe Norfolk had pulled

this off. Norfolk had spent months doing nothing more than insulting the men's characters and loyalty. Those thousand petty sallies had joined to form a deadly thrust when slurs had merged with truth in the King's mind.

It was an important lesson, this patience. The long view of a game. Siege rather than direct engagement. Norfolk, the great general, had even sacrificed small skirmishes to win the battle. He had allowed Sadler to receive a grant of lands, Wyatt a paid appointment to the Kent Commission of Sewers. Lulled them into complacency. Nothing threw off a man's suspicions like reward. Like Cromwell and his fool earldom – though that move saved him from a traitor's death.

Gardiner shivered. Burning was the penalty for religious sin. Some claimed it was worse even than being drawn and quartered. If Gardiner were ever convicted for his Catholic leanings, it would be the fire for him.

He shook his head to scatter the thoughts that plagued him. This was not the time to think, this was the time to act. The warrants had been signed so unexpectedly that he and Norfolk were unprepared. They had to find Sir John Gage, Constable of the Tower, to make arrangements. The arrests might have to wait until the morrow...

"What?" The King's voice was a snarl.

Gardiner jumped. "Sire?"

"You look upset, as if you think I am making a mistake."

"Just the opposite, Your Majesty. My grief was for you, having to endure the burden of such a betrayal."

The King nodded, and Gardiner relaxed. Gardiner kept his face calm, praying the King would not realize they hadn't really expected this success. That would make him question his decision, might foil all their plans.

God forbid.

January 20, 1541—Hampton Court Palace

Edward strode into the King's bedchamber, unnerved but not terribly so by the unexpected summons. It was a half hour before the Council meeting was due; the King probably just had a question. Edward needed to stay calm. Any display of anxiety made Henry skittish.

Again Edward blessed his old stable master, the man who'd molded him for his first real post, Master of the Horse to Henry FitzRoy, the King's illegitimate son. That had put Edward under the King's eyes and begun his career. Now it helped him manage a man who was as wild and as arrogant as any untamed colt.

Henry was sitting in the corner, alone, staring out the window past the gardens at the Thames. He glanced over his shoulder to acknowledge his guest and waved his arm to designate a stool next to him. "Sit."

"Sire, I—"

"Quiet." The order was sharp, the King's eyebrows knitted. Edward sat silently and waited as Henry continued to stare off, lips in a thin line. After a minute or so, a raise of the King's chin pointed Edward toward the window as well.

Edward turned, a picture of obedience. He took a deep breath, figuring that was the reaction the King wanted. The two watched as the royal barge docked and three men came toward the palace. Finally Henry spoke. "I thought more on what we discussed last night."

They had discussed Sadler last night, and Edward had defended him. Not confrontationally of course. No. Edward had used Cranmer's tactic, wistfulness. Edward had reminded Henry of late-night messages cheerfully delivered and other instances where the good Ralph had proved his worth and his loyalty. The King had not objected last night, but had something changed? Was Edward in danger or might this simply be melancholy?

"Your memories of Sadler spurred my own," Henry continued. "I remembered his devotion to Jane and to my son."

Henry turned to Edward, eyes boring. "Whatever he said to Wyatt, I don't believe he wished me harm. I don't believe it was anything more than love for my son and support for the proper succession."

Edward allowed his deep relief to soften his mouth into a smile. Still, he was careful to keep some regret on his face. It was safest that way.

"I have ordered him released," said the King. "He will be here any minute now."

The words were thrilling, but the King's face remained severe. Joy mixed with nervousness in Edward's chest – what reaction was Henry expecting?

"God bless and preserve Your Majesty," Edward said. "I believe you did right."

"I know I did," said Henry. The self-righteous tone reassured Edward. It meant he had correctly read the King's views, even if he hadn't responded properly.

"Both in releasing and in arresting him."

"Sire?"

"Norfolk was working some plot and I needed to test it."

The import of Henry's words went straight to Edward's stomach and he had to hold back a retch behind a gentle smile. The King had manipulated the manipulators. The realm of potential traps had just multiplied a hundredfold.

The King turned back to the window. "Most of my Privy Council are only temporizing for their own profit, but I know the good servants from the flatterers, and if God lends me health I will take care their projects not succeed."

Was he turning on Norfolk? Edward could not sift truth from madness. All he could do was nod slowly.

The page cut short further conversation by announcing Ralph Sadler. Henry lifted his chin and looked down his nose as Sadler raced over and prostrated himself. "I thank God for the sight of Your Majesty before me. I praise Him for opening your mind to my loyalty."

The King waved his hand. "Rise, Ralph, you are forgiven."

Sadler looked up but remained on his knees. "I ask no

more than this."

The King gave an exasperated sigh. "Do you say no more than this?"

Sadler spread his arms wide. "I will say whatever you will let me say. I will apologize for my carelessness in speaking words that might have been taken wrongly. For any actions that might lead you to think I had anything but Your Majesty's best interests always before my eyes. For any way I have failed to fulfill Your Majesty's wishes. For—"

"Up," said Henry, waving his hand again.

Sadler scrambled to his feet, not foolish enough to disobey a second command.

"Your apology is enough," said the King. "Especially given the things my men found at your home." The sound of challenge tinged the King's voice, and Edward found his own chest constrict.

Sadler narrowed his eyes. "I have few possessions."

The King nodded, as if checking something off a list. "That is true; the task did not tire them," he said with a smile. "They found nothing but a portrait of me and a painting of the Battle of the Spurs."

Smart move. Edward was transported back to the days after Cromwell's arrest, when the reports from the search of Austin Friars had somehow yielded evidence. Right afterwards, Edward had purged his own home of anything that could be considered dangerous, anything that could hint at reform. Tom had mocked his caution but there was no reason to take chances, and thankfully Sadler had felt the same way. Indeed, Sadler had been even more careful. The Battle of the Spurs was a wonderful association for Sadler to have chosen - the King was inordinately delighted by that victory against the French.

"My brother commanded a company there. I am proud of his contribution to Your Majesty's glory."

"Your brother did well," the King said. "Now it is your turn."

"Sire?"

"Hertford here leaves for France in three days to deal

with the vexing issue of borders. He will meet with the French commissioners to finally settle the frontier between Ardes and Guisnes."

"He certainly is in a better position than most to accomplish that task," Sadler said.

Edward had spent a great deal of time in France. At thirteen he had been a page to Henry's sister Mary when she was sent to wed King Louis XII, and then over the years Edward had returned several times – most notably to provide for the defense and fortification of Calais and Guisnes. But he knew even he would be unlikely to succeed in this – directly, anyway – so he had a plan that would insulate him from disaster, assuming the King approved.

"Though I thought your most vexing border issues involved Scotland?" Sadler continued. Absolutely true. Although Henry's sister Margaret had maintained close ties between the two countries while she acted as Regent for her young son, once James V was an adult he had taken a French bride who reminded him of centuries of English aggression against Scotland, and the equally long Auld Alliance that bound France to Scotland in friendship and protection. King James was no longer a friend to England.

"Norfolk is the man for the North," said the King. "My plan is to send him there right after we next hear from my nephew."

Again, Edward prayed a letter would arrive soon. He did not like the idea of leaving Norfolk and Gardiner free to plot while he was away. Without Norfolk, Gardiner would lose much of his power. And Sadler would keep them all in line.

"And I had a new thought too," added Henry. "To send Gardiner to speak to the Emperor. Which is why I will need your energies, Ralph, when so many of my chiefest servants are gone."

Edward was ready to cry with relief. Now there would be no one left at court to whisper poison into the King's ear. For at least part of Edward's absence.

Sadler bowed deeply. "I will be tireless, Your Majesty. I am honored."

The King rose. As he did so, he clapped Sadler on the shoulder. The gesture was odd for some reason. It seemed harder than a friendly sign, almost as it to give himself support. Maybe his leg was not as healed as it appeared to be.

"Let us go to the Council meeting now," Henry said to Sadler. "Keep out of sight behind me for as long as you can. I want to watch people's faces when they realize you've been released."

Marillac's words came back to Edward. Once again, the King was giving both succor and offense to both sides.

What did this mean?

March 16, 1541—Whitehall Palace

Edward spurred on his horse. The sixteen-hand gray courser was not as sleek as the destrier he usually chose, but it was faster. A better mount for the seventy-five mile journey between Dover and Whitehall, especially since Edward wanted to continue on to Hertford Hall that night after the hour or so it would take him to wait on the King. It had been a long time since Edward had seen his wife; he had a lot to discuss with her, things he was not so foolhardy as to commit to paper.

The *Primrose* had put him ashore only yesterday after his seven weeks in France, and he had missed a great deal at court. Henry had shut himself up in his apartments over a *mal d'esprit*, refusing admission even to the Queen. The whole court had gone dark and quiet, and the French Ambassador had remarked the atmosphere resembled more a private family than a King's retinue. Then just when people thought it couldn't get worse, the King's gloom had turned to anger and suspicion. He rejoined the world of men but with a vengeance, accusing everyone around him of being a lying timeserver and flatterer who looked only to his own profit. He had even come to the point of openly mourning Cromwell's loss. Henry raged one day that his councilors, "upon light pretext, by false accusations, had made him put to death the most faithful servant he ever had."

An interesting twist. The first execution the King had ever publicly regretted, even mentioned. Was he finally softening?

Edward approached the courtyard to Whitehall and was relieved to see the grooms were waiting for him. He had made the arrangements during his quick stop at Leeds Castle in Kent, sending a messenger on ahead while Edward took the little sleep he needed to break up the sixteen-hour trip. This readiness was the reward for his foresight.

One of the youth ran up to Edward to catch his reins. The lad had a bright look in his eye, though his tongue tripped from nervousness. "Sir Anthony Denny says the King'll see your lordship when you've changed, milord."

Denny. Good man. The King's closest confidant in his Privy Chamber. Edward grunted his thanks and made his way quickly to his rooms to shed his dusty travel clothes and don the finery necessary to approach the King.

The manservant handed him a small mirror.

"Thank you," Edward said. "You may go now, Barnaby, but make sure the stables know I am leaving for Hertford Hall after my audience. I want a horse ready for me." He snapped his fingers. "And have word sent to my wife now so she knows when to expect me."

As the manservant bowed out, their eyes met for a moment and Edward remembered Barnaby had been a messenger until Cromwell noticed his talent. Advancing someone assured their loyalty, and you never knew where you would need an able friend. "Find the youth who greeted us if you can. Ask him to do it."

Edward glanced at the ceiling in a quick acknowledgement of Cromwell's genius, then turned back to the mirror.

He raised his chin and donned the focused gaze that would signal his capability when he first bowed to the King, then softened it to the brotherly concern he would need to inquire about the King's state of mind. Those faces should keep him safe. With a last return to pride, he put the mirror down and embarked on his quest.

He was admitted immediately at the King's apartments. Edward knocked on the bedchamber door, and Denny opened it. "Ah, Hertford, His Majesty is waiting for you."

The room was dark with only a few lone candles here and there to brighten it. The King was sitting beside his desk in his favorite chair, his ulcerous leg propped high on a footstool. He was busily grinding a pestle against a mortar, looking isolated and lonely in the cavernous space.

"Greetings, Your Majesty." Edward's bow was low. "It does me good to see you looking well."

The lie was not outrageous: the King looked unchanged from when Edward had last seen him. Back when he was doing well.

"I am doing better now. Things were bad for a time."

"Praise God that time is done."

The King sniffed and waved Denny away. "Return to me in an hour."

When Denny was gone, Henry resumed. "It started with my leg. The wound closed like it did that time before." He took another pearl from the basin next to him and dropped it into his mortar.

"God's blood," Edward mumbled as he crossed himself. Five or six years earlier, they had rejoiced when the King's leg had apparently healed. Unfortunately, the closed wounds trapped the poison inside. After three days of a fever which turned the King's face black and came close to killing him, the doctors thought to lance the scars open with a red-hot poker. Gray pus burst from the skin and continued to ooze for hours afterwards. But within fifteen minutes the King was recovered enough to speak and curse them all roundly. And threaten them with death if they ever let such a thing happen again.

"This time we caught it sooner. I was not in the same danger." The King pounded on the pearl to crush it.

"Even so, I thank God you are well." Edward waited for

Henry to reply, but the King just shook his head and indicated the chair across the table from him.

Edward sat and saw that Henry was still shaking his head. What the devil was going on? "I heard you were melancholy," said Edward. "Was that the cause of it?"

The King's words came out in a staccato sequence, punctuated by the pounding of the pestle. "I have an unhappy people to govern," the King said. "Getting my country into line is the last grace I have left to me, but even that is exhausting. I find myself like Sisyphus, endlessly rolling the same ball up the hill."

What ball was he referring to? "Sire?"

The King looked up from under his eyebrows, pestle grinding. "But I know what they are plotting and I have my own plans."

Overwhelmed, Edward reached out to the King, placing a hand on the table before him. "I offer you all my help and succor in this. Whatever you command."

The King's lower lip trembled. "I am glad you are back. Someone I can trust. You are the only person I can say that about."

"Surely that's not true," Edward said, hoping it was.

Henry's eyes narrowed and, like a predator stalking its prey, he turned his head to Edward. "You heard about my melancholy? What did you hear?"

Edward withdrew his hand and sat back in his chair. He had rehearsed the answer to this question, but the suspicion on the King's face still unnerved him. "Marillac reported you had no interest in any type of recreation, even music." Marillac had also said the King was often of a different opinion in the morning than he was after dinner, but there was no need to mention that piece of information.

"Marillac is too damned observant," said the King. "But he was right. I was miserable. I'd never felt that way before and feared it would never end."

"You were laid low after my sister Jane died and the Lord gave you comfort then. You—"

"This was different," Henry said quickly. "This time I

couldn't even present a brave face to my people. That's why I had to shut myself away. Even from my gentlemen."

"And your doctors?"

"They finally helped return me to a public life."

Edward nodded. "I never could have understood if Jane had not explained it to me. I always knew you lived your whole life observed, but she explained the unexpected cumulative effect to such an existence."

"That's exactly it." Henry's eyes glowed for a moment then quickly extinguished. "She left us too soon." He stood and started to pace. "Look at me. My kingdom is safe, I've given it an heir. I have a beautiful wife and a new chance at love. And yet I would still take the old."

Was that it? He was still grieving Jane? *Pay attention,* Edward's brain shrieked. He needed to delve into what the King was saying to understand it, but he had to remain in the moment in order to react appropriately.

"I miss my sister too," was all Edward said.

"I care for nothing." Henry spread his arms wide. "I cannot bring myself to even pretend I do."

Edward kept his face sympathetic as he cast about frantically for a response. What did the King want Edward to say? What did he need Edward to say?

He reminded himself of the formula: praise first, then advice. As long as the advice reflected the King's desires.

"Of course you can't. You pushed yourself too hard for too long." Edward leaned forward and shook a cautious finger. "You should be gentler to yourself. Give yourself time and space. You don't have to be before the public all the time."

"My people need to see me."

"Your people need an active court, diversions. Let the Queen preside. You can attend as much or as little as you want. And then go out on progress during the summer, when the good weather has lifted your spirits."

"Aye. That is what I have started doing and it has worked well. But it makes me feel weak." The King wiped a tear from his eye, then put down the mortar to grab a handkerchief and blow his nose. "When I was young, I lived completely sheltered from the world. No one entered my chamber without passing through my father's. I spoke to no one save him and my confessor. My father's death liberated me from that prison, and now I enter it again."

"It is different when you hold the key."

Henry's thoughtful nodding encouraged Edward to continue. "You are the most public King who has ever ruled this land, you don't need to open yourself so much. Close the doors to your rooms against all comers. As much as you want."

"It's not a question of desire. I can't bring myself to do anything else."

"You can build yourself back up slowly. I will be with you - and I will bring the Prince to you every day if you like, to—"

"Not every day, that would be too much."

"Every week, I will bring the Prince to visit and cheer you."

"That would bring me joy," the King said.

The excitement of success spurred Edward on. "And talk to your wife," he said. "You always felt better talking to Jane. God gave us these helpmates for our glory."

Henry's face twisted. "You're a fool, Edward."

Edward's pride dissipated, but he did his best to keep encouragement on his face.

"I can't confess such weakness to her," the King said. "She thinks of me as her hero, her knight. I don't want her to see me as..." He sighed, and when he continued his voice caught. "I was once the handsomest prince in Christendom, with golden hair and a fine calf. I could best anyone at the joust, at tennis, at archery. I could dance without tiring and whisk a pretty maiden off afterwards. And now look at me." He waved an arm over his raised leg, the reeking bandage so prominent as to mock its wearer.

Edward's throat tightened. He was terrified, not by the secret shame but by the fear the King would come to hate Edward for having heard it. This was dangerous ground.

He took a deep breath, the better to offer the sympathy the King needed. The sympathy that would soften the ferocity that threatened the very country.

* * *

Edward felt the wind in his hair as he rode hard for his house. The chill was uncomfortable and yet strangely calming, reminding him he was getting further and further away from the panic the King's revelations had instilled in him and closer and closer to his wife's soothing arms.

Barely three falls of his horse's hooves in the courtyard, and Anne was already in the doorway to greet him. Edward was off his horse immediately, tossing his reins over the tired courser's back without waiting for the running stable boy. Edward wasn't worried the animal would wander off and forego the bag of oats and the brushing waiting for it; he cared more about embracing his wife.

He held her tightly for several deep breaths, reveling in the warm smell of her until she pulled away.

"I can't believe you came all the way home after so long on the road," she said. "I will make it worth your while though." Her hand slipped to his breeches and his heart fell.

"I will disappoint you there," he said. "I am weary to my bones and cannot shake off my conversation with the King."

"Oh? What is amiss?" There was alarm in her voice.

"Nothing to harm us. Just disturbing." He pulled her back into his arms.

"Must you attend the Council meeting tomorrow?" she whispered in his ear.

"It is but a short trip to Westminster. And I saw the King already, so I am prepared for it."

She gave Edward a squeeze and pulled away again. "Are you hungry?"

"More tired than hungry."

She grinned. "You can go right in to bed; there is already a tray waiting for you there."

Warm gratitude flooded him. "A tray?"

"One large enough to comfort the King."

As she spoke, the pit in Edward's stomach softened into hunger. He put an arm around her waist and led her into the house. Some of the servants came out to the hallway to welcome him home, but Edward gave only quick hellos and did not slow his pace.

The tray shone from its spot on the side table. He walked over to it. One hand reached for a slice of venison, folded it, and shoved into his mouth; the other followed with a piece of the crust from a meat pie. As he chewed, he sat on the bed and pulled off his boots, then stripped off his doublet and hose. He pulled down the blanket and crawled between the fine linen sheets. Anne laughed and handed him a nightshirt. He had barely put it on before he was motioning her to hand him the large round platter so he could avail himself of more food.

This time he picked a chunk of bread that he dipped in the gravy for the pie. As he chewed, he watched Anne prepare for bed. The return to normalcy relieved Edward almost to the point of pain.

The hood and jewels came off first, carefully set on the table. Then her rich sleeves and gown, her kirtle and finally her farthingale. Wearing just her chemise, she turned to the bed.

"Don't forget the wine," he called, and she placed a full goblet on the night table before joining him under the blanket.

Edward moved over so their sides were touching all the way down. She giggled and hooked an arm through his.

"So the King was unhappy with your news?" she asked. "Is that what happened?"

The reminder of the King dampened Edward's mood a bit, but not as much as he feared. "No, no. I had already written him the results; there was nothing new."

She looked at him with her lips pressed together, as if debating whether to push on. Edward wondered what she was thinking. Was his failure to agree on the borders considered failure behind his back? The French had proposed a compromise that would have involved a retreat. Edward had refused to entertain such a request and insisted they come to England to present their meager offer to the King.

"And you, were you satisfied?" she finally said.

It was a good way of phrasing it. Comforting. He nodded. "Yes, yes I was."

He had agonized for a time over whether continuing the border dispute was the right thing to do. He had finally decided it was the only thing to do.

"Were you frightened?"

"That the King would be angry with me? Of course." Edward ripped off a piece of bread and popped it into his mouth. "But," he mumbled with his mouth full, "he would have been far angrier if I had made the concessions the French were demanding."

"True."

Edward motioned for the glass of wine. "I threatened as much as I could - like haggling with a merchant who reduces the price of his goods only when you're leaving his yard. I moved them to the best deal I thought we could get, then invoked the King. Now when they come to England our new starting point will be this one - certainly more favorable than it had been."

She placed a tender hand on the blanket atop his knee. "But still not as favorable as the King expected."

"Ah, but we're not yet done. I told him before I left that this might be how I would handle it. He knew the strategy and appreciated the opportunity for a new round of negotiations."

Anne sat back into her pillows and laughed. "Of course you had a plan." She took the cup from him and took a sip. "I should have known - but I was just so worried for his mood given the way he skulked in his rooms for so long. You heard all about that from Marillac, yes?"

"I did." Edward took a bite of meat.

"You probably know more than I do, then, since his information is likely to be better than the stories Elizabeth shared. The King would not even allow Catherine to visit him during his dark days."

"So he told me," Edward said.

"Did he?" She sat forward, eyes wide. "Did he say why? She was afraid he was tiring of her."

Edward shook his head and swallowed before explaining. "Just the opposite. He didn't want her to see him weak. He feared she would be disillusioned."

Anne raised a single eyebrow. Edward shrugged. "All men want to be admired by their wives."

"And did he speak of Norfolk or Gardiner? I know you were happy those louts were not here to bend the King's ear in your absence, but that probably saved their lives. He is furious with them over Cromwell."

"Which makes it a good thing I was not here, or I might have been tempted to try to seal their fates."

Anne opened her mouth at Edward's words, so he spoke louder to stop her from speaking. "That would have been too dangerous – you never shoot your arrow unless you are sure of felling your target. There's no return otherwise."

Anne gave him a sideways glance but said nothing. She clearly doubted him. Now was the time to tell her of his fears.

Edward pulled off another chunk of bread and sat back. "The King is hearing voices."

"Voices? Is he mad?"

"Not those kind of voices. Echoes of his father's lessons, guiding him, goading him."

Anne narrowed her eyes. "Does that help him or hurt him?"

"Did you ever meet the old King?"

Anne shook her head. "I saw him from afar, but I didn't come to court until after he died."

"I did. He was a terrifying man who trusted no one. Sunken eyes that would bore into you and make you believe terrible things about yourself. Bony hands that looked like a dead man's claw and that were all too ready to sign a death warrant."

Anne blinked. "Like father, like son."

"Not in the beginning. The King rejected his father's cruelty for years, but now he is determined to exceed it."

Anne crossed herself and sat back to stare off for a time. When she spoke, her voice was a whisper. "We all hear echoes from the past. We are graced when they are gentle. The King's are harsh."

"And cunning." Edward shifted. "Whenever I try to guess what he's thinking, I find I am most likely to be right when I assume he is being devious. And the more deviousness I assume, the more accurate I am."

"This is not new."

"It's getting worse, much worse."

"It is nice he told you," Anne said, still staring off.

"He made light of it right afterwards."

"Well, it's important you know the malice in his thinking."

"Exactly," Edward said. He pulled her close, grateful for her calming perspective. "Now hush." He didn't want to contemplate danger any more. It was time to forget the world and seek renewal. His wife's arms were the right place for that.

Her warmth stirred him, and his exhaustion fell away. It was good to be home.

Chapter Eight

April 25, 1541—Greenwich Palace

The Council had concluded its main business for the day, arbitrating the price Anthony Marler, a London merchant, might charge for Bibles of the Great Volume. It had taken the lords an interminable hour to agree the price would be ten shillings sterling if they were unbound, and twelve if they were bound. Edward maintained interest throughout: the merchant deserved a fair hearing, and too many of the nobility didn't deign to give it to him.

The talk turned to the recent rebellion that had sparked the decision to pay such close attention to seemingly minor details. Again the Catholic North had risen to seek restoration of the old forms of religion. They wanted their abbeys back and their Latin Bibles. They would get neither.

"That's what I'll do." The King's eyes sparkled. "I'll go north to calm my people."

He had made the same resolution after the other northern rebellion four years earlier, the Pilgrimage of Grace. Back then, to assuage ill feelings, the King had promised to consider their requests and to crown Queen Jane at York. He did neither.

"Is that wise, Your Majesty?" asked Wriothesley.

"The country has been subdued, and the rebels will soon be executed. My subjects need to see me."

The King had never visited the far north of his country; it was past time for him to go. "It would be a good use of this year's summer progress," Edward agreed.

"Precisely," said the King.

"And Your Majesty could perhaps try to arrange a formal meeting with the Scottish king while you're there," said Norfolk. "Bind your nephew to you in a triumphant sweep."

Of course Norfolk would tie this trip to his own diplomatic work. And take all the credit. Edward kept his face calm, though inwardly he seethed.

"Yes, yes," the King said excitedly. "The greatest progress of my reign." He sat up straighter in his chair and turned his head to stare out the window at the verdant fields and hills far beyond the river's bends. That view was one of the reasons the King loved Greenwich Palace: it was in London but not of it, as he liked to say.

"You should go all the way to Newcastle, in Northumberland," said Norfolk, though the King was clearly not listening. No matter. The rest of the councilors turned to list cities to visit.

"Of course he must stop at Lincoln," said Cranmer.

"If it is to be the greatest, it should also be the largest," the King blurted. "What do we usually have, a thousand horses? I want four or five thousand this time. That will show England's strength and glory."

"That and a wife of an age to bear you sons," said Norfolk.

The King's face softened and he smiled. "You serve me well, Thomas."

Edward took a deep breath. In one move, Norfolk had parlayed a minor victory into the ultimate success, while Edward had been sent on a mission certain to fail, to determine borders that didn't matter.

Edward felt the bile rise in his throat over Norfolk's ascendancy. If only there was some way to marginalize him. Some weakness. Every man had one.

There had to be a way.

May 27, 1541—Eltham Palace

"You may rise," said the King with a grunt as he sat back in his chair and massaged the leg that rested on his footstool. "Tell us your news."

Edward watched Sir John Gage rise stiffly as he always did on such occasions. As Constable of the Tower, Gage supervised the executions of those who were unfortunate enough to become his inmates, and then reported on them to the King or the Council. The order to execute the illustrious Margaret Plantagenet Pole, the former Countess of Salisbury and the King's own aunt, had come directly from Henry; hence the report was being made to him as well.

Gage's forehead glistened and his eyes darted. He hadn't returned his cap to his head, and his hands clutched and kneaded its brim.

They were all unnerved by the King's mood that day: the hunt had tired him. But Gage's anxiety seemed to be something more. Probably just repugnance from watching a sixty-seven-year-old woman, especially one as thin and frail as Margaret Pole, suffer the ultimate penalty. The King had been undeterred, simply giving orders to execute her quietly within the Tower confines, without witnesses.

"It is done," Gage said, "but it was a difficult thing to get there."

"Oh?" asked the King. His tone was arch but bored.

"Your orders came quickly. Very quickly, Sire."

Was that complaint or excuse? Either one was ill advised. Gage was usually not so impolitic.

The King's lip curled. "I wanted the Tower cleaned out before I left for the North. Surely I did not impose too great a burden."

"No, no, of course not." Gage bowed in apology. "That's not what I meant. Allow me to relate the report from the start." He bowed again, and the King waved his hand absentmindedly.

Gage took a deep breath. "When I gave her the news

that she was to die within the hour, she found the thing very strange. She claimed not to know of what crime she was accused, nor how she had been sentenced."

Sad but naive. She had been sentenced by the King's signature on her death warrant; that was all the law required. As for the crime, followers of her son Cardinal Reginald had conspired to place him on the English throne and restore England to Catholicism, while Reginald himself had remained safely outside the King's reach. No one who knew the King was surprised he would inflict punishment where he could.

His face inscrutable, the King stared at Gage.

"I...ah...showed her the warrant and gave her time to prepare. When I came back for her, she was quiet. Wouldn't speak to me, or look at me. But many prisoners are veiled in prayers at such a moment; I thought nothing of it."

Edward's mind raced. Had the old lady made a scene on the scaffold? Is that what had happened? Railed against the King's justice?

"It was when she arrived at the block. She looked down at it, and said she would never place her head on it. Said it was for traitors, and she was none." Gage took a deep breath. "The guards tied her down but she struggled against her ropes."

Edward sensed the King's eyes flicker. With great effort he kept his own straight. And didn't flinch.

"The executioner was but a youth, Your Majesty. The man who usually fills the post was in the North on your orders to deal with the rebels."

"Your job is to be always prepared," said the King.

Gage swallowed. "The boy's inexperience, the prisoner's struggles...it was a difficult task." Gage's hands kneaded his hat harder. "The first stroke caught her in the shoulders."

"The *first* stroke," said the King.

Gage nodded. "She didn't stop. She kept turning her head every which way. So the executioner struck again. Still her shoulders. And again."

Edward stifled a gasp but could not prevent his hand from going to his suddenly queasy stomach.

The King's eyes narrowed. "She was still struggling?"

"She had stopped by this point. The fourth strike cracked the base of her skull. The fifth—"

"There was a fifth?"

Gage took a deep breath before answering. "There were eleven."

The questions stopped.

Edward kept his eyes on Gage, his face a careful blank. Everyone's face was a careful blank. Commiseration with a traitor was treason. Even general sympathy was suspect. The nausea Edward felt could get him killed.

The King had to speak first. Only then could they show some of their own sorrow.

"Well?" The King's eyes were blank, his lip was curled.

"We brought her to the Chapel of Saint Peter ad Vincula. I...I wanted to confirm with you that she should be interred there."

"Fine. Are we done?"

Gage nodded, bowed, and started to back out, in a daze at how the audience had gone. The King barely waited before leaning his arm over the chair and snapping his fingers. His spaniel trotted over, the pearled badge on its velvet-and-kid collar glinting in the light. The King bent down and picked the dog up, setting it on his lap so he could deliver quick kisses to its nose while it licked his face. "There, there, Cut," he said finally, pulling back. He reached into the purse attached to his belt and gave the expectant dog a treat. The spaniel jumped down and ran back to his corner of the room to enjoy the sweetmeat.

The rest of them in the room all stood, stunned. They had little choice but to wait, as if it were the most natural thing in the world.

"All of you may leave us," said the King. "Except you, Edward. You stay."

"Majesty," Edward said, bowing low. The King must need a sympathetic shoulder. He must feel terrible about

Margaret Pole.

"When shall we return?" asked Thomas Culpeper.

"Not before three hours," said the King. "I will call for you."

Culpeper smiled as if he had some pleasurable activity in mind and bowed out with the others.

After the door closed and left them alone in the room, the King sat at his game table, motioned for Edward to join him, then picked up the deck of cards and began to shuffle.

Edward poured two cups of wine and brought them over.

"Excellent idea," said Henry. He took a sip before dealing.

The King's face was neutral, as if nothing were amiss, and Edward wondered how much effort that was costing him. *Patience,* he repeated to himself. He needed to give his monarch time to open up on his own.

The King picked up his cards and looked through them. "Shall we wager?"

"Always," said Edward. The King loved to gamble, and was not too angry when he lost – as long as that didn't happen often.

Henry started to move cards around in his hand, but then paused and took a deep breath as if preparing to speak.

This was it.

"So how likely do you think it is that Scotland will join with France to war on me?"

The King must be worried the Catholics would try to avenge the Pole execution. "There is no good reason for your nephew to come against you. And Francis is too close to war with the Emperor for them to befriend each other now."

"She hadn't even considered the Emperor," said the King.

Edward hated to seem stupid, but he could not understand what the King could be saying. "Beg pardon, Sire?"

"Oh, that's why I had you hang back. I wanted to tell

you." Henry placed a pair of cards down in front of him and drew two more from the deck. "The Queen was upset two days ago."

Edward tried to mold his face into a show of interest. That seemed like the right response, at least the one that would not be completely wrong for the occasion. "Upset?"

"My dear wife was afraid I might consider taking back Cleves," he said.

It struck Edward that Margaret Pole was not in the King's thoughts at all. "Oh?"

"Of course I told her she was wrong to think such things."

Edward felt profoundly unsettled to be involved in such an innocent conversation following on the heels of such horror. His nausea returned and he kept his responses brief. "Of course," he echoed.

"Even if I were in a position to marry, I have no mind to take back Anne. Once my love is gone, it is gone. That has always been so..." His voice trailed off and Edward knew he must be thinking of Anne Boleyn...or Catherine of Aragon. Or Cromwell, or Carew, or any of the multitude of people he had killed. "And here it never even existed."

"True."

"Ah, I've won," said the King. He lay his cards down to show his hand.

Again the feeling of unreality. "Well done," said Edward. As if in a trance, he stretched out his hand to pick up the cards and deal a new hand. While he shuffled, the King sat back, kicked his legs out, took a deep breath, and lowered his chin. He stayed that way for a long while, eyes closed, until a slight snore indicated he had fallen asleep.

Edward shuffled more loudly, banged the cards on the table a bit, and coughed and sniffled to see if noise might rouse the King. Nothing.

He quelled his rising panic and continued to shuffle. He could not leave, much as he wanted to. It was too soon to get a book to read: it would make him look impatient. But if he waited too long, the King would be annoyed Edward had stared at him for a time.

And then the antidote and the solution appeared to him together. Edward lowered his head and closed his eyes, as if he dozed as well. Aping the King was always safe. Showing him how alike they were would build trust. And it would allow him to still his racing heart before he lost his mind.

October 17, 1541—Collyweston Castle

Gardiner stopped in the doorway and looked around the makeshift Presence Chamber created for the Queen at this stop on the progress: one of the family bedrooms pressed into service. Not the finest one, that would be the King's bedchamber; nor the second finest, that would be the Queen's. But one of the other family bedrooms, every inch scrubbed and shined and then carefully adorned with rich furnishings from the royal stores.

Several other gentlemen waited to greet the Queen. Most of the faces were not familiar, a sign of how long he had been away, but Wriothesley was there, and another member of the Privy Council. Gardiner smiled genially and made his way over to them.

It was a relief to be back in England after all those months on the continent where they tended to look down on their island neighbor and its despotic King. Their words, not Gardiner's of course, and he crossed himself against the errant thought.

He was glad to be joining the court at Collyweston, far to the north near Lincolnshire. The manor house had belonged to Henry's late grandmother, Lady Margaret Beaufort, and stood as a constant, if usually empty, reminder of the King's historic links to this part of the country. It was the perfect symbol of national unity, and would have presented the perfect *tableau* if this trip had been the diplomatic triumph it was supposed to be. The triumph Norfolk had planned.

Instead, the King had been snubbed by his nephew

James, who never made the trip to meet him in York. The King had waited like a jilted bride standing unwanted at the altar, incredulous and horrified, before finally bending to reality. After almost two weeks, pretenses and excuses finally gave way to wrath and the decision to leave – a decision made late one night after festivities that included heavy drinking. The King and his company had turned to mocking the King of Scotland, deciding he must be too intimidated by England's glory to face his uncle. But the King quickly grew maudlin over the irony that such a base individual had caused such insult.

"I have done that undeserving wretch too much honor by waiting," he slurred. "We will leave tomorrow, after Mass. Tell the Lord Chamberlain."

Somehow the command was carried out, and six hours later the royal cortege took off for the next stop on the progress, with all involved trying to recapture the festive air that had characterized the start of it. The Queen stepped in, holding dances every night until people forgot the snub.

But it was still a failure.

Before Gardiner could reach his friends, a younger man emerged from another room. His dark, shifty eyes clashed with his jaunty swagger, or perhaps just made it seem sinister. The man looked around and approached Gardiner, confirming him as the most important of the visitors. The cassock had its advantages.

"Your Grace?"

"Greetings." Gardiner's voice was tentative.

"I am Her Majesty's private secretary. Francis Dereham."

"Ah." Gardiner understood. "Of course. I am Steven Gardiner, Bishop of Winchester."

Dereham hesitated, his face squinting as if considering something. "The Queen is not available to receive you right now." His voice was self-important, haughty even. "Was she expecting you?"

"No. I just wanted to give her my greetings after waiting upon His Majesty."

"Well..." Dereham's voice trailed off and his nose wrinkled.

"Please leave word I came and I shall return another time."

"Yes, of course," said Dereham. He immediately turned to one of the many other younger men whom Gardiner did not know, and saluted warmly. Surprised and embarrassed, Gardiner stood there awkwardly. Wriothesley and the Bishop of Durham hurried over to greet him. While they were exchanging pleasantries, Gardiner could hear snippets of Dereham's conversation, including the words, "Come, I will insist Her Majesty receive you."

Gardiner's face flamed at this unexpected shaming. Sent away while a lesser man was admitted.

"We all dislike the man," Wriothesley whispered. "Think nothing of it."

"Who is he?" Gardiner asked. A simple question the two men jumped over each other to answer.

"Another member of the household of the Dowager Duchess of Norfolk, at Lambeth," said Wriothesley.

"He came to Pontefract Castle a month ago," said Durham.

"When we were in the North, a passel of them came to claim places at court," said Wriothesley.

"This one is the worst of all," added Durham. "He is too familiar with the Queen, and constantly acts as if their prior relationship gives him greater right to speak with her and attend her."

"Does he now," Gardiner said as noncommittally as he could.

"He's also got quite a temper," said Wriotheslesy. "And the Queen does nothing to curb him."

"Culpeper tried to recently, and they almost came to blows," said Durham.

Gardiner was shocked at this kind of behavior. It was appalling this man would act that way, but it was also upsetting that the Queen would allow it. Gardiner resolved to say something to Norfolk. This situation did not reflect well on Catherine, or the Howard family.

October 19, 1541—Hampton Court Palace

Edward added three letters to the stack already in his bag, taking care to carefully line up the edges to keep things neat and protected.

"Do you have a moment, my good Earl?"

The words drew Edward away from his focus. Thomas Cranmer was at Edward's office door with one of Cromwell's old messengers and another man Edward had never met.

Edward stifled a sigh. He was trying to leave to get home to Anne. Cranmer had a soft heart; he was always trying to help people with their personal causes, play the angel to men who had no right to such generosity. "A moment, because it is you who ask, my dear Archbishop. But I am pressed right now." Managing expectations.

"Thank you, my good friend." Cranmer swept his hand. "You remember John Lascelles, who was in service to Thomas Cromwell?"

"Of course," said Edward. An honest man and fervent reformer. "Greetings."

"This is his brother-in-law, John Hall."

Edward nodded his head at the newcomer.

"These fine gentlemen came to me with an issue that troubled them greatly. When they told me what it was, I feared for His Majesty."

Edward stiffened. Had something happened to the King? "Is there—"

"This is a matter that requires some thought and consultation," Cranmer interrupted. "And discretion."

Cranmer's lips were tight and his brow was furrowed.

Lascelles's too. Hall looked fearful. "Go on," Edward drew out the words.

Still the same worrying expression on Cranmer's face. "May we sit?"

"Please." Edward motioned to the chairs surrounding his desk and went to bring the tray with wine.

When they had all been served, Cranmer said a blessing and began. "John Lascelles studied law at Furnival's Inn, so when he learned of certain information recently he knew he must disclose it. To do otherwise might be misprison of treason."

Treason? Edward's chest tightened. And yet Cranmer had used the word *might.* Thus the "thought and consultation." Edward sat back, bracing himself.

Cranmer turned to Lascelles. "Tell him what you told me."

Lascelles took a gulp of wine. "Well, my Lord, I have a sister, Mary, who was a chamber woman in the household of the Dowager Duchess of Norfolk, when the Queen was young."

Servants always knew everything about a household; they overheard every conversation and cleaned up the detritus of every plot. Edward nodded for the man to continue.

"I thought it would benefit her house – and mine – if Mary sought a place in the Queen's household. Others had done the same – anyone would. Why not our Mary? But she refused."

Edward had no earthly idea how this would lead to treason. "Were they on bad terms?" he asked, hoping to move the story along.

"I asked the same, but Mary was firm. She said it was because the Queen was light, both in living and in conditions, and she could not serve such a one."

"Light?"

"She did not come innocent to the King's bed. There were two men."

The magnitude of the issue hit Edward like a kick to his stomach. "Two?"

"There was a music master, Henry Manox, who gave her lessons alone and they would... Mary tried to protect Catherine then, tried to stop Manox. She reminded him the Howards would undo him if they found out – but he told her to mind her own business, that Catherine's maidenhead would be worth any risk."

Edward could not believe what he was hearing. "And he succeeded?"

"He touched the secret parts of her body. But it was the Duchess's secretary who had her first. Francis Dereham."

"She told someone this?" Edward was cautious.

"She didn't need to," Lascelles said. "He used to sneak into the women's dormitory at night. They all knew. Catherine drew the curtains around them, so no one could see what they did. But the noises they made left no doubt. They called themselves married, my Lord."

The words shoved Edward backwards. *They called themselves married.* This was more of a precontract than had existed with Cleves; this was a true impediment. "Married?"

"Married."

Edward tried to wrap his mind around the enormity of all he'd just been told, the stark political advantage it would confer. And then the prospect of the King's reaction loomed. *God, poor Henry.*

"What shall we do?" Cranmer asked.

Edward swallowed to lubricate his dry mouth. "We shall investigate." He looked at John Lascelles, then at John Hall. "Where is your wife now? She must come to talk to Cranmer."

Hall hung his head. "She does not wish to—"

"This touches the King personally," Edward interrupted. "We must question your wife, look into her eyes and know she speaks the truth. For we will all die if she is lying."

Anguished, Hall nodded.

Lascelles spoke. "She's a good, honest, God-fearing woman."

"And there's many who can prove she speaks the truth,"

said Hall. "All the women from the dormitory."

All the women from the dormitory. All the servants. Henry could not back down from that. No. The King could not back down from that. Now the only question was who else would drown in her wake.

"You did right to come forward," Cranmer's voice was soothing. "Thank you both."

The two men took the dismissal and bowed out. Edward waited until the door was closed after them before turning to Cranmer. Edward stared at him intently.

"You see why I came to you?" Cranmer finally said.

"I do." Edward's ironic chuckle grew to a pained laugh.

"What demon possesses you?" Cranmer's face and voice showed concern, and his fingers covered the lower half of his face.

"Demon indeed." Edward stared into his cup. "Archbishop, is the Lord delivering His enemies into our hands, or is Satan tempting us like Christ in the desert?"

"I don't know how you see this as delivering our enemies," Cranmer said. "The King will not take well to this information."

"They had to have known, the Dowager Duchess and Norfolk. But they put her forward anyway."

"If he forgives her, he must forgive them." Cranmer looked down at his hands. "You see how enamored he is, how obsessed."

"He still has to put her away," Edward said. "If she is precontracted, she cannot give him heirs."

"He will hate us for telling him," Cranmer said.

"No." Edward steepled his fingers. "He will hate those whose ambition vanquished their sense of duty. Norfolk and Surrey – and all the Catholics if he's angry enough."

"We must be thorough," said Cranmer.

"We have two weeks before the court returns from the progress, two weeks to prepare. First you will question Mary Hall, then I will go to Lambeth and speak with the rest of the household. Then we will plan how to tell the King he was duped."

"That will be a delicate matter," said Cranmer. "After he falsely accused Anne of Cleves of that very crime."

"Cromwell's final revenge," said Edward.

Cranmer raised his glass. "To Cromwell."

"To revenge."

Chapter Nine

November 2, 1541—Hampton Court Palace

The bell rang to begin Mass in the Chapel Royal. Although he was not the celebrant, Stephen Gardiner was part of the ceremony for this holy All Souls' Day, and had donned the black vestments called for by the solemnity of the celebration.

Yesterday's Mass had been so much more public and joyful, as befitted the triumphant celebration of the Feast of All Saints. The King had observed the holy day with more solemnity than in recent years, joining the congregation on the main floor so he could approach the altar and give public thanksgiving for his blessed Queen. "I render thanks to Thee, O Lord, that after so many strange accidents that have befallen my marriages, Thou has been pleased to give me a wife so entirely conformed to my inclinations as her I now have."

Now, please God, she would give him a son and cement the great gains orthodoxy had made through her influence. It was time. There had been several times when it looked like she might be with child, but nothing yet. And so every month they prayed. And counted the days.

Movement in the King's box caught Gardiner's eye. It was not the King, but Cranmer, and he held a letter in his hands. Gardiner watched him place the paper on the King's chair then back out.

Gardiner closed his eyes for the penitential rite. When he opened them again, the King was in his booth with the letter in his hand, looking around but not finding anyone.

Gardiner watched Henry casually open the letter and start to read it as he took his seat.

"Dominus vobiscum. Et cum spiritu tuo," sang the priest.

Gardiner sang the response, then looked back up at the Royal Box. The King was gone.

* * *

Edward looked up when Cranmer entered his office. The prelate's ashen face made the Earl's stomach tighten.

"The King has summoned me," Cranmer said.

"You gave him the letter?"

The missive they had carefully crafted to begin the destruction of the conservative faction. A short message simply sharing that Queen Catherine had lived a dissolute life before her marriage, and that many knew of it.

"I put it on his chair."

That made Cranmer's pallor less disconcerting. "So you have not spoken with him?" Edward asked, just to be sure.

"No. I go now." Cranmer took a deep breath. "Come with me?"

Every fiber of Edward's being wanted to refuse, but he could not. All he could do was to make one small attempt to have this bitter cup pass from his lips. "This is a private moment. Are you sure?"

Cranmer nodded and walked out. Edward sighed and followed.

The King was waiting in his library. He stood in the middle of the room, its colorful floor at odds with the dark storm in his eyes. He faced the door with legs planted wide, a majestic posture intended to cow. His hands at his hips were balled into fists, the letter crushed in one of them. The library was the same room he used for Council meetings, and empty chairs circled him, suggesting the army ready to punish all those who angered him.

Henry stiffened when he saw Edward but recovered quickly. "You know about this nonsense?"

"I wish I did not," Edward said.

The King waved the paper. "So explain this to me," he said as he took his seat.

Cranmer bowed and began. "One of the women who served in the household of the Dowager Duchess of Norfolk came forward. She told us about light living that went on there, terrible stories that involved the Queen. There were two men—"

"Two?" The King froze and his focus on Cranmer intensified.

"The first was a music teacher when she was thirteen years old. She suffered him at sundry times to touch the secret parts of her body, which neither befitted her to permit nor him to require."

"I don't believe it," Henry said, adding a derogatory laugh to mock the outrageous claim.

Cranmer's voice dropped to a whisper. "Another man received her maidenhead when she was fifteen."

Henry's eyes widened. This was the man who had claimed to know the status of Anne of Cleves's virginity from the feel of her breast. "Ridiculous. That is vile slander."

Cranmer sighed. "I only wish it were. But the man crept into the ladies' dormitory and into the Queen's bed on more than a hundred nights, and they left no doubt of their activities."

The King was quiet for a moment. Then he took a drink and cleared his throat. "Rubbish."

"And during the day he would grab her buttocks when the Duchess was not present."

Henry cringed. "Such familiarity is inexcusable."

"And he referred to her as his wife."

Henry froze and his eyes narrowed. "Wife?"

Cranmer dropped to his knees. Edward quickly followed.

"Oh, Sire, I was forced to convey the news by letter as I had not the heart to tell you by mouth."

The telltale vein began to throb in the King's forehead and his face flushed, but he pressed his lips together and thought for a time. "I cannot believe there is any foundation in these malicious accusations. But they have been made, so you shall investigate the matter more thoroughly."

"Of course, Sire, and we will pray to find ourselves wrong."

Henry's eyes bored into Cranmer's, and he pointed a threatening finger at the cleric. "You are not to desist until you have gotten to the bottom of the plot. Because mark my words, a plot it is. Someone is trying to hurt me through lies about my wife. I will not stand for it."

"We will do all in our power," Cranmer said.

"And make sure your investigation raises no spark of scandal against the Queen." Henry waved at them to rise, then grunted. "Guard," he yelled.

The red-liveried sentry ran in from his post at the door and knelt immediately.

"Have the Queen confined to her apartments. There are ridiculous charges raised that must be investigated and dismissed," the King said. "But don't mention them to her."

"The women will gossip—" Cranmer began.

"Dismiss her women," the King said to the guard. "But let Lady Rochford remain with her. And a second woman of her choice. That will be enough to attend her."

"Shall I tell her you will come to her later?" the guard asked. Edward held his breath. The King could not resist his wife's excuses, accompanied by blandishments as they would be.

"No. I will not look on her face with such vile suspicions in my mind." The King waved a hand. "But don't tell her that. Don't tell her anything."

Edward and Cranmer exchanged relieved glances. The King was smart enough not to let Catherine close. He knew she might be guilty, however much he might pray she was not.

This was the King's way, to withdraw before he struck, to keep the victim far away.

"Leave me now," the King said.

Edward and Cranmer bowed out and walked back in

silence to Edward's apartments. With the door closed, Cranmer collapsed into a chair at Edward's conference table.

Edward poured the two of them tall goblets of wine; he noticed, surprised, that his hands were steady.

"What do we do now?" Cranmer asked.

"We bring more people into the investigation," Edward said. "More people to see for themselves the honesty of the witnesses, more people so he cannot turn back."

Now it was just a matter of making the case. Cromwell had taught them that. Assemble the details required by the law, however you get them. This time they had real ones.

"Audley will speak to Lascelles, Fitzwilliam will question Mary Hall again. And Wriothesley can go to Lambeth to arrest Manox and Dereham and speak to the rest of the servants."

"Are you sure Wriothesley will turn from Norfolk and Gardiner?" asked Cranmer.

The question made Edward nervous. On the one hand, it did not seem possible for anyone to lie about any of these matters. On the other hand, why take any risks? "Sadler should accompany him to keep him honest."

"I don't..." Cranmer's voice trailed off when the door swung open. It was Elizabeth Seymour Cromwell.

"They've confined the Queen," she said even before she was all the way inside. She gasped at seeing Cranmer, and her eyes widened. "Beg pardon, Your Grace," she said to the Archbishop.

Edward motioned her over. "Come sit," he said, and guided her to the table.

Elizabeth's eyes lidded as she took her seat with the two of them.

Cranmer immediately gave her sleeve a sympathetic pat. "What happened?"

Elizabeth glanced at Edward. He nodded. She straightened her back and took a deep breath. "We were practicing dance steps for a masque the Queen wants to hold. A guard knocked at the door and entered without waiting for a response. Not a page, but a guard. He had a spear and he waved it at us – his very look made me cross myself. He said, 'Ladies, it is no more time to dance.'"

She paused, her wide, unfocused eyes reliving the scene. They waited. When she resumed, the words rushed out of her mouth. "All he would say was, 'You are to be confined to your apartments with two women to attend you. Lady Rochford and one more.' That's when she fell to her knees."

"The Queen or Lady Rochford?" Edward was furious at his outburst: he should not have interrupted the narrative.

"Lady Rochford. Her face was stark, like she was about to faint. The Queen's was a deep red. She kept asking why she was to be confined, but all the guard would say is, 'I may not share that with you.'"

Edward and Cranmer exchanged a look, and Elizabeth caught them. "Tell me. Why is she confined?" Elizabeth looked Edward straight in the eye.

Edward kept his voice matter-of-fact. "While you were on progress, a woman who was in the Duchess's household with Catherine came to us. She told us the Queen had been intimate with not one but two men in her youth. The first was a music teacher, Henry Manox, the other the Duchess's secretary, Francis Dereham."

"Dereham?" Elizabeth looked shocked.

"You know the man?" asked Cranmer.

"The Queen took him as her private secretary this summer. He came to Pontefract to greet her and never left."

Edward saw Cranmer's jaw go slack. He realized his own mouth was open as well and snapped it shut. "She took him into her household?"

Elizabeth looked down at her clasped hands before answering. "Yes."

Dereham might have thought to continue the affair. The whiff of that possibility had just upped the ante considerably. "We must expand the investigation," Edward said to Cranmer. "The Queen may have been light after her marriage as well."

Edward's own pain rose like bile in his throat. *Adulterous woman, evil temptress.* His first wife had been such a sinner; there was no worse pain.

If it was true, if this woman had betrayed the King, there would be consequences to sin, he vowed grimly. If this meant the girl's death then so be it.

In the middle of Edward's misplaced rage it occurred to him that Norfolk and Surrey might know this too. It would mean their deaths as well. *This is the Lord's doing and it is marvelous in our eyes.*

November 7, 1541—Hampton Court Palace

Edward trailed behind Thomas Cranmer down the Hampton Court corridor, toward the Queen's apartments. They were on their way to question her.

The whole court had heard of the King's reaction to hearing his wife's past confirmed, how his sad lament had turned to rage and a promise that the wicked woman never had such pleasure from her wantonness as she would have pain in her punishment. But few understood how desperately the King needed her confession to remove the tiny grain of hope that she had not ceded her ultimate treasure.

They arrived at the door. Armed guards on either side blocked their passage.

"We are here on His Majesty's orders," said Cranmer.

"You are expected." The guard bowed before he pushed open the door for them, revealing the sad scene inside.

The Queen was curled up in her chair of estate, her head resting on the arms that cradled her drawn-up knees. She was weeping, shoulders shaking with plaintive sobs. Lady Rochford sat on a stool next to her, another lady on a cushion below. Both sewed as if nothing were wrong.

"The Archbishop of Canterbury and the Earl of Hertford," the guard announced.

They stepped into the room. Rochford lowered her

piece, and the sight of it startled Edward. It must have been started recently, since the fabric in the hoop was bare but for the crest in the center. It was a black bull, the Boleyn crest, horned. Cuckhold's horns?

Catherine rose quickly, head high and eyes narrowed. The ladies copied her. "Your Grace," she nodded to Cranmer. "My Lord," to Edward.

The two men bowed. "Your Majesty."

"What news from the King?" Catherine asked. Her seventeen-year-old face was drawn, and deep lines ran down her cheeks as if carved by a river of tears. Her eyes verged on wildness, as if she was about to throw herself into one of the frenzies her women described. Frenzies that were averted only upon an official visit. The girl could pull herself together in public; in private she fell apart.

Cranmer's demeanor softened in the presence of this piteous display, and tears assembled in his own eyes. "I have been instructed by the King to signal his most gracious mercy."

What? Edward worked hard to keep the shock off his face. This was not the plan. They had agreed the King's promise of mercy was to be extended only if she were honest – yet Cranmer had given it freely, without precondition? He was too soft for this work.

Still, Edward remained silent. He had to trust the prelate.

The Queen threw herself to her knees and held up her arms to them. "I give my most humble thanks unto His Majesty. He has shown me more grace and mercy than I thought meet to beg for, more than I could have hoped for."

She dropped her hands to the floor and leaned over her skirts, as if she were bowing to them. When she rose, she was more moderate. The weepiness had subsided, though a forlorn look remained.

Her two ladies exchanged looks. There was vague relief in them, and something else.

Then Catherine convulsed and wept loudly, worse than before. The women jumped up and led her back to her chair, where she bowed her head over the side.

"Your Majesty," said Cranmer, "what ails you?"

The sobs intensified.

"It seems some new fantasy has come into your head," Cranmer said. "Open yourself unto me. Tell me what it is."

Amazingly, the Queen obeyed. She quieted and lifted her head. "Alas, my Lord, that I am alive! The fear of death did not grieve me so much before as now does the thought of the King's goodness. When I remember how gracious and loving a prince I had, I cannot but sorrow. This sudden mercy, showed unto me so unworthy at this time, more than I could have looked for, makes my offenses appear much more heinous than they did before. And the more I consider the greatness of his mercy, the more I sorrow in my heart."

Cranmer put a sympathetic hand on her shoulder. "Dear lady let us pray," he said.

The two of them knelt together and prayed. Finally they moved on to gentle conversation, but they had very little of it before Catherine's eyes widened and she looked wildly around. "Is it six o'clock or thereabouts? Master Heneage was wont to bring me news of His Majesty around this time."

Edward was starting to get annoyed at the extended histrionics distracting them from the task at hand. She was ready to confess; why was Cranmer delaying?

Finally, the prelate moved on to their mission. "You do understand that His Majesty expects for you to admit your grievous sins, to earn the mercy he has shown you. We know you did not come virgin to his bed. You must tell us that now."

Her voice came low from her bowed head, and the men had to crane to hear her. "I am ashamed, truly ashamed. On too many occasions, I lay with Francis Dereham. Sometimes in his doublet and hose, and two or three times naked." She looked up at them, terrified. "But not so naked as he had nothing upon him. He always had his doublet on. And I do think his hose also."

Edward kept his face blank over the Queen's attempted

excuse. He considered pressing her to resolve the contradiction but decided against it - the state of their undress mattered little to their deeds.

"I was ignorant and frail and fell to the persuasions of young men. And then I was so desirous to be taken unto His Majesty's favor and so blinded with the desire of worldly glory, that I had not the grace to consider how great a fault it was to conceal my former sins."

"They were great sins," Cranmer agreed, "but you were a young girl who believed yourself married. Your conduct must be understood from that perspective."

Catherine narrowed her eyes again, and Edward thought he saw calculation glint from them. "There was communication in the house that we two should marry together," she said, "and I did call him husband and me wife. But I never promised him by my faith and troth to wed him."

Again splitting hairs - as she thought to do with Dereham's doublet and hose - but this went too far to accept. "But you promised to love him with all your heart," Edward blurted.

The girl was fully calm now, her gaze steely. "I do not remember that I ever spoke those words."

Edward froze. *What?*

"And my actions were not at my request or with my consent."

Edward's world spun. *Oh my God,* he repeated to himself, over and over. She was denying the facts that created the precontract.

"But you took him into your household," Edward said. "You...you..."

"He threatened to tell others of our past. I was misguided enough to believe my nightmare fully behind me."

"Do you know what you say?" Cranmer asked.

Of course she does, Edward thought. Despite her youth, despite her lack of counsel or advice, she was brilliant. Rape could be forgiven.

Catherine fell to her knees and again raised her arms. "I refer the judgment of all my offenses with my life and death wholly unto His Majesty's benign and merciful grace. I pray to be saved by his infinite goodness, pity, compassion and mercy, without which I acknowledge myself worthy of extreme punishment."

The Queen was channeling Jonah, that paragon of faithful repentance. Stuck in the whale's belly, he hadn't clamored for pardon but was grateful for punishment. Cranmer's misguided sympathy had opened the door for her to do that.

The girl might escape this trap after all. And Norfolk with her.

November 11, 1541—Hampton Court Palace

Gardiner's lip curled as Francis Dereham was led into the Council chamber. Despite the circumstances, neither the jaunty swagger nor shifty eyes had left the man. He was a fool, Gardiner thought, not to display more contrition. Though praise God he didn't, since his impertinent attitude would help convince the councilors the Queen was telling the truth about the rape – and help Gardiner prove the Queen had accepted Dereham into her household because he had blackmailed her, not because she thought to betray the King.

The Queen's confession was burned into Gardiner's mind: "He lay with me naked, and used me in such a sort as a man uses his wife, many and sundry times." As terrible as those words were, if those affections had indeed been forced upon her, there was no precontract, nothing to annul her marriage to the King. She could remain Queen. A Queen with a tarnished reputation, yes, but the King was past his initial fury. He loved her enough to accept this, Gardiner was sure of it.

This excuse had not figured in the record she had signed. But that had been drawn up by Cranmer, who wanted to see the marriage annulled. This was Gardiner's chance to save it, to keep the Queen on the throne. Gardiner needed her there, a factional figurehead. A sweet voice to whisper into the King's ear and sway his heart. Look at what she had accomplished already. Previously only Hertford could play the strong family card. Now Norfolk and Surrey had taken full advantage of their proximity to sway the King conservative. Cranmer's star was on the wane, and Gardiner was more powerful than he'd ever been. He had to save her.

He would do that by raising doubts in the councilors' minds. How hard would that be for a trained lawyer like himself?

Thomas Audley cleared his throat. As Lord Chancellor, he was responsible for the efficient functioning of the courts and he filled that function for the Council as well. "Master Dereham, we have questions for you that you will answer on your soul."

"Of course, my Lord," said Dereham.

Gardiner kept quiet while Audley went though some background information, including the dates on which Dereham had joined the Queen's household. Gardiner kept quiet when Cranmer took over the questioning and the probes became barbed. "You were sent away to Ireland by the Dowager Duchess. Why?"

"Someone sent her an anonymous letter. She wanted to separate us, for Catherine's reputation."

"For the Queen's reputation," said Audley. "Remember of whom you speak."

Dereham swallowed. "Of course."

"You left money with the Queen on your departure. A hundred pounds. Why?"

"It was my entire fortune, and I wanted her to hold it for me. To have if I died, to share if I lived." He leaned forward. "I thought of her as my wife, Your Grace."

Gardiner felt bile rise up in his throat at the word that would extinguish the King's marriage: wife. This he would address. "I find that difficult to believe," he broke in. "After all, what sort of husband forces himself on his helpmeet?"

Gardiner was mildly gratified at Dereham's widened eyes. He hoped the lout was remembering their last encounter, when he had shamed Gardiner by refusing him an audience with the Queen. Turnabout was fair play.

"I...I never forced her, Your Grace. I loved her as much as a man can love a woman."

Before Gardiner could press him, Hertford jumped in, his voice silky. "And so you returned to her this summer. To resume your relationship."

Gardiner stiffened. Dereham's response here was critical. Hertford was still trying to find adultery, another bulwark for his political attack on the Queen. What Dereham said and how he looked would determine whether the lords believed him or not.

"There was never a question of that, my Lord," Dereham said. The sneer disappeared, and only earnestness was left in the man's face.

Gardiner was relieved. Dereham was clearly telling the truth.

"You expect us to believe this?" asked Hertford.

Gardiner kept the smirk off his face at Hertford's failure.

"I returned from Ireland over a rumor the Queen was to marry Thomas Culpeper. I confronted her about it, and she told me her affection for me was done. I tried to change her resolve but...but the light was gone from her eyes."

"She was to marry Thomas Culpeper?" Cranmer broke in. "This is the first we are hearing of this."

Another potential precontract? Gardiner felt weariness spread over him, but then Surrey stepped in to rescue the situation. "This is the first I am hearing of this as well," said Surrey. "So it could not have been a family matter."

"There was once some talk between me and his father," Norfolk said. "But I thought my niece deserved better so it went nowhere."

"It was but a rumor," Dereham admitted. "But even that was enough to lose me her heart."

Sir John Gage, Constable of the Tower, left his seat at

the end of the table to whisper to one of the guards. The guard turned and left.

As Gage returned to his seat, Hertford and his reformist allies started in, posing interminable questions in a vain attempt to pursue any impediments.

Gage spoke up during a lull in the conversation. "I have given instructions to have Master Culpeper brought before us for questioning. Also to have his rooms searched."

Gardiner sniffed and tried to catch Norfolk's eye. Questioning the poor man and searching his rooms seemed a bit extreme. Such zealous vindictiveness would be remembered and punished.

"It is more important for us to question the Queen's ladies," said Audley to no one in particular. Grasping at straws now, since the women had already been interviewed.

Before Gardiner could respond, Thomas Culpeper was shown in. The handsome lad stood tall and dashing before them, though understandably wary.

"Greetings, my lords," he said.

"Master Culpeper," Hertford said, "we were told there was talk of a match between you and the Queen before she came to court. How do you answer this?"

Culpeper visibly relaxed. "I am of Howard blood, though a distant relation, and my father dared to hope. I would have been proud if such a match could have been made."

A guard entered and went right to Gage to hand him a piece of paper and whisper in his ear. Gage looked down at the sheet, then placed it on the table before Audley. "My lords," he said, "this was found in Culpeper's chest."

Culpeper lurched forward as if to grab it, but the guards at either side of him held him back. The Council members gathered around to examine it.

It was a letter, signed by a Catherine. It looked to be the Queen's own hand.

"Do you recognize your niece's writing, my Lord?" Audley asked Norfolk. "I believe I do."

Norfolk's voice was a rasp. "I believe I do as well."

The men began to read. The spelling was terrible: the woman was barely literate. Unfortunately, the most damning sentence was crystal clear: "It makes my heart die when I think I cannot always be in your company. Come to me when Lady Rochford be here, for then I shall be best at leisure to be at your commandment."

Worse still was the closing line. "Yours as long as life endures."

Pandemonium erupted. Norfolk drew his sword halfway out of its scabbard. "This deserves death."

Culpeper threw up his palms in a show of submission. "I never touched her."

Hertford snorted at those words. Not just Hertford, everyone on the Council. Gardiner himself came close to joining the rebuff despite wanting desperately to believe the lad.

"Truly, gentlemen, I know what you're thinking." Culpeper's face twisted into regret, and he brought his hands together to plead. "I wanted to, desperately. But I didn't—"

"Start at the beginning," Audley said. "Explain why the Queen would send you such a letter."

Culpeper straightened his back and took a deep breath. His lowered eyes bored into the floor in front of the Council's table. "I adored her. How could any man not? For a long time she would have nothing to do with me. But then she took pity on me and let me worship her, even calling me her 'sweet little fool.'"

"I never heard her refer to you as such." Hertford was not letting up. "On what occasions did she do so?"

"My Lady Rochford contrived for us to be alone at times."

"Times? What times?"

Culpeper looked pained. "At Pontefract, and several other stops along the progress."

"During the day?"

Culpeper's voice dropped to a whisper. "At night, my Lord."

Hertford leaned forward, his eyes glowing like the

Devil's. "What time of night?"

Culpeper looked up and took a breath to answer but dropped his head before doing so. He did that several times. Finally the words came. "I would come to tell her when the King had gone to bed, so she would know he would not visit her."

Late at night after the King had gone to bed. Could it get any worse? This would surely doom the Queen.

Sudden hope gripped Gardiner at a potential saving point. "So you were not actually alone; her other ladies could have come in at any time?"

"No, Your Grace. The door was closed."

Gardiner sat back in his chair, overcome.

The Devil leaned further forward. "For how long would you stay with her behind closed doors?"

Culpeper shrugged slightly as if trying to figure out the answer. "An hour? Sometimes more."

More than an hour.

"But I swear, my lords, we did not pass beyond words."

Hertford laughed. A short, ugly splutter. "You expect us to believe this?"

"I admit, I intended to do ill with her and I know the Queen was so minded to do with me. She even said she would have tried me if she had remained in the maidens' chamber at Lambeth. But I swear, my lords, I did not touch her."

The man's gaze was intent. As a priest, Gardiner had seen that look in many a penitent's eyes. Clarity, honesty. A glimmer of a chance returned to Gardiner. "Could your confessor confirm this?" They could figure out a way around the secrecy of the confessional later – right now the symbolic gesture was imperative.

Culpeper paused before answering. "I did not discuss this with my confessor. The Queen was afraid that if I was shriven of anything that had passed between us, the King, being Supreme Head of the Church, would come to hear of it."

Hertford jumped to his feet. "I think I speak for all the

Council when I say it matters not at all whether or not your lust was consummated. Your intentions towards the Queen were so loathsome and dishonest that they alone make you guilty of high treason." He turned to Gage. "Have him taken to the Tower."

The other councilors nodded and banged their fists on the table in agreement. Norfolk and Surrey were the loudest.

The truth of the situation hit Gardiner hard. He was the last person to have tried to defend the Queen. That made him vulnerable, like a freshly shorn lamb among wolves. "Hear, hear," Gardiner said and banged on the table with the others.

*　*　*

Edward admired the quick response of the guards who seized Thomas Culpeper, one on each side, and lifted him off the floor.

Culpeper's head twisted back and forth between his accosters. "Nay, unhand me."

They ignored him and dragged him backwards.

"My lords," he begged. "Nay, my lords. I did not touch her. We overcame temptation."

Edward snorted. His evil first wife had claimed that too, as had his father, before confessing the truth. Religious zeal welled up in him against all adulterers.

The guards hastened their pace. Culpeper raised his voice. "My lords," he shrieked. "My lords."

The page at the entrance closed the door to drown out the sound. It was done.

They had caught a sinner.

Edward was desperate to sit in the warmth of righteous indignation, but he forced himself to forego its lure. It wasn't over. "I cannot imagine the pain it will cause His Majesty to hear of this," he said. "Nor the best way to tell him."

The men looked around at each other, then every glance turned to Cranmer.

"Perhaps His Grace should be the one to inform the

King," said Gardiner. "He has been central to this matter all along. And he can offer spiritual solace."

Funny, thought Edward. Normally Gardiner would race to be the one offering spiritual solace. *Not this time, the coward.* And it made him no less cowardly that Cranmer actually was the proper choice. Gardiner was a weasel, little more.

"I think we all must go," said Audley. "This is a legal matter more than a spiritual one. We are the witnesses and we are his Council. We are also friends and we deserve the opportunity to try to shoulder some of his grief."

Perfect. Edward could not have done a better job himself. This forced Norfolk to go with them. The prey would be within the lion's reach.

"May it be God's will," said Cranmer.

"Amen," said Edward, and the other councilors nodded.

Audley rose. "Gentlemen, to the King," he said and walked out the door.

They all followed quickly, though their pace slowed in the hallway as each step reminded them how difficult this audience would be.

"The King's Council desires to see the King," Audley said to the guard at the entrance to the royal apartments. The fullest protocol, a signal this visit was of the gravest nature.

The King was in his chair in the corner of the library. His shoulders were slightly rounded, the closest he would come to cowering at the prospect of their report. He had a book in his hand; he closed it around his index finger as he greeted the intruders. "Yes?"

They bowed as a group. As they rose, Edward saw Henry looking at him questioningly and responded silently with all the sorrow his eyes could project.

Henry sighed as he turned down a corner of the page and rested his book on his lap. Then he set his arms on the rests as if bracing himself.

"We have arrested one of your gentlemen, Thomas Culpeper," said Audley.

The King's eyebrows drew sharply together. "What?"

Edward realized Audley was taking things too fast and decided to slow them down. Like a prize horse, the King had to be led gently into this grim gate. "Dereham mentioned during his questioning he thought the Queen might have been precontracted to Culpeper."

The King started sputtering. "Another precontract?"

"We quickly determined this was not the case," continued Edward smoothly. "But we brought Culpeper in as well."

"Good," Henry said, drawing out the word uncertainly.

"We also searched his rooms."

The King gave a slight shake to his head. "What did you find?"

Edward knelt. The rest of the Council scrambled to imitate him.

Kingston held up the letter. The King took it with a trembling hand and read it over. Edward could tell exactly what Henry was reading by the progression of tears that streamed from his eyes.

When he had finished, Henry looked around wildly, as if waiting for one of them to counter the terrible news with an explanation. When none did, he drew his sword. "I will kill her with my own hands," he declared, as Norfolk had before him.

He flailed his weapon forward and back before realizing how impotent a gesture that was, and dropped his arm. His lips curled, and Edward thrilled at the idea of the King's rage washing over Norfolk, drowning him as he deserved.

But before anyone could react, Norfolk prostrated himself fully, crocodile tears streaming from his eyes. "Oh, Your Majesty, how is my family so cursed as to have produced such horrible women?"

And instead of slapping him like a cur, the King raised the man and hugged him like a brother.

Edward's rage rose at the hollowing of his victory. Norfolk had used a simple annulment as a pretext to kill Cromwell. Edward had failed to use actual treason, true betrayal, to destroy Norfolk. The seventeen-year-old ninny would die and the old goat would live.

Edward shut his eyes tightly. This was temporary. He could yet prevail. *Please God.*

November 13, 1541—Hampton Court Palace

Edward looked in the mirror one last time. The King would be at Mass now; Edward should leave in the next few minutes to join him. That way, Edward would get there before the penitential rite, or at least the Kyrie.

Edward studied his reflection. He arched a single eyebrow. He hardened his eyes and marveled at their sternness, but then his thoughts sobered. Norfolk was still a free man. Edward still had work to do.

He walked down the corridor to the Chapel Royal. As he passed the Queen's closed door, his heart hardened against the young woman who would die for betraying the King. Again Edward felt himself flattened by the rage he himself had experienced in the dark days before Anne, when he had discovered his then-wife Katherine had lain with his father for more than two years. That the boys she had presented as his sons were actually his brothers.

He walked faster.

Admitted immediately to the King's box, Edward genuflected and took the place next to the King but one *banc* behind. The King turned slightly, lifting his head to grunt a sad hello. The gesture led the royal eyes to the empty box next to him, and the sight turned his gaze glassy, like a pond somehow freezing in an instant.

A mute reminder that Catherine Howard would never occupy the Queen's place again.

"A reading from the book of Malachi," intoned the priest.

"Thanks be to God," the congregation replied.

Edward was struck by the irony of that week's passage, and hardened himself not to react at the prescient admonition: "Then you will again distinguish between the just and the wicked, between the person who serves God, and the one who does not."

While the priest droned on, an unusual scuffling sound out in the hall caught Edward's attention. Clinking steel, whimpers and grunts. He looked back at the source of the noise, expecting the door to open. But nothing happened.

The King turned around too, and motioned to Edward to investigate. He jumped up; his fingers closed on the cold iron handle and pressed it to open the heavy door.

He was inches away from a struggling figure in chartreuse silk. Long auburn hair whipped around while two guards grabbed for her arms. White lace petticoats flapped as legs flailed, and a French hood bounced to the floor in the frenzy.

The world paused and the creature peered up at him, all wild eyes and gaping mouth. Edward's chest constricted from her inarticulate pain.

It was the Queen.

Edward froze from the shock, surprised by his natural pity, and uncertain what to do. The Queen froze as well, and in that instant the guards seized her and started to drag her away. She started shrieking. Piteous pleas to the one person who might save her. "Henry! Henry!"

Edward flinched and turned around to see the stricken King eyeing the door, his face deathly white and a trembling hand reaching toward the sound.

Edward quickly shut the Chapel Royal door. Henry dropped his gaze to his book of hours, an obvious attempt to hide his face. Perhaps not from Edward but certainly from the rest of the congregation, who were starting to whisper and squirm in their seats.

The muffled shrieks continued, receding gradually as the struggling woman was dragged, kicking and clawing, down the hall. Finally there was the clank of a door, then silence.

Edward forced himself to stumble back to his chair and bury his nose in his own book of hours. Out of the corner of his eyes, he saw courtiers turn in their pews, unsuccessfully pretending a sudden need to converse with a neighbor, unable to stop themselves from examining the Royal Box and assessing the King's reaction.

A tear made its silent way down the cheek of the outwardly unwavering monarch just as a guard appeared behind them. "Your Majesty."

Henry motioned him closer. The man knelt before the King, directly in front of Edward. "Apologies, Sire. The Queen escaped from her apartments and came to find you here. We will not allow this to happen again."

The King's terse question came from between tight lips. "Is she confined?"

"Yes, Sire."

The King waved the man away then fidgeted in his seat for a moment before turning to leave. "Come," he said to Edward.

Edward jumped to follow his sovereign, glad to be asked. As they walked down the empty corridor, Henry kept sweeping his gaze as if he expected to see Catherine still running through the halls. His pace quickened with every footfall.

As close as he was, Edward only barely managed to slip into the King's rooms before Henry closed the door behind the two of them and pressed his forehead into the smooth mullion between its intricately carved panels.

Edward put a hand on his shoulder. "I am so sorry."

Henry sighed loudly. "I must leave here. I cannot chance this happening again."

"Let us ride out to Greenwich," Edward answered. "The rest of the court can follow later."

Henry's eyes widened though they remained vacant. When he replied, his voice was unsteady. "The court can remain here. I want to go to Oatlands. Now."

Oatlands. That was a strange decision, given that this was where the King had married the woman. Edward wondered whether this might be some sort of magical wish on the King's part, a way of pretending this might change outcomes. Not that it really mattered.

"I will give the instructions to the Lord Chamberlain and your gentlemen," Edward said. "Then we can ride out immediately."

The King shook his head. "No, I want to go alone. Just Denny. Maybe your brother too. I want you to stay here for now and make sure all gets...done. Have her taken away someplace secure. Syon House. Then let me know when I can return."

"Of course."

November 16, 1541—Oatlands Palace

As Edward approached Oatlands after his intense eighteen-mile ride, the late afternoon sun gleamed warmly off the red bricks of the buildings. It was a soothing sight and yet he was nervous, wondering again how Henry was faring.

A page ran out in greeting. "The King is waiting for you, my Lord. E's in his bedchamber. And your brother'll be coming to greet you."

Edward smiled thanks between tight lips and handed off his reins. He hurried on.

As the boy had indicated, Tom caught up to Edward right as he made to cross the Great Hall. "Two days? That was fast."

Edward shrugged. "It didn't take much. The case is solid, and Syon House was quickly prepared. How is the King?"

"Miserable."

As always, his brother's nonchalance grated. "How, miserable? Praying to God miserable, crying miserable, dangerously silent miserable?" He repeated his original question, louder. "How is the King?"

Tom glared back. "Miserable," he said and strode off.

Edward had to hurry to catch up, and he was panting when they arrived at the King's rooms.

He caught his breath when he saw the curtains were open, an excellent sign. But that thought quickly faded. The rosy glow that filled the room also illuminated the ornate pearled bed that had been specially commissioned for the King's wedding night with Catherine Howard. The bed commanded attention, drawing the breath from Edward's chest. He forced himself to look around, to pick out Henry sitting alone in a dark corner by the fireplace.

The normally majestic King wore a rumpled silk night robe, its black jennet lining peeking over the lapels. A red nose and eyes loomed over an unkempt beard. His sore leg was propped on a stool, the hose unattached and barely covering the stinking bandages. The table next to him held wine goblets and a tray of half-eaten food. Edward was relieved so few people were here to witness this uncharacteristic degradation.

"What news?" Henry asked, his voice hoarse.

"Unfortunately, we have confirmed the worst. Your wife and Culpeper both admitted they intended to betray you, and her ladies testified as to the many late-night hours the two spent alone during the progress, in her bedchamber or in Lady Rochford's."

Henry raised his arms to the ornate plaster panels of the ceiling above. "Oh, Lord, why do you try your servant so?"

The King remained frozen in that posture. Edward squirmed, but he would not dream of interrupting.

Finally Henry nodded and lowered his arms into his lap. He turned toward the fire and motioned for Edward and Tom to sit with him. His throat caught around his words. "I almost discovered them once, did you know?"

"Sire?"

The King's lip curled. "I came to her rooms one night, after I'd sent word I would not. When I arrived, the door was bolted from the inside." His eyes hardened, never wavering from the flames. "It took that bitch Rochford an eternity to open it."

Edward's empathetic horror over the experience ceded in his chest to a grim satisfaction that the King accepted Catherine's certain guilt. The case against her was closed; only formalities remained. Though the formalities would entail their own difficulties. "You should know Lady Rochford has gone mad. Her mind snapped at the arrest. She is confused over where and who she is, and cries uncontrollably."

The King's eyes glowered and his lips curled. He turned slowly to Edward. "I want her dead."

"But, Sire," Tom said, "if she's insane she cannot be executed."

"Edward." Henry's voice was flat.

"That will be corrected, Your Majesty."

Henry shifted back to stare once again into the fire. "I will not be made a fool."

"It reflects nothing on you." Edward's tone was gentle, but firm.

"The whole world mocks a cuckold. I am unmanned."

"You are no less a man than you have ever been. Did you think less of me when my Katherine's sins were exposed?" Edward asked, knowing, in fact, the monarch had. Everyone had. It was the nature of the betrayal.

Henry lowered his face into his hands and wept. "It was the people around her. They corrupted her. I want them to pay for that."

Edward quickly pounced on that glimmer of wrath. "The Duke of Norfolk should be sent to search his stepmother's house at Lambeth. We know she was derelict in her duties, but she may also have concealed important information from all of us."

Henry's lips were a tight line. "I agree she did. I want her questioned."

Edward kept his eyes soft. With Margaret Pole, the King had made it clear he would not hesitate to impute a person's crimes to family members. The Duchess would be punished. Now there was just one more step...

"May I suggest, Sire, she be brought back to the Tower for that? I don't trust Norfolk to do a proper job."

"What do you mean?" Henry's eyes narrowed.

"I don't know how he could not have known," Edward said in the most reasonable tone he could conjure.

"And instead of warning you," said Tom, "he pushed her forward anyway, just to humiliate you."

Edward's heart sank. Tom's voice was too ebullient. The push was too strong, too fast. It would ruin everything.

Sure enough, the King recoiled. "I cannot believe Norfolk would be so cruel. Not without some proof."

"Of course," Edward added quickly, rolling his eyes at his reckless brother. "We seek only to punish the guilty. Give them the traitor's death they deserve, the first taste of their eternal fate."

The King nodded and a faraway look came into his eyes. "Culpeper is of gentle birth. He was my friend. Tempted by Delilah as I was..." The last words trailed off in a whisper. When he spoke again, his voice had recovered its strength. "I shall be merciful. He will die cleanly by the axe."

That was more mercy than Edward expected, and it made him worry Henry's moral pendulum was swinging back to clemency. Sure enough, Henry's next words proved Edward's suspicions right. "And Catherine... Catherine... perhaps I could find a way to forgive her too."

Edward's insides roiled. He could not let the King debase himself like that, or let Catherine regain her influence.

It struck Edward how much he had changed in such a short time. How only a few years ago he had struggled over the morality of political deaths, and now he was causing them. It was all because of Norfolk. Removing that evil would solve everything.

He girded himself. "The man may forgive. The King may not."

"I know." Henry squeezed his eyes together and tears flowed from them. "But the man wants to so much." The words came out in a choked sob.

"Of course you do." That was strategy, to agree with the King before twisting his reasoning. "But she is a symbol. *You* are a symbol. The choice is not yours."

The King's fat fingers covered his face and he sobbed loudly. "You are right."

That was better. Edward could soften his rhetoric without risking his progress. "We have all been fooled. The Devil works well; he always has. My own Katherine was such a liar."

"Ah yes," Henry nodded, and he reached out a sympathetic hand to Edward's arm.

Edward accepted the touch and continued, gentler. "I never forgave her. Even after I sent her away. Even after she died and I found a new wife, a good wife, nearer to my true heart."

Henry looked pained, but this was not the time to reassure. It was the time to press the lesson. "I admit it lingered, even after, oh, seven years. Just this year it surged again, and I disinherited the bitch's children from my honors and estates – even the ones inherited from her family. They are not my sons."

Henry's eyes widened and his hand jumped to cover his mouth. Edward dropped his gaze to cover his savage triumph. Out of the corner of his eye he could see Tom do the same, thank God. Edward wanted nothing to blunt the blow.

Henry sat up in his chair and straightened his robe. He ran a hand over his scalp. Finally he spoke, in measured words. "I will not have that...that thorn in my side. A lowborn boy to challenge my son. Praise God for sparing me that."

"Praise Him," Edward and Tom echoed.

Edward reached out and put a hand on the King's shoulder. "The worst is over. Now it is just a matter of uncovering the full extent of the treachery. And punishing it."

The King nodded and looked over at the tray of food. He picked up a chicken drumstick and started to gnaw on it. "You take care of this, Edward. Fix it for me."

The return of the King's appetite and the trust in his words reassured Edward. "I will do everything in my power, Sire."

February 13, 1542—Tower Green

The morning light was thin and cold. Edward crunched through the frost as he and the rest of the Council were conducted to Tower Green. Well, most of the Council: Norfolk had been spared this final duty. Such mercy did not extend to Surrey, who followed with the other lords and gentlemen of the court.

The group turned the corner and the scaffold came into view. Black cloth had been hung around it, and fresh straw strewn to catch the blood to be shed.

The spectators parted for the councilors, stepping back to give them the best vantage point. The men were all quiet. Respectful of the punishment that would soon be meted out, the penance that would soon be exacted.

Such a difference from the irreverent crowd that had witnessed the last moments of Francis Dereham and Thomas Culpeper. Those were public executions, at Tyburn, occasions for public merrymaking. There the shrieks of the tortured blended with the shouts of the street traders offering pies and gingerbread nuts for sale.

As he took his place in the front row, Edward's eyes fell on the weathered block, and he wondered when it had been replaced. Sir John Gage had told them how Catherine Howard - now stripped of her royal title - had asked that it be brought to her room so she might practice placing her head upon it. She said she wanted to make a good impression on the scaffold, a good Christian end that would signal her honest repentance. Edward could not help but admire such dark forethought.

A jostle at his arm made him turn around. Tom was there, a crooked smile on his face. "Try not to gloat at your big triumph."

Edward pressed his lips tightly. Anger, shame, and resentment twisted within him again. Norfolk had escaped his proper punishment. His elderly stepmother was lodged in the Tower, but the Duke remained a free man.

"Keep thy good humor, brother," Tom said. "This is not

the time nor place to show pique."

He was right. Cruel, but right. Edward relaxed the muscles in his face, which had bunched up into a sneer.

A murmur went through the crowd and Edward turned to see Catherine emerge from her lodgings, squinting at the dull sun. She wore a severe black damask dress with an equally stark charcoal gray kirtle. No jewels, no lace, no decorations to soften her appearance. Nothing but a child's face, which only increased the pathos.

Pity rose in him as the seventeen-year-old girl trembled, unsteady on her feet. Her mouth was slightly open and moving with what Edward could only guess was either a request she was too weak to voice or prayers that consumed her.

This was what Edward's attempts at scheming had brought about. Not revenge on an evil foe, but death for a child. Guilt and impotence mixed in his chest. To conquer them he reminded himself this was not his doing, only the wage of her sin. He reassured himself he had no choice, and likened her to his own evil Katherine. It helped, but not enough.

Catherine walked toward the scaffold, leaning heavily on the ladies at either side of her. Five paces behind, a visibly stronger Lady Rochford emerged, also dressed in plain black. Her eyes were wild but she had recovered her reason.

"Well done, brother," whispered Tom. "I should never have doubted you."

The King had insisted Rochford not escape her fate, so Edward had engineered a special Act of Parliament to allow for execution of the insane. Rochford's quick recovery after she was informed made people wonder whether the madness had been real or a ploy. Now it no longer mattered.

"Shut up," Edward answered.

Catherine mounted the steps to the scaffold, her ladies still supporting her. She swayed at the top but recovered herself. With hesitant steps she approached the center and turned to face the crowd. "Good Christian people, I have come hither to die."

Her voice grew stronger, her back straighter, as she continued. "Take regard unto my worthy and just punishment of death, for my offenses against God from my youth upwards, and because I have sinned against the King's Majesty very dangerously." It was clear she had practiced: her speech was well done.

She conceded she merited a thousand deaths and urged her onlookers to use her example to amend their ungodly lives. She prayed for the King's preservation and for people to obey him in all things. She made a good end. "I earnestly call to God for mercy as I commend my soul to Him..."

Her voice trailed off. She looked at the block, and her hand went up to check her hair, which had been piled high on her head to expose her slender neck.

She leaned over the block in front of her and set her palms upon it. From there, she lowered herself to kneel before it. For a moment she looked around wildly, as if hoping for a last reprieve, but she quickly regained her control. She closed her eyes and raised her hands, her lips moving with whispered prayer. After a moment she lunged forward, placing her head on the block and spreading wide her arms.

It took the executioner only a single swing to sever the auburn head.

Her two ladies rushed forward to shroud it in a black blanket and wrap it with her blood-soaked body so the yeomen could move the remains to the waiting coffin.

Tom leaned over and whispered into Edward's ear, "Let's hope the next wife fares better than this one."

Edward quickly elbowed him to stop – this was not the time nor place for flippancy. He prayed no one had heard Tom's idiotic comment – and prayed even harder no one would think Edward was the one who had said it. He knew how furious the King was with the members of his Council who were already urging him to consider a new marriage.

A whimper from Lady Rochford brought Edward's attention back to the issue at hand. The poor woman remained just before the scaffold, staring at the block with her eyes wide and her fingers convulsing over her rosary.

The guard took her arm. She jumped at the touch and her mouth opened, but she didn't scream as the man guided her up the stairs. Once on the platform she lurched to the spot where Catherine Howard had so recently stood, then put her hands on the railing before her to steady herself.

"Good Christian people, I am come hither to die."

Edward found himself holding his breath to hear whether she would speak of the evidence she had given all those years ago that helped send her husband and Anne Boleyn to their deaths. Part of him wished she would avail herself of the opportunity to take quiet revenge on the King in the perfect guise of religious obligation. It would be another Howard relation shaming Henry, one that might finally change his mind and reverse the whole sordid failure.

Instead, Lady Rochford knelt before the block. She shied like a frightened horse at the sight of the blood: when she laid her head down, her cheek would touch it. Edward recoiled from the thought, his mind feeling the wet wood on his own cheek. He prayed he would never be in such a position.

But still harboring hope Norfolk would.

Meanwhile the executioner waited, unmoving and pitiless in the face of Rochford's whimpers.

Eyes tightly pressed, her head bowed, her arms swept out. The axe rose then struck.

Edward sighed and joined the single file of men walking away in silence.

PART THREE: KATHERINE PARR

Never a Wife More Agreeable to His Heart...

Chapter Ten

February 20, 1543—Whitehall Palace

Edward struggled to contain his mounting excitement and slowed the steps that kept quickening on their own. As they approached the end of the hallway, Edward felt Anne rest her hand on his sleeve. "Wait a moment," she said.

Edward whipped around. "Is anything amiss?"

Anne shook her head. "It is just strange to think...another time returning...to this."

It was a little more than a year since Catherine Howard had met her end on Tower Green. Everything had changed, yet nothing had changed.

"Shall we?" he asked.

Anne nodded, and they rounded the corner to the Queen's apartments at Whitehall. Not that there was a Queen right now, but the Lady Mary had been playing that part for the court on those occasions that benefitted from a female presence. And was doing a much better job than that flighty Howard parrot had. For one, the King's eldest daughter was twenty-seven, not seventeen: she had the *gravitas* to fill the office properly.

"Are you ready?" Edward asked Anne, glad again she was here. Her six pregnancies had kept her from court for a long time, but now the children were old enough for her to return. Things moved so quickly in Henry's court, it would be good for Edward to have his wife's sage advice close by. Especially if they went to war with France, as looked imminent. Edward stifled the sneer that threatened to creep across his face. Norfolk and Surrey were strongly pro-

French, but Howard advice was seldom heeded nowadays. There was little to restrain the King's warrior aspirations.

Except that Cromwell had always hated war.

Edward could not fully tame the feeling of doom that arose whenever he went against a core Cromwell strategy. But Anne agreed times had changed. Another reason Edward needed her here. Hopefully Mary would insist Anne remain with her at court.

Anne smoothed the skirt of the new overgown she wore for the occasion. A rich blue, heavily embroidered to obviate the need for expensive jewels. "Aye," she said with a brief clasp of her hands that resembled prayer. Edward's heart filled to bursting.

He nodded to the page to announce them, and was pleased by the warm words he overheard: "My aunt and uncle are always welcome."

They entered the room and quickly took in the scene. Mary sat on a chair of estate in the center of the Presence Chamber, surrounded by her ladies. They were sewing but had lowered their cloths in smiling anticipation of the guests.

With a loving smile, Mary rose to greet Edward and Anne. "Welcome, Lady Hertford, it pleases me to see you," Mary said, kissing her friend. "And you as well, my Lord," she said to Edward.

"The pleasure is entirely mine, my Lady," said Anne. "Especially since I find you looking so well."

"It is all the hunting I have been doing." Mary looked around to acknowledge the appreciative laughs of her ladies. "Four hours each day in the saddle – my father says the exertion has brought me good."

"It is a blessing to so enjoy your duty," said Anne.

It was Mary's turn to laugh at the words. "Lady Latimer said the exact same thing to me." She turned around and pointed her out. "You do know my Lady Latimer, do you not?" Mary asked. "She has just joined my household."

Mary's stress on the word *household* disconcerted Edward. He worried Mary was hinting that there was no more room for Anne, but his descent was halted by his sudden decision that it didn't matter: Anne could return to court anyway, just form her own household. That would solve things if she were willing.

"Quite well," said Anne. She looked over at Lady Latimer. "Greetings, my Lady. It is wonderful to see you."

"For me it is always a pleasure," said Edward with a small bow to highlight his rank and his gallantry.

Katherine Parr – or Kate as she was known to her friends – was an attractive thirty-one-year-old woman with red-gold hair and hazel eyes. More importantly, she was warm and intelligent and zealous toward the Gospel – the hallmark of a secret reformer. And she would soon be quite rich once Baron Latimer died, as he had been threatening to do for some time. Kate had recently returned to court, nursing her dying husband by night and serving Mary by day.

With Latimer in what was expected to be his final coma, Tom had started to court Katherine. Discreetly, of course. The one unequivocally smart thing Edward had ever seen Tom do. Edward could scarcely believe how receptive the woman had been to the suit, but she was the perfect mate for Tom – the entire Seymour family agreed on this point. Tom was thirty-five years old now, and it was long past time for him to settle down. But the wait would have been well worth it if he ended up with this woman.

The conversation was interrupted by the arrival of the King. More blessings.

He hobbled in on his own with a cane, not in the travel chair he typically chose now. In the last year, Henry had aged considerably; he seemed much older than his fifty-two years. He had also grown more irascible and short-tempered – and fatter than ever before. Three of the biggest men that could be found could fit inside his doublet.

"Daughter," he said with a heavy breath as his men fanned out around him.

Mary made her *obéissance*, as did her ladies. Edward and Anne followed suit.

"Ah, Lady Hertford," said the King. "It is a pleasure to see you at court."

"The pleasure is mine, Sire. I am honored to see both your daughter and yourself during my visit."

The King nodded. "I hope we shall have your presence for some time. Indeed, I insist you remain."

Edward's heart soared. The King, not Mary, had insisted. So much the better.

Henry turned to his daughter. "I must thank you, daughter, for bringing good female company to court. You have turned my court into a gay place."

"I pray I shall continue to so please you," said Mary. "And with the King's preference matching my own, Lady Hertford, I would be honored to have you attend me. You would be a most welcome addition to my household."

"Though it would be hard to be more welcome than my Lady Latimer," the King said in between pants. "Wearing her new sleeves I see."

"Yes, thank you, Sire," Katherine Parr said with a curtsy. "I continue to be most grateful for your gift." She turned and held up her arms to display her pleats and sleeves to Mary. "Your father made me a wonderful present so that I might be attired properly for your service. Apparently styles have changed since I was last at court."

Henry looked around, and his men raced to bring a chair for him. Tom won, and presented it with a flourish. Henry grunted as he lowered himself into it.

"Your Majesty made a fine choice," said Tom. "Beautiful sleeves suit a beautiful woman."

Lady Latimer blushed.

"In such a contest, the sleeves fall far behind," the King said.

Lady Latimer gave a small curtsy but her smile was pained. "I follow Saint Paul, and do not seek glory from men."

The King opened his mouth, but Tom, failing to notice, spoke first. "Ah, but Proverbs tell us that an excellent woman is far more precious than jewels."

The King waved his hand dismissively to claim his theological dominance. "Saint Paul warned only against flattery - which is naturally duplicitous because it seeks to obtain an advantage. I offered praise, and was right to do so." He seemed peeved, though Edward was not sure why.

Katherine Parr curtsied again. "Your Majesty, my modesty at receiving a compliment thanks you for assuring me of your honesty in giving it." Her eyes twinkled. "Though I persist in thinking it undeserved. Not even my husband calls me beautiful."

The King smiled and held out his hand expectantly. "My Lady." It was a command.

She extended her own and the King brought it to his lips to kiss. "Your husband is a fool," he said and turned back to his daughter. "I am glad to have you at court, Mary. You and your ladies will stay, I hope, at least until the summer. I find your presence helpful."

Mary lifted her chin. She lived for praise from her father. The poor thing had suffered so much being kept from him by Catherine Howard's jealousy. "I am honored."

"I will rest for now," the King said, "but we shall dine together tonight. A banquet with all the court. Including your newly returned aunt."

Edward put a hand over his heart to signal how deeply touched he was over the King's thoughtfulness.

"It is I who am honored," said Anne. "Thank you, Your Majesty."

"We have missed your wit," the King said. "We are glad you will be staying." He turned to Tom. "Go tell the Lord Chamberlain to arrange everything."

Henry started to push himself to standing. His men crowded around him but he waved them away angrily. "I do not need your cosseting," he roared.

The room bowed and he smiled quickly, as if catching himself. He nodded to Mary and her ladies.

With that, he walked stiffly over to leave through the connecting corridor to his own suite. Edward had almost forgotten it existed: after Henry's first bout of melancholy, even Queen Catherine had been required to go through guards to visit him.

"With your leave, dear Lady, we will retire as well," said Edward.

"Thank you," said Mary. "We should all rest for tonight's merriment."

Her words caused a quick dispersal of the room. Edward held out his hand for his wife, to lead her back to their apartments.

He did a quick mental check. Both the King and Mary had shown enormous public deference and affection. Anne had a place at court, in whatever form she wanted. Tom was soon to wed a rich and well-placed woman.

Edward reveled in the triumph.

April 15, 1543—Saint James Palace

Saint James Palace was a royal residence built with the same red bricks as Hampton Court, bricks that lent a soft hue to the air of an afternoon. But while Stephen Gardiner loved Hampton Court, he hated Saint James. The number of apartments was limited in this smaller royal residence where the King went to escape the formality of court life; Gardiner's lack of even a bedchamber constantly mocked his relative unimportance and made it all the more infuriating that Hertford had a three-room suite even though Hertford House was closer than Gardiner's Winchester Palace.

For now, Gardiner sat in the formal study in Norfolk's apartments, in a private meeting that was not going the way Gardiner had hoped.

Hertford had made another evil move, the latest in a year's worth of opportunistic overreaching. He had Norfolk's son, the Earl of Surrey, convicted and caged in Fleet Prison for riotous proceedings and eating flesh during Lent. "*Imprisoned*, for sweet Jesu's sake," said Gardiner, pressing his lips together tightly. "Among debtors and other miscreants."

Norfolk looked down at his hands and shrugged. Stephen Gardiner's anger swelled at such indifference. Norfolk was a warrior, he should know such deliberate provocation had to be met by revenge. Any opponent would expect retaliation; you put yourself in danger if you didn't. But for some reason the Duke was ready to turn the other cheek, as if he, not Gardiner, were the clergyman.

"It is unfit to proceed thusly against a Howard," Gardiner said.

Norfolk raised his eyes. His unfocused look held resignation and irony. "The Earl of Hertford argues the rules must apply to all men, not just commoners."

"The Earl of Hertford cares too much for commoners. Always has. But this is unthinkable impropriety."

Norfolk shrugged again, and Gardiner bunched up his hands. That was an appropriate signal of his disagreement: no greater display of rage was wise despite the Duke's cowed state. The action also helped Gardiner stem the contempt that threatened to escape and flood his voice. "How can you remain so calm in the face of such treachery?"

"What choice do I have?" came the laconic answer.

"He must be stopped," Gardiner said. How could the Duke not understand this?

Norfolk rolled his eyes. "I am not the man to lead the charge. My voice is seldom heeded these days."

"How can you say that, as the conqueror of Scotland?"

Norfolk had led the campaign at the Battle of Solway Moss, where the Scots had been completely trounced and James V killed. The King needed such talent. And that decisive victory had returned Norfolk to favor.

"That was six months ago, long enough for my contribution to be forgotten. All that is remembered is the glory – enough to make the King long to war with France, against all my advice. I tell you, my counsel is ignored."

Gardiner waved his hand. "We will lead the charge for you."

Norfolk narrowed his eyes, though that could have been a reaction to Gardiner's use of the royal *We*. "And how do you propose to do so? Hertford is untouchable."

"I am going after Cranmer. That is the first step." Gardiner was glad to hear his voice sounding assured.

"You have a plan?"

Gardiner was stung by the sarcasm that dripped from Norfolk's voice – enough that he considered leaving immediately for effect before thinking better of such a rash action. "As a matter of fact, I do."

Norfolk plastered a smile on his face but it didn't reach his eyes. It was little more encouraging than his open contempt, but Gardiner persisted anyway.

"Several conservative clergymen from Kent approached me several weeks ago with a list of misdeeds by two reformers – a Richard Turner and John Bland, if it matters. They asked for my help in having them denounced to the Council. They could be burned for those charges."

"And how does this affect Cranmer?" the Duke drawled.

Gardiner swallowed his anger. "I had my nephew add denunciations of Cranmer's own sins." He paused to let the information sink in. "The list goes back to 1541, when he was more vociferous in his heresies."

Norfolk's eyes shone for a moment, then he shook his head. "You'll never make the charges stick; the King loves him too dearly." His voice was a cackle. "More than he loves you."

The rage Gardiner had hoped to quell escaped. "Are you a part of this or not?"

Norfolk snorted. "My son is barely home from a sojourn in the Fleet for a trifling charge. I have no path to the King's ear, no way to defend myself. I am in no position to take such a risk."

"I find it hard to watch a soldier like you retreat with his tail between his legs."

Norfolk drew himself to his full height, pride giving him the extra inches his body lacked. "A solider knows enough to retreat from certain failure. You would be smart to learn such tactics."

Gardiner shook his head. How could Norfolk not

consider that Gardiner's star was on the rise? How did he not appreciate Gardiner's loyalty - and give him the gratitude he deserved? "I don't need them. I am not tarred with your brush."

The words had their desired effect, and Norfolk deflated like overrisen dough in a barely warm oven. "Of course. I am honored you still count me as a friend. It just hurts to be so weak."

The man's pain soothed Gardiner, enveloping him with grace and renewed determination. "We will prevail," he said and made the sign of the cross. "God is on our side."

May 2, 1543—Whitehall Palace

Once again, the court congregated in Mary's apartments thanks to another royal visit. So as to keep her close-set eyes fixed on the King, his daughter set down her needlework the moment he arrived. She relished the attention and did everything she could to encourage it. Periodically she tugged at one of her dark purple oversleeves, making sure it fell properly over her burgundy skirt.

With great difficulty, Edward kept the smile on his face as Henry crowed to Mary about the latest "improvement" he had made in the country's religious life. The Act of Advancement of the True Religion, inspired by that weasel Gardiner, gutted many of the hard-won reformist innovations. For one, it restricted the reading of the Bible - besides clerics, only noblemen, the gentry and richer merchants were now entitled to such divine comfort; lesser people were unfairly excluded from grace. Another papist victory. At least Gardiner had failed in his attempt to remove the Great Bibles from the churches; their chains had protected against this evil aggression. It hurt Edward to remember when the first volume had been completed, the way Cromwell's hands had trembled the first time he held the giant tome in his hands.

But of course Mary, the darling of the Catholics, cooed

her approval of the restrictions.

Anne, sitting behind her, caught Edward's eye. Her steady stare expressed her own dismay.

At least this gathering gave Tom a chance to press his suit to the recently widowed Katherine Parr. Discreetly, not directly, letting the affection grow naturally. Slow seduction was Tom's specialty, the technique he had used to bed half the women of the court without a whiff of scandal attached to his name.

A lull in the conversation spurred Edward to rack his brain for a topic to introduce. Happily, his efforts were not needed as the King's smile brightened and he pursued his own interest. "I have seen your translation of the Latin Psalms," he said directly to Katherine. "It was excellent."

The woman looked startled. She must have been trading glances with Tom and lost track of the conversation. Now deep red spread quickly over her face. "How did you see this, Sire?"

"Cranmer showed it to me," Henry said smugly. "He was quite impressed, and asked for my opinion."

Edward's head spun. Had the King reversed his thinking again? Here he was praising a translation that brought the Bible closer to the people right after restricting the realm of its readers. These flips were exhausting and completely unpredictable. There was no way to determine safe theological ground.

"I asked for his guidance." Katherine Parr's nod turned to a shake. "I did not think it was worthy to be seen by anyone."

The King laughed. "On the contrary, my Lady. I propose to have my own printer, Thomas Bertelet, publish it so all men may be inspired to love the Lord by the beauty of the words. I have summoned him for this very purpose." The King looked around, basking in the polite applause generated by his announcement.

Katherine looked abashed. "I could not, out of modesty."

The King waved his hand dismissively. "Your name

need not be attached to the volume."

"You must do it," Mary broke in. "And you must let me read it too."

"And I," said Anne.

With further resistance clearly futile, Katherine clasped her hands together and stood in order to curtsy deeply. "I would be honored despite my misgivings."

"I think I speak for all the King's men when I say every man at court should read this," added Tom. "We could all use gentle instruction from a lady as wise as she is beautiful."

Katherine's face lit up. "You are quite the peacemaker."

"Indeed he is," the King boomed. "Enough to make me see his talents are wasted here." His voice turned sly. "It occurs to me, Thomas, you are very respected by the Spanish Ambassador."

The King's eyes narrowed, and that made Edward's want to do the same. Tom and Chapuys were friends, yes – Jane's sponsorship had benefitted all the Seymour family – but what did the King mean by this?

"I should make better use of you," the King said. "You shall have a promotion."

"Sire?" Tom's smile was cautious.

"I shall send you to Brussels, to represent us to Charles's aunt in the Netherlands. Especially as relations with France are deteriorating, your presence there will become ever more important to demonstrate my friendship with the Low Countries."

Katherine's face fell. Tom hid his own disappointment better, though his response was accompanied by seriousness rather than smiles. "I am deeply grateful, Sire, but I thought you had chosen Nicholas Wotton for that post."

Nicholas Wotton. Far more senior, far more reliable. Did the King really trust Tom that much? He had never seemed to.

"You will accompany him," Henry said. "It will be good work for the two of you." He turned to Katherine. "And now, My Lady, I shall ask you to accompany me to my apartments, where we will await Master Bertelet. And perhaps discuss your work and its process."

The King stood, not fully successful at muffling a grunt, and held out a hand to her. Katherine reddened a second time, curtsied to Mary, and placed her hand over the King's. His men stood to follow them, but the King waved them off. "I intend to discuss the word of God with Lady Latimer," he said. "The topic is too holy for rascals like you. Attend me later."

The King looked at Katherine. The intensity in his eyes was unmistakable.

The King desired the Lady Latimer.

Edward silently berated himself for not seeing this sooner. He looked at Anne, and her widened eyes told him she had drawn the same conclusion. He glanced at Tom, who was staring, mouth agape, after the King and the woman they both loved.

"I would be alone as well," said Mary. The poor girl looked sad. Was it just that the King had left, or was she, too, jolted by sudden understanding that she would soon be ceding her place to another?

The three Seymours assembled in the hallway. "I fear you shall be a bachelor for the rest of your life," Anne said to Tom. Her quiet voice was arch.

"It is a good thing I am a patient man," said Tom as he walked off in a huff.

July 2, 1543—Greenwich Palace

"Yes?" Edward looked up at the messenger whose livery entitled him to enter any room without knocking. Well, other than the King's.

"Greetings, my Lord." The man bowed. "His Majesty asks you attend him in his apartments. Immediately."

Oh Lord. Edward rose and ran out without another word. The monarch would be counting the minutes; it would not do to tarry.

Fastening his doublet as he hurried down the corridor,

Edward considered the different possibilities. He first prayed this was not bad news from France, on whom England had formally declared war just a fortnight before. Had there been an attack? Or what if Scotland was reconsidering the Treaty of Greenwich they had just signed, the one that gave their infant queen, Mary, as a bride to the young Prince Edward? Or perhaps someone was ill. Pray God that was not the case. Except Norfolk or Gardiner of course; that would be a blessing.

The demons in Edward's mind scattered like bats at dawn when he arrived in the King's Privy Chamber and the guard at the door smiled and good-naturedly waved him in to the office.

The King was standing at the window, looking out.

"Sire?" The word was a question as well as a greeting.

Henry turned around, his face devoid of expression. "I asked the Lady Latimer to marry me."

Edward exhaled a quick *Deo Gratias*. The news was excellent and long overdue. Indeed, Edward and Anne had been cultivating a deeper relationship with Katherine Parr ever since they had seen the gleam in the King's eye. Friendships nurtured before royal favor struck were always deeper.

But the look on the King's face – or rather, the lack of a look on the King's face – gave Edward pause. The King had noticed the great pains those around him took to never react incorrectly, never hold an offensive opinion. Now he withheld the signs that would indicate the proper reaction, though an astute courtier might still wrest some clues. In this situation, where the news should have been delivered with unmitigated joy, the King's expression made Edward worry a happy response was somehow dangerous. So what to say?

Start with yourself, one of his ghosts whispered to him. Jane or Cromwell, Edward couldn't tell. Usually Edward would listen more carefully to Jane's voice since the King had never turned on her – not irrevocably, anyway. That was the image he wanted to be associated with, although in this case it didn't matter. Both had taught that the King loved to hear what people thought of him, as long as it involved admiration. "I had noticed your great respect for the woman. Well, we all had – have – great respect for her." Edward paused and smiled, recognizing his words were not coming out properly but knowing this would not be a problem. Confusion added to authenticity. "What I am trying to say, brother, is that I am glad for you."

The King gave no reaction. Still that dangerous lack of expression. Beady eyes boring. A fist raised to his hips, inches from his sword. "She refused me."

"Refused you?" Edward controlled the knees that threatened to buckle under him. Was this related to Tom? If that idiot had pressed his suit somehow, his foolhardy action could get him killed. And Edward with him. *What else could have prompted a refusal?* The answer came to Edward like a warm breeze, and he arranged his face into compassionate sympathy. "Was she unready to move on, so soon after her husband's death?"

The fist came off the hip, and Henry broke out into a broad beam. It had been a test, Edward thought, with the King daring him to give the correct answer. This was a new twist for Edward to keep in mind. Another layer of suspicions to consider in all his dealings with the King.

"That is what I thought," Henry said. "She said she would rather be my mistress than my wife."

Edward's confusion reduced him to echo the King's words. "Your mistress?"

"I think she may also be worried I will react to her as I did to Anne of Cleves. Charming modesty in such a silly lamb."

Charming modesty? Brilliant strategy. Edward couldn't blame Katherine Parr for trying to refuse. And he truly admired how the woman had enchanted the King instead of incurring his wrath. Like when Jane had refused the purse of gold the King had offered, and he had swooned at her modesty. But that thought was for later. For now, Edward nodded. "All women should show such humility."

"She reminds me of Jane in many ways," Henry said. "I

think I will be happy with her."

"So she did finally accept your suit?"

"Not yet." Henry shrugged. "She wants to pray on it."

Pray on it? Not quite the response of a woman overcome by passion, but happily the King appeared little bothered. "Well, it seems only fair," Edward said with studied nonchalance. "Since I am sure Your Majesty was guided by God before taking this step."

"Precisely what I said to her." The King's smile was smug.

Edward made a mental note to have Cranmer visit the woman. The prelate offered the ultimate counsel and comfort; even Catherine Howard had bowed to his power. If anyone could guide Katherine Parr's prayer and its response, it was Thomas Cranmer – and there was clearly only one response that was possible here. The woman who offered her body rather than her soul would know that. God willing.

Chapter Eleven

July 12, 1543—Hampton Court Palace

Stephen Gardiner raised the host high. He twisted it slightly to catch the light, his own way of reminding reformists of the Real Presence they tried to deny. There were many secret heretics in this group of twenty, dressed in their finest clothes and crowded into the Queen's Closet, the wood-paneled oratory right off the Queen's apartments at Hampton Court. The magnificent room was just large enough to hold them all standing shoulder to shoulder. The close quarters gave an intimate feel to the room that was at odds with its gleam of gold and jewels, though they made the room warmer than Stephen Gardiner liked. Not that he really cared right now. He was too full of pride at having been chosen to perform the private ceremony.

Him. Not Cranmer.

Cranmer's role had been limited to issuing the license. The kind of clerical function Gardiner had always pretended to love since it was the only one offered him. But not today.

Today he was gratifying the King's closest desire, holy matrimony with the Widow Latimer. Gardiner's face would be the one she associated with this moment. Forever. And she would love him for that.

Like everyone, Gardiner had been happily shocked at the announcement of the marriage, though of course he joined the many others at court who claimed to have spotted the signs. After all, power did not stem only from being close to the King – some of it accrued from people *thinking* you were close to the King. And such prescience, or claims at least, were important indicators of that closeness.

Gardiner gave the host to the King, then to Katherine Parr. After her prayer, she raised her eyes to look at the man about to make her his wife, the man resplendent from head to toe in cloth of shining silver, the man who commanded body and soul of every good Englishman. The King looked back, and Gardiner swore he saw fear cross the royal brow until the moment the woman's rigid stare softened into a happy smile. At the shy return of her gaze to her feet, the King cast his eyes toward the ceiling in praise.

Again, Gardiner wondered about the woman's religion. Catholics had embraced Katherine Parr as one of their own based on her dead husband's allegiances – Lord Latimer was papist enough that he had been suspected of supporting the Pilgrimage of Grace some years ago. The couple had been forced to avoid court afterwards, at least until Cromwell died and reformist supremacy along with him. The woman must be conservative.

Or was she? She enjoyed disputing theology, and she knew an enormous amount about Old Testament texts. That combination was often the sign of a secret Lutheran.

Gardiner brought himself back to the moment, reminding himself he was performing the King's wedding Mass. Gardiner had craved such a mark of favor for a long time. He needed to savor every syllable.

The resolve strengthened him, helping him to infuse every gesture with the stateliness the situation demanded. Gardiner was even fortunate enough to experience the detachment that sometimes came to him, where he could watch the skill with which he performed his office and even feel the admiration that rose from the onlookers. Or at least the admiration that *should* arise from onlookers.

Katherine's voice was low as she repeated his prompts. To have and to hold. From this day forward. For better, for worse. For richer, for poorer. In sickness and in health. To be bonaire and buxom in bed and at board. Until death do us depart.

"I promise," she said, and held out her finger for the

King to put the ring on it.

As the monarch's fat, trembling fingers fumbled with the simple band, Gardiner called for him to proffer the rest of the gold and silver that would seal his commitment. But instead of summoning a page laden with a tray, the King merely described to his new wife the jewelry he had chosen for her – much of which she was already wearing. The magnificent necklace of diamonds and rubies was one such gift, as were the large golden cuffs on her wrists. Gardiner hazarded a glance at the bride out of the corner of his eye to gauge her reaction. She didn't seem angry, or look like she felt cheated. Her gaze was steady and calm. Unreadable.

She seemed much more interested in the benediction, closing her eyes and bowing her head even before Gardiner began. A Lutheran would not care so much about a priest's intersession; that was a good sign.

"Those whom God hath joined together, let no one put asunder." As the sound of those final words faded, all attention turned to the next step, and the curtain descended on Gardiner's glory.

The King raised an arm and called to the prothonotary who stood in the corner, respectfully apart from the illustrious guests. "Watkins, you can go make the public instrument of the promises."

Watkins bowed and left as the others cheered and shouted "God save King Henry" and "God save Queen Katherine" while the bells of the Chapel Royal jingled a joyous psalm for the occasion. The King's daughters, Mary and Elizabeth, received the first embraces, followed shortly by Lady Margaret Douglas, the King's niece. Then the room split. Hertford and his wife hugged the King first, then the Queen. Next came Sirs Anthony Browne, Anthony Denny, and William Herbert, the new Queen's brother-in-law through her sister, Anne. Meanwhile, Anne Herbert, Lady Lisle, and the Duchess of Suffolk crowded around to kiss the Queen first and then the King. The rest of the company congratulated Gardiner while they waited, as if no insult had been done to them, as indeed none was. They were all lucky to be there, each of them envied by the thousand people who comprised the rest of the court.

"Do you follow the royal couple to Oatlands?" asked John Russell, Lord Keeper of the Privy Seal.

"No." Gardiner's quick, dry answer was intended to curtail any rejoinder. No, he was not following the royal couple to Oatlands. And Gardiner didn't want people's pity over that fact. What newly married couple wanted a priest to accompany them on their wedded bliss?

"Oatlands?" asked Thomas Heneage, Groom of the Stool. "That was where His Majesty married...the late Queen. Why would he return to the ghosts that must haunt those rooms?"

"He loves that palace," said Russell. "It is where he goes to truly retire."

Gardiner wrinkled his nose in disbelief and noticed Heneage do the same. "Well," said Heneage, "I can't see him relaxing very much there, unless he replaced the special bed he commissioned for the last occasion. I'll wager that will make him leave soon on his progress."

Gardiner remained silent. He would not be the one to explain how the King was unlikely to choose a location for its ability to relax him. The King was motivated by anger more than gentle thoughts. If he was returning to Oatlands for another marriage, it was more likely to involve an exorcism. A ghost to be slain on this wedding night.

October 12, 1543—Windsor Castle

The King had drifted from the conversation to clean his nails. Edward politely looked around the room, glad to be back at Windsor, glad the summer progress had finally come to an end. The King and Queen had chosen smaller hunting lodges for their accommodations this year, and while this made for a more intimate setting, it also made it more inconvenient for courtiers.

"Edward, you shall dine with us later in our Presence

Chamber."

"Gladly, Sire," Edward replied, happy to return to relevancy. It didn't matter that he didn't know who else - if anyone - would be there, he was just happy to dine with the King.

"The Prince has arrived from Hertfordshire and is resting. We will prepare him for his role in tomorrow's celebration."

It was the boy's birthday. Six years old and healthy, by the grace of God. Also kind and intelligent, and comfortable with his uncle. Edward was reminded of his duty to the boy, his obligation to earn the place his nephew had cemented for him. "Excellent idea, Your Majesty. It will give him great comfort." Edward chuckled. "The lad does love to be prepared for things. His curiosity and desire to excel are rare in one so young."

The King's lower lip quivered. "He is the perfect son. Your sister would be so proud of her accomplishment."

Edward bowed in acknowledgement, blessing Jane yet again for the legacy she had left.

The King put his hand on Edward's shoulder. Edward clasped the royal elbow and stayed perfectly still, happy to accept as long an embrace as the man desired.

After a moment, the King straightened and composed himself. "The Queen has persuaded me he should come to court more. She wants all my children to join us."

Edward weighed the proper response to this delicate situation. Tact required he ignore the reference to Elizabeth - the girl was a reminder of uncomfortable times. He also decided not to mention the King's longstanding fear of sickness, his terror of risking his son to the unwholesome air of court. This was a step that would be good for the boy, and Edward would be a fool to discourage Henry from taking it. "It will be nice for you to be surrounded by family. You deserve such a pleasure."

"God bless my wife for giving it to me."

Edward donned a warm smile of encouragement. Yes, God bless Queen Katherine Parr. Finally a woman worthy of the office she held. Most importantly, a woman who would keep the King in a better – certainly more even – temper by offering the quiet family life more appropriate for his age, not the vain revelries of youth with which he had entertained the last wife. "It will do your heart good to keep your son close, but the truth is it will do him even better to watch you, to learn from you." Edward paused for effect. "It will make him a better man."

Henry nodded. "It is time. He's been brought up among women long enough; he must look to his future." He looked off, as if watching something far away, then clapped Edward's shoulder and nodded again. "Not all the time of course; he's best in the country. But I shall enjoy having him next to me at some audiences. And I'll soon have him welcome ambassadors."

Edward laughed obligingly. "See there, you are already planning his political instruction. How about the rest? Have you given any thought to his tutors?"

"Bishop Richard Cox, my chaplain, to start. There's no one better for theology, and he also excels at Latin, Greek, and arithmetic."

"Good choice." Edward smiled, and not just because Cox was a reformist. "A man of God who is also a brilliant scholar. And then you can choose the others based on the boy's talents."

"Exactly."

The important points seen to, it was time for Edward to turn the King's attention to more enjoyable topics before returning again to serious matters. Alternating experiences was important, Edward had learned. More and more, the King grew bored of doing any one thing for too long and would summarily dismiss anyone attending him when that happened. At the same time, his "too long" was getting shorter – all the man wanted to do was lock himself in his rooms to mix tinctures in the hope of finally curing himself. "And I am sure Your Majesty has not forgotten about the gentler pursuits?"

The King brightened. "Of course not. He started riding

this past year – a beautiful Welsh pony – and he can shoot a bow already. We will accelerate those lessons in between his academics."

Good. It was working. If Edward kept bouncing between topics, Henry was happy. It was exhausting but worth it for its results. "He'll be ready for hawking soon," Edward said. "I've brought him a merlin for his first bird. I will present it to him tomorrow at his birthday masque."

The King raised an eyebrow. "A merlin?"

Inwardly, Edward groaned. Did the King want his son to fly a gyrfalcon just because of his rank? That would be a mistake. Outwardly, Edward widened his smile. "Absolutely. The smaller size will be a good match for him."

The King's voice was as flat as his eyes. "A merlin?" he repeated.

Edward's insides tightened as all his senses screamed danger. *Don't show fear,* he commanded himself. The King was like an aggressive dog. If you showed fear, he would attack. It was instinctive.

"The merlin's equitable disposition makes it one of the easiest birds to train," Edward said confidently. "It is the perfect way to learn mastery."

The King's eyes narrowed. "A steady hooded peregrine would be as easy to train."

Edward's heartbeat thrashed in his ears. He wasn't sure of the source of the King's anger. Was the King angry Edward had chosen a bird that a simple squire could fly? Or that he was not displaying reckless confidence in the young Prince's untrained ability? Perhaps the King was insulted at the reference to the boy's slight size? How could Edward apologize properly without knowing which slight rankled? He would risk adding ammunition to that fire. He closed his eyes and plunged. "I meant no offense, Sire. I was thinking back on my own childhood. Jane's first bird was a merlin, as was mine. I did not stop to think a prince should be challenged more than others."

The reference to Jane, as hoped, struck a chord. As did the reminder of the Seymour expertise. Still the King sniffed. "I had been thinking a tiercel peregrine," Henry said.

That was something. Male falcons were at least a third smaller – and lighter – than their female counterparts. Did Edward dare to take the next step? He had to. "I must say, I was thinking a tiercel merlin as well."

Henry knotted his eyebrows and drummed his fingers on the arm of his chair.

"I wanted him to experience overwhelming success with his first bird," Edward continued. "To keep him loving the sport for life. Of course, as your son – and Jane's – this is likely inevitable."

Henry harrumphed like a dog shaking off water and nodded. "Fine. But give it to him privately, not in front of people. And plan on moving him to a peregrine quickly."

"Of course, Your Majesty," Edward said, bowing to hide the blush of relief that flooded his face. "Indeed, the peregrine could perhaps be your own present to the boy when the time comes. A reward that would mean a great deal to him."

"Just so," said the King. He glanced over to his table, the one at which he mixed his potions. Edward knew what that meant. "You may leave us now."

The words panicked Edward for a moment. He had not thought to ask earlier whether Anne was invited. Was she? That would be her first question, and she would be furious her husband had forgotten about her, however temporarily.

"My wife and I will return with great joy," Edward ventured.

The King just waved him away. Hopefully that signaled his agreement, though Edward would work out a ruse with Anne to have her retire quickly if it turned out she had been slighted. She could say she just wanted to bring the boy a present; the King would understand that. Hopefully.

At least that might forestall her cold anger. Edward hated those moods, though not as much as he feared the King's. He bowed out.

November 13, 1543—Whitehall Palace

Thick gray clouds portended an imminent storm, the threat magnified through the thousands of small glass squares in the heavily mullioned windows that lined the corridor. Edward kept his back straight and his step measured as he walked down the hall, but once he got into his apartments he closed the door behind him and sank to his knees.

Anne looked up from her reading. "What is wrong?" she asked, alarmed.

Edward's throat tightened so he could only stare mutely at his wife.

"Husband, what is wrong?" she repeated as she jumped to her feet.

Edward waved her back and lurched into the room to take the seat next to her. "Cranmer is to be arrested tomorrow. The King has signed the warrant."

Anne gasped. "Cranmer? What is this?"

"A trick of Gardiner's. Remember I told you about the reformers his nephew denounced to the Council?"

"The ones you examined over the summer?"

Edward nodded. "The same." He looked around the room. Anne caught his meaning and rushed to bring him a goblet of wine, which he quaffed deeply before continuing. "You remember Cranmer was also questioned then?"

Anne's eyes widened. "But the King laughed and joked about it. He even announced in open court that he had learned the name of the greatest heretic in the land. I remember watching him, he was leaning over and clutching his great belly, sighing between rounds of mirth."

"Well he is laughing no more. Somehow Gardiner pursued the matter - and persuaded the King to his side."

"But Cranmer is no fool," said Anne. "He has always trimmed his views to match the King's."

Edward shook his head. "The accusations included conversations from years ago, before the King reverted to orthodoxy."

Anne sat back, mouth agape. "But surely poor Cranmer cannot be in danger now for things that were permitted then."

Edward closed his eyes. How in the world could he explain to his wife the full extent of the King's lunacy, the full extent of the danger they all ran from every conversation?

"What will happen to him?" Anne pressed.

Edward opened his eyes and held her gaze. "Heresy is punishable by death."

"Lord Jesu!" Anne exclaimed. She brought her hands together to pray. Edward didn't bother. It wouldn't help.

Like Cromwell before him, Cranmer had been tarred with crimes he had never committed. And once the questioning began, the salvation of his immortal soul would force him to take positions that would tighten the noose around his neck. Gardiner was no fool: it was one thing to waffle over the number of sacraments, or the doctrine of salvation through faith alone, and so he would quickly move to the ultimate issue, the only one on which the King had never wavered, the only one that mattered. Denying the Doctrine of Real Presence was death; accepting it was damnation. Sobs began to rack Edward's body. This could have been him.

Anne fidgeted, uncomfortable as always when Edward showed deep emotion. "How did the conservatives regain their strength?" she asked. "You said Norfolk had been subdued of late."

"It was Gardiner. That snake."

Anne's eyebrows knit. She picked up her book and played with the edges of the pages. "I thought the King disliked the man," she said in a faraway voice.

"He chose him to perform his wedding ceremony. That was a sure sign of favor," said Edward.

Anne waved the small volume dismissively. "That was the King's effort to keep things even between reformists and conservatives. He doesn't like the man."

Edward had always felt the same way, but it was helpful

to hear his wife confirm it. And her rationale. "Why do you say that?"

Anne shook her head. "His lip curls when Gardiner speaks. And he cuts off the bishop's sentences."

Edward sighed. "You are right in all you say. But that matters little to the facts."

Anne paused and looked down. With a shrug, she ran a finger over the book's stitched cover. "How did you hear of this?"

"I saw the warrant on the King's desk." Edward closed his eyes against the memory of his own impotence. How the King had pushed him away and covered the paper with a "This is no concern of yours." How Edward had stuttered about loyal friends and mercy until the King had yelled at him to be silent and had asked whether he, too, was a heretic to be questioned.

Edward raked anguished fingers across his head.

Anne broke the heavy silence. "When will Cranmer be seized?"

"Tomorrow at the Council meeting."

"Can you get a message to him?"

Edward raised a single eyebrow at his wife. It was a ridiculous idea; happily, she didn't have them often. "Why? So he can escape? I'd be arrested the second they knew he was gone, and he'd be caught before he reached the coast."

"True."

"Nor is it in his nature to deny the Lord's plan for him."

"I should not have suggested it. It is just so unnerving to think something so momentous can be hidden from a person like that."

Edward shuddered. "At least he will have a last night of peace."

"It still feels as if we are missing something."

Edward had no answer. The King's whims were uncontrollable and unfathomable. And the conservatives had once again used this to their advantage. Until the reformists learned to do the same, they were vulnerable. "The conservatives are killers," he said. "We are not."

"You must learn to be."

"Unfortunately, that is not my strength."

Anne shook her head. "Neither is asserting your dominance, but both these traits are essential."

The disapproval cut deeply and triggered Edward's fear again. As did the guilt over how he'd failed his friend. He staggered over to the *prie-dieu* in the corner.

"I must pray."

November 15, 1543—Whitehall Palace

Gardiner rested his elbows on the Council table and steepled his fingers as he waited. As they all waited.

The amethyst in his episcopal ring caught his eye and made him smile. He'd likely be replacing it soon with the one from the See of Canterbury. After all, who else would the King appoint to take the post Cranmer was about to vacate?

His chest pulsed with the anticipation of power. It was difficult to appear nonchalant. Was this how Norfolk had felt during the Council meeting at which Cromwell was brought down?

"Can we let him in now?" asked Hertford. "We've kept him waiting outside for more than half an hour." The Earl had a sheen of sweat on his upper lip.

Gardiner decided to torture Hertford a little more. "We were conducting business of import to the King. Would you prefer to appease a traitor than serve His Majesty?"

Gardiner felt a violent glee when Hertford dropped his gaze. The other councilors did the same. All but Norfolk, and the two men exchanged grateful and triumphant glances over this moment Gardiner had created. The moment that would right the world, when Norfolk would arrest Cranmer just as Norfolk had arrested Cromwell.

It was time.

"Bring him in," Gardiner ordered and sat back to enjoy the spectacle of his own making.

Cranmer entered, his cassock pressed as if this were a holy day. He wore a gentle smile on his face and greeted the men as if he had not been forced to wait out in the hall like a commoner. *The fool.*

As Cranmer took a step toward his usual place at the massive oak table, Hertford covered his face with his hands. Gardiner said a quick prayer that this gesture would not communicate the ambush. Not that it would change the outcome, but it would ruin the moment Gardiner had imagined over and over since the King had signed the warrant. Another reason to hate that idiot Hertford, as if Gardiner needed one.

You are next, Gardiner thought.

As he continued to his seat, Cranmer patted Hertford's shoulder but was forced to halt when Norfolk rose to block the prelate's path. "Archbishop," Norfolk said without bowing, "I arrest you in the name of the King."

Gardiner scrutinized Cranmer's face, searching for the terror he hoped to see there, but nothing. Even when the guards approached and surrounded the two of them, the smile remained.

Cranmer raised a hand. "Just one moment, gentlemen."

"I command here, not you," said Norfolk.

Cranmer held up a ring. "The King commands here." His voice filled the room, as if booming from his pulpit.

Norfolk turned to look at the ring, and the rest of the men followed suit. Twelve mouths gaped at the large gold signet ring emblazoned with the royal arms. Gardiner had often seen it on the King's finger. It made no sense that it was in Cranmer's hand now.

"What trick is this?" Norfolk asked.

"The King gave it to me to show that you may not proceed against me without his presence."

Gardiner's temples pulsed from the beating of his heart, and his vision blurred. This was not possible. It could not be.

"But he signed your arrest warrant." Norfolk's eyes narrowed.

"So he told me." Cranmer's brow was smooth, his voice tranquil. "Hence the need for the ring."

Gardiner could not contain himself. "You really expect us to believe he gave it to you?"

Cranmer turned to him. There was a sneer on his face Gardiner longed to slap off. "You think it more likely I pried it off his finger?"

"Enough," said Norfolk. "Let us attend the King so he may guide us in this."

Gardiner let the other men file out before him. He should have been at their head but panic tightened his chest and hindered his breathing. He needed a moment to calm his racing pulse and try to make sense of this impossible twist.

Hertford looked back at Gardiner as he walked out. Gardiner averted his eyes, realizing their roles had been fully reversed from just moments ago, even down to a damp upper lip. The thought propelled Gardiner to join the line lest he be the last one out of the room. Perhaps there would be one more spin of fortune's wheel. This triumph could not be gone like dew on a sunny day.

In the King's Presence Chamber, His Majesty was sitting tall in his chair of estate, resplendent in silver cloth as if awaiting an important audience. Gardiner felt sweat dampen his armpits.

The Duke of Norfolk spoke first, holding up the warrant like a priest elevating the host. "Your Majesty, I apologize for disobeying your clear command, but your Archbishop claims your signature does not reflect your desires in this matter."

"My Archbishop knows my mind." The King swept his gaze across the councilors. Gardiner shriveled when the beady eyes found him, bored into him, sucked out his confidence and hope. "Gardiner," Henry barked.

Gardiner quickly approached the throne. "Yes, Your Majesty?"

The King pushed himself up slowly to stand, then descended the first of the platform's three steps to tower over Gardiner. The King's great bulk dominated the space between them so much so that Gardiner felt as though he were shrinking.

"Your nephew denied my supremacy, and I have ordered him arrested."

Gardiner's mouth gaped.

"Aye." The King's voice was a snarl. "Germaine Gardiner is no friend of mine - but Cranmer is and I will not see him so used. Who loveth me will love him."

Gardiner opened his mouth, ready to try to defend himself, but the King's eyes narrowed and his nostrils flared. Stunned and defeated, Gardiner quickly snapped his mouth shut and dropped to his knees.

The King looked around the room, and the rest of the councilors joined Gardiner. "You should all be like Cranmer," he said to them. "Strive for the truth unto death, and the Lord shall fight for thee."

Gardiner flinched as his mind jumped to the immediately preceding verse in Ecclesiastes: "Make not thyself an underling to a foolish man; neither accept the person of the mighty." He pressed his lips tightly lest his anger force those words from his lips, for then he would be the one lodging at the Tower this night.

And he bowed his head.

November 15, 1543—Whitehall Palace

The Hertford apartments at Whitehall were merrier than they had been in some time. Edward had brought Cranmer and other friends to celebrate the stunning rescue of the man the King had once laughingly termed the greatest heretic in the land. God bless Anne, who had quickly arranged for a feast, which they now enjoyed around the oak trestle table that dominated the outer room of the lodgings. Cheese and bread, pears and sweetmeats. And good wine.

Edward looked around the table at the group, the heart of the Reform faction. Cranmer was there of course, and

Sirs Anthony Denny and William Paget, men well placed at court whom Edward was courting for the future. Also John Dudley, Viscount Lisle – a good Protestant gentleman who, having launched his career as Master of the Horse to the former Queen Catherine, reminded Edward of himself and his own start at court. Now Lisle was Lord High Admiral of England; both men had done well for themselves.

Gregory Cromwell, too, had come, having clawed his way back to royal favor after his father's fall. Elizabeth had helped her husband here; the King loved her well.

And these were but a few of the people who were safe now that the King had made such a strong statement with Cranmer. It was maddening Henry hadn't shared with Edward his plan to save the cleric, but this was not a time for pique. This was a time to celebrate the gains of the true Church.

A maid set another platter of sweetmeats on the table then began refilling wine goblets. Edward waved her away. "Thank you, you may leave us. Leave the pitcher though."

They would serve themselves in a deliberately family style. Protocol had to be observed with those above you, such that an easy informality with others asserted rank. One of the thousand tiny opportunities Edward had learned to seize: a man was as powerful as others thought he was.

A shadow crossed his field of vision. He looked, but there was nothing there. His balance shifted slightly. *Damned wine. Go slower.* He could have sworn the shadow was Thomas Cromwell, a reminder that, despite Cranmer's good end, it could too easily have gone the other way. Or perhaps just an angel had come to join the celebration.

Edward willed himself to relax. He had to trust. After all, Henry had just proven there was a limit to his madness, that there were some people around him who were safe. As long as Edward did nothing terrible, the King would give him the benefit of the doubt. *Please God.*

Now Anne called out to the table, her glass raised. "I salute you, Archbishop."

"Hear, hear," said Paget.

Cranmer shook his head and proposed a new toast. "To the King's Grace."

"To the King," they all agreed.

Edward sighed, still amazed over the turn of fortune's wheel. The world was not the same as yesterday, just as yesterday had been a change from the day before. Life to death and back to life. Edward could not tell whether his joy was tempered by soberness, or his soberness relieved by joy. "And to righteousness," he added.

"To righteousness," they all agreed and sipped their wine.

Paget broke the silence that followed. "So is it righteousness, Archbishop, that makes the King love you so? It must be more than total devotion, or he would love us all as much."

There was a rueful note in Cranmer's laugh. "The King is a compassionate man. I think he pities my frail humanity."

Denny snorted at the mention of the King's compassion. To steer the conversation to safer waters, Edward spoke up. "We are all frail humans, friend Cranmer."

"Ah, but I share my struggles to help him with his own," said the prelate. "And let his own struggles teach me in turn."

"What struggles can you share, Archbishop?" Paget's tone was arch, digging for gossip.

Cranmer responded with his characteristic honesty. "In his darkest days I told him I knew what it was to regret a marriage with every fiber of your body."

Edward was shocked. "He knows of your wife?"

"He does."

"And he trusts you all the same?" asked Paget, his mouth agape.

"He trusts me far more for having told him, and that honesty likely saved my life. It was certainly better that he had heard it from me when Gardiner came for my head."

Cranmer was right about that. Right enough that it made Edward wonder whether there was anything in his life that he would not want Henry to hear from anyone but him. He quickly dismissed the idea: there was nothing.

Anthony Denny reached out to the center tray and grabbed a walnut. "It was a wonderful thing to see Gardiner being disciplined." He cracked the shell as he spoke, picking at the halves to extract the meat inside. "To see him finally understand how far he had overstepped."

"Praise God the King saw through Gardiner's plotting," said Edward.

Elizabeth, who had been quiet in the far corner of the table, leaned forward. "He did far more than that." Edward could tell from the way her mouth worked that she had more to say.

Sure enough, she continued. "I just can't understand why he went through such a charade. Why would he sign a warrant? Has he really no understanding of how serious such an action is?" She shuddered. "Does he sign them all so easily?"

"There has been a great harvesting of warrants lately," said Gregory Cromwell.

Edward's jaw tightened. It was unwise for Gregory to remind people of his father's end, even if the King had publicly regretted the death.

Denny sidestepped the subject. "And how terrifying that the King has made a warrant dangerous to more than just the person it names."

"I just can't stop thinking about how carefully he set this trap," said Anne. "How he waited and watched the whole time. It makes the hair on my arms stand up."

Paget patted her hand. "It is even more sinister to experience it. Everything is a test. You always have to assume he knows the truth and is just hoping to catch you in a lie."

Elizabeth clucked as if she had more to say, and from the set to her jaw Edward knew the words would be dangerous. Edward shook his head but still she let fly her words. "You make it sound easy, but it is so much more complicated. What about when he is wrong?"

There were indeed many such times, but it was

foolhardy to speak of it so openly. Edward opened his mouth to soften her statement, but Gregory spoke first. "You never know what the King will fault you for. The things that keep you safe one day will get you killed on the next."

Edward's hand tightened around his goblet. If such words were reported, they would all be in danger. Paget and Denny fidgeted, even Cranmer seemed uncomfortable. Edward shot Anne a look and she rolled her eyes back in response. He had to rein this in. "The King recognizes trust and sacrifice—"

"Not always," Elizabeth snapped.

"No," Edward said, raising his hand and his voice to stop her. "But at least you can improve your odds."

"I never thought of you as a betting man, Hertford," Denny said, grabbing on to the new topic like a man overboard to an oar. "Your brother, yes, but you, no." The table laughed, breaking the tension.

"I bet when I am likely to win. And never more than I can lose."

"A noble ambition," Anne said. "Elizabeth, you and I should go wait upon the Queen while you are here. She will be delighted to see you."

Elizabeth looked annoyed as if she were considering a refusal, but Anne was already on her feet and on her way to the end of the table to grab her sister-in-law's arm. "Gregory, you must come too, to present your wife."

Anne glanced at Edward with a gleam in her eye. Edward put a hand over his heart and blinked back his thanks for saving them all. Anne touched her necklace, and Edward was not sure whether the gesture was meant to reassure or to signal that she wanted another stone for the chain as her reward. No matter, he would get her one anyway. Two, actually – the second one for knowing to remove Gregory as well.

What a lucky man he was.

December 18, 1543—Hampton Court Palace

Edward sat with the King in the recently rebuilt royal apartments at Hampton Court. This was the sixth time the King had made extensive changes to these rooms, spending insane sums on minor differences in decoration - spades to replace the linenfold carved on the wooden paneling, new white marble to replace the previous grey veins with blue. But as much as Edward hated the expense, he dared not lecture. No one did.

Right now they were discussing the King's planned New Year's gift to his wife: magnificent emeralds reset into an *ouche*. Edward recognized the stones from another wife's necklace but was discreet enough not to mention any names.

"That would be an excellent choice, Your Majesty," said Edward. "They will bring out the green of her eyes."

"Yes, but will they earn me her loving gratitude?" the King quipped before turning serious again. "This is the last gift I will give in the ceremonial exchange, and it must eclipse the rest."

Edward looked down at the Gift Roll, the carefully curated list of New Year's presents the King would give to every member of court. "This is finer than anything else you will give that day. And certainly than anything you might receive."

The annual exchange was a carefully measured social and political event. Every important person at court (and many not-so-important people) would give the King a thoughtful gift - decorative needlework, fanciful clocks, perhaps even a sleek racehorse - and the King would reciprocate with something of value.

Edward's mouth twitched, and he worked hard not to smile. Cromwell had taught Edward to encourage the King to reduce the size of the gifts he gave, except those to allies. And Queen Katherine could well be considered an ally. "This is magnificent," he repeated. "You have—"

A page appeared at the door and Edward bit back annoyance at the interruption. Finalizing the Gift Roll was an intimate moment, offering connection and information Edward could trade on for days. And part of that magic was now lost.

"Thomas Maynman, Sire."

Edward sniffed. It could have been worse – at least this would likely keep it a private setting. Maynman was Keeper of the Wardrobe at Greenwich, and had been pressed into expanded service while the Keeper of the Great Wardrobe, Ralph Sadler, was away in Scotland.

Maynman strode in with a wide smile on his face and bowed deeply. "This is a day when I am most honored to hold the position that I do." As he rose from his bow, his eyes filled with a reverence that was echoed in his voice. "Your Majesty, they are ready for you. The tapestries."

The King drummed his feet against the floor and shook his hands excitedly. "Have the Prince brought to me here. Now. We will see them together."

Maynman's smile grew even broader. "Your Majesty, I made sure he'd be close by. I'll fetch him myself."

Henry nodded. He turned away and brought a hand to his mouth to cover his emotion. Edward used the same gesture to show his.

The tapestries. Ten enormous panels, commissioned right after the birth of Jane's son. The King worshiped tapestries; he had already collected more than four hundred. He also competed with both Charles V and Francis I in displays of courtly magnificence, and this commission had been calculated to be finer and grander than either of them had ever sought. It was the highest homage the King could pay to the woman who helped him fulfill his ultimate duty, the siring of an heir.

Again Edward was flooded with the bittersweet. *If only she'd lived.*

"It is so hard to wait – I want to see them all now." Henry shook his hands again.

"You set a wonderful example with your patience," Edward said. "Your son's gratitude for this moment will increase forever."

And Edward would be there. His feet itched to do their own celebratory dance, but such excess would be inappropriate. Excitement was to be doled out in careful measure.

Edward was a trusted advisor and guide to two generations of English rulers. *Move over, Norfolk,* he thought. The Seymours would soon erase all vestiges of the Howard preeminence.

The miniature Henry, all red-gold hair and padded shoulders, was quickly at the door, his slim face shining and his slight frame drawn to its full height. In his own rooms he looked like a normal six-year-old, but here, near his father, he looked tiny, delicate. But not sickly, thank God, despite the pallor the boy had inherited from Jane.

"His Royal Highness, Prince Edward," announced the page.

The boy bowed proudly, then raced over when Henry leaned forward in his chair and spread his arms wide. "Father!"

Edward bowed to his nephew, and the boy smiled widely before embracing him too. Edward's heart swelled.

"Today is a wonderful day, my son," said Henry. "A day I have been awaiting since your birth." The King's attention snapped to Maynman. "Did you tell him?"

"No, Sire," Maynman said quickly. "I left the happy news for you."

The King relaxed, and Edward realized he'd been holding his breath even though Maynman was the one at risk – the King's anger could too easily escape its logical borders.

"Come," the King said. He clapped his hands on the armrests and leaned heavily to stand. He had to pause twice but it was still a relatively fluid motion. Edward was quick to hand him the cane that leaned against the chair.

"Onward," Henry said and led the way to the Great Hall. The boy clearly knew there was something exciting afoot as he walked with a skip in his step, but his lips were pressed together to keep the silence that protocol demanded. It reflected well on the careful training he'd been given, and Henry patted the boy's head.

The arched wooden doors to the room were theatrically closed inside their carved marble frame. Edward nodded approvingly to Maynman, to let him know he'd done well even if the King was too preoccupied to comment.

Henry paused and tears rose to his eyes.

"Father?" The Prince reached out an arm, uncertain.

The King put a hand on his son's shoulder, the look on Henry's face stately yet paternal. "When you were born, I commissioned Master Peter van Aelst to make me the finest tapestries in the world." He wheezed a moment but recovered quickly. "A series devoted to the life of Abraham – a righteous man like me who fathered a son in his old age."

The boy's eyes widened.

"Hundreds of unparalleled artisans have been working on them for more than six years. They are here now, hung now, for us to gaze upon them for the first time."

The boy sucked in his breath and peered at the door reverently.

The King nodded, and the guards on either side swung open the panels to admit them. "Come, let us examine the treasures together," said the King.

Each of them gasped upon crossing the threshold and finding themselves surrounded by a sea of massive magnificence. Dazzling blues and reds and greens, not to mention enough gold and silver to fill a treasure chest. And woven with such skill you could swear the fabric contained actual leather and bark and water instead of wool and silk and metal-wrapped thread.

Each panel was designed to pull viewers deep into it by the beauty of the scene itself and the poignant holiness of the moment evoked, then keep them there while they delighted over the cleverness of the allegorical figures and symbols. Edward actually felt a part of the *tableaux*, standing there with the greater-than-life-sized figures.

"They are hung in order, Sire," said Maynman.

"Like the Stations of the Cross in a church," said the

boy.

Edward smiled. "A quick wit," he said.

"Exactly," said the proud father. "Now tell me what they are."

Edward tensed even though he was not the one being questioned. He glanced at the boy. He might not be able to read the Latin description given to each in a *cartouche* at the top set off by scrolling acanthus, but surely Bishop Cox had taught him enough to recognize iconic scenes from the patriarch's life.

Sure enough, the Prince was relaxed. A small smile played around his lips, the kind of smile Jane used to have when she knew something no one else did. Yes, the boy did have a lot of her in him.

With full assurance, the lad turned to the first tapestry. "This would be the return of Sarah," he said, pointing to it, "and that would be the separation of Abraham and Lot." He squinted to see the two at the other end of the room. "The circumcision of Isaac, the expulsion of Hagar." He paused for a moment, and his eyes flickered to his father before he continued, more slowly. "Meeting with Melchizedek; and Eliezer and Rebekah at the Well."

"Your son does you proud, Sire," said Maynman. Henry clapped Maynman on the shoulder.

"But that is only six, Father," said the boy.

"Three more are in the Watching Room behind," Maynman said quickly. "And the appearance of God to Abraham will grace the King's bedchamber. I gave the orders to have it ready for our return."

"Excellent, excellent," said the King with another clap and started his triumphant stroll around the room.

They oohed and aahed dutifully as the King raised his cane to point at each in turn and play the patriarch himself, expounding wonderful details about the stories. "See here, where Abraham is meeting with the King of Righteousness, he is surrounded by Faith, Hope, and Willingness of Spirit. These figures are Fame and Honor."

When they were done perusing the tapestries, Henry

turned back to the room and sighed contentedly. "This series is a fitting testament to the glory of England." Henry put his hand on his son's shoulder, and the boy straightened even more. "Part of your legacy. *Our* legacy."

The boy looked around, eyes wide.

"I should commission a portrait now. Something to befit this masterpiece. You and me and your mother in the center, your sisters to our sides."

The boy's beam turned pained. "Father," he said, "I am thrilled to have my mother honored, but what about Queen Katherine?"

Edward's throat tightened. Of course the boy was close to the woman, the only mother he'd known.

"This will be the portrait of a dynasty," said Henry. "Your mother sacrificed all for it, to her will go the glory. She was my one true wife."

Edward exhaled the breath he had been holding, relieved. The King would never again let lust get in the way of the kingdom. He had learned his lesson finally. It had taken not one but two Howard girls to teach it to him, but he'd learned it.

The boy's eyebrows drew together. "But is not Queen Katherine also your true wife?"

The King ignored the question and answered a different one. "You can't be so caring of those around you. It is weakness in a ruler. You must do what you know to be right, regardless of how it makes people feel."

The King looked around. He grunted and pointed his cane at a chair that a guard came racing to bring over. Waving away all help, Henry lowered himself to sit, then leaned forward to add urgency to his words. "All my life I have been cursed by people who loved themselves more than they loved me."

Fear twisted the boy's face. Even Edward's cheeks heated.

"Are you speaking of Queen Katherine?" The boy's lower lip quivered.

"No, of course not. I am speaking of traitors." The

King's lip curled and his voice lowered. "Men and women who harbor greed and vice, who would sell their souls for the riches that come with a crown. They all have it, everyone around you, and you must learn to recognize it. The second they act on their evil thoughts, you must cut them out of your life. Out of life itself."

The boy's eyes widened. "But—"

"I would join your mother tomorrow, but I cannot leave you like that. You are not old enough yet to bear the mantle, your eyes cannot yet see. You would be cheated like Edward V, stripped of your crown. And so I will hold on, claw to life for as long as I can. For you."

The boy was trembling now, close to panic, and Maynman was visibly shaken. They were not as familiar with the King's fits as Edward was.

The King continued his rant. "If someone betrays you, it is your duty to execute them. God's anointed is the law of the land and the Church, and no one can be allowed to commit treason and live."

The boy hung his head at the weight of the obligation. "I understand."

"No one." Henry pointed a crooked finger in the boy's face, forcing him to cross his eyes at it. "No matter how close, anyone who betrays you must die. Else it encourages others to think they can do the same. You are not an ordinary man. You are England as I am England. You must be worthy of her."

"I will, Father." The little Prince's eyes watered and his voice trembled.

Edward wondered how much the boy had been told about Catherine Howard. He resolved to explain all to his nephew, to help him understand the King's tirade.

Edward caught the boy's eye and gave him a nod meant to reassure. He would help the boy make sense of the world, to understand the nuances of these important lessons. And remind him there was one person he could always trust. His uncle Edward would always be there.

They all startled when Thomas Wriothesley burst into

the room. The man gave a bow deep enough to make up for its brevity. "Your Majesty." He rose, eyes blazing, ran to the King, and bowed again.

Something has happened, Edward thought.

"What is it?" the King asked, putting a protective hand on his son's shoulder and drawing him closer.

"The Scots have repudiated the Treaty of Greenwich and renewed their Auld Alliance with France. Their infant queen is to wed the Dauphin."

Her dowry would hand Scotland to the French. Edward felt as if he had been kicked in the stomach, though at least this wasn't his own failure.

Henry drew himself up and placed a hand on the sword at his side. "Send word immediately to Simon Preston in Edinburgh. We will war on them to avenge this insult to me and to my son. And bring them back to the terms we agreed."

"Sire," Wriothesley agreed and rose. He paused as if he expected the King to continue, but quickly realized he had in fact been dismissed. He bowed out to execute his assignment.

"Father?" The boy's voice was plaintive, unsure.

Henry patted the boy's head. "Treachery must be punished, just as I was saying."

The King, his eyes and voice flat, then turned to Edward. "I have a mind to torch the realm, put it all to fire and sword. I want Edinburgh so razed and defaced as to remain a perpetual memory of the vengeance of God lightened upon them for their falsehood and disloyalty."

Those would be some tall orders, if he gave them, but Edward knew his duty. "I am Your Majesty's servant in all things," he said. "Just say the word and I will see to it they regret this decision."

Chapter Twelve

Edward sat back into the arras that covered his chair, surrounded on both sides by his men. The seat was a formal chair of estate, set up for him in the tower of Blackness Castle, the great Scottish garrison fortress and prison on the shore of the Firth of Forth. He looked down his nose at Simon Preston, the Provost of Edinburgh. The gesture was deliberately Henry-like, provocative and threatening.

Ten thousand men had landed in Leith the day before, reinforcements for the troops Edward had led there already. With the four thousand English horses that joined them from Berwick, they had quickly captured Blackness as a base from which to attack Edinburgh. The show of force had terrified the Scots, who had come now to beg.

"My Lord, we offer you the keys to the city," Preston said with an expansive wave of his arms that belied the sweat on his upper lip. "We ask only that you allow those who desire to depart to do so. With their effects."

Edward, careful to mask the triumph he felt, nonchalantly picked at a spot of dirt on the leather doublet he had chosen to convey his readiness for battle. "Only?"

"Good Protestants, my Lord, who are as angry as you and I with the Scottish Catholics who have subverted our government policies."

"Are you so angry?" Edward said, his tone arch, provocative.

"I offered to try to raise a force to aid in your invasion." Now Preston's arms were forward, pleading. "I offered my colleagues to try to assassinate Cardinal Beaton."

Edward shrugged. "You did neither of these."

"I offer you the keys to the city," Preston repeated, arms still open.

"Another empty offer." Edward glanced at Sadler, who had prepared him for this meeting with a list of all the perfidious tricks the Scots would try to use. Tricks that Sadler had discovered through painful experiences over many months in the country. Tricks to which Edward would not fall prey. "I will accept no less than an unconditional surrender."

"My Lord, I think the result will be the same." Worried wrinkles no longer crossed Preston's forehead; he obviously thought his childish overture had worked.

"I disagree," said Edward with deliberate joviality. He leaned forward to punctuate his words. "I have been sent to punish Scotland."

Preston's eyes widened. "But we do not wish to resist."

Edward put a hand on the hilt of his sword. "Then my men will have an easier time taking control."

Preston's mouth fell open. "You will not allow friends to leave?"

"These friends have done nothing to demonstrate their friendship. They allowed the betrothal of their Queen to England's heir to be broken off; worse, they gave her to the French." Edward picked at his teeth. "Ratify the Treaty of Greenwich, give us your Queen, and then we will speak."

Preston raised his chin. Scottish defiance coming out. "And in the meantime you will war on us?"

Edward raised his own chin. "I am commanded to show the force of King Henry's sword to all those who would resist him. To all who would stand against a marriage between our countries."

Preston's hand found his own sword hilt. "I like not the manner of your wooing. And I expect my countrymen will feel the same. Good day, my Lord."

With a bow that was no more than a nod, Preston turned on his heels and stormed out. Edward's men exchanged worried glances, but Edward was not concerned. Preston's defiance was his only gambit: to test Edward's resolve like he would test a merchant's on market day. But Edward would not back down. Henry wanted blood, and savagery was required. Now Preston knew that too.

That was the way to govern: through fear. Henry had taught Edward as much, and now Edward would prove how well he had learned the lesson.

That's what this commission was designed to do, Edward was sure of it. Henry was aging and needed to know that, if something happened to him, Edward would be strong enough to keep his nephew safe. Edward was being groomed for greater power – he just had to show he was ready.

"Should I order him detained, my Lord Hertford?" Sadler's look was calculating. "So that he does not raise the alarm?"

Edward shook his head. "They know we are here, they know we will attack the city. There is no danger in allowing him to spread fear. Only advantage."

"You think he'll return with a better offer?"

Edward waved his hand. "The only offer I will accept is the surrender of their Queen."

Sadler's grimace and shrug concerned Edward. Did Sadler not understand the strategy – or was Edward perhaps missing something? "You think there is a middle ground, given the King's instructions?"

"I don't think we should throw away the goodwill of the Protestant lords because of the bad faith of the Catholic Regent," said Sadler. "I fear that is a mistake."

That was fair. Naive, but fair. "The King wants them punished."

Sadler rubbed the back of his neck. "His letters suggest this, but I thought it was posturing for any spies who might intercept them. Or the pain from his leg."

"Norfolk has parlayed for years and gotten nowhere. The King is angry and done with them."

Before Sadler could reply, a messenger was at the door.

"Your Lordship, I bring you a letter."

"From the King?"

"From Lady Hertford."

"I'll leave you," said Sadler.

Edward sat back in his chair and ran his finger gently over Anne's seal before opening the letter. It was hard to be away like this.

"Husband," it began. He hoped the lack of an adjective or other endearment was just Anne's clipped way of writing, and not a harbinger of bad news.

It was. "Thomas Audley has died and Wriothesley was appointed Lord Chancellor in his place. I am sorry you were not here to be considered for the post, though I understand the King chose him to keep both papists and reformists at bay, and you are more associated with progress."

Edward pounded his fist on the table in annoyance. Wriothesley, Gardiner's puppet, was now the highest-ranking officer of the land. The appointment angered Edward, but only because of his own personal competition with the man. Truthfully, when Edward considered the reality, it made little difference, as the King would give Wriothesley little additional power.

"Preparations for the King's departure for France continue apace, and it looks like nothing will stop him now. He is determined to appoint the Queen as Regent in his absence and to create a Regency Council for her. I have heard both Cranmer's name and your own associated with this, and also that you would be named Lieutenant of the Realm, and thus the head of the Council."

Despite this special mark of favor, Edward's stomach roiled. The Queen would serve as Regent, not him.

Edward stood and trudged mechanically over to pour himself wine. He sipped it as he stared out the window.

Things could be worse. Katherine Parr had little love for Gardiner or Norfolk and had already shown that she would rely strongly on Edward. More importantly, Anne had managed to become one of the Queen's close friends, a confidante. Edward would retain much of the influence he had won, though he would still find himself ranked behind the Parr brothers for trust and advice.

Please God, let the King survive France, thought Edward. The Parrs were not leaders, much as they thought they were. They would ignore Edward's advice. They would also keep him away from the boy. Edward might lose all his standing in the world.

"Certainly you fare much better than Gardiner. He is deep in the muck lining up supplies of cheese, butter, herrings and stockfish. Indeed, the Duchess of Suffolk has started the court calling him 'Stephen Stockfish' behind his back."

God bless the Duchess of Suffolk. Some time ago she had named her spaniel Gardiner for the express purpose of calling it loudly – and often – to heel. This was even better.

The rest of the letter was little more than a recital of the King's pains and ailments. But it closed with a tender "I count the days until your return" that made Edward smile.

He went to the desk and took out a fresh sheet of parchment. He flicked through the stack of quills, looking for one whose point was crisp, and tested its width on his finger.

He wanted to respond in kind, with equally important insights. But faced with the blank page, all he could think was a guilty *I was wrong.*

Anne had told him he was an idiot to push himself forward for this military command, that he should keep all his focus on France. But Edward had been too sure that the King would abandon the idea. Edward should have remembered his wife was rarely wrong.

Power came from proximity to the King; how many times did that have to be demonstrated to Edward? It was stupid to leave court, stupid to remove his face from the King's daily sight. He had lost the chancellorship and the regency. And for what? The title of Commander, and arras on his chair?

Stop it, he ordered himself. He had fought for this opportunity to prove he could lead. That is what he must do. He would torch the city, destroy the countryside. He would wreak the destruction the King craved, then return home in triumph. The next time the King chose a regent, it would be Edward.

July 15, 1544—Calais

Gardiner glanced heavenward, at the skies above Calais dripping with gray clouds. A foreboding sight, yet God might have intended some comfort since it did feel like home.

The King had arrived last night with more troops after a quick Channel crossing; now he was mounting his horse. He planned to ride to Boulogne, encourage Suffolk's men, and then continue on the day after to review Norfolk's attempted siege of Montreuil.

Gardiner watched as the complicated process began, his face just one in the sea of deliberately impassive onlookers. The fully armored King mounted the stool next to his massive charger, a gift from Charles V. As Henry swung his leg, the heavy rope creaked as the winch struggled to heft him into the air. Four pairs of arms guided his swaying figure as it slowly lowered onto the waiting steed, a Spanish Andalusian built through generations to offer the strength required of this feat. Even so, it groaned as the King's full weight bore down upon it.

Solidly seated now, the King cut an imposing figure in shining Italian steel etched with gold displays of foliage, *putti*, and running dogs. He pranced his steed over to Suffolk and Norfolk, who had come to greet their leader and escort him with glorious formality. And to excuse their failure to capture their assigned towns by blaming others for their inadequacy.

The King looked over at Gardiner. "What are you waiting for? We ride to Boulogne."

"Did you not wish to review your troops, Sire?"

"I shall judge them on the journey. You as well," the King said and guided his horse away.

Gardiner hoped this meant he would help judge the men – but knew it didn't. He pursed his lips. Such a terrible commission he had been given, that of provisioning and victualing an entire army. He had inadequate funds and little help, few people in the field to oversee and confront provisioners so that supplies did not run late, stocks did not rot, and horses did not turn out to be naughty nags. Gardiner took a deep breath to quell his rising frustration. This was not the time.

"Here," Gardiner called to a page for a horse. "Hurry, knave."

It took them too long to fetch a mount, and Gardiner had to spur his horse to catch up. When he did, the King slowly turned to him, his lip curled. "There you are. Finally. Try to keep up from now on, try to be useful."

Gardiner tried to swallow his anger, but resentment still twisted his lips. *Try to be useful?* No one would be here but for Gardiner's efforts. And he received no gratitude. Instead, over the last three months Norfolk had sent letter after whining letter complaining how he lacked what he needed to complete his charge. He needed more money, more gunpowder, more rope – one of the endless lists had even begged for more beer. The King had yelled at Gardiner – but never authorized the necessary funds.

The King was stubbornly blind to the true cost of goods and to the extent of the preparations Gardiner had undertaken. Henry also ignored all entreaties to stop changing the plans on which all of Gardiner's calculations relied. Hopefully now that the King was here he would understand his fault and forgive his good servant.

Gardiner opened his mouth to respond but the King cut him off. "The men's packs look too large for them."

"They needed to be of a size to hold all the gear you specified."

The King sniffed. "They look half empty."

"You modified the list, Sire."

"Is that your defense? Will you say nothing of the rampant embezzlement I see before me?"

"Your Majesty?"

"The provisioning – as Norfolk describes it and as I see here – should not have cost more than thirty thousand pounds, yet the forty I sent was not enough. Where is the rest?"

Gardiner lifted his chin. "Your Majesty, at your command I have been the purveyor for the largest invasion force ever assembled. Your forty thousand pounds moved forty-eight thousand armed-and-booted men across the Channel, along with sixty-five hundred shod horses to transport the guns and the ammunition and seat the officers. It also provided every one of them with cheese and butter and herrings. And everything goes scarce quickly in times of war. Prices rise significantly."

The King bit his lip, uncertain as most bullies are when they are thwarted. "We should have gotten more value from our gold."

We would have if you hadn't debased the coinage, Gardiner thought to himself. For the last two years, the Treasury had sought to overcome its near-empty state by mixing copper in with the silver of the coins. As these aged, the base metal shone through the royal portrait stamped on them and lent the King the nickname Old Coppernose. But that could not be said out loud, of course.

"Beg pardon, Your Majesty," Norfolk said quickly. "I only meant to say that the money received did not go as far as it should have."

The King shook his head. "I am ill advised," he said to the ground with a sneer. "I shall send for Hertford to join us. He will know how to fix this."

The bile rose in Gardiner's throat. Somehow Hertford was triumphing in Scotland. Report after report had come back detailing the terrible punishment he was inflicting upon the Scots, flaunting lists of cities and towns burned and looted and the mushrooming numbers of able-bodied Catholics killed. And then a letter had come from the young Scottish queen herself, asking for safe conduct for her ambassadors to come and negotiate peace with her good uncle.

Gardiner's cheeks flamed.

He hated this place.

September 18, 1544—Boulogne, France

Edward looked across at the now useless arrow slits of the walled city of Boulogne. The city was surrounded by fifteen thousand proud English soldiers, and from his perch atop the hill opposite, Edward could see the castle within that had held out for three long months despite – or perhaps because of – its lack of a central keep. Circular towers, each equally important. Many targets, but many strongholds.

A grateful lump in Edward's throat rose at a sight that had become common to him: a figure ceremoniously throwing wide the defending gates to wave a white flag. Victory. *Praise God.*

Edward chuckled ruefully over the way he was making up for so many years spent avoiding war. And with a vengeance. He had proven that he could lead men and achieve all the King's most lethal goals, decimating the Scottish capital and burning all the towns between it and the English border. For twenty years, Norfolk had failed to subdue the land, now Edward had. That kind of success had led the King to want him here, now, to force the surrender of Boulogne before the French army could arrive to save it.

And force Edward had. But with diplomacy this time. He had bruited through the camp followers in the village that those who submitted would be spared – the English did not seek a slaughter. It worked. Boulogne had formally surrendered on the thirteenth, and English forces had secured it completely so that Henry could take control of it.

A row of gaunt, filthy defenders emerged, lining up sullenly before the gates. More skulked inside, stationed according to instructions from the English officers. Sixteen hundred remained out of an initial force of sixteen thousand – stubborn and valiant men who had held out for longer than anyone else would have. The castle had been built to withstand much, but the daily onslaught of English explosives made the undermining of the fortifications inevitable. Surrender was the better option.

The King, fully armored and beribboned for this moment, rode up to Edward. His councilors, also armored, clustered immediately behind him. They were flanked by officers bearing flags. Foot soldiers hurried behind, lining up for their triumphant march into the city.

"Your Majesty," Edward said with a grim smile.

The King smiled back, a tear of pride in his eyes. "Nothing compares to a well-earned victory," he said to Edward. "See how the Lord prospers my cause."

Edward was careful to display only joy at the triumph, not disappointment that his own decisive part was disregarded. The King did not share glory easily.

"We shall enter our city now," the King called to his men. "The city you have earned."

The Marquis of Dorset shrugged his red velvet cape over his shoulder and held aloft an unsheathed sword. He raised it as if to pierce the gray clouds, remnants of the cannon smoke that capped the area. Then he pointed it toward the town with a yell to set the procession in motion. The air was immediately filled with the sound of trumpets and fifes, in tunes that complemented and clashed at the same time. The foot soldiers advanced, four abreast, the trumpeters and fifes dancing around them then fanning out to take up places on the walls of the town where they called out the villagers and prepared the stage for the King's entrance. The officers on horses came next, and then the line of precedence crowned by the King.

This was the culmination of all the work and preparation, the reason for all the deaths. So that the King could play the noble and valiant conqueror. This spectacle would accomplish that - it already had. But so much time and money and effort had been poured into this one town. Montreuil would not offer a similar success - that town was too strong to fall, too stubborn to capitulate.

So what would happen tomorrow, when the cheers and flowers were past?

Edward sighed and fell in behind.

September 19, 1544—Boulogne, France

Edward's eyes snapped open at the urgent sound of hooves thundering in the distance. For a moment he did not remember where he was, then it registered. Boulogne. He rose to look out the window of his room in the castle, next to the King's apartments. The light of the moon lit up the silhouette of a lone rider from the direction of Paris.

Stifling a curse, Edward pulled on his boots and ran to the courtyard. He was not alone – Norfolk and Gardiner were also scrambling to make sure they would be privy to whatever news was on its way.

"Halt," called Norfolk as the rider entered the gates.

The messenger jumped off his horse and bowed. "I bring urgent news for the King."

"We are his Council," Edward said. "Can you tell us?"

The messenger bit his lip, but continued. "Spain and France have concluded a peace treaty."

The blood drained from Edward's face, and he saw the same ashen reaction from both Norfolk and Gardiner. The Emperor no longer warred with them against France. England was isolated. Now what?

"Any details?" Norfolk asked the boy.

"Yes, Your Grace," said the messenger. "A copy of the treaty they signed."

Edward held out his hand. "Give it here."

Edward unfolded the parchment. The three men crowded around to read it and assess its full significance. Edward's eyes skimmed over sections promising perpetual peace and arranging marriages. Then he found the list of rights relinquished and the central problem: the Emperor had included England's acquiescence to peace but without consulting the King and without including any of the terms upon which the English would insist. Henry would be furious at the Spanish betrayal but impotent because of his isolation. A fearful combination.

"We are done here," Gardiner said. "Without the Emperor we have no way to push on and take Paris. We should stop this senseless bleeding of funds." The whine in his voice made Edward shiver in disgust.

"The King must return to England," Norfolk said. "This also threatens his safety."

"It does," Edward agreed. "I expect Francis will try to retake Boulogne from us now that this is the only front on which they are fighting."

"Or worse, invade England," said Gardiner.

The three men nodded at each other. For this one time, Edward had to trust and work with them. The country had to be preserved or they would all perish.

"Let us wake the King," Edward said.

Norfolk and Gardiner exchanged glances. Edward pretended not to notice and spoke instead to the messenger. "Come with us. Your work is not done."

They walked in nervous silence to the King's rooms and gave a quiet knock. Denny responded immediately.

"We've been expecting you," he said and led them in.

The King sat up in the richly ornamented bed that had been brought for him from England. Papers and correspondence were strewn among the furs that covered him, and the remains of a snack that would have fed a farmer's family graced the table next to him. "What news?" he asked.

No one spoke. No one wanted to be the one to impart the terrible tidings. No one wanted to brave the King's reaction.

Edward put his hands on the messenger's back and pushed him forward. But Norfolk quickly moved to quash that by saying loudly to Edward, "My Lord Hertford, will you do the honors?"

Edward stifled a curse at Norfolk's maneuver. Edward longed to treat the responsibility as if it were a tennis ball,

either lobbing it back to the messenger – or smashing it into
Norfolk's face. But that was not seemly. Great power led to
great responsibility – and the reverse was also true. Edward
should deliver the blow. He steeled himself to take the risk,
and took a physical step forward to spur the plunge.
"Charles betrayed you. He and Francis – may they rot in hell
– signed a peace behind your back."

"What?" Henry sat up straighter and his eyes narrowed.

Edward turned to the messenger. He plucked the paper
from his hand and brought it to the King. That also garnered
Edward the choice place next to the bed, while those other
two idiots lingered by the door. *Good,* he thought.

Henry read the treaty, poking his finger violently at the
phrases that enraged him and repeating them for the room.
"Perpetual peace." Poke. "Rights to territories – what about
English rights?" Poke. "What is this? Charles dares to speak
for England?"

"He does more than that." Edward leaned over. "The
next section says Charles has 'passed the present articles with
the comprehension of the King of England.'"

"That devil," said Henry. He looked numb, like a man
punched.

Edward turned to the messenger. "There will be no
answer tonight. Wait on the King tomorrow morning – or
better yet, be prepared to wait on the Council. We will send
for you when we are ready."

Pressing his advantage, he waved his hand at Norfolk
and Gardiner. "Go share the news with the other councilors.
Let them consider their advice over the night."

Gardiner opened his mouth as if to speak but stopped
when the King's hand waved his own dismissal.

Edward allowed Norfolk to see the small smile play on his lips. The man had gambled and failed, and now he had to preside over fools who would have nothing new to suggest beyond a quick retreat to England. If only Edward were not so worried about the consequences of this treaty for the English – *would France now turn aggressor?* – he would be gloating right now.

If only.

July 19, 1545—Portsmouth Harbor

Thunderclouds loomed dark and ominous, adding a chill to the sea air. Stephen Gardiner shuddered as he looked out over the waters of the Solent from the thick stone ramparts of Southsea Castle, unnerved as always at how dramatically the tables had turned. After England's tactical retreat from Boulogne, France had indeed decided to invade. But unlike the cowardly Francis, who had skulked in Paris while his coastal cities were under attack, Henry had hied to Portsmouth to encourage his men.

The fortress was new, barely two years old, part of the defenses the King had constructed around England's shoreline to protect the country from aggression. At the time it had seemed like an overabundance of expensive caution, but now that a major naval battle raged only two hundred meters from shore, all Englishmen praised his prescience.

Since the day before, the English ships had danced with the two-hundred-strong French fleet attempting to break through and land. So far the vagaries of wind and currents had prevented either side from getting within boarding range or even musket span, and the heavily outnumbered English ships held the advantage thanks to long-range cannons that were the envy and dread of any opponent.

The spectators huddled on Southsea Commons. A great chair had been set out for the King, and a half a tent of Tudor green was erected around him both to shield him from the worst of the sea wind and to frame his bejeweled figure as an inspiration to his fighters. Most of his Council crowded around him at this dread moment, the greatest threat England had faced. They all cheered and cringed by turns; it was all they could do. Just watch. And pray.

Next to Gardiner, the King wheezed in his chair and pointed his finger to direct the Almighty. "May God smite those French bastards."

"Amen." Gardiner made the sign of the cross to seal the request.

As if to obey, the King's premier warship, the eponymously nicknamed *Great Harry*, turned about to start the next attack.

Like its namesake, the *Great Harry* was a massive structure: one hundred sixty-five feet long, with masts that soared more than a hundred fifteen feet in the air above the fore- and stern castles. Overweight, but imposingly so.

"They heard you, Your Majesty," Paget laughed.

"They want to do you proud," said Denny. "Especially after last night. How they cheered you."

The King had dined on the *Great Harry* the night before. It had given him the opportunity to finalize the navy's defensive strategy. More importantly, the traditional visit had spurred the thousand seamen lucky enough to man it and the thousands more who watched from the neighboring ships.

Henry nodded gleefully. "It was a moment blessed by God. All the more so given how He cursed the French King's visit. I'm surprised Francis did not abandon his evil plan after such a sign."

Francis too had paid the ceremonial sendoff visit to his own flagship, the *Carraquon*, and had insisted on bringing his own chef to regale the seamen with fine food. The poor man, unused to the cramped quarters of a ship, had been careless with the galley fires, which quickly reached the sixty-three barrels of gunpowder packed in the *Carraquon*'s hold. The royal family barely escaped the explosion.

"I think the crew expected him to," said Wriothesley. "After all, it took them three days to outfit the new flagship.

That should have been done much sooner."

"It was folly." Henry sniffed sanctimoniously and adjusted the blanket that covered his legs. "Now they must attack from a position of weakness. That surely will drag down their morale, their resolve."

Gardiner crossed himself to thank the Lord for His intervention, and the others followed him. "So different from your own men, inspired to glory from the strength of your speech."

Though the flattery could have continued, their attention was drawn to the *Mary Rose*, the finest English warship ever built. And more deadly than ever now that she'd been refitted to double the number of cannons she held.

The *Mary Rose* hoisted her sails to follow the *Great Harry* and fire from her starboard side. More petite than the *Great Harry*, the queen to his king, she was a graceful, easy to maneuver, eight-hundred-ton beauty. The pride of the nation.

The *Great Harry* was advancing, its giant sails billowing, and bearing down on the French fleet. The men waited for the *Mary Rose* to do the same, but in the middle of her turn she floundered, heeling farther and farther.

"Was she struck?" asked the King. "Did you hear cannon?"

"There was a blast of wind just before she turned north. Maybe the captain could not handle the shift," said Sir Anthony Browne.

"That's ridiculous," Gardiner said, bristling at the implication that his friend, the Catholic Sir George Carew, was not up to his job. "There must be something more than that."

"Well, isn't this the first time she has sailed since the retrofit?" Browne's voice was indignant. "With ninety cannons now, it could well be her weight or balance."

Gardiner froze. As always, the critical question sprang to his mind: *Could I be blamed?* The cannons were the new larger, heavier, cast bronze models, adding greater accuracy but also more than twenty tons from the old wrought-iron ones. The King had personally made that decision but he had consulted with the Council. Would they now be accused of giving bad advice?

Gardiner was not known to be an expert in weaponry, though he was in procurement. Praise God he had nothing to do with these choices...

Who would be blamed then? The answer sprang to Gardiner's mind: John Dudley, Viscount Lisle was the Lord High Admiral. A Hertford ally. And Hertford had been Admiral himself until two years ago; there might be a way for Gardiner to pile fault on his doorstop as well.

"The retrofit is surely where the problem lies," Gardiner said with carefully infused innocence, trying not to gloat. "I cannot help thinking that the Admiral made some terrible miscalculation."

Browne's eyebrows raised. He was a friend to Lisle and Hertford; of course he would fear the implication. "It's a bit early for blame," he said.

"And a bit insensitive at a time like this," the King added.

Gardiner flushed, embarrassed. He turned his attention back to the ship, and was even more appalled. Both at the situation and at his own misstep.

The men on the upper deck were crowded on the windward side so as to create a countervailing force while the waves slapped higher and higher on the leeward side. Sailors were clambering up the masts, tearing at the rigging to lower the sails. But despite all their scurrying, the ship was still and silent as though stunned into shock.

When Gardiner was a young priest in the service of the King's early wars, a soldier right in front of him had been pierced in the chest by an arrow. The light left the boy's eyes but still he remained standing for a time. Now it looked like the light had left the *Mary Rose*.

"The water is almost up to the gun ports," a quiet voice said, too raw to distinguish. It didn't matter who it was. Nothing mattered more than the sight in front of them. They all stood, gaping in horror. Gardiner tasted death in the sea air that filled his mouth.

"Why can't I see them trying to close them?" asked the King. "Can you see? They should have closed them before the turn."

No one, certainly not Gardiner, would dare to point out that seamen would never close gun ports in the middle of a battle for what should have been a simple maneuver. It was only because the new cannons pointed out from holes that had been cut close to the waterline that, in retrospect, closing them was exactly what should have been done.

The water was now level with the highest gun ports on the port side, invading the ship and tilting it still further.

Some sailors jumped from the masts into the roiling sea; others scurried like rats to climb to higher ground but were thwarted by the netting that covered the ship to prevent boarding by aggressors. Their screams and shouts carried only faintly to the shore, all but lost in the cannon fire from the other ships around them: this was but one skirmish in the larger battle that raged on.

The heavy gray clouds held the ship from above as the whitecaps attacked it from below. The water had reached even to the fighting deck. There was no hope of saving the *Mary Rose.*

She went quickly, her lifeless body slipping into oblivion and leaving nothing behind but random debris – barrels and broken bits of masts – floating in the roiling water. Absence amid warships. Emptiness where a small city had once stood.

Gone.

The moment lengthened, aching. Still they stared at the empty sea as if intense concentration and prayer could change things.

Gardiner paused. Who would speak? Should they wait for the King to break the silence? Or was he waiting for them? Which one of them should express his deep sorrow? Denny had the closest relationship with the man, but Gardiner was the senior cleric. Did this mean he had to be the one? *Please, Lord, let this cup pass from my lips...*

A sniff came from the King. Gardiner looked over at the stern face and was surprised to see a tear make its way down the royal cheek. He wasn't the only one. Paget emerged from the shadows of the corner to place a compassionate hand on the King's shoulder. "You should retire for a bit, Sire," he said softly.

The King shook his head and straightened his back. "This is not the time to hide myself from my men. This is the time when they need me the most. I will remain here until the battle ends."

Gardiner felt a grudging respect for the man's sense of responsibility, but the moment quickly ceded to frustration. The heir to the throne was a seven-and-a-half-year-old boy. They needed to keep their leader safe. "If the French land..." he began but let the words trail off.

The *Great Harry* unleashed forty guns all at once with an intensity that rumbled the ground beneath the men and broke the tension between them. The warship charged, with two sister ships flanking and seven more fanned out behind. Lisle's aggression felt heartening, yet it was hard to see how the eighty English ships could overpower more than two hundred French ones. It would be so much safer to continue the defensive game; at least it would keep them safe. And prevent further demoralizing losses.

The King turned to Gardiner. "If the French land then we will repulse the invasion."

There was really no other response possible at this point, and Gardiner nodded as if fully convinced. "Amen," he said and turned back to the sea. It was too soon to admit to fear, too soon to suggest retreating to London for safety. That would come later. Or hopefully not.

The real question was how well the country would rally. Gardiner could not help but think about Boulogne's base example – its villagers capitulating to save their skins. Would Englishmen do the same? It was hard to say. The country was bankrupt, the coinage devalued. Now the *Mary Rose* was gone – a sign from God? Only twelve thousand – now eleven thousand – English soldiers against thirty thousand

Frenchmen. The King would need local support to hold London.

Dread and fear tightened Gardiner's stomach. He needed to leave, needed to do something. And he needed to look brave.

"It seems to me that your troops could use prayers right now," he said to the King. "With your leave, I will go and walk among them, pray with them, let them know you are here with them."

The King looked over at the armed men on the shore who were watching their comrades fight, who could only scan the coastline as they waited vainly for something to do, some brave contribution to make to England's dark hour. He nodded. "Go now."

July 27, 1545—Newcastle

At the head of the table, Edward sat in his chair of estate. The arras that covered it gleamed red to hint at war and power. Around him sat his commanders, that group of men he had strategically named The Council in Scotland to show the King that Edward could take advice.

He had called this emergency meeting to share the new report from London. He had already read it, considered the possibilities, and decided on his response. This gathering was just to make his men feel they were involved in the decision and to give it their full support.

He motioned to the messenger to begin reading while he watched his men carefully. Henry had taught him well: never trust anyone who showed fear. And fear was too rife after the loss of the *Mary Rose*. Even though the battle itself had not been lost, men still believed the hand of God had wagged its angry finger.

The messenger cleared his throat, mumbled over the formal greetings, then began in earnest. "'On 22 July, the French landed some fifteen hundred men on the Isle of Wight and burned ten or twelve small houses, but were ultimately driven to take refuge in a small earthwork fort, and a large force of good Englishmen, eight thousand, assembled to oppose them. The French Admiral d'Annebault recalled the troops and his fleet departed.'"

"Praise God," said Sadler.

Bless the man, Edward thought. Bless him for knowing that Edward would want him to help rouse the others. Edward nodded and motioned to the messenger to continue.

"'The next day, the French sent six galleys carrying above twenty thousand men. They landed some men but all Kent repaired thither for their repulse.'"

"Here, here," said Sadler, and they all banged fists on the table. This time the messenger knew to continue once the reactions quieted.

"'Some say they have given up for good, but others believe they will try again to land. The coast is ready. There are no cannons, demi-cannons, culverins or demi-culverins remaining in the Tower. They have all been sent to our towns, along with shot, powder, and munitions to supply the key defenses.'"

"Amen," said Cuthbert Tunstall, the Bishop of Durham, over the sound of more banging. The defense of England was the one point on which Edward could agree with the Bishop, a friend of Gardiner's. Like the rest of the conservative faction, Turnstall's only split with Roman Catholic doctrine was his acceptance of Henry as head of the Church of England.

"'Though without any sightings these defenses seem little needed. God willing this truth shall hold.'"

"Thank you," said Edward with a dismissive wave of his hand.

As the messenger retreated, Edward leaned forward and looked searchingly at each one in turn, stopping on Lord William Stourton, who was the key man Edward wanted to win over. The seventh Baron Stourton was a gruff man five years younger than Edward, and married to one of Viscount Lisle's sisters. Lisle was a firm friend of Edward's, but

Stourton's long-term mistress was one of Norfolk's lesser nieces, so it was hard to trust the Baron's loyalties. Nevertheless, Edward would cultivate him. "Did you hear the same thing I did?"

"That they have abandoned their plans?" Stourton said with a wide smile.

Edward stifled a curse. "Just the opposite."

Stourton waved his hand. "Their treasury is as bankrupt as ours, and with their lack of success on these *sorties* they have surely returned home to lick their wounds."

That was the obvious inference to be drawn. And precisely the reason this little charade was so important. Edward needed to dampen the overconfidence to which his men would otherwise succumb even as he roused them to action. "I agree in principle," he said, knowing such a concession would make Stourton more likely to listen to the analysis to come. "But I worry they will try one last offensive. And if so, they will try it here."

"Are you sure?"

"Not at all," said Edward. "But wouldn't you, if you were they?"

Stourton nodded slowly. "Yes. They could land among allies and double their troops while most of our men and equipment expect them elsewhere."

"Exactly," said Edward. "Which is why we must put things in such order that their malice would be well encountered."

The nodding quickened. "Berwick," said Stourton. "We must fortify Berwick. It's the gateway to the country."

Perfect. That was the idea Edward had hoped to elicit. Berwick was the northernmost town in England, an hour's hard ride from the Scottish border. More importantly, it was also the town that would resonate with the King: back in his father's time all invasions had been launched from there.

"Go there now," said Edward. "Take five thousand men with you, into the town if you think best."

That woke Bishop Turnstall. Of course he would be the one to object. "But what if we are wrong and they land elsewhere? That will not leave us enough to defeat them. Or to defend ourselves properly."

Eyes darted and Edward pretended not to notice. He forced joviality into this voice, the better to cauterize this well-justified fear. "If we've bet right, we will ambush them for a decisive victory. And if they land farther north, we still intercept them and hold them off until reinforcements arrive. The entire country is on alert. This is our best chance to hold the North." He did not share his final thoughts: since Berwick was below their main position, they would be insulated from all blame if the French landed farther south.

Around the table, chests puffed. Good. The King would appreciate that Edward had cultivated this attitude – and applaud Edward's cynicism. Edward would wring out yet another round of praise in this stupid and overdone war.

August 1, 1545—Newcastle

Newcastle was an old motte-and-bailey fortress constructed on a site that had defended England since Roman times. It was an important border stronghold against the Scots, its safety assured by the weathered gray stone walls that surrounded the entire town. This had allowed industry and commerce to flourish, attracting workers and craftsmen from miles around. Edward marveled at the coal miners, ship builders, glass blowers, wool merchants and more who crowded for space. If only all England were this strong, no one could threaten her.

The messenger found Edward in the Castle Keep. Edward's hands trembled as he opened the short letter from his friend William Paget, Secretary to the Council. Barely ten lines on the page. Were they official or advisory? Would they announce an English defeat or victory? Or would they contain nothing new, just more conjecture and planning?

It was exhausting to wait for an uncertain attack. To remain prepared and conquer the complacency such delays encouraged. But such was war, and therefore such was

Edward's life, with no respite in sight.

"Well?" Sadler's sharp tone brought Edward back to the moment and to the opening lines of the letter. "Good news," it began. And it was not written in cipher.

Relieved, Edward handed it to Sadler. "Read it to me." Edward walked over to the thin window and surveyed the countryside, the flat fields on either side of the River Tyne stretching out as far as the eyes could see. It had become a compulsive habit for him, to search for any sign of enemy troops. Only a fool was attacked unawares.

"'We are confident now that the French have retreated, as their forces have been reported in Boulogne. Despite this, the King applauds your decision to fortify Berwick. Wriothesley tried to call it a waste of men, a weakening of your main forces, but the King told him to hush, that you understood strategy and danger better than any of them. He would name you Governor of Scotland if he could; he wagers you might see a way to take this role for yourself. Well done, sir.'"

Despite the comforting words, Edward slammed a palm on the stone jamb next to him. Governor of Scotland? That meant the King was not planning to recall him, at least not for some time. And the letters from Anne made it clear the King's health was weakening. Edward needed to be there to secure his own future.

He took a deep breath. He had to make the best of it, and pray. Just pray.

"We should respond," said Sadler. "Would you like to dictate your answer to me?"

Edward nodded. With his eyes still peeled to the horizon, he began. "It is good to hear that the French ships have returned to their own waters – I will have it bruited here to discourage the Scots, who continually expect to support a landing on this coast. But again, as I have said, we remain prepared. If they do come here they shall have no cause to boast of their welcome."

"Amen," Sadler said as he wrote.

"You may leave," Edward said.

"Would you not like to celebrate?"

Edward shook his head. "Tonight we will celebrate. Now I will rest."

He needed it. He hadn't slept soundly in weeks from the strain of vigilance. It was not just the emotional toll, it was also the financial one caused by the vast sums needed to keep troops so prepared. The King had provided only a limited amount of funds, and would be furious to hear his money was almost gone. This new change solved two problems, though Edward's cynicism did not allow him to fully believe it. There would be no true rest while he was here, only enforced calm. But that would have to suffice.

Until he could return home.

Chapter Thirteen

March 29, 1546—Greenwich Palace

It was Good Friday. The day every true Christian man came reverently to church, removed his shoes and crept on his knees to the cross, even the King. Especially the King. He adored the ritual, perhaps because it was the only time he experienced humility and submission. The reformists decried the practice, arguing such public display polluted pure intentions. Another reason Stephen Gardiner resented those heretics who did not understand that intentions could be elevated by display. At least Hertford and Sadler were still in Scotland, unable to incite further mischief. That was some consolation.

The Chapel Royal was stark for this day, its low lights further obscured by the smoke from the heady incense. It turned the congregants who crowded the pews into dark outlines, ghostly apparitions who matched the somber mood of the celebration.

Since Gardiner was officiating, he had the honor of being the first to creep. Starting at the chapel doors, he slowly inched down the black-and-white stone center aisle, his sixty-two-year-old knees protesting with each movement.

The slow pace gave him ample time to worry that the King would never make it, and would resent that Gardiner had. He finally decided he would complete the task but exaggerate his own agony. He would offer a humbling demonstration of valor and perseverance, but not so much as to incur His Majesty's jealousy.

Last year had been so much easier. Last year Easter had

fallen just three months before the war with France, when the King was strong from the anticipation of glory. His youth had returned – or a semblance of it if he squinted hard enough, and the King was better at squinting at himself than most.

Now, at fifty-four, the King was unquestionably old. The Scots' repudiation of the Treaty of Greenwich had aged him. Charles's betrayal in making a sudden peace with Francis had aged him. The sinking of the *Mary Rose* had aged him. The death of his childhood friend, Charles Brandon, had aged him. And his increasing corpulence had aged him.

Still, Gardiner reminded himself, the King had never missed a year, even after Catherine Howard's fall. He might yet rally for his audience. Besides, he could use his arms to bear some of his weight and just crawl the whole way.

Gardiner groaned again for good measure.

Finally, he was at the cross, and he gratefully kissed Christ's feet. *The die is cast, and cast well.*

The King barely waited for Gardiner to finish before having his travel chair pushed into the aisle. It was an amazing contraption, a chair of estate fitted with wheels so he could go anywhere in the palace at will. The King used it all the time now.

Two of his men crouched before him to remove his shoes and hose. Even from his distance, Gardiner could swear a faint suggestion of rot descended on the chapel, undermining the gloriousness of the incense.

The men braced themselves to help the King move to his knees. He grunted but knelt unaided, and looked up at the cross. One knee moved forward and he groaned. The other advanced and he gasped, falling to his hands to breathe deeply. His fingers twitched, causing his rings to glint in the dim light and reflect the sweat on his forehead.

"Sire?" his attendant asked, uncertain.

"Help me back up," the King whined.

Back on his knees, he gave it another try, equally unsuccessful. After a third, he kept his hands on the floor and tried to crawl but made no real progress. He wheezed loudly, the hint of a whimper hiding in the breath. Four times a hand inched forward and a knee followed, but that only gave him half a pew. The grunting pants grew louder and the hidden sobs more prominent.

Gardiner's chest tightened at the sight of the infirm King overcome by his efforts. This was more than mere weakness. The King's health was failing.

Stephen Gardiner cursed his failure to recognize the danger before now. The prohibition against speaking of – or even imagining – the King's death had created a world in which such an eventuality did not exist.

Except that it did.

Gardiner closed his eyes, but still he was losing the fight against the muscles in his face. He turned away, toward the cross, and hid his face in his hands. The deeply pious gesture allowed him to hide the silent screams that mounted inside him until he could master his emotions and turn back around.

Just in time, because silence descended on the room as the kneeling King froze in place. Gardiner could tell from the way His Majesty's shoulders shifted that his attention had turned away from his own efforts and pain. His eyes darted from side to side, clearly aware of the people around him, of his courtiers judging him. He looked up and caught Wriothesley's eye. The Lord Chancellor quickly took a step forward, but the King turned away and leaned back on his haunches. "I can't," he said. "Help me back into the chair."

Once he was there, he crossed his arms and harrumphed but caught himself and reasserted control. He raised his gaze to the figure on the cross and stretched out his arms, forestalling any action by the congregants. Gardiner took a deep breath, relieved that no pretense of normalcy would be required: no good could come from it. It was one thing that the King failed to make it down all thirty feet of the aisle, it was quite another that he could barely make it out of his chair. And such heavy breathing. From barely crawling.

"Lord, my mind praises you even when my body

cannot," said Henry. "This, then, is the ultimate submission I can make to you. To come to you not on my own knees, but on those of others."

He waved toward the altar and Denny quickly went to push his chair.

"No, no," said the King. "You must do for me what I cannot."

"I would be honored, Your Majesty," said Denny, slipping off his own shoes and dropping to his knees to push the chair.

The angle was awkward and he grunted. Quickly Will Somers slipped off his shoes and joined Denny. Together they slowly pushed the enormous chair to the altar.

As they advanced, Gardiner let his mind race. How close was the King to the end of his days? He had already outlived his father by three years, though Henry VII had always been sickly. The King had recently launched a plan to secure the succession: his latest will anticipated a Council that would help the young Prince govern if aught happened. He had – believably – claimed this plan was due to normal prudence, but now the sudden interest seemed to Gardiner to be more sinister.

Did the King fear imminent death?

Again Gardiner howled inside. The members of the Regency Council would be the men who were closest to the King at the fatal moment. If the King died from this exertion, majority rule would go to the reformists.

Gardiner's dread was interrupted by the chair's arrival at the wooden cross, raised before the altar. The King's men helped him to his knees again so as to kiss Christ's feet as he always had. He seemed more agile now, less feeble. Some of Gardiner's fear left him, but the part that remained knew he needed a plan to swing the King's pendulum back to orthodoxy, and quickly. With him weakening, they could not afford patience. Gardiner had to act now to save the Church.

And Gardiner knew how he would do it. He would raise the King's wrath against the Protestant faction. Not the ineffectual way Gardiner had done it before – hoping to build momentum by starting with smaller fish – for that had just wearied the monarch, and he had veered back before they had achieved real impact. This time they would start with the Queen. The instrument had already presented itself. All Gardiner had to do was figure out how to use her.

The plan consumed Gardiner's thoughts, try as he might to keep his mind on this holiest of days. Of course, his posture was such to make people think he was experiencing religious ecstasy. And indeed he was. After all, the Lord had lit these thoughts in Gardiner to save His Church.

With that observation, Gardiner gave himself over to his fantasy until the end of the service. After the last congregant had been absentmindedly greeted, Gardiner hurried to the evening meal to share the plan with Norfolk, to put the good Duke in Gardiner's debt.

The gloom of the sanctuary ceded to a beautiful spring evening, the sun still relatively high in the sky. The King had gone to his rooms, but most of the court was outside in the center courtyard between the chapel and the palace. Benches had been arrayed around long tables covered with black cloth that lent formality rather than ominousness to the display. Trays were piled with food, properly sober for the day but still including blessed treats like oysters and porpoise that almost made up for the Lenten prohibition of flesh, butter, eggs, and dairy foods.

The Queen had chosen to have her ladies read devotions aloud for the court, a common pastime of theirs. Today's fare was Bible verses, though Gardiner doubted their choices were as conservative when they were in private. He'd wager the Queen harbored forbidden books. A search of her rooms might yield a rich reward – if not Lutheran pamphlets, then at least perhaps something written by Tyndale. Enough to prove heresy.

Gardiner bowed to her as he passed, and she nodded absently in return. It irked Gardiner that her response was not more gracious. Did she think so little of him?

A command ripped through the air. "Gardiner!"

It was one of the Queen's ladies, Catherine Willoughby Suffolk, Dowager Duchess now that her husband had died. Her husband who was close in age to the King.

"Gardiner, heel," she repeated as the cowed spaniel shuffled over to the Duchess's side.

The Queen's other ladies kept their faces bland, though Gardiner could swear he saw a smirk on Anne Seymour's face and heard a muffled snicker from that tired joke.

You will not smile while you burn, he thought.

Norfolk approached and clapped Gardiner on the shoulder in greeting, then moved him away from the group.

"I have a plan that will change her tune." Gardiner's voice was raw.

Norfolk glanced around to confirm there were no prying ears about. "A plan?"

"A woman known to be a friend of the Queen's, Anne Askew, was arrested last month for preaching heresy."

Norfolk wrinkled his nose. "The woman was released. The charges would not hold."

"I intend to seize her again, and this time I will question her myself. Question her until her song sends the Queen and all her ladies to the Tower. God willing their husbands will inevitably follow behind."

"That would eliminate the entire Protestant faction in one stroke."

"Wriothesley will help me," Gardiner said. "This will be a chance for him to shine."

Norfolk scratched his chin. "Be careful you don't get greedy. Concentrate on the dangerous ones."

Gardiner glanced back at the Dowager Duchess of Suffolk. His voice dropped to a whisper. "They are all dangerous."

June 20, 1546—Tower of London

For the first time in a long while, Stephen Gardiner was glad that his residence was directly across the Thames from the Tower of London, the realm's first and foremost royal stronghold, the palace that served a reign's highest moments. The Tower was the soaring sanctuary from which sovereigns emerged to receive the holy anointment at their coronation, the luxurious palace where the King met foreign ambassadors and showed off his formidable menagerie. But the Tower also served a reign's lowest moments: it was the fortress to which sovereigns retreated when their subjects rebelled, and it housed the buried dungeons where traitors met their fates.

Today, Stephen Gardiner had come to the Tower's underbelly, past the locked door flanked by guards, past the row of chambers small enough for prisoners to feel the thick stone walls close in on them. Here, Anthony Kingston, acting Constable in John Gage's absence, gestured to Gardiner to precede him into a space that was larger but no less foreboding.

Gardiner lifted his cassock to step over the doorstep and into chilled air infused with must. He paused a moment for his eyes to adjust so he could take in the scene. Anne Askew was tied to a chair in the center of the dimly lit room, her chin lifted. Wriothesley and his henchman Richard Rich circled, launching sharp-toned questions and receiving only monosyllables in response from the proud twenty-five-year-old. Gardiner put up a finger to quiet his men, then motioned with the other hand for a chair to be brought to him facing the prisoner.

There was no fear in the brown eyes that bore into him, which was surprising as even brave men often needed new trousers when they were brought to this fearsome place. "Mistress Askew," Gardiner said. "Do you know who I am?"

"No, Your Grace."

"I am the Bishop of Winchester," he said.

The eyes widened slightly.

"I am here because these gentlemen have told me of some highly improper answers you've given, answers that could endanger your immortal soul. They have sent for me to press you on these points. You understand?"

"Of course," she said with a quiet calm. "But my soul is not in jeopardy. I believe as Scripture has taught me."

Wriothesley advanced. "She has few words, Your Grace," he said to Gardiner, almost spitting. "Ask her why that is."

The woman looked down her nose at Wriothesley. "Solomon says a woman of few words is a gift of God."

"Careful how you speak, or you will burn," Wriothesley threatened.

She grimaced. "I have read all the Scriptures, but never could I find that either Christ or his Apostles put any creature to death."

Wriothesley drew back his hand, but Gardiner blocked the intended violence. He wanted the woman to believe she might obtain mercy from him; it might loosen her tongue. "Thank you, my Lord," he said to the Chancellor, "but I shall deal with Mistress Askew now."

Wriothesley harrumphed but stepped back. Gardiner continued, his voice honeyed. "Do you have the spirit of God in you, Mistress?"

"If I do not, then I am reprobate or cast away."

This was what Wriothesley had reported – that she answered questions without answering them. Gardiner would have to lead her better. "I have heard say that you would rather read five lines in the Bible than hear five Catholic Masses."

"Yes."

"How could this be? Five Masses are five opportunities to join with the living presence of the Lord. Surely this should be preferable to five lines of Scripture."

"Ah, my Lord, no," she said. "The one does greatly edify me, and the other not at all."

Her calm smile had returned, and Gardiner understood Wriothesley's impatience. It took enormous force of will for Gardiner not to slap the thinly veiled contempt off her face.

It was time to hone in on the testimony that would kill her. "It is alleged you have said that priests could not make the body of Christ. Is this true?"

"I have read that God made man; but that man can make God, I have never yet read, nor I suppose I ever shall."

Bile rose in Gardiner's throat. "Do you believe, Mistress Askew, that private Masses help the souls of the departed?"

"I find it great idolatry to believe more in those Masses than in the death which Christ died for us."

Her half-answers were infuriating. Enough cat and mouse. "You speak in the riddles of the guilty, but that will not serve you forever. Do you believe the Eucharist is Christ's body?"

"Why was Saint Stephen stoned?" she asked. "What part of his speech was blasphemy?"

Gardiner jerked back, flummoxed. "I can't say." Saint Stephen had denounced the authorities who sat in judgment on him, but his actual quarrel had not been recorded. Of course, that was the girl's point: she was being questioned for her politics rather than her theology. As if there were a difference.

"Don't you know?" The girl's voice was taunting.

"You see, my Lord," Wriothesley broke in, frustrated. "This is what she has done for the last two days. She alternates half-answers and half-truths with ridiculous accusations."

Wriothesley was right. Enough was enough. Anne Askew did not deserve the hearing they had given her. She had forfeited that right long ago. It was time to move on to the real purpose.

"To not affirm the Real Presence is to deny it," Gardiner said. "This makes you a heretic, Mistress Askew. And a traitor."

"These are your words, not mine. I love the Lord and our King."

"A heretic," Gardiner continued, "who has been admitted to the highest circles. Have you spread your poison at court? Have you infected others with your beliefs?"

"No."

Gardiner stood and shook his head as he moved his

chair to sit near the window. "We will see if the rack will change your answers."

Wriothesley's gaze never faltered, but Kingston snapped his head around and looked at Gardiner as if he had grown horns. "Rack a woman?"

"Rack a traitor," Gardiner answered, uncaring.

Kingston's chin rose. "This goes against all our laws. I cannot allow you to do this."

Gardiner met his gaze. "Then leave."

Kingston started to sputter. "I will speak to the King."

Gardiner waved a dismissive hand. "Go ahead. I do his work."

Kingston gave an abbreviated bow and hurried off. The stomp of his boots echoed on the doorjamb, and the heavy wood door slammed behind him. The quiet afterwards was all the more deafening.

Gardiner turned to Wriothesley and Rich. "It will take him at least three hours to get to Greenwich and back, even if he is admitted to the King's presence immediately. Untie her."

Wriothesley nodded, his jaw set, and fumbled with the ropes.

The woman was pale now, and there was fear in her eyes. Good.

"Unless you have something to say to us?" Gardiner tried.

She shook her head. No matter. Many prisoners stayed brave until they saw the instruments.

"Come," Gardiner said. He picked up one of the lighted candles from the holder and led everyone through the gloom to the adjoining room. It was even darker and colder than the one they had left.

The stained stone walls enclosed a sinister jumble of metal cages and tools. The room was said to contain every device of human torture, though only a half dozen or so had been fully explained to Gardiner. It was enough.

Gardiner paused and pointed at a large upright post, one of the wooden pillars supporting the roof. He raised the candle to show a row of iron rings one above the other. "You are lucky we let you sit during your questioning. Many prisoners are hung by their arms here until they confess. Those who have endured it say it feels like all the blood in their bodies has rushed up into their arms and hands, as if it would ooze from the ends of their fingers."

A mighty roar from the Tower lion tore through the room.

"He sounds hungry." Gardiner's voice was a purr. "The smell of treason does that to him."

The woman's eyes bore into him. "Or he's a Roman lion who smells a true follower of Christ."

Anger rose in Gardiner at the way the woman was twisting the situation. He pushed her past areas marked by iron forms and chains, driving her to the rack.

"But no, this simple device shall be your fate, Mistress." He paused to let her take it in. "Your wrists go here," he said, pointing at two rope rings at the top of the frame. "And your ankles here." He pointed to their counterparts below.

The woman bit her lip and swayed but said nothing.

Gardiner kept his voice quiet, reasonable. "I only want to know who else at court shares your views. You have had dealings with my Ladies of Suffolk, Hertford, Denny, and Fitzwilliam. And the Queen. Tell me about them."

"There are no ladies or gentlewomen of my opinion," she said.

"As you wish," he said. "Take off your clothes. All but your shift."

"Your Grace!"

"You will not hide behind modesty," Gardiner said. "Do it yourself or these gentlemen will do it for you."

The woman complied, slowly as if she kept expecting them to change their minds. The fool.

Finally she could dally no longer and was made to climb onto the rack. Her hands and feet were fastened. When she was firmly tied down, Gardiner approached her head.

"Now I will ask you again," he hissed, "give us details about the Protestant sympathies of the women at court. Do any of them deny the Eucharist as you have done?"

"I know nothing of anyone's beliefs," she said. There was a catch in her voice. She might well be close. One prod might do it.

Gardiner nodded and Wriothesley turned the handle. The woman grunted then screamed, then her cries slowly subsided into a moan. Gardiner waited for her to catch her breath, then leaned his face close to her ear. "Give us names."

"Never."

Gardiner straightened and nodded again. Wriothesley grabbed the handle and gave it a turn hard enough to lift the woman's stretched frame five inches above the bed. "Give us names," he raged loud enough to be heard over her screams.

Wriothesley let go of the wheel and the woman slumped, unconscious.

"Good," Gardiner said. "Now she understands the consequences of her stubbornness. Revive her and we will speak in earnest."

July 24, 1546—Whitehall Palace

A large linen cloth, thin as lace, shaded the King's private garden. Like his chair, the cloth could be moved on command to shelter him from the worst of the sun's rays.

The corner of Gardiner's cassock fluttered in the breeze, and he crossed himself in gratitude for this further reprieve from the late afternoon swelter. Hopefully the King would be equally soothed; he had been irritable all morning from the pain in his leg, and the heat had exacerbated the problem. The Queen was trying to distract him by disputing Scripture.

"The charity which stands at the root of God's universe begins in the hearts of men," the Queen said.

"You place too high a premium on inner devotion, and not enough on the sacramental side of religion," the King replied.

"Why is ritual more important than the love and fear of God, joy in God, godly meditations and thoughts, patience and humility? You yourself wrote that, Sire, years ago."

"Before men took it too far." The King sounded peeved.

It came to Gardiner in a flash, the recognition that he could use the King's foul mood to rile him over the Queen's religious views. This was how he might snatch victory from defeat, now that Anne Askew had, impossibly, kept her silence even after five miserable days on the rack.

"You look surprised," Gardiner said to the Queen. "But I am even more so. I find it shocking that anyone would try to twist the views of a theological master."

"You seem overly proud of yourself, Bishop." The Queen's voice was bitter.

"Your Majesty?" Gardiner asked, his face carefully bland. *Please, Lord, let this opening hold.* "'Tis not pride but comfort at the words of a master. And gratitude for the chance to do God's work."

"His work?"

"I help to curb the Lutheran excesses, to bring the people back to the proper observance of the Church of England. This is the ultimate honor for me."

The Queen's eyes widened, and her lips twitched like a spitting cat. "You racked a woman until she was near dead. You plucked her bones and joints asunder. Tell me, did it serve the Lord that she had to be carried to the stake to burn?"

Gardiner tried his best not to smile. He could not have asked for better. The King had quietly ratified the racking, so to criticize Gardiner was to criticize her husband. "The woman Askew denounced the Mass. The men burned with her did the same. Surely you do not condemn me for seeking God's justice?"

Two other heretics had been burned with the Askew woman. One of them was John Lascelles, the man who had brought Catherine Howard's past to light. Another slap to the reformists, and a reminder to them that vengeance could be taken at any time. *Yes, Lady, I have good reason to be proud,* Gardiner thought.

"The King himself was appalled by such an extreme handling of the woman," said the Queen.

They both turned to the King, who was squirming in his chair to find a more comfortable position. "Hmm?" he said when he realized they were waiting for him, then quickly supplied an answer. "And yet she did not recant."

"None of them did," said Gardiner with as much righteousness as he could infuse into his voice.

Katherine raised an eyebrow but did not comment. Instead it was the King who responded. "If I had spared them they would have spread more filth with their rebellious preaching. I don't need more of my subjects infected with Protestant poison."

As gratified as Gardiner was with the King's verbal support, he fumed inwardly that it had interrupted the Queen's ramblings. Gardiner needed her to continue talking if he were going to catch her.

He added new bait to the trap. "You are so right, Your Majesty. Why, the woman Askew even had the temerity to tell her investigators she would rather read five lines in the Bible than hear five Catholic Masses."

The Queen leaped back into the conversation. "Is it heresy to prefer the words of our Lord to idolatry?" She turned to the King. "Sire, to the glory of God and His eternal fame, you began a good and godly work in banishing that monstrous idol of Rome, the Pope. I urge you to thoroughly perfect and finish that work, cleansing and purging your Church of England. Too much superstition remains in the dregs."

"Where else would that lead but to a Protestant state? Commoners thinking they are equal to bishops, to peers – and entitled to share in the riches of their betters." The King's voice was sharp and the Queen's eyes widened.

"Nay, nay." She flushed and her fingers fumbled with her book. "That was not my meaning."

Gardiner honeyed his voice. "You seem quite agitated, Your Majesty," he said to Katherine. "This heat is dangerous. Perhaps some rest might help?"

"Aye, Kate," said the King. "Leave us."

Her hands trembling, she swallowed and answered. "Yes, Sire, thank you. I will retire."

Gardiner was careful not to smile. How stupid, to leave an angry King alone with her enemy. And how fortunate for that enemy.

The King watched her retreat, his head shaking. "A fine thing it is when women become clerks," he said, his voice dripping with sarcasm. "Is this my fate, to be instructed in my old age by my wife?"

Gardiner steepled his fingers. "I would say it was a sad thing, Your Grace, to watch the most brilliant theologian of our day being so lectured. It was quite unseemly for any of your subjects to argue with you so malapertly as the Queen has just done, and a grievous thing for me to hear."

The King sucked his teeth and shifted his leg again with a grunt. "There is no excuse for such behavior."

Gardiner leaned forward, arranging his face to display commiseration and hide his mounting excitement. "Hearing her dispute Your Majesty's learned judgment in matters of religion, it occurs to me the Queen may be a misguided woman who must be shown the error of her ways," he said with exaggerated sympathy. "Already it is whispered at court that she holds opinions dangerous to the policy and public government of princes."

"Is that so?" The King's eyebrows both furrowed and raised.

"I am sad to say it is, Your Majesty. As you yourself noted earlier, Protestantism preaches that all things ought to be shared in common – the ultimate danger – so when she pushes to destroy ritual she brings the people around her closer to this sacrilege."

The King's eyes darted in anger and he harrumphed.

Gardiner pressed on. "Perhaps a discreet inquiry should be made to look into her activities? To allay the suspicions –

your own most of all."

"My own?"

Gardiner adopted a sad look and shook his head slowly. "You surely have worried that her views are offered in a heretical tone. It is essential to know you are not harboring a viper close to your bosom."

Henry narrowed his eyes but Gardiner held his gaze unflinchingly.

"And you think a formal inquiry is necessary?" the King finally asked.

"I do, Your Majesty," Gardiner intoned. "If only to show that a high position is no protection from the law. It is a symbolic gesture, but an important one."

More importantly, a formal inquiry left no route for escape. But that was not the argument to make right now.

"Fine," the King said. "She may be investigated."

The speed of his victory urged Gardiner on to the next phase of his plan. "May I also suggest some of her ladies be questioned with her? In case the influence comes from them?"

The King's eyes were slits in his face. "Which ladies?"

"The women she spends all her time with. Ladies Herbert, Lane, and Tyrwhit. And of course—"

Before Gardiner could mention the Dowager Duchess of Suffolk or the Countess of Hertford, the King started to shake his head. Rather than lose all his ground, Gardiner abandoned this final ambition and hastened to plead his existing case. "Again, just to be sure."

The head shaking continued. "I find it hard to believe my wife could be guilty of heresy."

"As do I, Your Majesty. Any of them. But gentle questioning will establish her innocence beyond a doubt," he lied.

"Hmm."

The King looked to be wavering. Gardiner needed to press on, and press on hard. "And, perhaps more importantly, a search of their possessions. Hidden heretical books will speak volumes. As will their absence."

"Very well." The King shifted again in his chair. "Bring me the warrant and I will sign it."

"Sire." Gardiner bowed his head to hide his trembling lips. "I will go do that now. Shall I send your musicians to play you something soothing?"

"Fine."

Gardiner left, triumph lifting his soul until his feet barely touched the ground.

July 26, 1546—Whitehall Palace

Edward walked into his apartments at Whitehall, tired from the long journey, grateful to be home after his many months in Scotland. The Highlands were a rough place, and Edward had been happy to leave them. With every mile on this trip home the grass had gotten greener, the houses larger, the formalities greater – until they were all crowned by the extravagant magnificence that was Whitehall Palace.

The King had retired for the night, so Edward was free until the morning. Anne was not there, of course: she would be attending the Queen. He sent a messenger to tell her of his arrival then sat on the bench at the foot of their bed to remove his boots while he waited. The corners of his mouth turned up, and he hummed a happy tune as he imagined the tender moments ahead.

The door to their apartments opened and he stood quickly, arms open wide. Anne scurried in, hood askew and eyes wild. "Edward, thank God!" She flew at him and threw her arms around his neck.

His relief at having her in his arms was scattered by the terror he saw on her face. His heart felt like it had stopped in his chest, and he held his breath. "What is wrong?"

"The Queen is to be arrested along with three of her ladies – Herbert, Lane, and Tyrwhit. What if they don't stop there? We are all in danger."

"What?" He pushed Anne's shoulders away so he could look into her face. "Arrested?"

"For heresy."

His vision went black for a moment. It had never occurred to him Anne could be in danger.

Anne buried her face in his shoulder. "Oh God, Edward, they will burn."

"How is this? What happened?"

Anne pulled a handkerchief from the purse that hung from her belt and blew her nose before answering. Edward felt he would jump out of his shoes from the interruption but kept silent.

"The other day, the King's leg was bothering him, and Gardiner provoked the Queen into talking about Anne Askew."

Gardiner. Edward shuddered and clasped his wife tightly. Again she spoke into his shoulder. "Oh God, Edward. Will he come after us too?"

Edward had no doubt Gardiner would indeed try, but he could not say that to Anne. Instead he stroked her hair. "Only if she answers wrongly."

Anne drew back, eyes narrowed. "What do you mean? How could she not?"

Edward broke away and strode over to the table. He poured a glass of wine for himself and another for Anne, which he held out to her while he drank deeply. This was not the way he expected this night to unfold.

He started to pace. The movement helped him think, help him weigh possibilities. He would need all his skill to escape this intrigue. "Did they find any books?"

Anne shook her head and dabbed at her puffy eyes. "The Queen keeps only devotions in her rooms. She is no fool."

"And you have not taken any chances, have you?"

The look Anne gave him included a slight eye roll. "Of course not. Have you?"

He did not mind the question; she was entitled to his answer as he was to hers. "So there is no proof against her. Only what she might say to his questions."

"True." Anne's voice came out slowly. "But you well

know that will be enough. Gardiner is trained as a lawyer, he will know how to trap her."

A vision flooded Edward, one of the young Stephen Gardiner, back when they were both clerks to Cardinal Thomas Wolsey. Gardiner always had been a priggish pedant. And he brought that trait to his theology.

Edward shook his head. "Gardiner is master of logic, but he lacks grace. The Queen is more thoughtful. She holds the advantage."

Anne furrowed her brow. "All the grace in the world will not save her when the Bishop asks her whether she believes Christ present in the Eucharist."

"She can tell him she believes as the King commands."

This time Anne's eyes did roll. "And what if he presses and asks her to describe what that is? She cannot do so without perishing. There is no salvation. For any of us who will be questioned."

Edward's head jerked around. "I thought only three of the Queen's ladies were named?"

"Yes, but all of us were part of the warrant."

Edward's knees weakened. He looked around and quickly found a chair to drop into. When he spoke, he was glad to hear his voice was calm. "Well, it is still a good sign she is not lodged in the Tower."

The Tower was a fearsome place, and many minds snapped when they arrived. The relative safety of her apartments would help prepare her for her questioning.

"Aye," Anne said as she sat beside him and twined her fingers with his.

"When does the questioning begin tomorrow?"

"We don't know."

"When do they come for her?"

"I said we don't know. She has not been arrested yet."

Anne's words made no sense, and Edward wondered whether his mind had heard a happier phrasing than the words she had spoken. "What?"

"The warrant has not yet been served."

Cautious hope returned to Edward like a raptor to an

old nest, and he prayed his ears were reliable. "Not yet served? Then how do you know of it?"

Anne put up a hand and took a deep breath. "Edmund Bridges showed it to Dorothy Bray, one of the Queen's maids of honor."

More nonsense. "Why did Bridges have the warrant and not Wriothesley?"

"The King gave it to him to deliver to Wriothesley."

Edward scratched his head. Bridges had a loose tongue, and he and Bray were affianced, but that was not important now. "Did the Queen consider pleading with the King?"

"She could not consider anything, poor woman. But Doctor Wendy might intercede for her; we are praying for that."

"Wendy? Why would he do so?"

"The Queen made much lamentation, as I am sure you can imagine. She wailed so loudly the King heard it in his chamber. He sent Wendy to see to her health and comfort."

"Did she tell him her distress was related to the warrant against her?"

"He came twice. Before and after the wailing. The second time, he told her that her enemies were working a terrible plot against her and she must take care."

"The King sent him twice?" Edward sat back and pondered the barrage of conflicting facts. The utter lack of logic suggested its own solution, and hope glimmered warm within.

"What is it?" Anne's voice was sharp.

"The King might be wavering."

Anne's eyes widened and her mouth rounded. She looked hopeful, but the fingers that played with the carvings on the arm of her chair betrayed her doubt. "Thanks to Wendy?"

"He is just a part of it." Edward put up his hand and started counting points off on his fingers. "The King signs the warrant and instead of giving it to Wriothesley, gives it to a man who cannot keep a secret to deliver it to Wriothesley." He leaned forward without adding another finger. "I wager he also told Wendy before he sent him in the first time – to offer another avenue by which the news might spread." He sat back and added another finger. "Then when he knows the Queen has heard, he sends Wendy to explain the source of his anger." Another finger. "And offer hope."

Anne stared at Edward's fingers. "But..." Her voice trailed off.

Edward leaned forward again. "This is but a warning."

"But why?"

"He only wants to teach her a lesson."

Anne sat back in her chair. "What a terrible lesson." She looked down at her handkerchief and fussed with the lace. "How can you be so sure?"

"I'm not. But this is what he did with Cranmer."

Anne started to protest, but Edward drowned her out. "He does not want to execute another queen. You saw how poorly he felt after Catherine Howard."

Anne sniffed. "Only because he had no other woman waiting for him."

Edward swallowed his annoyance. She was right, of course, but their focus belonged elsewhere. "As he has no one waiting now. Gardiner may have managed to pique his anger on one bad day, but now he wants a way out of his rash decision."

Edward waited, watching as she wiped away her leftover tears and blew her nose.

"So what now?" Anne finally asked.

"She must go to the King. Quickly, before Wriothesley arrests her."

"And say what? Thank him for rescuing her as he did Cranmer?"

"No!" His vehemence made her jump. Edward gave her an apologetic look then continued, quieter but just as intense. "He did not come to her directly. She must play the game. He doesn't want to be told of her submission, he wants to experience it."

"And how should she do that?"

Edward suppressed the condescension that threatened to creep into his voice. Anne was terrified, and terror clouded judgment. "She should thank him for his loving message, speak of how it comforted her. Display softness, femininity. Change his bandages. Rub his feet. Anything she can think of – anything that does not involve politics or religion."

"I understand that part," Anne sniffed. "But what if the King insists on discussing what happened? How should she respond?"

Edward shrugged. "Deflect the issue and center it around him. Tell him her purpose in disputing with him was merely to take his mind off his pain. Slip in a compliment – that his learned answers provide wonderful guidance and soothe her soul. And quote Saint Paul about the obedience of women."

Anne sat back and pondered, her face slowly brightening. "You think that will work?"

"I know it will." It had to.

Anne nodded. "If only it were not too late to do this tonight."

"She must go to him first thing tomorrow morning. Maybe hear Mass with him, or right afterwards when he likes to sit quietly in his garden."

"I will go to her now so she can prepare."

Edward was heartened by the determined look in Anne's swollen eyes. She understood. They had a chance.

Anne stood to leave, and Edward felt her absence even before she took her first step away. It had been so long.

"I hate to leave you so quickly after your return," she said. "But—"

"This is more important." He leaned back. "Stay with her. Help her practice her answers. And be there to delay the guards if they come too soon – enough so she can sneak out to the King through her private corridor."

"I will help with her answers, but someone else can delay the guards. We have been separated for a year, and I do not intend to sleep apart from you tonight."

Relief flooded him at the reprieves - political and emotional - he'd been granted. He needed his wife's arms around him, his arms around her, to replenish his soul. It had been too long.

Anne was halfway to the door but ran back to hug Edward, her eyes filled with tears. "Thank God you returned."

Thank God indeed, Edward thought.

July 27, 1546—Whitehall Palace

The great stained glass windows on the eastern wall of Whitehall's Chapel Royal shone with an unearthly brilliance from the morning sun, casting a soft green hue that bathed Stephen Gardiner in warmth and approval. With his heart full, Gardiner intoned every syllable of the Mass. The exercise helped him both to savor the moment of his greatest success and to beg for the strength and grace he would need in the coming days.

Gardiner loved the chapel at Whitehall; it was the only thing he liked about the palace. Built by Cardinal Wolsey back when it was the main residence of the See of York, no expense had been spared to infuse awe into worshippers' souls. The carved timbers of the arched ceiling held even more gilded stars and pendants than the one at Hampton Court Palace, and painted angels covered every inch of flat surface. A fitting monument to the glory of the Church.

A glory Gardiner would soon restore.

Later that day he would question the Queen. He would never be allowed to torture her, but he would not need to. She would condemn herself as the Askew woman had, as all heretics did, over the issue of the divine presence in the Host.

And this time Gardiner would not tarry. This time he would turn directly to that question and doom her before the King could change his mind. Then Gardiner would attack her ladies. One by one he would purge the court of the reformists and save the Church. And then he would be given the glory that was his due.

The sacred Latin words vibrated like tuning forks in his mind, offering ecstasy and radiating approval. He gave himself fully over to the sensation, reveling in the divine gift and promising over and over to be worthy of it.

Ite, Missa est. Go, the Mass is ended. The closing rang in his heart, which whispered the response: *Deo gratias,* thanks be to God.

With a catch in his throat, he turned to kiss the altar and prostrate himself as a further show of gratitude. He lost himself in thanks and praise, so much so that, by the time he rose, the chapel was empty of its celebrants. Only the assistants remained in choir, patient as only churchmen could be with such expressions of devotion.

Gardiner maintained a contemplative silence even after they took his stole; he left with just a nod, still marveling at the beauty of the world.

His feet took him to his apartments, which were off the Long Corridor in the East Wing, close to the courtyard garden where the King spent so much of his time. Evidence of Gardiner's favor since only those who were important to the King merited such proximity, and only those who were trusted by the King were allowed to catch occasional glimpses of his repose. The garden mitigated this ability somewhat with vines that trailed down the outside of the covered walkways, and dwarf trees obscured entire sections, but a careful courtier might catch a glimpse of gold and be reassured by the knowledge that the King was close by.

Like now. As Stephen Gardiner passed the window that gave onto the garden, he noticed the telltale glint of jewels in the western corner, and he stopped to look more carefully. The King was already out enjoying the fine morning. *Good.* That would keep him far removed from the activities in the palace; he would miss any screams or scuffling that might result from the Queen's arrest.

Motion from the corner caught his eye. It was a soft green brocade gown. The Queen had entered the garden and was approaching her husband.

Damn, Gardiner thought and quickly moved to the side to watch without being noticed.

He could not see the King's face, only the Queen's. She wore a French hood without a coif. The fashion flaunted her hair, which cascaded over her shoulders. *More a style for a loose woman than a queen,* Gardiner thought.

Clanking from down the hallway drew his attention. It was Wriothesley, marching with a detachment of soldiers. Not quickly enough. "Hurry, man," Gardiner called. "You must serve the warrant quickly."

Wriothesley looked slightly abashed at the scolding, but all confusion melted when he glanced out the window and saw the royal couple. "It will take us but a moment."

As if to underscore the need for speed, he dashed off with barely a nod, his men jogging along behind him without breaking formation. Normally Gardiner would have called him out on such diminished protocol, but in this case the haste demonstrated greater respect.

Gardiner made the sign of the cross at the hallway where Wriothesley and the soldiers had just been. He lingered over the emptiness before turning back to the window to monitor the situation.

What he saw chilled his blood.

The King was holding out his arms. The Queen smiled and moved toward the embrace. After receiving a kiss on the forehead, the Queen settled back, a gentle smile on her face. What had happened?

It was then Wriothesley appeared, the signed warrant in his outstretched hand. He spoke, and the Queen paled and brought her hand to her mouth.

The King grabbed his cane and slowly pushed himself to standing. He turned, and Gardiner gasped at the rage on the King's beet-red face. His yells of "Fool," "Knave," and "Beast" could be heard even from this distance, and then he raised his cane and brought it down again and again on Wriothesley's shoulders. The Lord Chancellor's legs buckled and he dropped to his knees, covering his head with his arms to shield himself from the continuing blows.

It was the Queen who calmed the King, grasping at his doublet to get his attention. She put her arm through his and pulled him toward her. The King gave one last kick to Wriothesley before returning to his chair and waving his cane to dismiss the whole lot of them.

Nausea swept over Gardiner as he realized he too would be the target of this anger. The King and Queen had obviously reconciled. Gardiner had miscalculated.

Badly.

He pulled away from the window and scurried down the hallway back to his apartments. That would be the safest place for him until the King's anger blew over. Until then, Gardiner would be indisposed.

Back in his apartments, he stumbled over to the *prie-dieu* in the corner and knelt for guidance.

His thoughts roiled over how once again he had been used as a puppet. Once again he would be shamed before the rest of the court but privately reassured he was still one of the King's favorites, doing the King's work.

Resentment boiled up, and bile burned Gardiner's throat. Over and over the King had prospered others before Gardiner. It was not right.

Gardiner allowed himself to descend into fantasies of challenging the King, of retiring from court. But after several melodramatic scenes – all of which somehow led to his being taken to the Tower – he calmed down and realized the futility of such an approach. He could not challenge. He would not leave. He had to continue to represent the Church and conservative thought. This was his cross to bear.

Gardiner pushed himself to standing and walked over to the mirror. He donned a serene expression and tried out some responses. "My only concern was to make sure the Queen was true to you. If you are happy, then my job is done." That would work. "If your wife is more conforming to your will, I am happy to have been of use." Better.

This would be a temporary setback, he vowed. *I am not yet defeated.*

July 27, 1546—Whitehall Palace

A soft twilight obscured the King's giant bedchamber. The curtains were drawn, though not fully, while the candles had not yet been lit. The scene reminded Edward of an ancient mausoleum.

Edward ignored the stench assailing his nose and pulled his chair closer to the grand bed where the King lay propped up on pillows, overexerted from the beating he had administered to Wriothesley. Edward was thankful his return from Scotland had made him the lone exception to the King's instructions he not be disturbed.

The months had not been kind to Henry: he looked terrible, far worse than anyone had let on in letters that might have been intercepted. His face was puffy but seamed, his complexion sallow enough to turn any blush in his cheeks to orange. He wheezed and coughed and groaned with every breath. Only his eyes had gained strength; they were more beady and dangerous than ever.

"It does my heart good to see you, Sire."

"Why? I am old and sick and weak."

Edward ignored the petulance and smiled. "A statement belied by the way you overcame Wriothesley."

"Ha!" Henry roared. "I did deliver a strong punishment."

"I don't believe the Lord Chancellor will hazard such a risky feint again," said Edward.

Henry sucked his teeth. "It wasn't him, it was Gardiner. This was the second time that man has attacked someone I love. First Cranmer, now my wife."

Edward kept his face neutral. "I know you value his counsel, but I have never fully trusted him."

"Nor I," said the King. He braced his arms to lean forward on the bed then pulled out papers from the pocket of his robe. "Hand me that pen."

Edward picked up the quill and inkwell and brought them over. Henry dipped the nib and then made an *x* on the page with a flourish. "Done."

Edward squinted to see what it was. "Sire?"

"It is a list of all my councilors. With my notes."

Edward did not quite understand the purpose of such a list, nor why Henry would look so smug about it. "Notes?"

Henry leaned forward, his voice conspiratorially low. "I have started to compose the Regency Council. For my will."

His will? Was the King so near to death? Anne's letters describing the King's recovery from dangerous fevers had been carefully crafted to let Edward read between the lines. And the sight and smell of the King should have alerted Edward. But still he was shocked. "Your will? A Regency Council?"

Henry looked down, embarrassed. "I have been weak of late."

Edward focused on that fine line between commiseration and sycophancy that conversations with Henry increasingly required. "I had heard you were closeted much of the time from episodes with your leg. I know that is not your preferred state."

"I hid my illnesses from people. I don't want them to see me weak. I am arranging my affairs in case anything happens to me. My son will need help to govern."

"Pray God that day will be long in coming," Edward said quickly then turned the conversation to the key issue. "You think a council rather than a single regent?"

"There is no single man who could govern my kingdom as I do, no one person who has the judgment – and personal power. My son will be safer with a group of trusted advisors who will each have like and equal charge to rule collectively, by majority decision."

Edward felt as if he had been punched in the stomach. Edward should be the one to govern for the Prince, not merely add his voice to a group. But he stopped those thoughts, acutely aware of Henry's narrowed eyes carefully gauging his reaction.

This was clearly a test, but Edward was unprepared. The King admired – and rewarded – bravado, but he struck down all grasps for power. Would Edward expressing his disappointment at the news demonstrate his worth, or would it suggest disloyalty?

Choose, he ordered himself, but he could not. Instead, he sidestepped the issue to deliver the required reply. "Well, then I am glad Gardiner got a black mark from this. As I said, I don't trust his judgment. Or Wriothesley's, since you're making a list."

"Ha!"

With the broken tension came the better response. The real issue Edward needed to address, more than just his own vanity. "And I worry about Norfolk, who will surely try to seize control."

Henry narrowed his eyes. "The Council will stop him from doing that. Will stop anyone from doing that. All of you together will keep things evenhanded."

Evenhanded? Just the opposite. How could Henry not see the danger – he'd always distrusted Norfolk's pedigree as much as he'd honored it. "Norfolk is rich enough to bribe every one of the lords to get his way. And once he crowns himself Regent, what stops him from going further? Few men can resist the urge to power. Your son would not be the first boy to be killed in the Tower, nor even the second."

There. It was said. But astonishingly Henry shook his head. "Norfolk has always been loyal, despite many provocations. I cannot ignore that."

"I worry more about Surrey. His rashness, his vanity. And the love the people have for him. Surrey is the real threat."

"Some would say that about you."

Edward resisted the urge to shudder. "I have neither the ambition nor the bloodline. I exist only to serve you and your son."

Henry nodded. "And you will do so by providing the counterweight to the Howard influence. And giving your wise counsel. I have missed that of late."

Although Henry had closed the conversation, Edward had one last theatrical point to make. He placed his hand over his heart. "You are the head of the realm, the head of the Church, and the head of my family. You and your son will always have my unadulterated loyalty."

"I know." The King's lower lip trembled, which made his next words all the more unexpected. "You may leave now."

"Sire? Do you not wish to discuss Scotland?"

"Later. I would rest now."

Edward bowed out, his mind racing. Why a dismissal at such a time? Was it really fatigue, or a trick?

No matter, he told himself. This would be a good chance to plot with Anne. No Regent? Ridiculous. A kingdom needed a single ruler. Decisions needed an ultimate arbiter with a clear vision, not a shifting blend of selfish compromises. Power would inevitably flow to a single person, and a shared regency would favor Norfolk.

Edward had to overcome this shortsighted idea, had to make the King see how wrong he was. This had to be a slow build, a careful strategy. Every day, Edward would point out indications of Norfolk's power and then comment how the King was one of the few people who could curb it. Question whether Norfolk would try to overturn the King's will. Or Surrey.

Edward needed to create a thousand tiny drips, like a small stream carving a vast underground cave. That would be Edward's single-minded goal.

He only hoped he wasn't too late.

Chapter Fourteen

November 29, 1546—Winchester Palace

Since the twelfth century, Winchester Palace had served as the London townhouse for the Bishop of Winchester, much as Lambeth Palace housed the Archbishop of Canterbury. But while Lambeth was across the Thames from Whitehall, Winchester was across from the Tower, which was now used only for celebrations. Another slap.

Gardiner inclined his head to receive Wriothesley's bow. He needed to keep his composure, but it would not be easy. The reassuring glow of the magnificent Rose Window, a constant reminder of the historic importance of his own See of Winchester, would help.

Wriothesley had come to see Gardiner at Winchester Palace rather than wait for him to appear at a Council meeting. That told Gardiner two things: first, that Wriothesley thought this meeting important; and second, that he did not want to wait the week or two until the King's expected return to London. His Majesty had retreated to Oatlands Palace, as if on a progress, so that he could regain his strength through the hunt. A delusional goal, since he could no longer sit on a horse for long. Nowadays he would ride out only barely beyond the manicured lawn, and the beaters would drive the stags to him for slaughter.

"To what do I owe this visit?" Gardiner asked.

Wriothesley's eyes widened slightly at the lack of light banter. *Good,* Gardiner thought. Wriothesley had studiously distanced himself from Gardiner after the fiasco involving the Queen and was now courting the reformists. Well, there were consequences for betrayal. Wriothesley would learn that when Gardiner refused to accommodate him now.

"I come to ask a favor on the King's behalf."

Gardiner twisted his face into a wry smile. "I would be happy to oblige His Majesty. How may I do so?"

Wriothesley shuffled his feet and wrung his hands. He was clearly uncomfortable, and Gardiner reveled in the unspoken acknowledgement of guilt. The King, because of his deteriorating health, was obsessed with securing the throne for his son. Right now he was in the middle of a scheme to make his dominions easier to manage. It required those around him to make unfavorable exchanges of their properties, some more unfavorable than others.

Finally, Wriothesley spoke, the words coming out in an unending jumble. "You have seen the lists that I prepared with my lords Paget and Rich, of the properties you would cede and those you would receive in return. You have had a week to review the proposal but have said nothing. What is your response?"

Gardiner had indeed seen the lists. There were dozens of them, for every member of the Privy Council – they all were affected by this strategy, since they had all received generous gifts over the years. The last month had been consumed with this seemingly interminable process, the King opening the conversation then the person involved requesting a small tweak to soften the impact of the plan. But no such opportunity had been given to Gardiner. Indeed, Wriothesley's visit meant that none would.

"The three of you prepared these lists?" Gardiner asked.

"With the King, of course."

Gardiner doubted that. This was a Hertford ploy. The King didn't just want to expand his son's dominions, he also harbored hopes of renewing the attacks on Scotland to force the marriage between the Prince and the young Queen of Scots. This would require an infusion into his depleted treasury, and the reformists had once again dangled Church assets before the King's eyes. With all the great riches from the dissolved monasteries dissipated, that damned Hertford was looking to seize chantry lands from the clergy. From Gardiner. That was unacceptable.

Gardiner curled his lip. "I say that I will not discuss this matter with you. I did not hear this news from His Majesty, as his other councilors did. I do not trust your intent."

Wriothesley clenched his jaw. "My Lord, you are making a mistake. This will provoke an unfavorable comparison with Cranmer. The Archbishop was happy to surrender the advowsons of several rectories in exchange for a number of messuages."

Gardiner sneered. How dare Wriothesley pretend to advise him? This from his former ally was no more than currying favor with his new friends. "How much did Hertford pay you to say that to me?"

Wriothesley's hand found the hilt of his sword. Gardiner smirked, unimpressed. "Sit down, my lord," he said. "And calm yourself."

Wriothesley shook his head. "I am in no man's pocket, especially not Hertford's."

Gardiner waved his hand as if accepting the explanation. It was true that Wriothesley disliked Hertford, but that did not prevent collusion. Only a naive fool insisted on liking all his co-conspirators.

"If you say so," Gardiner said. "But I still insist that any discussion of this matter should take place between myself and the King. I do not trust this invention of the Council."

"This was not an invention of the Council, my Lord," said Wriothesley.

Out of habit, Gardiner opened his mouth to explain himself – that his refusal was intended to demonstrate to the King how untrustworthy Hertford was – but closed it just as quickly. He owed Wriothesley nothing. And with Wriothesley no longer an ally, it was safer to let Gardiner's refusal stand on its own than to take a chance that his words might be twisted.

"Good day," he said as he stood and curtly left with no further word, his heart warmed by Wriothesley's obvious shock.

November 30, 1546—Oatlands Palace

The handful of lords attending the King during this quasi-progress sat around the table in the Council room at Oatlands. Wriothesley had just arrived from London and had been describing to the Council his conversation with Stephen Gardiner.

For Edward, the revelation caused the small, dark room to be bathed in white light. His ears stopped hearing Wriothesley's words.

"I'm sorry, what?" Edward said before he missed too much. He needed these details; they were important.

"He called the request an invention of the Council," Wriothesley repeated.

Edward was nonplussed. What kind of lapse was this on Gardiner's part? Visions of Nicholas Carew filled Edward's mind. A man who had died from a similar stupid choice.

That didn't matter. This was Edward's chance. Much as he hated to act without the benefit of a well-considered plan, he needed to rise fully to this occasion.

"How dare he?" Edward's roar was loud enough to shake the room, and he quickly turned to bow to the King, who was wiping sweat off his blotchy face. "Forgive me, Sire, but this selfish insult to your person was more than I could bear."

William Paget quickly moved to calm things down. "Did he say why he came to that conclusion?"

Edward grimaced. Paget's question opened the door to an exculpatory explanation, which Gardiner, the lawyer, had surely offered. Edward berated himself for not speaking further and preventing this potential mitigation of the harsh facts.

"No," said Wriothesley. "Only that he thought this was a scheme by Hertford to deprive him of his lands."

Spoken as if Wriothesley were still friends with Gardiner. Edward's longstanding enmity for his old rival rose to his throat. He glared at the Lord Chancellor but willed himself to focus on his proper goal. His mind found his attack and he thrust hard. "These exchanges of land have been discussed for a month. Gardiner knew they were important to the King - vital to England - but still refused with only a flimsy argument."

"And I made him a generous offer." The King sniffed and wagged his finger at the men before using it to wipe his nose. "More generous than it needed to be."

"And still he sneered at it. At you," Edward said. "That is inexcusable."

"Actually, he was sneering at you, my Lord Hertford," Wriothesley said, falling right into the trap Edward had laid for him.

"I see how a simple mind might think that." Edward infused silk into his voice. "But in fact his words reveal his true thoughts, like a peasant emboldened to honesty by too much drink. He is not content with disregarding His Majesty's wishes or the safety of the realm, he also attacks the King's offer as mean."

"He overstepped," said Denny. Several other lords rapped their agreement on the table.

Edward opened his mouth to add more censure, then closed it just as quickly when he saw the King's lower lip tremble. Cromwell's old lesson still echoed in his mind. *When your argument succeeds, stop.* It always surprised Edward how few people were disciplined enough to follow that advice. Too many people were too fond of their own voices.

Right now Edward had no time for fopperies. No softness. No mistakes. Not now. He waited for the King's obvious verdict.

"Bishop Gardiner does not deal lovingly with me," said the King. His eyes hardened and his chin lifted. "I could have demanded a surrender, but I offered an exchange. By God, he will get nothing now."

"I believe we can find a method to authorize this measure through other spiritual and temporal officers. One way or another." Edward felt safe in saying that - Henry had, after all, seized mountains of Church property. There were precedents. "But he should also be required to submit."

"I care only for the measure," the King said. "As for the man, let it be known that I do not ever want to see Gardiner's face again. He shall not get the chance to mistreat me further."

The words sang like a choir in Edward's head. Without access to the King, Gardiner was nothing. One providential move had neutralized an important foe.

But would things stay that way? How serious was this ban? Now was the time for Edward to set the limits of this victory, before the King's anger faded. "Is he dismissed from the Council?"

Edward noticed Lisle and Denny hiding smiles behind their hands. They too knew that triumph was illusory without specifics. It was good to have friends who appreciated your finer moves.

The King shook his head. "It is the position, not the man, who sits on the Council. Gardiner may attend on days when I do not. But he will be banned from my rooms."

Edward stifled a curse. That left a chance for Gardiner to return to power. Unless Edward could make sure any access was completely barred.

His mind started the list. He would hold more Council meetings at Hertford Hall. Exercise constant vigilance – let nothing skip his attention.

Edward stood and whirled around to the door. "Guard," he called, a hand in the air, and the soldier was before him immediately. "The King has given instructions that the Bishop of Winchester is not to be admitted to the royal presence. Regardless of what Gardiner might try to claim, he is not welcome in the King's apartments or anywhere near His Majesty. Make this known."

The guard bowed and disappeared back behind the thick stone doorframe.

The room fell silent, complementing its darkness. A harsh contrast from the light and hum of words from the hall. The men listened for a while, then the King broke the spell. "Thank you, Edward. Thank you all." He beckoned to

Denny. "I would be alone now, to ponder this betrayal in private."

Denny jumped to his feet, but before he could approach the King's chair, the guard was back in the room.

"Have my instructions been relayed?" the King asked.

"Aye, Sire. The Bishop of Winchester shall be turned away without announcement. But right now Sir Richard Southwell is returned to court and begs leave to wait upon the Earl of Hertford after the meeting."

"Southwell," Henry called to the door. "Welcome. And explain why you do not beg leave to wait on your sovereign."

Richard Southwell was a great favorite at court, beloved by reformers and conservatives alike. Years earlier, when he had joined Cromwell's household as a tutor to Gregory, Southwell and Edward had become friends; but later, when Southwell took on offices in Norfolk - he currently served as that county's sheriff - he had also become close to Norfolk and Surrey. Southwell had not yet stepped out of this easy center to favor either side, but Edward was confident the man would prove loyal when the time came.

Southwell entered, clearly abashed despite the King's cordial tone, and bowed deeply. "I was not aware you were in attendance, Your Majesty. It does me good to see your face."

The King sniffed. "A good that you denied yourself - choosing to see your Council rather than your King."

Edward was not sure whether the King was joking. Normally this kind of banter would be jest, but in light of Gardiner's recent selfishness the King might have formed one of his sudden sinister opinions. Edward needed to save Southwell. Besides, such altruism was good politics. It was an effective strategy at court, to place people in your debt. Proclaim your own friendship before asking for evidence of theirs. Though not foolishly often, of course.

"A loyal man after your own heart, putting duty ahead of pleasure," Edward explained. The King loved to be seen as industrious and responsible.

The King thought for a moment then smiled. "I cannot

scold you for that. Come," he said, extending his hand.

Southwell was on his knees immediately to kiss the gold signet ring, lingering long enough that the King had time to twist his wrist to clap Southwell's cheek with a chuckle. "Duty ahead of pleasure. Good man," he said. Then he nodded to Denny to carefully lower his legs from their perch and wheel him out. The bandages were already badly discolored, after less than two hours. No wonder he was sweating so.

With the King's departure, the men grew quiet.

Southwell's eyes swept the room. His gaze hesitated at Wriothesley and his lips pressed together, then he shrugged and faced Edward. "I bring you greetings from your sister, whom I had the pleasure to see lately."

Wriothesley stood. "I will leave you to hear your family news."

Others followed him out; Lisle and Paget remained.

"So tell me," Edward began, sitting back and putting his boots up on the table. He raised a hand to signal the waiting servant to bring them wine.

"Elizabeth can wait." Southwell sat back, a smile playing on his lips. "You will be glad you saved me from the King's wrath."

"Will I?" Edward's tone was playful. "And why is that?"

Southwell looked pointedly at the page who was filling their cups.

Edward reached to take the jug. "We can do that," he said, waving the lad away. "You may leave us."

When the door was closed and their privacy assured, Southwell picked up his cup and looked at its contents. "I had occasion to call upon the Earl of Surrey at his home in Kenninghall. The Earl seems to think he deserves a higher estate than he has."

Edward's levity scattered like quail before a hawk. He placed his feet back on the floor and leaned forward. "Oh?"

"He told me he thought his father should be sole Regent if the young Prince were still a child when aught happened to the King."

Thank you, thought Edward. Southwell would add another voice confirming Edward's warnings to the King. "That does indeed take precedence over news of my sister. I have been trying to persuade the King that Surrey believed this; I am happy to have this proof. Will you come with—"

"If wishes were horses, then beggars would ride," said Lisle, cutting in. "We need more than this or the conservatives will tear the argument apart."

Southwell's lip twitched. "Ah, my Lord, I might dismiss it too, except he took the matter much further. He was quite free with his explanation of why that was the case, as if seeking advance support for a scheme he planned to launch."

Lisle shook his head. "This still is not proof of a treasonous intent. Not without more."

"There is more," Southwell said. "Much more. Our good Earl has had a new shield painted for his Great Hall, and it includes the arms of King Edward the Confessor."

Only the reigning monarch or his heir was entitled to use those arms. This was an assertion of royalty.

"The Confessor?" Edward's voice was a whisper.

"Nor did he seek to hide it," Southwell added. "He said it was his heritage, and asked if I would have him deny his bloodline."

Lisle raised a hand. "Wait a moment. The Earl of Surrey has long quartered the Howards' cross crosslets with the leopards of England. This is pretension, yes, but not treason."

Despite Lisle's doubts, Edward felt himself shaking. This news took Surrey's head half off his neck.

"Nay, my Lord," said Southwell, "this is not the heraldry we have all seen. This shield had the arms of England in its first quarter."

The first quarter. Not an escutcheon of descent, but the escutcheon of claim.

Paget whistled tunelessly, eyes unfocused. "I would have thought him smarter than that."

"I as well," said Southwell. "I even challenged him. I

said the second quarter would have been enough to show his line, and the King might not trust such a sudden change."

Edward could not help but admire Southwell's technique: a sentence that could work for divergent audiences. The King would hear condemnation where Surrey would have heard a friendly warning.

"And did those words not move him?" Edward asked.

Southwell sneered. "He probably hoped his sister would persuade His Majesty to forgive the act."

"His sister?" asked Edward. "Why would he look to the girl to persuade the King? The family relationship is all but gone." Surrey's sister, Mary Howard, had been married to Henry FitzRoy, the King's bastard son, and when the lad died she lost most of her influence.

Lisle answered, his voice matter-of-fact. "Over the summer, when their Majesties...er...quarreled, Surrey suggested his sister seduce the King so she might better rule here as others have done. Those were his words."

"How did I not know this?" Edward was furious over the opportunity that had sat wasted for so long. "The King would find this abhorrent." The marriage had never been consummated because of the couple's youth and the boy's frailty, but the idea was repugnant nonetheless.

"Are you surprised a Howard would try a third time to dominate the King through one of their own? I thought you knew."

"No."

Edward sat back in his chair, shaken by a mixture of awe and fear over the ammunition that had just dropped into his hands on this glorious day.

First Gardiner, now Surrey. Edward felt faint from the good fortune that had been cast his way, and he wished he had a moment to compose himself. He didn't want to miss a piece of this wonderful puzzle.

Surrey's reckless arrogance – and his impatience – had offered Edward a marvelous gift. This was everything he needed to condemn the Earl – especially with Gardiner neutralized through his own stupidity. This time Edward would show no mercy. "Was his father, the Duke, aware of the plans?"

"He surely saw the shield," Southwell answered.

Edward let the words fade into the air, savoring them like the final note in a *pavane*. Failure to report treason had killed Sir Nicholas Carew, Margaret Pole, and so many others. Norfolk would die for this.

Paget squirmed in his seat and spread his arms out across the table. He looked at Edward, pain in his eyes and as much sweat on his brow as the King had recently shown. "My Lord," he began, and Edward found himself exchanging confused glances with Southwell and Lisle. "I had a conversation with the Earl that did not seem harmful at the time but in light of this information must be disclosed."

Edward's pulse quickened still further, and he feared his heart would explode in his chest. *More ammunition?*

"When the King was ill last month, Surrey told me he hoped to see the idea of the Regency Council abandoned."

Paget's revelation would add wood to the fire, but it did not warrant this kind of fear. "And so?"

"You too fear the Regency Council is unwieldy. We all do. I thought it no more than that and did not want to condemn a friend."

Edward patted Paget's hand. While it wasn't much, Paget's discretion then would make his revelation more inflammatory now.

Paget screwed his eyes together. "I should have known it was more sinister when he mentioned he would see me as Lord Chancellor if the matter were up to him or his father."

There it was. Surrey had actually started to form a council. He was a dead man.

"I thought at the time it was pure flattery," Paget continued, "but now I see the potential of something more serious in his words."

Surrey was right: Paget was an important ally. Edward needed to echo some of that praise. "While the flattery might have been well deserved, I believe there was evil behind it."

"He also mentioned a private meeting with the French Ambassador."

More evidence. This day had handed Edward a dukedom and the keys to the kingdom.

"We must investigate this matter formally," said Edward. "We must investigate all his dealings." He pointed to Southwell and Paget. "You will both need to testify to these matters."

"Of course," they said in near unison.

"But we must act immediately," Edward continued. There was no time to waste. Delay would soften the royal outrage – he needed the King's anger to explode.

"Before an investigation?" Paget asked.

"We have two different sources with damning testimony. This is more than enough for His Majesty. The investigation will be for the prosecution to undertake."

Southwell rose. "I am ready now."

Edward turned toward the door to the King's chamber. Lisle followed quickly, the others more slowly.

"We pray the King will allow us a moment of his time," Edward said to the guard.

The soldier nodded and knocked at the massive wooden door that was locked against the world.

It took a long moment before Denny popped his face out. "Yes?"

"Will His Majesty see us? It is important."

Denny looked back and mouthed something to the King before nodding and opening the door to them.

As they entered the room, Edward was struck again by the strength of the stench. He had not noticed any abatement when the King left the Council room, but being closer to it again made it hard to breathe.

The King was propped up in bed with a small bottle of rhubarb clutched in his hand. He had been taking these tinctures for years to mitigate the excessive yellow bile of his choleric disposition, but now his doses had multiplied drastically – enough that the royal accountant had questioned the expense. Edward had instructed him to keep quiet, lest anyone else grasp how sick the King was. The telltale red stains on his fingers were harder to hide, though it was easy to imagine the Almighty was creating a physical sign of the blood on his hands.

Henry took a swig and wiped his mouth with his sleeve. "What is so urgent?"

Edward quickly relayed the basic facts himself. While he longed to make an emotive argument, he kept his recital dry so the King would not suspect manipulation. Though he did allow himself dramatic pauses for effect.

The King questioned the others to get more details from their stories. The telltale vein in his forehead throbbed blue, and the royal face deepened to purple. "By God, they presume too far."

Success.

"I want them seized immediately," said the King. "Have Wriothesley do it."

That meant Norfolk would be arrested by a former friend. Was that more or less hurtful than being arrested by a longstanding enemy? It didn't matter; the result was the same.

"You were right about Norfolk," Henry said to Edward after another swig and wipe.

Most men would console right now. Edward would not make that mistake. Instead he would use as a weapon a piece of information he had long ago discarded. "He always did aim high. Surrey too. Remember how it was rumored he desired your daughter? Whether or not it was true, it says something of his hubris that men would believe it of him."

"Praise God that Southwell saw evidence of his perfidy," Henry said.

"And praise God that honest men will come forward against their interests," said Edward.

"You will all be richly rewarded for this. And Norfolk's own holdings will pay for it, every penny." Henry's voice was a snarl. "God blesses my endeavors, as you know."

Edward's heart began to race. Norfolk was the richest

man in England after the King – perhaps even before, since the Duke's purse did not open as easily. The day he was attainted, all his lands and titles would default to the Crown. The Treasury would be restored, and the boy's reign would be assured – even Henry could not spend so much money that quickly. And the spoils would be huge, especially for a sole Regent, which Edward was now more likely to be.

Now to finish the job.

December 2, 1546—Winchester Palace

Stephen Gardiner stood with his nose high, fully ready to receive Thomas Wriothesley back to Winchester Palace for the second time in two weeks. Obviously, the Lord Chancellor had decided not to wait for Gardiner to attend a Council meeting. Since the King was expected in only two or three days, they must be getting desperate to steal his lands before then, parade their victory. They were dealing with the wrong foe.

Wriothesley entered the Great Hall and gave barely a nod. Strange. Few people were unimpressed by the room, no matter how many times they'd seen it. Even Gardiner was still thrilled by it every time he saw the fine tapestries that lined both walls along its hundred-foot length, and the books housed on both walls of its forty-five-foot width. But Wriothesley's eyes remained directly ahead of him, unmoved.

Nor did Wriothesley give any further reaction as he approached Gardiner's dais, the one the Bishop cherished for just these moments. The raised platform featured a chair that dominated the seat on the floor in front of it: a reminder of the imbalance of power that would afflict any visitor – unless Gardiner specifically negated it. And this time he would not.

Thwarting Gardiner's silent message, Wriothesley ignored the seat and instead chose a posture of power, legs spread and his fist on the hilt of his sword. Gardiner lifted his chin against the attempted intimidation.

His face inscrutable, Wriothesley began. "You have been absent from the Council, my Lord."

The Council. A ragtag bunch of people whom the King had left behind in London. None of them friends to Gardiner. "The King is away. The real Council is with him."

Wriothesley screwed up his face as if he tasted something bad. "Both Councils have been busy. This morning I detained the Duke of Norfolk and the Earl of Surrey."

The unexpected announcement sucked the air from Gardiner's chest. Detention was death. Surely Wriothesley had used the wrong word. "Detained?"

"They are being held at my own Ely Place for questioning."

"What?" A mental image seized Gardiner: his palace bricks crumbling into a pile around him. Destruction. Utter destruction.

"It is said Surrey aimed too high and plotted to overturn the King's plan for a Regency Council. If you have any information about this, you should share it with me now."

Gardiner's attention was caught by movement at the end of the hall. Wriothesley had brought soldiers with him. Ten armed men had entered the Great Hall and were lined up at the door.

Gardiner wondered whether he was in danger, but try as he might he couldn't see how. He had not been part of any plot and had no information. Still, the sight of the men was unsettling. Suddenly his chair seemed a feeble feint.

Gardiner brought his focus back to the more immediate issue. What the devil had Surrey done? "Overturn? How?"

"Surrey intended that he and his father would take control. Of the Prince and of the realm."

Gardiner's lawyerly mind twisted around this explanation and calmed his terror. The charge was nebulous; it sounded fake. Another Hertford plot? Probably. And an unartful one at that. This was not something that could pull Gardiner down. It shouldn't even pull the Howards down, if Gardiner was skillful. "I know the Earl of Surrey – and of course the Duke – have hopes of being included on the Regency Council when the King determines its members; the world knows of their great pride in their lineage." He nodded for a dramatic pause. "I also have heard the Earl speak – we have all heard the Earl speak – of his preference for somehow giving preeminence to his father's sound judgment." Gardiner paused and shook his head. "But that is a far cry from treason. I will want to hear more specifics before I believe such evil of him."

Wriothesley, a lawyer himself, smirked. "That is fair. I had not yet mentioned the alleged ambition was accompanied by action."

"Action?"

"Surrey did his best to solicit accomplices in this goal. If he had such conversations with you, it would be best to reveal them now."

Accomplices? Again Gardiner felt as though Wriothesley was trying to trap him, though again he could not see how this would be possible. "Any good advisor will discuss ideas with members of the Council. That is statecraft, not treason."

"Except Surrey also quartered the arms of Edward the Confessor on his shield."

Gardiner's knees buckled, and he grabbed behind himself to make sure the chair would catch him. Why would Surrey do something so stupid? That was unlike him.

Maybe it isn't true. The thought burst fully formed into his mind like Athena in her armor. Surrey was ambitious, but he would never be so overt about dangerous aspirations. No one would. This had to be a Hertford plot. But how far did it go?

"And Norfolk? What did he do?"

"He did not report the crime."

Maybe he hasn't seen it, Gardiner thought. Athena parried her sword. This might be one of the King's deadly games: allowing a favorite to face a threat and then turning the tables on the accuser. Finally, Gardiner was not on the troubled side of that pattern. Norfolk would escape this trap, as had Cranmer and the Queen before him. Gardiner would help him - and destroy Hertford in the process. "I must speak with the King."

Wriothesley's eyes steeled. "You do not seem surprised by this revelation. You knew of this?"

A wave of nausea came over Gardiner as he realized his enemies would try to use even his lack of condemnation against him. How could he have missed that trick? Especially after Wriothesley had not initially mentioned the shield in his explanation of Surrey's arrest. He had deliberately withheld information, as if interrogating a common criminal.

"Of course not." Gardiner kept his voice haughty to lend credence to his words. His enemies would pounce if he showed fear. "I just cannot conceive that the Duke would be a party to treason and—"

"But you conceive the Earl might?"

Gardiner drew himself up. "This is the second time you have tried to trap me. I have done nothing wrong."

Wriothesley shook his head. "That was the second time I gave you the chance to supply an explanation that will satisfy the Council. You give me credit for nothing, despite all my years of loyalty."

Gardiner wrinkled his nose at Wriothesley's melodrama. "You know me well enough to know I work within the law. I have nothing to fear. Enough that I intend to speak to the King on this. Someone has to give voice to reason."

The annoyance returned to Wriothesley's face and he shrugged. "The King will not see you."

"Of course." The King was at Oatlands, and when he did return to Whitehall he would want a day or so to settle in. "But once he is in London and—"

"The King will not see you. That's another development you missed in your absence."

This had to be nonsense. More of Hertford's plotting. "What kind of development?"

"His Majesty is furious over your refusal to exchange the lands he requested. He says you love him little to treat him so uncharitably. I must say I understand his pique."

"The King is angry about that?" Again, mental bricks tumbled and white cliffs crumbled. And, again, Gardiner's lawyerly reasoning took over. "But I didn't refuse. I just wanted to speak with him first. As others had done."

"To negotiate?"

Wriothelsey's arch tone turned Gardiner's fear into rage. "How dare you? Is that how you twisted my meaning? Is that what you told—"

"I did no such thing. If anything, I gentled your words. This was the King's interpretation."

"Why was any gentling needed? Surely you of all people understand my accusations were directed at other councilors, councilors who wish me ill."

Wriothesley shook his head. "That is the problem. There was nothing ill in the proposal. You were no worse treated than anyone else, and far better treated than many. Yet you called the King a miser."

Gardiner cursed his mistake. That was an epithet people had once said of the King's father, a man from which this King had always distanced himself. Of course he would be angry.

Gardiner massaged his aching temple. "Who spoke for me? Defended me?"

"I did. And Sir Anthony Browne."

Two people. Only two people. And Gardiner had just attacked one of them. "I see."

Silence stretched between them until Wriothesley ended the moment. "I need no thanks. I will leave you now. You are still a member of the Council, so you have a chance to beg forgiveness. Perhaps a letter might soften him."

Wriothesley was right. A carefully crafted missive would offer the chance to explain. That was Gardiner's only hope. "Will you—" Gardiner began but Wriothesley ignored him and strode out.

The room felt strangely empty with him gone, but

Gardiner was glad he had left and taken his soldiers with him. The incident could have gone the other way far too easily. Gardiner was close to gagging over the danger he had just survived.

There was work to do.

Gardiner seated himself at his desk and centered a sheet of paper. Its whiteness intimidated him, and he had to force himself to begin. Context first. "Sire, with no opportunity of making suit to your presence, I beg pardon for molesting you with this letter. But molest I must."

He took a deep breath. Flattery and apology were next. "I have always esteemed your benefits and felt great joy in your favor. And if for want of circumspection my doings or sayings were otherwise taken in this matter of lands, I on my knees desire pardon."

Finally, he could explain. "I never said nay. I never intended to resist your pleasure but only to be a suitor, a position to which I was wrongly emboldened by past favors. I would gladly supply anything you want could I but have such help from you as others have had."

He sat back.

This was a good first step. The King would be back in London in a few days. Gardiner would prostrate himself at the first glimpse of the royal robes in the Council chamber, and hopefully end this terrible episode.

December 10, 1546—Whitehall Palace

The hallway in front of the King's apartments was empty, and Gardiner took the opportunity to approach the guard at the door. "May I wait on His Majesty today?" he asked as he did every day.

"Not today, Your Grace," came the reply.

Gardiner was about to complain but he heard voices approach, and he quickly turned away as if he had just left the apartments, then nodded hello to the arriving courtiers.

Gardiner walked over to a window and studiously

looked out its leaded glass diamonds as if an important answer were to be found among the white bricks of Whitehall Palace. Anything to fill the interminable hours.

He was cast off and at the end of his wits. He needed to see the King, then all would be well. But all paths were closed to him. Every day he came early to meetings of the Privy Council and stayed late in the vain hope the King would attend. Every day he was refused permission to wait on His Majesty, even before the request was passed on. And every day his panic grew.

But he couldn't let anyone see that. So he lingered in the outer chamber as if all were well, and told his rosary as if meditating on a question the King had asked of him. Anything to not seem excluded. It was important that people not recognize he was out of favor; that would spiral him downward all the faster.

Gardiner felt himself abandoned like Christ on the cross. There were no friends left around the King to defend him. Or Norfolk. There seemed no way to get back into favor.

For the hundredth time since dawn, Gardiner quelled his rising panic. He just had to hold on for a little while longer. The King would remember his faithful servant. He had to remember. He would.

Wouldn't he?

December 24, 1546—Whitehall Palace

Edward let himself into the apartments at Whitehall where Anne awaited him. These rooms were new to the Hertfords, larger than their old ones. They had been Norfolk's before his arrest, and every linenfold panel stirred thoughts of Edward's not-yet-completed political victory, inspiring both triumph and anxiety in him. Not that this was a surprise. Everything now inspired both triumph and anxiety in Edward.

Anne sat at the rosewood marquetry table in the corner,

in front of Norfolk's chessmen. But this was accidental, or perhaps prompted by spite, as she was sewing, not playing. She looked up when she heard Edward and smiled. "I'm glad you could come. The Queen has just decided to go on to Greenwich with Mary and not wait for the King. We leave within the hour, and I wanted to make sure I wished you Godspeed."

The Christmas season was traditionally celebrated at Greenwich Palace. Normally the court would have repaired there the week before, though the real celebrations would not begin until after Midnight Mass at Saint Paul's Cathedral. The service, celebrated by the entire city, would, more so than any others during the year, rely on the traditional superstitions. But Christmas was Christmas, after all.

Edward would miss his wife, though he was somewhat relieved to be free of the infectious nervousness that plagued her nowadays.

"Did the Queen expect anything different?" Edward asked. "Did you?"

"Of course not. But we all had to pretend we did."

The King was recovering from yet another fever. Like the others, it took a greater toll than its predecessors. Also like the others, its severity had been downplayed to the world.

Edward walked over and sat with her at the table. He picked up a castle and admired the fine carving of the jade. "It will be easier once you get to Greenwich."

Anne grimaced. "People will still ask where he is."

"The season's rituals are more for the people's pleasure than the King's. They care mainly for the music and feasts, the wine that flows in the fountains. As long as the Queen and Mary are there, no one will really question the King's absence."

"True." Anne bit her lip. "Besides, she can tell people he hopes to join the court for Twelfth Night."

"I don't think he'll make it." Edward looked around out of long habit and normal prudence. Speaking of the King's death was treason even if plans did need to be made. Especially if plans needed to be made. "He'll need more time than that to rise from this sickbed."

"He cannot stay away so long without rumors flying. They already are."

"Well, they would be worse if the King showed himself in his current state," Edward said. "If he recovers enough we can have him receive ambassadors at Whitehall and make much of those visits. But the celebrations would be too much for him – they'd make him look sicker by the contrast. And the travel alone would kill him."

Now it was Anne's turn to look around. "Pray God that does not happen before he signs his will. Will he do that this time?"

Edward was cautious. "Perhaps."

"How can you be so calm?" Anne's voice was a hiss.

Edward looked deep into her eyes, plumbing them for the understanding he needed. "Because power cannot be wielded by the fearful," he said softly. He could not let himself get any closer to breaking, even with Anne, or he would never put himself back together.

He sat back, and his voice became matter-of-fact. "The conservatives have lost their majority in the Council. The proper order will be preserved no matter what."

"The betting in London says Surrey and Norfolk will be acquitted. What if they regain the King's favor?"

Edward took a deep breath. "The King, thank God, is determined to strike Surrey down. He spends every waking hour on the legal case against him."

"But today Surrey is still alive. What if the King dies before the trial? The country will rise for the Earl, and he'll come after you like Simeon and Levi avenging Dinah. Surrey calls us low born and base now – and that's despite the King's protection."

Edward willed himself to remain calm despite Anne's rising panic. "To Surrey, even Tudor blood is base. That is why he is lodged in the Tower right now. But the King will live through the trial." Another thought came to him. "Did I tell you? Norfolk's wife and mistress both testified against him."

"His wife has hated him for years, but Bess Holland surprises me," Anne said. "That must have enraged the old Duke, another commoner getting the better of him. The only commoner, the only person, he ever really trusted."

"The world has gotten the better of him," Edward said. "The claims have been corroborated. The Duke and his son will be brought to trial and condemned to death."

Anne bit her cuticle. "I still worry London won't allow it."

"Just the opposite. The trial is the ultimate rule of law. No one can argue with justice, let the bookmakers say what they may."

"I know." She fiddled with her hands. "I hate to leave you. I worry things are not progressing the way they should. Is the King still determined to have a council rule instead of a regent?"

This topic was more sensitive. "Unfortunately, yes," Edward said between clenched teeth.

"But did you not explain to him the Council needs a figurehead to implement its recommendations?"

The faint sound of steps in the adjoining room. Edward froze.

"My maid, Catherine," Anne explained. "She is preparing my trunks."

Edward took Anne's hand and led her over to the window seat at the far end of the room. The alcove was a more private spot. Less to worry about. A wise man always minimized dangers, even when none were visible.

"It is not so simple. This is the very argument that landed Surrey in prison. I did offer the King a gentler version, and he argued everything would be implemented by the individual office holders - the Secretary, the Lord Privy Seal."

"But what about the vision for the country? What happens when the Council is divided? What then?"

Edward shook his head. "The King does not understand

that argument. No one has ever openly disagreed with him – not for long, anyway. And never vehemently."

"It is disingenuous for him to think this will not happen."

"Ah, but with Norfolk, Surrey and Gardiner neutralized, it is less likely."

"How are you not enraged over this?"

Her voice was a wail that pushed Edward over the edge, and he slapped his palm onto the window's stone jamb. "I cannot allow myself to be. And I cannot listen to this from you anymore. I must remain calm to be effective, how can you not see that? I want to be Regent more than anything, sole Regent, Lord Protector. I work towards it every day. What more do you want me to do?"

His head ached. He lowered it to cover his face and hide in the dark for a moment. He'd spoken treason. God help him if he had spoken the words to anyone else.

A soft touch on his shoulder. "Forgive me, husband. That was selfish of me. I should be giving, not seeking, reassurance."

Edward grunted, not quite yet ready to pick his head up and emerge, though happy his wife had calmed herself.

"I think I am eager to see Surrey dead because I see the situation differently than you," said Anne. "You see a dying man—"

"Hush." Edward's eyes flew open and he looked around to make sure the maid hadn't entered. The King was too suspicious right now to take any chances.

"We are safe." Anne swallowed and continued on. "You see the actions of a man concerned with posterity, of ensuring his son has the proper councilors around him. I believe the King wily enough to know that a government by committee can never work. He knows one man will rise to power. With the boy only nine, it is inevitable."

Edward knew this – it was why he was hell-bent on destroying the Howards. But Anne was saying something different. "And so?"

"I think it is more a question of timing. Of delaying as

long as possible until he can delay no more. Which is why I push you – we have learned how quickly his whims can change."

"But why delay?"

"If he names you – or anyone – now, he loses his power. He becomes irrelevant. This scheme is concerned with the now, not the later."

Edward considered it, and it did make sense. "What do you advise?"

"Start to share this interpretation with people. Start them thinking about who it is that should keep power for the Prince. You are the only logical choice. Once Norfolk is dead there is no one else powerful enough to do it."

"The topic is too sensitive while the King lives."

"So broach it without words. Let them see you at the King's side, speaking for him. Train them to listen to you now so they will continue the habit later. And when Surrey and Norfolk are dead, you can be even bolder."

He brought her hand to his lips then turned it around so it was cupping his cheek. She was brilliant. This would offer success with no risk to his head.

"Thank you," he whispered.

Chapter Fifteen

December 30, 1546—Whitehall Palace

Edward pushed another pillow behind the King to help him sit up more comfortably, then straightened without moving away from the great bed. It made for a powerful visual: him at the King's right hand while the rest of the Council amassed behind the footboard. Anne was right: this context would train people to accept Edward's authority.

"Gentlemen." The King wheezed and coughed then waved his hand as if nothing had happened. "I thank you for coming today for a most important event."

This was the moment. The King was finally ready to publish his will. And though it did not contain all the terms Edward sought, it was a step forward. Anne was right about this too. The document established a power structure only treason could deform. It omitted Gardiner, Norfolk, and Surrey – and Edward could improve things from there...

"Master Secretary, please read the document to this company."

Paget stepped forward and bowed. He turned to the group, cleared his throat self-importantly, and began. "'Remembering the great benefits given him by Almighty God, and trusting...'"

Edward's mind wandered during the lengthy preamble. He kept his eyes on people's faces, to gauge their reactions. He noticed with satisfaction the way their eyes flickered at the King's desire to be buried next to Jane at Windsor, another measure of his connection to the Seymour family.

All attention rose when the important portion began: the

appointment of the Executors and Regency Council.

"'All these shall also be councilors of the Privy Council with Prince Edward,'" continued Paget, "'and none of them shall do anything appointed by this Will alone, but only with the written consent of the majority.'"

Edward could feel the sidelong glances directed at him, but he kept his face serene. Fingers twitched as people counted up the names. Lisle, Paget, Denny... Yes, reformists outnumbered conservatives. Not by much, but it was enough. Majority vote with this list would give Edward control on all key issues.

When the list ended, Edward could see frantic questions behind the eyes of the witnesses who had been left off the list. But all the men calmed when Paget began a new paragraph and added new names to the mix. "'And the following persons shall be of counsel for the assistance of the foresaid councilors when required.'" Paget read the list of advisors, the consolation prize for those not chosen to rule. Southwell and Sadler were on it; so was Edward's brother, Tom.

Another list in which reformers outnumbered conservatives. Another list of friends.

Edward kept his face impassive as the gifts clause began and excitement swept the room. The King had promised the Howard lands, incomes, lordships and offices would be given away as rewards for loyal service. They had not yet been formally seized, but every councilor had dreams of riches.

Henry took a sheet of paper out of his pocket and handed it to Paget to read. Edward could see Paget's face fall and wondered what that meant.

"'Hertford shall receive a dukedom, Lisle and Wriothesley earldoms, Seymour and Rich baronies,'" read Paget.

His dukedom. With Norfolk attainted, Edward would be indisputably the most important peer in England – the only other duke in the land was Suffolk's nine-year-old heir. Edward smiled and nodded his thanks, first to the King and then for the congratulations of the others. He noticed their smiles were guarded now, waiting for more to be mentioned.

"'Hertford shall receive lands worth one thousand marks, Thomas Seymour three hundred, Lisle two hundred, Wriothesley one hundred.'"

More nods from the four men, but now the smiles of the others turned to grimaces as each heard his own number, all lower. This was a retreat from the King's earlier hints.

Paget lowered the sheet, done with reading, but still he kept speaking. "Sire, I urge you to consider that perhaps the rewards should be higher for some of these gentlemen. Also, the excellent Sir Anthony Denny has been omitted from this list. His long service to Your Majesty deserves some reward."

"Let me see that."

The King looked over the list and nodded. "Thank you. Yes, Denny belongs on this list. As for the amounts, consult with each other. Recommend the revenues suitable to the new honors and I will consider them."

The men looked around, relieved. There might be higher bounties after all.

Sir Anthony Browne added his own voice. "Sire, I fear that you might have made another inadvertent mistake. Bishop Gardiner is nowhere mentioned in this document."

Edward kept his face bland, though his jaw clenched. He had not expected this, and he should have. What if the King relented? Worse, what if the King relented before this entire company?

"Hold your peace," coughed the King, and Edward's nerves calmed. "I remembered him well enough, and of good purpose have left him out."

Praise God, Edward thought even as he again cursed his own lack of preparedness. It was hard to think of everything during these trying times. Too many moving parts, too many changes. Too many personalities, too much fear and self-interest. Too much of everything.

But still Browne persisted. "What purpose could that be, Your Majesty?"

Henry waved his arm. "He is of too troublesome a nature. I myself could use him, and rule him to all manner of purposes, but he would just cumber you."

"And yet—"

"Have you not done molesting me in this matter?" The King might no longer roar as loudly, but his menace had not diminished. "If you will not cease to trouble me, by God I will dispatch you out of my will. Let me hear no more of this matter."

Browne dropped to his knee and cast down his eyes. "Of course."

The King waved his hand.

"Would you like to sign it now?" Edward asked.

"Not yet," answered the King. "I will wait to hear the recommendations as to the gifts, then sleep and dream upon the matter."

Edward stifled a curse. Unsigned, the will was not enforceable. Though the reading aloud would preserve the gist of it, the comfort was cold. Gardiner was still a member of the current Privy Council, and Norfolk and Surrey were not yet condemned. The wheel of fortune was still in spin.

"Will you sleep now?" Edward asked before his thoughts could continue their descent.

"Aye."

"Thank you, gentlemen, for your service to the King," said Edward, implementing the implied dismissal - and reminding the men of his position as the King's chief advisor.

One step at a time.

January 13, 1547—Guildhall

Edward sat back in his judge's chair, his face stony. Despite the chill of the day, beads of sweat clustered on his temple, partly because of nervousness, partly because of the heat generated by the fifteen hundred bodies crammed into Guildhall's vast Great Hall to witness Surrey's trial.

The massive stone building, built by Henry IV on the site of a Roman amphitheater, was one of London's main gathering places, and its Great Hall had been used for many notorious trials. Nonetheless, this was the first time that a man of gentle birth had been tried here instead of Westminster; the choice was intended to remind the Earl that his title was merely a courtesy one; his father was still its substantive holder.

Cheers from outside alerted Edward that the Tower boat had docked and Surrey was arriving. A fearful number of people thronged the riverbank and streets, driven by their strong national pride for the inventor of the sonnet. Of course, Surrey had not actually invented the sonnet, only its rhyme scheme, but that was too fine a distinction for the masses who credited him with poetry itself. Hopefully that would change as a result of the trial – people hated traitors.

John Gage, Constable of the Tower, led Surrey to the defendant's stand where a chair had been placed there for him. It was one which Edward had chosen specifically because it was low, to shrink Surrey's stature and ensure that everyone in the room would be looking down on him. Unfortunately, Surrey kicked it aside, choosing to stand. Edward gritted his teeth over the aura of authority such posturing gave the Earl – and over the dashing figure he cut in the black satin coat, furred with cony, that Gage had given him to wear at trial.

"You are lucky Constable Gage gave you a new jacket for your appearance today," Edward said. "The muck from your old one would have been too offensive."

Murmurs spread throughout the room. The remark was intended to invoke Surrey's hapless attempt to flee: He had tried to escape his cell through the cistern that drained to the Thames – low tide left only two feet of water at the bottom of the shaft – but by chance the guards had noticed his cell was empty, or perhaps they saw his servant waiting with a boat, and caught Surrey halfway down. He tried at first to press on, but the space was too tight for him to gain ground, so he had no choice but to allow himself to be hauled back up, covered in sewage. News of the incident had quickly spread, and Edward was gratified at the way people were relaying the story. The episode would, of course, also form part of the prosecution's case – it was well known that only the guilty feared judgment – but Edward, impatient to tear Surrey down, was introducing it now.

Edward needed to burnish his own personal legend, and the worse Surrey looked, the better Edward did. It helped that he was seated at the center of the judges' table, presiding in the name of the King over a debased traitor. That was the image that would stick in people's minds. Again, Edward thanked Anne for reminding him to paint the proper political picture.

"And yet I was in better company in that shaft than I now find myself in," Surrey said.

Arrogant bastard, thought Edward. He still thinks he will get away with this.

Edward nodded to Wriothelsey, who opened the trial by reading the indictments. His voice was low, and the twelve jurors in the box to Edward's right leaned forward to hear. Lords and nobles, crowded in the other front benches, also leaned forward, and the throng in the vast space crowded hard against the bar. Edward could almost hear the wood release a soft moan against the crushing crowd.

"How do you plead?" Edward asked.

"Not guilty."

More murmurs from the crowd, though no one should have been surprised. Edward glanced at the high-arched ceiling that soared fifty-five feet above his head. The colossal figures of London's legendary guardians, Gog and Magog, winked back at him from atop their carved marble pillars. *Victory is at hand,* their eyes said.

"Proceed with your case," Edward ordered the Lord Chancellor, unleashing the prosecution that Henry himself had directed for maximum effect. Carefully assembled evidence, a case that even Cromwell would have admired. But somehow it fell flat again and again as Surrey responded to the charges with wit and character. Such was the magic of the Earl's name and the gilding of his tongue that he constantly seemed to overcome the evidence. Edward could not understand how there could be any hesitation in the face of such overwhelming facts.

Wriothesley's parade of witnesses included former friends of Surrey's, men who understood that Surrey was unsuited for power, that his tempestuous temperament would make him even more deadly than the King. The jurors, Norfolk residents under the law and therefore more likely to support one of their own, were careful to remain inscrutable; but the throng of Londoners – Londoners, for goodness' sake, not conservative northerners! – seemed persuaded by Surrey's rebuttals.

They nodded when Surrey argued that his father was indeed the most qualified person in the land, both on account of his services and his lineage, to be entrusted with the government of the Prince and of the realm. And when Surrey insisted on listing those merits and services in comparison with those who had been preferred to him, the crowd glanced sidelong at Edward.

They nodded when Surrey emphatically denied that, in furtherance of his plan of domination, he had exhorted his sister to lay herself out to please the King and gain his favor.

"Do you see this paper?" Wriothesley asked him. "It is written in your sister's own hand, signed and sealed by her."

Surrey looked down his nose at the document, a sneer curling his lip. "I see it."

"In it she swears before God that you pushed her to become the King's mistress." Wriothesley shook the paper in the air. "She claims you cajoled and harassed her to endear herself to the King, that you spoke of her wasted life."

"Will you condemn me on the word of a wretched woman?" Surrey asked. This time the crowd shook their heads.

They went back to nodding when Surrey swore that he had taken no treasonous action. But that was not a valid defense: action was not required for a conviction. The King in his wisdom had long ago updated the law to match the theological understanding that intent to sin was sin itself. Men's intentions determined their guilt, on earth as in heaven.

"What do you say to this confession, written and signed by your father and under his seal, where he admits that he is guilty of keeping secret your 'false acts' in using the arms of Saint Edward the Confessor, 'which pertains only to kings'?"

Edward hid a smirk. Norfolk had written his confession only that morning, throwing his son to the wolves in an effort to save himself. *Overcome this,* Edward silently challenged.

"These arms have been on my family's escutcheon for centuries, without challenge or impeachment. Will you condemn me for paint on a board?"

The jurors' heads shook, and the sight roiled Edward's insides. How could this be happening? It looked more and more as if they might acquit. And who knew what would happen then? Surrey and Norfolk – for if Surrey were acquitted, Norfolk could not be guilty – would steal the throne once the King died, if not before. Edward would be the first one they came after. He was beside himself.

The clock chime from Saint Lawrence Church announced the hour. Edward's panic mounted with every clang, and there had been many of them over the eight hours since the room had lightened with the rising sun. At long last, now that the sun was setting, Surrey was making his summation, his final plea. It took all of Edward's reserve to keep the rage off his face as insolence poured from the Earl's mouth.

"Gentlemen, I ask whom you would believe," Surrey said. "I am a true nobleman, brought here by inferior men. I would never lie, but the Hertfords, the Pagets, and the Lisles of this world would condemn their fathers for a piece of gold. I have honor; they do not."

Edward could not let that accusation stand uncensored before such a crowd, and he broke in. "Is that the same honor that led you to counsel your sister into whoredom, or propelled you down a shaft more suited to men's shit?"

That stopped the nods and started the whispers. Edward's hopes perked up, and he could see that Lisle too was excited by the crowd's reaction.

"Yes," Lisle added. "How can you claim honor when you tried to escape?"

Surrey's eyes flashed. "I tried to avoid coming into the very pass where I now stand. The fallen are always found guilty."

"Are you saying that innocent men can be found guilty? Is this your judgment of the King's law?" Lisle's tone was arch.

Edward looked at the members of the jury. "That arrogance should be part of your deliberations," he told them before giving them further instructions. He reminded them of the law, of the edict that stated that anyone, other than the King or Prince, who bore the arms of Edward the Confessor was a traitor. There should be no need for more.

Edward waited while they filed out, then stood to leave himself. It made him nervous to leave Surrey with the crowd, but he had no choice. Precedence was precedence, and Edward was not about to cede an inch of it to that cur. He nodded at the other lords, letting them know they were welcome to wait with him in the special chamber set up for the purpose, then walked out with his head high.

The room was arranged like a Presence Chamber, with Edward's seat on a raised dais at the end of the room. The men were thus forced to come wait on him as they would on the King.

Train them to listen to you now so they will continue the habit later. Again, Edward blessed Anne for words that had become a habit.

John Gage entered to report on the formalities that he had overseen. "My Lord," he said bowing, "the Earl of Surrey has been settled in a room of his own where he is close confined."

"See that he is watched," Edward said. "He may have friends in the crowd."

"The room is secure," Gage said. "The jury has also

been settled. They asked for wine, which I brought them. Though I must warn you, they don't think to be there long enough to drink it all."

"Oh?"

"They mentioned they expect to quickly acquit. They were uncertain with the strength of the case."

Edward's fear rose, but his rage shoved it aside. *How could this happen?* "Uncertain?"

"They mentioned to me that the evidence might not be enough for them."

Edward rose from his chair on the dais and went to stand directly in front of Gage, both to keep their conversation private and to heighten the threat. Their eyes were level with each other, and Edward leaned in until their noses almost touched. "Do they understand the King will accept nothing less than a guilty verdict?" he asked. "That he will question the loyalty of any man who disagrees?"

Gage's eyes widened. "But he ordered a trial rather than attainting Surrey directly. That means he expected that reasonable men might differ."

Idiot, Edward thought. "Just the opposite. The King ordered this trial as a courtesy to Surrey's Howard ancestors and to the people of London who might otherwise seek to excuse such a well-known figure. But the King has no doubt the Earl is guilty, and neither should the jury."

Gage blinked uncontrollably, and beads of sweat broke out on his upper lip. "I wish I had known this earlier, to mention it to them."

"Go tell them now."

"That would be intervention and I could not—"

Edward leaned in even closer to heighten the menace. "To not go could be far worse. For them and for you."

Fear swam in Gage's eyes and he moved away. "I will tell them what you've said." He bowed immediately and was out of the room in a blink.

Edward forced himself to breathe deeply to calm his racing pulse. He took papers out of his pocket and made a show of looking at them. He could not chance speaking with anyone right now, not in such a delicate state. Instead he let his mind range over the possibilities. Should he send a message to the King to solicit a further royal threat? What if the note didn't get there in time?

Too many minutes passed. Edward was not quite ready to emerge from the protection of his papers, but he could delay no longer. It looked wrong for him to be alone.

But all he had to do was look up and Paget and Lisle were upon him. "What did you say to Gage?" they asked in near unison.

"I told him the King expected a guilty verdict."

"And why did he look so surprised?" Paget asked.

"Somehow he did not realize it."

"But the King himself developed the questioning," said Lisle. "Everyone knew that."

Before Edward could act, word came back the jury was done. Edward felt a chill. Had Gage gotten to them in time?

"What did they decide?" he asked.

"No one knows, my Lord," the page answered. "No one ever knows until they announce it in court."

"Let us go there then." Edward rose and forced his knees to work despite their weakness. Fear clutched his chest, and he had to force himself to breathe fully. He needed to look as if nothing were amiss.

The Hall's two huge Gothic stained-glass windows were dark now, except for light from a spindly moon. Despite all the candles, the room seemed smaller. Gog and Magog, from atop their shadowy perches, now portended defeat.

Edward worked on calming his breath as the gentlemen of the jury were marched in. They glanced at Surrey as they entered, then pretended they hadn't. What did that mean?

The jurors took their seats; the foreman remained standing.

"What say you?" Edward asked.

"Guilty and he should die."

A thousand shocked murmurs of "guilty" echoed down the Great Hall as each spectator repeated the verdict for the people behind. A flood of relief surged through Edward's limbs. Surrey came unhinged. He pointed at Edward but looked back at the mob, shouting. "The King wants to get rid of all noble blood around him." He had clearly expected an acquittal, was obviously hoping to incite revolt.

Gage motioned to two guards, who grabbed Surrey's arms and started to drag him away. As the other guards turned the blades of their axes to face him, he screamed and twisted back to face his judges. His bulging eyes flashed at Edward as if they could unleash a hail of arrows. But they couldn't. Surrey had lost. Edward prayed that his triumphant look would haunt Surrey just as Norfolk's face must have haunted Thomas Cromwell.

As he was dragged away, Surrey surged like a fish on a line and kept shouting. "He will have none but low people around him. This is a conjured league that has destroyed me." But the people did not react. They merely looked at him with a mixture of confusion and sorrow on their faces, as if the family pet had turned rabid and was being taken away. Such was the magic of the King's justice.

It was only when Surrey was dragged outside that his shouts seemed to have any effect on the crowds. But even then the response was less than expected. Calls of "be strong" and "God save you" were as far as people went. All those thousands who had cared enough to assemble, yet none but Surrey protesting. And the harder he fought the more they turned away.

Still Edward sat frozen, listening for sounds of uprising as if his intense concentration were helping to avert it. He did not move, he did not twitch. He would not leave the battlefield until every last ember was extinguished. Until then, the world would see him as steady and strong.

Finally the sounds of agitation died away, and Edward knew Surrey was securely in the barge, being rowed back to the Tower. It was over. Surrey would remain in that cell until his execution, which would not tarry.

Now for Norfolk.

January 23, 1547—Whitehall Palace

The King was propped up in his great bed, with books and papers strewn about. Edward, along with Denny, Paget, Lisle, and Browne, circled him, standing now but with their chairs close by. These were the King's closest advisors; they spent a lot of time around that bed.

The King's doctors had just filed in quietly; their voluminous scarlet coats formed a stark wall against further interruption as they waited patiently for the King to finish his conversation with Edward.

"Again you urge me to execute Norfolk?" The King's voice was silky.

Edward found himself holding his breath. The King believed more than ever that fear begat obedience, and no one could ever be sure if a question was a trap. But this was important policy and Edward had to push. Surrey had gone to the block on January nineteenth, but Norfolk still languished in the Tower. The King was still considering a courtesy trial, and delay was dissipating his anger. He needed to be pushed to a decision, and soon.

"I merely remind you that we lack a legal path to execute a traitor."

"I have a mind to commute his sentence to life imprisonment." The King's voice lilted and his eyes hardened. That signaled a snare and Edward backed off.

"That of course is your right. But before you may exercise that choice you need a sentence imposed."

It worked. Henry shrugged and picked at a tooth. "Send it to Parliament. Have them vote on it."

Warmth radiated throughout Edward's body, and he looked down to hide his elation. He didn't even want to show relief for fear of pushing the King back from this key line he had just crossed. Parliament would undoubtedly vote to convict, and then Edward would be only one royal bad mood away from securing Norfolk's death.

"I will inform the lords when I go to Westminster for the Council meeting later," Edward said, as if no urgency spurred him. "Unless you want to change your mind and hold the meeting here?"

"Not unless there is something that needs me. I would prefer to rest."

"There is nothing on the agenda that would require your advice," said Lisle.

Lisle had wormed his way into the King's inner circle right before these latest bouts of illness. As the newest member of the core group, he had the spot at the foot of the bed. But he was visibly grateful just to be there, since few others were even allowed into the King's apartments: only a small number of servants, a severely reduced number of the Gentlemen of the Privy Chamber, plus such of the Council as Edward invited.

"Enough talk of death," said Doctor Wendy, the King's most trusted physician. "The King must turn his mind to pleasantries so that I may properly measure his humors."

As Wendy began his examination, an unexpected knock jolted the door to the King's apartments. Everyone jumped. Edward exchanged glances with Denny before going over to see who it was.

He noticed with satisfaction that the flute player in the antechamber had not stopped his soft playing. It was no more than the proper choice, but Edward nodded at him anyway as he passed him. He opened the main door a crack to see what was wanted.

"The Lord Warden of the Cinque Ports, my Lord," said the guard. Then at Edward's blank stare, "Your brother."

Edward had indeed forgotten Tom's latest title, the one the King had given him to avoid anything greater. He blinked. "Here?"

Thomas Seymour stepped confidently forward. Edward smiled cautiously, glad to see him though concerned about the havoc his arrival would automatically wreak. Tom did have a tendency to roil things up.

The face that smiled at him was older, wiser, the reddish beard longer. His skin had toughened though his clothes were still as showy. Of course, between Tom's semi-exile to keep him away from the Queen, and Edward's stints in Scotland, it had been almost two years since they had seen each other.

Edward embraced his brother, determined to be glad for another ally, before shutting the door behind them.

Tom's nose crinkled from the stench the scent of rose oil and ambergris could not mask. His eyes darted around the room. The drawn curtains lent a somber air, and the random candles lit the distressing disarray caused by the deliberate paucity of servants allowed to witness the King's decline.

"How goes our brother, the King?" Tom said. "I understand he is recovering from his last fever. This one quite short."

Words that could be overheard. *Good.*

"Shorter than the last one," Edward answered in kind. "He was well enough to receive the French Ambassador only six days ago. This fever came on him then resolved in five days."

That was the politic way of putting it, the way they chose to look at it when in the King's presence. They did not mention the fact that these bouts might be shorter but the time between them had almost disappeared. It was dangerous to speak of such things..

Denny, Paget, and Lisle emerged from the bedchamber for an embrace. "It is good to see you, my Lord," said Denny.

"You come at a good time," said Lisle. "The King is improving."

Tom smiled. "My brother was just telling me that. It was a comfort to hear. May I see him?"

"His doctors are with him right now. I'll let you know when they're done."

"Perfect. I will give family news to Edward in the meantime."

"We will be in the library," said Edward, well aware that Tom cared nothing for family. Tom cared nothing for anyone but himself.

The library had only one entrance; they would not be overheard. Tom undoubtedly wanted news, news beyond the letters that were carefully crafted to attract no notice when they were read by spies. It was good they would have this opportunity before Tom saw the King. It would help Tom react appropriately.

Tom chose a chair that was closer to the door than Edward would have liked and immediately put his feet up on the table. Not even ten minutes and already Tom was annoying his brother.

"That looks disrespectful."

Tom shrugged. "And who will see me?"

Edward slapped Tom's boots, and he had the grace to lower his legs. Edward immediately poured himself a cup of wine, as if to take control of the situation. He breathed deeply to calm himself so that he could begin.

Instead, Tom smacked his lips appreciatively and took matters upon himself. Of course. "So I saw Surrey's head on its spike above the Tower. Why is his father's not next to it?"

"It will be," Edward said between clenched teeth, questioning his earlier assessment that Tom looked wiser.

"Are you sure?" Tom's voice was haughty. "Well, now that I am here I can help."

Edward pulled himself back from his annoyance. There were more important things to discuss. Tom was not entitled to set the agenda. "What are you doing here, anyway?"

Tom swallowed his wine and poured himself another cup. "I came because I heard the King was—"

"Tom!" Edward quickly interrupted.

Tom rolled his eyes. "Sick. I also heard that no Regent has been chosen for the Prince, but rather that a group of councilors will share power. And you couldn't even squeeze me onto that Council?"

Edward pressed his lips together. "I tried but the King refused."

Tom banged a fist on the table. "I want to be on the Council. You need me on the Council to vote with you."

"You *are* one of the named advisors," Edward said. Tom shook his head. "That's not enough."

The truth was, Edward really could use another vote on the Council – it was the body that would have to vote him in as Lord Protector – but the King had been adamant. So adamant that Edward thought it better to wait until Henry was in a better mood. With Tom here now, able to add his own plea, they might have a chance.

For a second, Edward considered hinting at his plan to seize power. But the plan was treason.

"The King is ready for you." Denny's voice at the doorway made Edward jump. Thank God he had kept silent. Edward took a surreptitious breath.

"Thank you," said Tom. On their way to the bedchamber, he looked over his shoulder at Edward. "If you will not help me, I will help myself."

The King was speaking when the three of them entered. Lisle and Paget nodded briefly without taking their attention from the King. Doctors Wendy, Owen, and Heycke glanced over at Tom, stretching their grim faces into an approximation of a smile.

"Your Majesty," Tom declared during a lull, narrowing his eyes at the sight of the weakened King and the white mound of diseased flesh he'd become.

Henry was the only one to ignore the greeting. Tom went to the side of the bed and planted his feet wide, arms akimbo. He remained silent, complying with protocol that demanded he delay further conversation until the King acknowledged him, but his pose commanded attention. Edward groaned inwardly over his brother's lack of judgment.

Doctor Wendy stopped talking and looked at him, and the King slowly followed suit.

"There is the royal fighter," Tom's voice boomed. "The most valiant of the English soldiers. No fever can get the best of you. Please God, none ever will."

Henry smiled, and Edward was both relieved and resentful that his brother's jovial nature once again had allowed him to get away with behavior that should have been chastised.

"Your tongue is as silky as ever," said the King. "If these are the compliments you give, no wonder you fared so well as our ambassador these past years."

Tom bowed with a flourish. "I must say, Sire, it is easy to compliment you. I have to work much harder to find virtue to highlight in others."

The King laughed and the rest of them bleated along.

"I am surprised not to see the Queen here, giving you special comfort," said Tom, always ready to pander to the King's appetites.

The King's eyes narrowed. Did he still view Tom as a rival for the Queen's affections? Tom must have seen the change too, since he continued with a different tack. "Or do your doctors tell you to conserve your energy? Not that you know how to rest - I see all your books and work beside you."

"There is too much to be done to rest," said the King. "Did Edward tell you? I want to war on Scotland in the spring. I will not rest until their young queen is married to my son."

"It will be a glorious day," Tom said, "when the two nations are united."

Henry's lower lip trembled with pride, as if he would be the one to straddle that double throne. "It will indeed."

"And you should consider finding a husband from Spain for Mary - or at least pretend to. The Emperor would be pleased with that plan, and in a single move you could completely isolate France."

"Ah Tom, your strategy is sound."

"If it is sound it is because I learned it from Your Majesty, and I thank you for it. I also thank you for making me one of the Prince's advisors, as much as I pray the day will never come when I am needed."

The King waved a finger. "I was thinking more about that list." He turned to Edward. "The Queen's brother, the Earl of Essex" - he took a breath, as if working up to the next words -"move him from the list of advisors to the Council itself. The boy will trust his uncle."

"Excellent idea," Edward said. "It will give him great comfort to have his family around him. Shall I do the same for Tom?"

The King struggled. "No," he cried as a paroxysm of coughs overcame him. Edward rushed to get him some water and help him drink.

Tom's face drained of color. *Good,* thought Edward. Tom had never believed that the King dismissed his abilities. Now he'd seen it himself.

Finally the King relaxed into his pillows, eyes closed. "Where were we?"

Edward's stomach tightened. This was the time to be bold. "You were just giving instructions that Essex and Tom be added to the Regency Council."

The King shook his head. "No. Tom has no judgment."

"His diplomatic skills served you well in Brussels and Vienna. His acquitted himself well with his command of your army. He was rash when he was younger, but he is seasoned now. He will be a good addition."

Henry was silent.

"Our brother will be a good addition," Edward repeated.

Henry waved his hand in a gesture that could have indicated either agreement or disagreement. Edward was at a loss. Retreat or pursue? Instinct told him to retreat, that he had more important issues than Tom's advancement. But this was a small step that might pave the way for other achievements, the important ones. This had to be the time to act. Especially with Tom watching. Edward had to show his brother he was trying, had to earn his trust. And support.

"Thank you, Your Majesty. I will make sure Essex learns of his own good fortune as well."

Denny looked at him sharply, then back at the King, who did not react at all to Edward's apparent victory. Lisle was quick to speak up. "Perhaps Seymour should swear his oath at the Council meeting?" he asked.

The King remained immobile.

"Yes, thank you," Edward said. "In fact, we should leave now and let His Majesty rest."

The King waved a hand again to send them off.

Edward caught Tom's eye and lifted a single eyebrow.

January 26, 1547—Whitehall Palace

Everyone's whispering blended together in the King's bedchamber. Everything was subdued, quiet, with flute music in the background to lull the soul and distract from the suffocating reality.

The King had not left his bed for days. He no longer scolded them for speaking among themselves and not directly to him. He was too tired to be bothered. He was often too tired even to sit up.

Edward sat in his chair at the King's right-hand side, reading aloud once again the proposals for provisioning the army in Scotland that spring. The King would immediately forget the details, but he never tired of hearing them. His main pleasure came from planning the invasion; it distracted him from his pain and often lulled him to sleep. Denny sat to the King's left, adding an "Oh?" or "Ah" here and there to demonstrate his involvement.

They all startled when Paget ran into the room, waving a large sheet of paper covered in seals. "Parliament has finally delivered the Act of Attainder against Norfolk."

Norfolk had been attainted. His titles and properties were now forfeited to the Crown and available for distribution. More importantly, his head could now be severed from his body. Edward's heart pounded. Unfortunately, the King still needed to assent.

Edward turned toward the King. His beady eyes opened and nostrils flared. He looked like a raptor about to choose his prey. Edward prayed it was Norfolk, but the King might equally turn on Paget for interrupting. Or Edward for ceasing to read.

"Sit me up."

Edward and Denny grabbed the King's fleshy arms and pulled while Paget stuffed pillows behind him, gradually building up support.

"More pillows," the King demanded.

They added more as the King squirmed to find a comfortable position, slapping at the cushions. Bedsores on his buttocks had joined the ulcers on his legs, and there was no way to console him anymore. Or to dampen the stench of rot more appropriate to a three-week-old corpse.

"Enough," the King grunted, his face waxy. "What day is it today?"

"Still Tuesday, Sire," said Denny.

Another grunt.

"We should discuss Norfolk," said Edward.

"Not now. I have urine to make. Get my physicians."

Another delay. Edward stifled a groan but quickly calmed himself. The attainder was less than two hours old, the wax on its seals barely hard.

Paget turned and ran but stopped at the doorway. Doctors Wendy and Ayliffe were waiting in the Presence Chamber, expecting the call, and came immediately to collect and inspect the liquid.

The King still bragged of his sanguine humor, easily diagnosed in his youth from his red hair, ruddy cheeks against white skin, and of course his enthusiasm and activity. Although he knew from his frequent thunderous outbursts that age had changed his temperament to choleric, he fumed when doctors addressed only that trait. It made treatment difficult at times.

John Ayliffe carefully dipped his little finger into the cup and tasted the liquid, eyes darting. He repeated the process twice. "Your urine tastes sweet, but there is a hint of sharpness," he said. "We could try more chamomile."

Thomas Wendy, Ayliffe's senior, shook his head. "But it is dark, almost green, and smells of hartshorn. That and the fish smell in his sweat calls for more rhubarb."

"I cannot take any more rhubarb than I am taking," said the King. "And I don't see any results. I want to be cupped."

"Not until the third phase of the moon," Wendy said. "It will do your blood no good until then."

"Then consult your books and find me something else. I will rest for now."

"Would you like to recline?" Wendy asked.

"No."

The doctors bowed and made to leave. Wendy signaled Edward and the others that he wanted to speak.

"Shall we allow you a moment?" Edward asked.

Edward took the royal grunt as agreement and bowed out as well.

Wendy continued through the privy chamber into the library before turning to speak to the men following him. He wrung his hands and glanced back at the gaping door to the bedchamber. He opened his mouth but then closed it, shuffling from one foot to the other and glancing again at the door.

"What is it?" Edward finally said.

"My Lord." Another glance. A deep breath. "We are commanded to try, but there is nothing we can do. I know it is treason to speak of the death of the King, but there comes a time when...it can't be treason if..."

They all waited.

"My Lord, there is nothing more we can do for His Majesty. He is failing rapidly. It is but a matter of days." Wendy bowed quickly and darted out, Ayliffe following close behind. The rest of the group gaped dumbly.

The unthinkable was at hand. The King was about to die. Edward cursed himself for not reading the signs. The King had been dying for so long that the true nearness of the event was a shock.

The familiar surroundings felt suddenly dreamlike. In the tapestry on the wall, Judith brandished the severed head of Holofernes and spurred Edward to act. He filled a cup of wine, then grabbed the King's Assent from the top of the pile on the desk and handed it to Paget. "Be ready to bring me this."

Moments later Edward was next to the great bed, his

face lowered to the King's. Edward's senses screamed from the fetid air that rose from the man's mouth and skin.

"Yes, Sire?"

The eyes opened and blinked.

"You called for me?" Edward asked.

"No...I..." The King looked confused. "Did I?"

"I thought I heard you ask for wine."

The King nodded. "I would like some."

Edward handed Henry the cup and waited until he had taken a couple of sips before coming to his real purpose. "Sire, you must give the orders about Norfolk. He has been attainted and should die."

"There is no rush," said the King. "I want to make sure the furor has died down."

"Sire, it has been two weeks since Surrey's execution; the moment is slipping away. If you tarry much longer it will seem that you pardoned him, and that will stir things up again."

The eyes blinked and watered a bit. "Fine. Sign it."

Edward turned to Paget, eyes blazing. "Did you hear that?"

The King had signed almost nothing with his own hand since September 1545. Instead, a dry stamp was used, a facsimile of his signature impressed on the document and then inked in. Paget had control of the dry stamp.

"I did," Paget said. "Your Majesty, it shall be done."

"And you are free now to distribute his properties," Edward continued. "I know you want most of them for your own treasury, but you mentioned you were still considering gifts for faithful servants."

"I was but I'm tired now. I will tell you my plans later."

Paget bowed and retired to the library to begin the formalities that signing for the King required. Edward and Denny followed him, watching. Trembling.

The second the ink had filled its borders, Edward grabbed the paper out of Paget's hand. Edward went straight to the outer door, to the guard whose eyes widened at the sudden appearance. "Take this to John Gage, Constable of the Tower. Hurry, man. Hurry if you love our King."

The guard took off. Edward exhaled. Norfolk would die within a day.

Edward suddenly noticed that no one was attending the King. *Damn,* Edward thought, but before he could go back Denny grabbed his arm.

"We should tell him. Much as I hate to take away his hope, we have to tell him. He needs time to prepare his soul."

"I agree with you in principle," Edward said, "but the King is loath to hear any mention of death, least of all his own."

Denny looked back into the bedchamber and shuddered. "How can we send him off to God unshriven?"

Denny spoke the truth, but Edward could not imagine having that conversation with his brother-in-law. It was still too dangerous - even now - to risk enraging him. He had just signed Norfolk's warrant, after all.

"Perhaps we could wait until the moment is closer," Paget said. He clearly didn't want to do it either. No one did.

"I'm sure the doctors delayed telling us," said Denny. "I'm going to tell him. In a moment."

He left the room in the direction of the privy. It occurred to Edward that his own bowels were roiling, but this was not the time. He looked at Paget, whose face was twisted as if something weighed on him. "Paget?"

Paget's words came out in a rush. "You mentioned the other day that Surrey was right to consider me for the post of Lord Chancellor. What did you mean by that?"

Edward shrugged, uncertain. "Your advice and counsel are worth more than anyone else's."

Another rush of words. "I could help you become Lord Protector. I think this is what the King wants. I think it is what he expects."

Edward heard a choir of angels sing. Paget was known to be a close confidant of the King's. His support would sway the others more than any other factor. "If you do that, I will listen to you before any other man. You will be my right hand in everything I do."

"I think your brother expects to occupy that place."

Edward shook his head. "My brother has learned that he must be content with far less. He will not displace you."

Paget opened his mouth to say something, but just then Denny returned and motioned to them to follow him into the King's bedchamber.

He went straight to the King's side. Edward and Paget glanced at each other and followed halfheartedly. They paused at the doorway, reluctant to enter.

"Sire," said Denny, "it is the opinion of your doctors that you are not likely to live."

The King's face did not change. "Is it?"

"Aye. It is time to prepare yourself for death, to recall the sins of your life, as becometh every Christian man to do."

The King was quiet for a bit. "The mercy of Christ is enough to pardon me all my sins, even if they were greater than they are."

Edward bowed his head, relieved that sanctimony had carried the day. The others did the same.

"Sire," Denny's voice was quiet, "would you like to see the Queen?"

Henry just shook his head. "I shall see Jane soon enough."

As always, Denny nodded as if the King's answer made perfect sense. "Is there any learned man you would like to confer with, to open your mind to?"

For a moment, Edward panicked. What if he called for Gardiner?

"I would have Cranmer."

Thank God, thought Edward.

"He is at Croydon," Denny said. "Shall I have him sent for?"

"I will first take a little sleep. When I feel myself again, I will advise you upon the matter."

The King's face was ashen, his voice reedy. Edward

backed out of the room and went to the outer door. "Send for Cranmer," he ordered the guard. That way he could be there when the King awoke, prepared for any request. He should have been with them all along. "Send for my brother as well."

After an hour or so the King awoke, exhausted from the rest he had taken. He waved a weak arm to call them over. "Cran...mer." Henry's voice was barely a whisper.

Edward leaned over to share that Cranmer was on his way, but the King's eyes were vacant. Edward started for the door to reiterate the King's request and add some urgency, but stopped when he heard the rustling behind him in the bed.

He turned around to see the King's arms and legs shaking, eyes bulging in fear. Edward took a cautious step back to the monarch. "Sire?"

The King's agitation continued and his mouth started moving. Was this the moment? Was the King even now staring into the abyss of the afterlife?

Again Edward tried to break through, to quell the terror. "Sire?"

The King turned to look but his gaze was unfocused, as if he saw someone else in Edward's place. What ghost haunted him so? Was it Cromwell? Anne Boleyn?

The lips continued to move and finally an agonized wail came out. "Monks."

That single word chilled Edward, and the hairs on his arms stood straight. To establish his Church, the King had killed dozens of those austere brethren, hanging some in chains, drawing and quartering others, and starving still more. Now they were taking their unexpected revenge.

The King's eyes closed but the whimpering continued. Edward put a hand on Henry's shoulder, unsure what else to do for the man.

Just then Tom arrived. "Where is Cranmer?" Edward asked him.

"Directly behind me," Tom said. "Are we in time?"

Edward shrugged, unwilling to put his fears into words.

The cleric rushed to the King's side. "Sire, you sent for me?"

The King opened his eyes. He tried lifting his hand to Cranmer, but only the fingers obeyed. Cranmer took the hand in his. "Put your trust in Christ. Call upon His mercy."

Again the mouth moved but no sound came out. The King was beyond speech.

"Tell me that you trust in the Lord," Cranmer urged. "Give me a sign."

The breathing slowed. Then nothing.

He was gone. Only his mountainous carcass was left, like the heap under a triumphant goshawk. A rush of life throbbed in Edward's ears.

"He squeezed my hand at the end. He died in the faith of Christ." Cranmer lowered his head onto the King's body, and they all closed their eyes to pray tribute to the life that had passed. The irresistible force that had ruled their every deed and thought since they were lads. The dazzling flame extinguished.

Suddenly the world felt out of balance. The King's death had left the ship rudderless. It was up to them now.

The eyes were already starting to film. Edward reached out and closed them. The feel of the clammy skin and the sight of the lifeless body created urgency. There was much to do before this news could be shared.

"We must bring the Prince – the King – to London to secure his person," Edward said. "No one can know of this until we do that. No one."

"We should have had him here already," Tom said.

"And alert the rest of the court that the King might be so near to death?" Even to Edward's ears Paget's voice sounded condescending.

"He is not far," Edward said soothingly.

"What about the Council?" Paget asked.

"We make no announcement until they can kneel to the boy."

That would be when the power was transferred, the magic moment. When people heard of the death of the

King, they would immediately drop to one knee and cry their allegiance to the new one. The news would spread through the palace from knee to knee, room to room, then outside through the stables and the surrounding village and thence the countryside. Edward had to be ready for that moment, ready with the focus of that new loyalty. Or someone else might try to steal it.

"It will take three days to get the boy back here," said Denny. "We cannot keep the secret for that long. The servants will know when he does not eat his food."

Edward waved a hand. That was easy. "Keep having his food brought in every day. Just close the bed curtains so no one can see."

"What about the smell?"

"Do you really think he can smell worse?"

Someone knocked. They all jumped at the sudden sound. Heart beating, Edward closed the bed curtains on his side and motioned to Denny to do the same on his, then walked to the door of the antechamber. It was John Gage.

"I have made all the arrangements for Norfolk's execution. I just need the King to approve them."

Edward felt his heart shrink. He felt defeat flood his face, and tried to disguise it with a more appropriate reaction. "Alas, the King is sleeping right now. Unfortunately, he may be developing another bout of fever, which will make him want to delay a day or so. But he will call for you when he is ready to speak about it."

Edward closed the door quietly and rested his head against the carved wood to calm his nausea. That fateful delay was one mistake it was too late to correct. Hopefully there would not be others.

He walked back into the bedchamber, where Paget, Cranmer, and Denny sat around the bed's velvet tent, staring at it as if the curtains were still open. Tom stood alone behind them, eyes on the door and ready to spring.

"That was Gage, ready to execute Norfolk," Edward said.

"Another problem solved," Tom said.

"Just the opposite. He wanted to speak with the King first."

"Well it's too late for that," Tom said. "Did you just instruct him to proceed?"

"No. I told him the King was sleeping."

"That was stupid." Tom wrinkled his nose. "Now he'll be back. You should just send word that the King does not want to be bothered with the details."

"It would be much better to end the old reign with such a death than to start the new one with it," said Paget.

"Agreed," Tom said.

Cranmer sighed loudly, seeming to deflate beneath his silk cassock. "We do not have that choice. The King's passing means it is up to the Council now."

"We could have them vote," said Paget.

"What if they release him? It is customary to pardon all prisoners on a new accession. What if they follow tradition?" Denny asked.

"We must follow the law," Cranmer said. "For our own consciences and the good of the realm."

Spoken like a priest, Edward thought, but Cranmer was right. Cheating would delegitimize their rule, would make Norfolk a greater danger dead than alive.

"We must get the boy," said Edward, taking a step closer to loom over the seated men. "Then we can assure an orderly transfer of power to him."

"So we don't tell the Council until then?" Paget's brow twisted.

"There is always danger when a void in power is created, even when the succession is clear," Edward said, straightening his spine. "Surrey and Norfolk were attainted because of the threat they posed to the new sovereign, and Norfolk still lives. We cannot take chances."

"But—" Paget began.

"The minute we tell them, sixteen men will be in here arguing over which chair they will occupy in the Council room," said Tom, shaking his head vigorously. "And demanding votes when they disagree."

Edward silently thanked Tom. If there was ever a moment when he welcomed his brother's brashness, this was it.

"Our late master did create an unwieldy system," said Cranmer. Paget and Denny nodded. Tom smirked.

Edward suppressed his rising excitement. It was starting. The time when they could finally give voice to the topic that had consumed the court's thoughts for months, if not years. The question of what would really happen after Henry died. Summoning all the sincerity he could muster, Edward launched into his case. "I think he knew that a single hand was needed for England's helm, and he wanted it to be me. He told me he trusted me to take care of his son and his realm when he was gone. He certainly groomed me for the position."

"From afar I certainly assumed that was the case," said Tom. "That Surrey's jealousy prompted his treason."

The men nodded at that perfect argument. Edward wondered whether his brother had made it up on the spot; it sounded like the kind of ammunition Anne would have supplied him.

"I agree this is what our late master wanted," said Paget. "I did hear him speak of a future where you would guide his son."

That testimony would do it for Edward. Especially during these early days when men were still shocked and saddened by the news.

Cranmer nodded and made the sign of the cross over Edward. Clear acceptance.

That made three votes of the sixteen, plus his own. *A quarter of the way there.*

Edward turned to Denny. Denny was a friend and a strong reformist. *But would he corroborate?* Edward steeled himself to remain silent and wait for Denny's reaction. Forcing the issue would spook the man, and Edward needed Denny.

Denny shook his head. "I agree shared power is not a good solution. But—"

"Who else could take the helm?" Paget asked. "You? You're not a politician."

"And you're too new a man," Denny shot back.

"Well, if you're going through the list, Browne is too old, and Lisle here is no good with money," Tom said. "I could do it."

"You're too rash," Denny said. "Wriothesley could do it, but he's a traditionalist."

"You see, there is no one else." Edward smiled as he said it.

"True," Denny said slowly. "And I suppose the King had indeed said things that could be construed as passing power to you. I just don't know whether the rest of the Council will agree."

Edward had already thought about that, *ad nauseum*. He only needed nine votes, though to make such a statement would sound too calculating. Instead he pushed Denny to help. "So what would you suggest?"

"Wriothesley will be the hardest to persuade. Bishop Bonner too," Denny said. "They will do everything they can to tip the balance of power to the conservatives. Maybe if you leave them for last, so they know themselves isolated. Browne too – he's another secret Catholic."

"You can't leave Browne," Paget said. "We need him. I say try the opposite – take him into our confidence early. Maybe send him to Hertfordshire Castle to get the Prince."

Edward nodded. "I think it important I go myself, but I will bring him with me. It is a proper assignment for the Master of the Horse."

It was the right way to handle Browne; bringing him would demonstrate respect for his position and influence. That would help him believe – that would help the whole lot of them believe – that Edward would not abuse the authority he was requesting, that he would still give the others their due.

They only needed to believe it long enough to vote him Regent.

"I will count on the three of you to persuade the others,"

said Edward. "Paget and Denny, your words will be our greatest asset."

"Not mine?" Tom's voice was sarcastic.

"You came back too recently," Edward said. *People know you as a liar,* Edward didn't add.

"But does this mean we tell them of the King's death?" said Paget. "You said we should not."

Edward nodded. "Tell them privately, one at a time. And instruct them to keep the secret. They will think themselves more important that way."

Paget nodded. "What about the ports? We need to close those until things are settled. If Spain hears, they might try to force Mary on us."

"Have Lisle do it, not the Council," Edward said. Lisle was Lord High Admiral; no one would question his orders. "And see that the Lady Mary" – he stressed the word *Lady* – "is watched."

"But what if we cannot persuade them all?" Denny looked nervous. "It does go against the instructions in the King's will. Where is the will, by the way?"

Edward smiled. "I have it."

The men nodded. "That he gave it to you shows the King's state of mind, his intention that you should wield power," Paget said. "That alone will help persuade most of the lords."

Edward nodded. But he had another trick left, one that would dominate everyone's thoughts during these crucial early days. "We should make a list of the other instructions the King gave us before his death," he said. "The ones that are not reflected in that document."

The King had spoken of many more gifts than he'd made. His generosity had waxed and waned; it was not clear where he ended up, but Edward was determined the will should not cumber them.

"Oh?" Paget drew out the syllable.

"You remember he said there were other gifts and plans?" Edward said. "He told me more details of your title, my Lord. First Baron Paget of Beaudesert."

Paget stared at him hard. Edward met his eyes and continued. "Just as he chose the dukedom of Somerset for me."

"I heard those instructions too," said Tom. "But I was too distraught to pay attention to his plans for me. Remind me what he said about me?"

Edward looked at his brother, grateful enough for the fake corroboration that he was happy to overlook the hidden threat beneath his brother's words – but at a loss for words.

"Of course." Tom snapped his fingers as if remembering. "He also mentioned Sudeley Castle to me. That must have been part of it. Baron Seymour of Sudeley."

A grab, but Edward was not about to complain. His brother would not be the only one doing this. "That makes sense," Edward said laconically.

"But how can we implement these gifts if they were not formally made?" Paget said. "There is nothing that allows us to do so."

"Ah, but there is," said Edward.

Edward reveled in their puzzled looks, glad that he had been as discreet as he intended. "The King's will explicitly authorizes his executors to appoint legacies to his servants." Technically the will allowed the executors to appoint legacies to "other" servants "not mentioned," but no one would quibble. Gardiner, the lawyer, might have, but he had been left out.

"Do you remember if he settled his bequest to me?" asked Denny.

"Absolutely," Tom said. Edward kept his face expressionless at Tom's "recollection."

"He mentioned a manor and annual revenues," Tom continued.

"I knew he would," Denny said.

Paget turned to Edward. "My Lord, let me be the first to congratulate you," Paget said. "I am sure you will be fully loyal to our new King."

"Just remember," Edward warned, "that the two issues are intertwined. Either we add all the King's spoken wishes or the will stands as written. If they want their gifts, they must accept me as Lord Protector."

"I am confident they will," said the new first Baron Paget. "It is the only conclusion to draw. It was the will of our late King."

Edward nodded. "It was indeed."

January 28, 1547—Hertfordshire Castle

The horses' hooves clattered urgently beneath Edward and Browne, breaking the silence of the early morning. They were on the twenty-seven-mile journey to Hertfordshire Castle, and making good time.

Sir Anthony Browne lifted a hand and reined his horse to a stop. "Enfield Castle is just down the road," he said. "We should secure the Lady Elizabeth."

Edward looked up at the sky. "It is early for that. It might alarm the household. I would rather secure the Prince and then get her on the way back."

"The King you mean."

Edward pressed his lips together. He would have to get used to that. They would all have to get used to that.

"You're probably right," said Browne. "Though we would lose a day, unless we traveled at night."

"I don't want to do that." Edward thought a moment. "With or without Elizabeth we will overnight at Hertfordshire. I'd rather without."

"Fine. We'll still be back to London within three days."

"That's the important piece. We need that speed to make sure the secret holds until the people can be confident in the new King's rule."

Browne grunted. "He will have good men around him."

That was the opening Edward had been waiting for. "But just as the court needs a focus and a head, so does the Council."

Browne grimaced. "Let me guess. You think that should be you?"

"Yes," Edward said with all the intensity he felt. "Because of my blood ties to the new King. Because of my great experience in all affairs of the realm. And because King Henry himself came to this view at the end."

Browne's eyebrows raised above narrowed eyes. "Did he?"

"At the last, the King understood a strong hand was needed to guide England during the boy's tender years."

Browne stared at him; Edward held his gaze and lifted his chin. *Now for the bait.* "Strong hands, actually. He had a better view of some of the bequests."

Browne's hands jerked, and the pull on the reins almost caused his horse to shy. Suspicion narrowed his eyes still further. "What?"

Edward infused even more sincerity into his voice and reached down to pat his horse's neck. "As he contemplated eternity, he saw he needed to strengthen the men who would provide the key support to his son. You were one of those men, and he assigned you yearly revenues of a hundred sovereigns."

Edward could see the greed in Browne's eyes. That sum would cover all his household expenses, right there, without any of his other revenues or offices.

"I wish he had signed something to reflect the changes, but he weakened too quickly." Edward paused to let the words sink in and hardened his tone. "But I intend to see that his wishes are carried out, and I hope I can count on you to do the same."

Instead of answering, Browne jingled his reins to resume their ride. But he chose to walk his horse instead of gallop, and he seemed lost in thought. Edward kept quiet. And prayed.

They rode for a quarter mile before Browne broke the silence. "Wriothesley will never agree."

"His is but one vote among many. But I hope he will do the honorable thing, especially since I intend to honor the King's wishes for him as well."

Browne's eyes narrowed. "What were they?"

"A title to grace his existing lands and revenues," Edward said. "Earl of Southampton."

Browne settled back in his saddle. "So he gets a title?"

Jealousy on top of greed, Edward thought, exhausted. He took a deep breath. "The King raised every man from where he was. Wriothesley already had the revenues." He decided to add a mild reminder of their relative positions. "And he *is* the Lord Chancellor."

Browne grimaced again and returned to riding in silence, his brow furrowed. "This is a time when all men must be honorable," he finally said. "You have my vote."

Edward had guessed right.

Six votes. With Lisle, seven. Plus the ones that Denny and Paget would shake loose: William Herbert and Anthony Wingfield at the very least.

Nine of sixteen, with more likely once the outcome was assured - no one would want to be on the wrong side of this thrust.

The taste of victory was on Edward's tongue. *Not yet,* he warned himself. *Not yet.* He was too close to let down his guard now.

He nodded to Browne and dug his spurs into his mount's flanks.

January 30, 1547—Whitehall Palace

Edward strode in to Whitehall, one hand on the young boy's shoulder to both guide him and calm the slight quiver that gripped his small frame. Edward intended to make good use of that posture until the Council had been fully trained to follow his orders.

They strode through the halls, Elizabeth following immediately behind, Browne a step after her for protocol's sake. When they came to the King's apartments, Edward ordered the doors opened wide. The smell that assailed them was not as oppressive as he remembered, but still the boy cringed from it and his eyes went to the closed bedchamber door at the far end of the room. Edward squeezed his shoulder.

Edward's key allies were already assembled in the Presence Chamber. Tom, Paget, Denny, Cranmer, and Lisle - almost all the votes he needed - all leaped to their feet and bowed to their new monarch. And smiled intently at Edward. That meant he had the numbers he needed. Hell, he only needed two more beyond this group here, and he certainly had that.

"Summon the rest of the Council," Edward ordered the page. "You should receive them on your throne, Your Majesty," he said to the boy.

All eyes turned to the King's chair of estate. It stood slightly to the right of the fireplace, facing out into the room. In the tapestry hanging behind it, Julius Caesar was crossing the Rubicon.

The nine-year-old's eyes widened but his mouth pinched into a thin, resolute line. After another furtive glance at the closed bedchamber door, he mounted the three steps and sat in the massive seat that had been large even for his enormous father. The new King's jeweled doublet commanded respect, but his feet stuck out awkwardly.

Edward followed him up and leaned over to whisper. "Move forward so the edge of the chair is right behind your knee."

The boy quickly complied, sitting tall and proud, though his feet still reached only halfway to the floor. For a moment Edward considered fetching a smaller chair, but he quickly discarded that thought. Every man here was accustomed to bow before that throne; it still conjured the old man's specter.

Edward positioned himself at the new King's right, as he'd stood at Henry's right, and waited. As the lords began to file in, each followed the same pattern: a nod for the King to show their respect, then a nod for Edward to show their support. Edward tried not to let his fingers twitch as he counted his votes. Thirteen of the sixteen were there and smiling. They were all in place, their eyes all upon him.

Edward made the quick decision not to wait for the final three. He didn't need them – he had more than a quorum – and he didn't want them because they were his opponents. With all the force he could project into his voice, Edward called out the announcement. "The King is dead. Long live the King."

As one, the room dropped a knee to the newly created Edward VI, long to live and reign over them. The guards at the door followed suit, and from the corridor a soft echo rose from falling knees, the gesture rippling out through the palace like waves in a pond. The making of a new monarch was indeed a momentous event.

He returned his hand to the boy's shoulder. "Given our King's tender years, I have been asked to act as Lord Protector, to safeguard the King's person and the realm, to guide His Majesty to the wisdom of maturity." Edward paused and spread his arms to the room. "You are His Majesty's Privy Councilors, those trusted men appointed by our late King. You are here and able to act on this matter. I call for your vote now, as the first act of His Majesty's reign."

Edward held his breath in prayer and anticipation for the moment that would be even more magic than the one before.

"I move to confirm," said Paget. The words filled Edward like lightning.

"Seconded," said Browne.

"Aye," said Tom and Lisle. One by one, they all agreed. With each new *aye*, Edward's chest expanded. With the last one, it was ready to explode. Several times in Scotland he had played the victorious general surveying his conquered terrain, but the triumph had never felt this glorious.

He pointed to Paget. "As the Council's Chief Secretary, you will record the result."

Paget bowed his agreement. The others did the same.

Looking out over the lowered heads, Edward imagined Gardiner gnashing his teeth, Norfolk growling, Surrey howling. And Cromwell smirking.

Female voices were at the door. Katherine Parr entered

with Mary, followed by their ladies. They all curtsied immediately to the new King, though Anne shot a quick look at Edward. When she saw his slight smile, she visibly relaxed, even exulted. *I am blessed to have her here,* he thought.

"God save you, my son," said the Queen. No. No longer the Queen, now the Queen Dowager.

"God save you, my brother," said the Lady Mary.

"God save you," repeated her ladies.

"Thank you," said the boy.

Edward felt the King's questioning glance and responded with a nod. *You're doing fine.*

"I don't know if they have informed you yet," said the Queen Dowager, "but I will not be acting as Regent for you as I did when your father left to war on France." She smiled thinly, clearly peeved at this demotion. "Still, I shall remain at court and be available to serve Your Majesty in any way I can."

The boy looked up at Edward to respond for him. Edward palmed his shoulder reassuringly.

"I know I speak for my nephew and all the court when I offer my great condolences on the death of your husband, and my deep thanks for your courageous offer in this your time of grief."

"Yes, I am so sorry for all of us," the boy said, clearly grateful for the hint at what to say. "Though I must not be sad, for the sake of my people."

Edward patted his nephew's shoulder.

"And I understand congratulations are in order for you, my Lord," Katherine said to Edward. "I understand the Council intends to name you Lord Protector. I know how much my late husband thought of you, how much he valued your advice. The King is lucky to have his uncle guide him." She looked at Tom. "Both uncles." Another look, this time at her own brother, the Earl of Essex. "And even a third."

Edward found himself vaguely annoyed at her *largesse,* much as he understood her reluctance to cede the control she had expected to be granted. "The vote has already occurred," he said. "We will formally address Parliament tomorrow."

We. The royal we. Edward was officially the ruler of the land, and tomorrow or the next day he would have the boy sign the patents that named Edward Duke of Somerset, a reminder of Edward's familial tie to the Tudor line. It was the title the late King's grandmother, Lady Margaret Beaufort, had first inherited from her father, one that had briefly been held by the King's son FitzRoy. A semi-royal title. And while it still would not have been senior to the Norfolk dukedom, the Norfolk dukedom no longer existed.

The Dowager Queen bowed to Edward, and the rest of the room did the same.

The nine-year-old King inclined his head in response, as if the deference was for him. Edward was not about to correct him. The deference was for the power, and the boy didn't yet have it, couldn't yet have it. When he was grown he would, but for now Edward did. A pack of dogs could have only one head.

The image of a disembodied head flashed in his brain. A vestigial fear from the days that had just ended. Though now that his brother-in-law was dead and could never turn on Edward now, the record had been sealed. Edward was free to remember only the affection that had existed between them, free to bless him unreservedly for raising him to this – without fear that the wheel of fortune would reverse itself in a new spin.

He had won.

Epilogue

February 16, 1547—Windsor Castle

Stephen Gardiner looked around the congregation, at the faces of the people who had come to pay their respects to the passing of England's greatest monarch. Or, rather, the man who considered himself England's greatest monarch. Saint George's Chapel at Windsor Castle was draped in black, as were the Yeomen of the Guard, three abreast, their halberds pointed to the ground.

In the chancel with Gardiner sat the great King Henry in effigy, clothed in golden robes of estate and bearing a jeweled scepter in his wax hand.

So incredibly lifelike, and yet Gardiner could tell it was not the King because it inspired no fear, no anger. Nothing but awe at God's great mystery, death.

Where was the King's soul right now? Heaven or hell? The figure's wax face bore a smile to suggest heaven. Gardiner thought hell.

Again Gardiner felt the knife twist in his heart. He had served the man faithfully for decades, even when it meant denying his own beliefs, and this was his thanks. Left out. Not a part of the will, not a part of the new Council. Like the runt of a stray dog's litter, he had been abandoned completely.

No, not completely. Gardiner had been chosen to officiate at the King's funeral. What kind of half-eaten bone was that? Not good enough for anything that mattered; only good enough to offer half-hearted, sycophantic, sarcastic praise.

Speaking of sycophants, the members of the new King's Privy Chamber were there. And those of Henry's old Privy Council who had wasted no time crowning the new Duke of Somerset as Lord Protector of England.

That pompous ass was there, sitting in the royal seat. Wearing black as if he were sorry over this turn of events.

Not like Gardiner. Gardiner was devastated.

The King had died with his face turned away from one of his oldest servants. Gardiner had done everything he could to beg forgiveness, everything he could do to contact him. But nothing had worked.

And yet Gardiner was delivering Henry's funeral sermon. Was this a longstanding plan or had the late King regretted his rash decision? Had he remembered his love for Gardiner at the end?

Gardiner so wanted to believe that he had. That he hadn't gone to his death with that anger, that barrier in his heart. Or if he had, that he regretted it now that the eyes of his soul had been opened by the eternal. The old King would be learning a great deal of truth on that other side of life. He already had received an important lesson, if last night's incident was any indication.

The funeral procession had stopped for the night at Syon House, one of the abbeys the King had closed – and the sad property where Catherine Howard had been imprisoned for months before her execution. His enormous lead coffin was left for the night in the old chapel, and must have somehow expanded because it had opened enough for his blood to leak onto the stone floor below. The attendants who discovered this in the morning had run out to find a plumber to solder the coffin's joints shut again, so that the cortege could complete the final leg of its journey. And when the group returned to the chapel, a red-eyed dog was avidly licking the blood from the stone floor. They had an almost impossible time chasing it away from its macabre task.

Gardiner could still hear Friar Peto warning this would happen. *The dogs will lick your blood as they licked Ahab's.*

That was twenty years ago, when the King had repudiated his first Queen Catherine for that Jezebel Anne Boleyn, the prophecy forgotten until it came true.

Should Gardiner preach that story?

He should, but he wouldn't.

No, once again Gardiner would do what was right for his master. He would conjure the King they had all loved, the one who cared deeply about his people. Gardiner would eulogize the Supreme Head of the Church who still wanted to keep the old ways, the God-ordained monarch whose only quarrel with Rome was the identity of the Pope.

That was how Gardiner would save England. Hertford–Somerset now – and his henchmen hoped to turn the country Protestant, but Gardiner would thwart them at every step.

He still had allies. Norfolk had escaped death, though he was still in the Tower. With life came hope.

The usurpers would make a mistake.

Gardiner would rise again.

Patience.

AUTHOR'S NOTE

For forty years, I have been fascinated by the Tudor era. I have always hated when stories ignored the facts and so I have tried to be as accurate as possible - leveraging the inherent precision of a timeline.

From there I pulled back. Long ago, my developmental editor taught me that the objective story is significant only in terms of what it means to the main character, that everything needed to be filtered that way. Since a single character couldn't capture the complexity of Henry's court, I use two to round out the goings-on. In *Jane*, it was Cromwell; in *Somerset*, it had to be Gardiner. I focused on their perspectives, their sides. And between the two rivals, I could triangulate Henry and show just how duplicitous he really was.

But I still had to push a bit to get the story right. The scenes plot much better when Edward (or Gardiner) is actually in the room and when Edward (or Gardiner) has some agency in the events. So there were places where I prioritized the interests of drama over accuracy, and made calculated stretches. In all likelihood, Edward was likely not in the room when Cranmer went to question Catherine Howard, nor with the King when she was dragged screaming down the corridor (though they often did sit together at Mass). Edward did not give Katherine Parr the strategy she used to save herself from Gardiner (though he did get back that very night), he was not the one who threatened Surrey's jury with Henry's wrath (that was Paget). And of course, Edward was not proclaimed Lord Protector until the actual Council meeting the next day...but that would have been so anticlimactic. This was just the right place to end his story.

Also in the interests of narrative, I (over)simplified storylines and characters (and STILL came in at more than 110,000 words). I didn't go as far as Showtimes' The Tudors and conflate Margaret and Mary Tudor into a single sister for Henry, but there were a number of people I simply never mentioned (Will Somers made only a single appearance for goodness' sake!). This part of Henry's reign is fascinating - but incredibly complicated. So many courtiers and so much intrigue makes the story difficult to follow, especially when names change as people advance!

Speaking of names changing, I was not fully faithful to the conventions of protocol. For example, my copyeditor tried to correct my references to use people's titles instead of their names (Margaret Douglas became "the Countess of Angus" and Margaret Beaufort became "the Countess of Richmond and Derby") - but while this may have been how they were addressed then it is not how we know them now. Similarly, I was a little anachronistic with language: I used the word "cryptologist" to describe Burke's function (so that I could get Marillac's letter in front of Henry!) even though the term did not arise until the 1640s.

I hope you appreciate the choices I made - and I hope you love the book! I hope you will consider leaving a short review on Amazon or Goodreads to help other readers discover it - it would mean a lot to me.

Janet Wertman
Pacific Palisades 2018

ALSO BY JANET WERTMAN

The Path to Somerset is the second book in the Seymour Saga trilogy. The story of the rise of the Seymour family begins with a 27-year-old Jane who is increasingly desperate for the marriage that will provide her a real place in the world. It is Jane who pulls the Seymours deep into the Tudor court's realm of plot and intrigue, when she captures the heart of its volatile king. *Jane the Quene* is available now at Amazon.com.

Hopefully in 2020 I will be releasing adding the third book in the trilogy. *The Boy King* will chronicle the reign of Edward VI, who had to grow up enough – and still before his 16th birthday - to execute both his uncles for treason. Tragically, they ended up more loyal to him than the men who succeeded them in the King's service...

While we're on the subject, you do subscribe to my blog, don't you? I publish a new post every week or so (though admittedly during the runups to a publication day I rely a little more on the "or so"). It's a great way to get a regular dose of the Tudors in between my books coming out! Find me at www.janetwertman.com. Hope to see you there!

Made in the USA
Columbia, SC
15 January 2020

86814652R00226